PRAISE FOR

## *The Duke Undone*

"I loved *The Duke Undone*, and so will my readers!"  —ELOISA JAMES,
*New York Times* bestselling author of *My Last Duchess*

"A beautiful blend of seductive suspense and heart-tugging romance that I
could not put down. Romance fans should make room for this author on
their keeper shelves!"  —LYSSA KAY ADAMS,
national bestselling author of *Crazy Stupid Bromance*

"Joanna Lowell's skillful storytelling and dazzling characters create one of
the most exciting new voices in historical romance today."

—JULIA LONDON,
*New York Times* bestselling author of *A Princess by Christmas*

"A charming romance with an atypical heroine and a to-die-for (and hot!)
hero in this unique tale of a duke and a struggling artist in Victorian
London."  —JENNIFER ASHLEY,
*New York Times* bestselling author of *The Stolen Mackenzie Bride*

"I really loved this book—in fact, I couldn't put it down. It's a fabulous
feast of a story that plunges you into the Victorian era with all its levels
and complications—into the art world and among aristocrats and slum-
dwellers. There's tension, adventure, derring-do, a fight against corruption
on several levels, a rich cast of characters, and a hero and heroine to admire
and cheer for. All in all, a rich and heartwarming historical romance.
Highly recommended."  —ANNE GRACIE,
national bestselling author of *The Scoundrel's Daughter*

## Titles by Joanna Lowell

THE DUKE UNDONE

THE RUNAWAY DUCHESS

# THE RUNAWAY DUCHESS

## Joanna Lowell

JOVE

New York

A JOVE BOOK
Published by Berkley
An imprint of Penguin Random House LLC
penguinrandomhouse.com

Library of Congress Cataloging-in-Publication Data

Names: Lowell, Joanna, author.
Title: The runaway duchess / Joanna Lowell.
Description: First edition. | New York: Jove, 2022.
Identifiers: LCCN 2021031465 (print) | LCCN 2021031466 (ebook) |
ISBN 9780593198308 (trade paperback) | ISBN 9780593198315 (ebook)
Classification: LCC PS3618.U568 R86 2022 (print) |
LCC PS3618.U568 (ebook) | DDC 813/.6—dc23
LC record available at https://lccn.loc.gov/2021031465
LC ebook record available at https://lccn.loc.gov/2021031466

First Edition: January 2022

Printed in the United States of America
1st Printing

Book design by Katy Riegel

For the witches.

# PROLOGUE

London
May 1883

THE DUKE OF Cranbrook did not kneel to propose. Over the years of their acquaintanceship, Lavinia Yardley had thanked the heavens more than once for the man's rheumatic joints, which limited his range of motion. She'd been able to sidestep his pinching fingers, dodge his kisses.

Most of the time.

*Nasty old goat.* Of course, she'd never had the satisfaction of addressing him thus.

"Would you do me the honor of becoming my wife?" The Duke of Cranbrook repeated the words. Oh, he was goatish indeed. Staring back at her hungrily, lips curling away from yellow teeth. His hair, tufted above his ears, thinned to wisps near the crown.

"Miss Yardley," he said. "Or should I say, Lavinia. *Dear* Lavinia. I want to give you so much more than trifles, these little tokens of my regard."

His gaze trained on the bouquet of bloodred roses sitting atop a battered cabinet. The room was hot—uncomfortably so—but Lavinia felt cold, cold to her very bones. How foolish she'd been, to believe her mother.

*The roses? I bought them. Aren't they cheerful?*

What other *tokens* had her mother accepted on her behalf?

"I know you'll give me much happiness in return." The way he dropped his voice, the insinuating note. He slid his knuckles down the side of his face, tugged at his silver whiskers. She crossed her arms over her breasts.

Her throat tightened. "In truth, I've known little happiness of late. I'm in no position to give it out." She spoke haltingly.

The Duke of Cranbrook took a step forward, lips twitching. The eagerness of his expression revolted her.

"I was stunned to hear that the prosecution pressed the matter, took things to such an extreme. Stunned. Stunned and frankly aghast. To be dispossessed of your very *home*."

He laid a hand on his chest, moved more by his own reaction to her plight than by the plight itself. He hadn't removed his gloves. A relief, to be spared the sight of those puffy white fingers. She still remembered the night they'd kneaded her thigh below the table at Lady Chatwick's dinner party, how her stomach had seesawed with disgust. She'd kept silent. Her father's architecture firm had just submitted plans for the renovation of one of Cranbrook's country houses.

"It was a great miscarriage of justice, I believe that firmly," he said. "Weston acted out of turn. But alas, a man abandoned by the woman he loves is capable of anything."

He referred to the rumor—one of many that had circulated in the winter months—that heartbreak explained her former fiancé's ungentlemanly insistence on bringing her father to trial, standing by when she and her mother were turned out of their residence at Chesterton Gardens. An enduring bit of gossip, its juiciness guaranteeing its popularity. Even she could see the appeal. A notoriously hotheaded aristocrat, jilted and vengeful. A capricious beauty whose family was ruined by her faithlessness. Pure romance.

Pure nonsense.

Miss Yardley's brilliant engagement to the Duke of Weston had been short-lived. According to the papers, she had ended it.

She hadn't, though. *He* had ended it. Anthony had never wanted to marry her. He'd been manipulated into the engagement by her father. One of her father's many abuses of power. Her dear, doting papa had exploited his position as the trustee of Anthony's family estates. He'd lied, and he'd stolen, and worse. He'd wronged Anthony, and he'd wronged Effie, Anthony's sister.

In so doing, he had wronged her, his own daughter. She, too, had been betrayed.

"A man *in* love is also capable of anything." Cranbrook parted his lips. Those yellow teeth protruded. He took a step toward her, and she caught a whiff of something sweet and rancid. The scent of his sweat and cologne mingled with the roses spoiling in the heat.

There was no mirror in this dim suite of rooms—the Rossell Hotel was shabby, even squalid—but the windows gave her back her reflection, confirming she was just as beautiful as she'd been when she debuted. Every social column of 1880, of 1881, had agreed that she was perfection itself. And yet . . . perfection wasn't penniless. Perfection's father did not reside in Holloway Prison.

She'd taken comfort in her old gowns, toiling to dress herself each morning without the help of her maid, but now she wished she were wearing sackcloth. Something that hid her body. Or at least something that squared better with her surroundings.

She was standing near the window, behind a chair, and she gripped its back. She would ram it into him, if need be.

"Perhaps shame holds you back. I confess, visiting you *here* . . . seeing the reduction in your prospects, knowing you are quite cut off from Society . . ." He shook his head. "Most men would hesitate to connect themselves with a woman in your situation. But I am not most men. My wealth and status confer upon me absolute freedom in my choice of spouse. Fondness is my first and only guide."

A pause, while she stared at him blankly.

"Love," he clarified. "Will you deny that a certain sympathy exists between us? My heart has ached for you these past months, as though your suffering were my own."

A strange sound escaped her. Perhaps a strangled laugh. *Sympathy?* Was that what he labeled his furtive, repulsive liberties? She would say it, finally.

*Nasty old goat. You disgust me. You have always disgusted me.*

She drew a breath, but before she could speak, she heard a faint squeak. Every hinge in the Rossell Hotel wanted oil. Her mother had cracked the door that separated bedroom from parlor. Her mother was listening. Why didn't she burst out and interrupt this preposterous scene?

An ugly old lecher, twice widowed, spouting vileness to her only daughter in a tawdry hotel! It couldn't be borne. Her mother, for all her meekness, would surely charge forward, outrage transforming her from mouse to lioness. Mothers protected their young.

Lavinia waited. A pulse fluttered her eyelid, and she tried to pin it down with the pad of her finger.

"You weren't meant for such a dreary existence," continued Cranbrook with a sweeping gesture. "No soirees. No evenings at the theater. Nothing gay. How long can you stay in these rooms? Mr. McCabe is a generous man, but his charity isn't limitless."

She started. Mr. McCabe owned several hotels, some grand, some—like this one—decidedly less than grand. Her father had helped him win his election to the Metropolitan Board of Works. How did Cranbrook know that Mr. McCabe had offered up this vacant suite?

"I worry for you, *dear* Lavinia. I worry for you, and for your mother."

There. Almost too quick to catch. He'd cast a glance toward the cracked door. Ah. So he knew her mother stood behind it. He knew . . . because they had planned it.

The edges of her vision softened, then everything snapped into focus. Sudden mental clarity sharpened her perception. The dark pores studding Cranbrook's nostrils. The soot streaked on the ceiling. That smell . . . roses, musk, dirt, lust, desperation, spoilage.

Did it matter in the end, if Cranbrook had approached her mother or if her mother had gone to Cranbrook? They'd arranged this meeting. No doubt they'd already settled the terms. What would those terms be? A June wedding. Her mother would want to move into Harcott House as soon as possible. Or perhaps Cranbrook would set her up in a house of her own. Even better. What else? Could it be that her mother had negotiated for Cranbrook's intervention on her father's behalf?

She tried to bore a hole in the door with her gaze, to meet her mother's eyes. Was this truly the only option? She'd assumed that her mother—pale and calm, even when the bank accounts were emptied, the house seized—was devising some plan, some solution. She'd hoped—foolishly—every day for an unexpected announcement. A distant relative, an American millionaire, had invited them to New York. The queen had commuted her father's sentence.

Lavinia saw clearly now. *She* was the plan. She was to be sold like meat.

*Breathe.* She had to remind herself. *Breathe. You can refuse.*

Refuse and do what? Wait in the Rossell Hotel for someone to save her? Her mother? That invented millionaire? The queen?

She'd been bred for marriage, nothing else. She could dance, hold a tune, play the piano, speak French, flirt, sulk, decline cakes and pudding at a banquet, appear fascinated while half-asleep. Skills that didn't possess value beyond the drawing room, the ballroom, beyond her cossetted little world. For most of her life, she hadn't regretted it. She'd believed she'd marry George. She'd *acted* on that belief. She'd ruined herself. No one knew. But a husband—a husband would find out. And that meant marriage was no longer an option.

She had no future.

*Governess.* But who would trust the moral education of their children to the daughter of a convicted thief?

*Shopgirl.* She'd have to live in a filthy dormitory with *real* shop-girls who picked their teeth and tinted their hair. And what if someone she knew came up to buy a bottle of scent? Why, she'd die right there, behind the counter!

*Parlormaid?*

Her eyes were beginning to water. She blinked rapidly. She wondered if her mother *was* looking back at her, if she would be able to read her expression.

"Lavinia." Stars above. Cranbrook was reaching inside his frock coat, producing a round ring box. He thumbed it open. One large diamond flanked by sapphires.

"Or should I say . . . Duchess of Cranbrook?"

Her breath exploded. How grotesque, that her destiny should have gotten so hopelessly knotted.

She'd spent years waiting to be styled *duchess*. Dreaming of the day. Ever since that spring afternoon when she'd run after George, waving his mislaid cigarette case, and he'd reached out to pocket it, then ruffled her curls, smiled, and said, *That's my Vinnie.* She, a girl of seven. He, already grown, broad and golden and gorgeous—the infamous Marquess of Stowe. It was more than a decade before anything happened between them, but that afternoon she apprehended everything at once, in a flash.

His Vinnie.

Her George.

Duke and Duchess of Weston.

Then George had died, and he'd taken it all with him. Love. The fairy-tale wedding at St. James's. The holiday afterward in Paris. The two children she'd already named, a boy and a girl. The title. She'd grieved in secret. Then, for a strange, short interval she'd thought she'd been reprieved. Anthony was the closest she could get to George himself. She might have unburdened herself, confessed her love for his older brother, told him, even, that George had been her lover. He might have understood.

She hadn't had time. In quick succession, he'd broken the engagement, married his outlandish painting teacher, and ruined her family.

She looked up at Cranbrook's face, at the greedy, red-rimmed eyes, at the bloated cheeks, permanently flushed by wine, at the abundant jowls and insufficient chin.

The marriage might be, in a sense, a success. A man so old, so besotted, so doddering and goatish, perversely fixated—she'd be able to wrap him around her finger. If he noticed she wasn't a virgin, he wouldn't protest. No, he would pinch and knead to his heart's content. And she, his wife, his duchess, she would live a life in which luxury offset loathsomeness.

To refuse, to choose dignity—that path led to poverty, to utter abjection. How long would she preserve her dignity then?

Here it was. The solution. The future.

Her lips were glued together. Her arms hung limp at her sides. Cranbrook gripped her forearm, lifted her hand, set the ring box on her palm. The jewels glittered.

At least she was selling dear.

She closed her fingers around the ring box. It felt good to make a fist. To squeeze.

*Yes* was an impossibility. She nodded and didn't flinch as he peeled off his gloves, trapped her face with his naked fingers. When he forced his mouth hard upon hers, she heard a click.

Her mother, shutting the door.

# CHAPTER ONE

Bodmin, Cornwall
One month later

"YOUR GRACE?" THE maid at her elbow was young and pretty. All the maids in service to the Duke of Cranbrook were young and pretty. This one—Beth, Bess, something like that—had tried to play nurse in the train compartment. If Lavinia so much as twitched, she brandished the bottle of lime water or leaned in with a dripping cloth. By the time the train reached Reading, Lavinia's bodice was soaked and she'd declared herself recovered, just to escape the girl's clumsy ministrations.

She lifted a hand to her tight, inflamed face. She was not recovered. Every step further impressed the fact upon her.

"You're going in the wrong direction. The carriage is behind you."

So it was. Lavinia kept threading her way along the crowded platform. Porters trotted back and forth, unloading the ducal luggage. A fat red hen ran over her right foot and a moment later a shrieking young boy in feverish pursuit ran over the left. She stopped short and the maid trod on her heel. *Too much.* Lavinia wheeled about.

"Give me *space.*" Her voice emerged as a growl from her parched throat, and the maid fell back a step, a fretful line appearing between her brows.

"Apologies, Your Grace," she said.

"I don't want your apologies. I want you gone." Lavinia felt a familiar wave rising within her, hot and heady. Her fits of temper had been legendary in the Yardley household. And extraordinarily effective. Papa had hated to see her cry. Even as a woman grown, she'd found that a storm of sobbing was all it ever took to produce her heart's desire. Up to a point. There were some things Papa couldn't fix. She could cry until the end of time, but no one could bring the dead back to life.

"Very well." The maid rested her chin on her interlaced knuckles, a childish gesture. She was little more than a child, really. Round-cheeked. Blond. If she wasn't in livery, getting scolded, and Lavinia in a pink silk faille day dress, doing the scolding, onlookers might have mistaken them for sisters.

"Shall I tell His Grace . . . ?"

*Tell him to go to the devil.*

"Tell him I went to the station house." Lavinia said it softly, becoming aware of those onlookers. West Country families in home-spun clothes gaping or chuckling knowingly. She knew what they saw. A high-handed lady berating her poor, long-suffering servant. How *dare* they judge her! It wasn't like that at all. If they only knew the night she'd had . . . that this was her first full day as a married woman and that it was vying to become the most awful day of her life.

The maid persisted. "Are you seeking refreshment? There are still cakes and sandwiches in the basket. I could—"

"I'm *seeking* the water closet," Lavinia snapped. "Or do you prefer I call a porter and vomit in a hatbox?"

That silenced her. And produced a guffaw from a pair of market women. A loutish farmer in a smock shook his head. Lavinia tried to strike a gentler note.

"I'll be along shortly. Thank you, Beth."

"Nan." The maid shrugged, blue eyes flicking toward the farmer. He took the pipe stem from between his teeth.

"No water closet," he called, grinning. "Privy across the tracks, by the brown oak."

Nan grinned back, then curtseyed to Lavinia, thin-lipped.

"I will tell His Grace you've gone to the privy," she said, and whirled, the spring in her step mildly suggestive of a flounce.

*Disrespectful chit.* Lavinia spun on her heel, stalking in the opposite direction. It didn't matter one whit whether or not she got off on the right foot with the staff. Not when her relationship with the master of the house was already doomed.

A railway worker was moving down the train, smearing something that looked like butter on the wheels. Soon the train would pull away, her last connection to London, to her old life, disappearing. Her stomach lurched. She intercepted the gaze of another farmer—Cornwall was experiencing an *epidemic* of smocks—and tossed her head. *Nan* might flirt with laborers, but *she* did not stoop.

As she swept past, the farmer's jaw dropped. In London, the men didn't let their chins hang so low. Couldn't. All those chins were propped by collars. Another benefit of civilization.

"Do you intend to address me? Or does your mouth always hang open?" She paused, fisted hands on her hips. She'd already yelled at a maid to the general amusement of henwives. Why not set down a bacon brains?

The farmer looked behind him doubtfully as he straightened.

"Yes," she said icily. "*You.*"

She waited for abashed stammering. Chagrin. Amazement at her condescension. The farmer, however, did not seem overawed. And, like any shallow-pate given a chance to act on the stage of life with his betters, he botched his lines. What emerged was *not* a stuttered paean to her beauty.

"I've never seen 'em that bad before." He peered at her more closely, then whistled through his teeth. "And 'ee came from Lunnon, did 'ee?"

He turned to a stout, travel-stained woman approaching with a basket and jerked his thumb at Lavinia.

"What do I always say about Lunnon?" He shook his head. The woman stared at Lavinia, eyes widening.

Lavinia's hand flew to her cheek. Of course. She must look a *monster*. The blood rushing to her face renewed the itching. Mortified, she whirled.

The farmer's eager voice pursued her. "I hear as they've got 'em in Buckingham Palace."

She clambered gracelessly up the steps of the footbridge, bunching her skirts. The farmer was still spouting.

"Cook the mattresses!"

She reached the far platform, heart pounding. That farmer thought she'd been chewed up by *bedbugs*. She'd been terrified of bugs at the Rossell Hotel, but thank heavens she'd never been bitten. If she had been, she certainly wouldn't speak about it. The Cornish were *dreadful* people. And Cornwall was a dismal, backward, common sort of place. Good for boors, dullards, and invalids. Small wonder Cranbrook retreated here whenever he could. Nothing for an aged widower to do but lie out on the patio in flannels taking the sea air. Fondling the maidservants. Only a Bluebeard would dream of bringing a wife to such a place for their honeymoon.

She eyed the station house, an unprepossessing building. No water closet indeed. Probably still lit with oil lamps, and the agents nailed up charms to guard against the pixies. Sighing, she paced past the station house to the platform's edge. Trees started up low and gnarled, their crowns the dense wet green of mashed peas. A gust of wind disarranged the branches and cold droplets scattered down. *Nan* had her bonnet. Blast the girl. Butterfingered Florence Nightingale. Belle of Bodmin Station. Out of habit, she raised her arms, shielding her curls, then she let them drop. A little late to worry about her coiffure. Lank hair befitted a ghoulish countenance.

Let the rain pelt.

She glared at the countryside. Which was the "brown oak"? The trees were all brown. They were *trees*. What made one oak browner than another? You had to solve a riddle to use the blasted privy. Not to mention soak your shoes wading out into the mud.

Although . . . She pressed her middle experimentally. Perhaps she wasn't going to vomit after all. Simply crossing the tracks—putting the train between her and Cranbrook—had soothed her stomach. Stopped its shivering.

"Oh!" She sucked her breath, jolted by an impact. The biggest dog she'd ever seen knocked her sideways so that her foot splashed in a puddle. A sharp bark accompanied the splash.

"Alfie! Alfie!"

At the sound of his name, the shaggy, filthy creature bounded off. Farmers were bad enough on their own, but they all seemed to travel with retinues of sheepdogs and poultry.

She daubed ferociously at the pawprints on the pink silk. Habit again. She gave the skirt a final shake. Her eyes wandered to the wagonettes and station flies parked on the grass, doors open. In one fly, a small child curled on his mother's lap, head on her breast. The father was standing in a wagonette, helping the porters load boxes, suitcases, umbrellas, rugs, and handbags. She'd like to sleep as that child slept, secure in the knowledge that his parents were close, that everything had an appointed place, that long journeys ended in joyous reunions and soft beds.

She'd scarcely closed her eyes in days. The night before the wedding, she'd sat up in a chair listening to her mother's even breathing, wrestling with her bitterness. *How could she rest so easily?* Last night, she'd retched and scratched, moon-faced and wheezing.

The wedding ceremony had unfolded like a bad dream. Four hundred bejeweled guests packed into the church. Bustles overspilling the pews. Fans fluttering. Cora, Agnes, and Elise had buzzed around her in the antechamber, plucking at her veil, effusing sweetly on the joys of second attachments. She understood them perfectly.

Once tarnished, she'd never be welcomed back into their set. Marriage to Cranbrook wouldn't restore her shine.

Mercifully, the reception was small. Cranbrook's friends and family circulated through a pair of flower-decked rooms at Harcott House. Her mother murmured ceaselessly with Lady Chatwick and Lady Sambourn about God knew what. As for herself, she had remained motionless in the corner of the salon, refusing to be drawn into conversation. Ignoring the snickers of Cranbrook's half-grown sons. Each passing second weighed on her. Finally, she'd broken from her trance and stumbled out onto the balcony for air.

Cranbrook and fat Lord Browning had been leaning on the railing, their backs to the room.

". . . damiana, phosphide of zinc, cocaine, and syrup of ginger. That's the tonic I take for a cockstand. So, old boy, shall I send a crate?" Browning was clapping Cranbrook's shoulder.

"No need." She could hear the smile in Cranbrook's voice. "I married the best tonic I could find. Do you want to know the secret?"

She'd watched, horrified, as Cranbrook drilled his index finger into Browning's chest.

"Fresh ingredients." He chuckled. "Fresh. Ingredients."

More clapping. Snuffles of laughter.

"Ho, is that the secret? These days, I wouldn't know." Browning sighed with mock envy. "Well, get to it, you scalawag. Don't you have a train to catch?"

Cranbrook drained his glass of champagne.

"Indeed. But if we miss it, we'll go tomorrow. You can't rush the first time. It's when a man makes his mark."

Browning was laughing again.

"Soften the wax," he crowed. "Press the seal down hard. No wiggling. Eh, Cranbrook?"

Her heart didn't change its rhythm as she stole away. But the beats sounded darker. *Doom-doom. Doom-doom.*

Her heart was still beating darkly. *Doom-doom. Doom-doom.*

Tonight, Cranbrook would claim what he'd been denied. And he would discover himself deceived.

Her gorge rose. Pure panic. No way to purge it.

"That's not ours." The father had climbed over the side of the wagonette to wave away the porters, a trunk suspended between them.

"Oh." Before she could think, she'd darted forward. "Oh, that's *mine*."

The porters sidled toward her and lowered the trunk to the ground. Tears sprang to her eyes. *Her* trunk. The one piece of luggage that didn't bear the Cranbrook coronet. Dear God, it had almost been lost, and with it the gowns she'd worn in happier times, her diaries, her notebooks, her albums and fashion magazines. *Home.* She wanted to throw her arms around it, greet it like an old friend.

"Sorry about the mix-up," said the father, unnecessarily. No fault of his. But she nodded at his courtesy. He was blond, with an extravagant mustache, his clothing neat, his expression cheerful. His eyes skipped tactfully over her face as he smiled at the middle distance. A Londoner, a banker or stock dabbler, she'd wager, with a Cornish wife and a large, young family. Off to visit the country cousins. She'd always enjoyed embellishing upon observable reality, scribbling her fancies in those packed-away notebooks. This family seemed to have stepped from the pages of a storybook about jolly summer adventures. More children kept tumbling out from between the trees, boys and girls, both sexes armed with sticks that they clattered together with alarming ferocity.

"Surrender!" The command rang out again and again as the melee approached the station house, followed by the inevitable chorus.

"Never!"

Lavinia's lips curved, tugging the little blisters. Smiling hurt.

"Time to go." The father began to wrangle his progeny, grabbing at the ones who rampaged too close. "All of you. Even Admiral Nelson."

The smallest girl threw down her stick in disgust. After many more shouts, no surrenders, and one tragic death performed in several heroic stages, they'd all packed into the flies and the cabmen were whipping the horses. The flies rolled away from the station, and Lavinia let loose the breath she'd been holding. She felt emptied out. A profound loneliness, akin to a more uncanny feeling.

Inexistence.

She was no longer Miss Lavinia Yardley. But she wasn't—couldn't be—the Duchess of Cranbrook.

The crowd on the platform had thinned. She bent down to lay a hand on the trunk's lid. How silly she was. Trying to derive comfort from a leather box. She should stand up straight. Summon the porters. Walk back across the footbridge. Cranbrook—Peter, he'd told her to call him, her *husband*—awaited. She laid her other hand on the trunk. She closed her eyes.

"Mrs. Pendrake?"

Her eyes opened and she rose, dusting her gloves. Another rustic, this one approaching at an alarming clip. He wasn't smocked, but his brown canvas hunting jacket flapped open, and she could see his shirt, the collar flopping, tied loosely with an olive-green scarf.

He'd emerged—like the boys and girls—from between the trees. Did Cornish woods possess some strange power to multiply children and produce men out of thin air?

"I've kept you waiting. The train's always late, but then . . ." The rustic slowed as he drew up beside her. "I was later," he finished, ingeniously. He dropped his bags, shook his hair from his eyes. His chest rose and fell, but he didn't sound remotely out of breath. Or, for that matter, overly repentant. Strong hands gripped hers.

"Mrs. Pendrake," he said with unaffected warmth. "I am delighted to meet you."

He wasn't Cornish, not by his accent. But no young gentleman from town would tramp about hatless, in a *canvas* jacket. Nor had any gentlemen from town ever met her gaze with such . . . *levelness*.

Not that he was short. He was medium tall and had to look down into her eyes. But he did so without any superiority and without a trace of supplication. As though social distinctions—to which she and her erstwhile friends had always paid such jealous attention—were so much frippery. He saw through it all. He saw *her*.

Except he didn't. He saw . . . Mrs. Pendrake? Who, pray tell, was *Mrs. Pendrake*?

"Oh. I'm not . . ." She tugged her hands from his with odd reluctance, but before she could continue, his expression changed, eyes narrowing with concern as he examined her. She fought the instinct to duck her head. How embarrassing. To make an introduction—even as someone else—with red lumps disfiguring her face. But there was something almost soothing about his intent, methodical inspection. She lifted her chin and returned his regard.

*His* face was completely ordinary. Somewhat square. Nose over-large. Ordinary brown eyes. She was used to men who composed their features, who held their heads at the angles that made the most of their jawlines, who paid good pounds sterling to have their hair styled until it achieved a manly artlessness. George had been a peacock.

This man was utterly devoid of artifice. Artifice, it turned out, came in useful. Deployed to attract, it also created a buffer.

Their eyes met. He was very close, and his gaze was very direct. She dropped her eyes. *Good Lord.* He was wearing gaiters.

"Looks painful," he said. "Was it the *Alstroemeria*?"

At this extraordinary question, she looked up. Their eyes met again. Ordinary brown. It was only the fringe of dark lashes that gave them such shadowy depth. She cleared her throat.

"In fact . . ." She paused and settled on the truth. "It was strawberries."

At this, he stepped back, brow furrowed. "You were breeding strawberries? What varieties? Was it the leaves?"

"Breeding?" She blinked. "No. Eating. I was eating them." As one did.

His face cleared. "Ah. A *dietary* complaint. I feared the lilies I'd sent had caused the irritation."

He mistook her incredulous expression.

"Of course you know the sap is an irritant." He gave a rueful shake of his head. "I didn't mean to suggest you wouldn't have handled the specimens properly. But the sap spreads. I've gotten festering boils from it myself, in the damnedest places."

"Have you," she said faintly, but if he heard the reproach implied by her tone, he made no sign.

"When did the reaction start?"

"Yesterday." She shifted uncomfortably. He was altogether *too* frank. And what sort of man sent a woman lilies as a specimen instead of in a bouquet?

"Then the worst is over." The assurance in his voice made her swallow hard. Of course, this misguided stranger hadn't the faintest understanding of her situation. The worst was yet to come.

Suddenly, the platform began to vibrate. The train roared to life. She'd been gone too long. At any moment, Nan would come to collect her, or worse, Cranbrook himself.

"Most women would have taken a few days to recover," he said. "But then, most women wouldn't have trekked through the Tapa Shan mountains during a relapse of pernicious malaria."

What on earth? She turned to stare at him. Was Mrs. Pendrake an explorer? A brigadier general? Whatever she was, one thing was clear: this man *respected* her. His tone had been teasing but laced with appreciation.

"Not *women*," he corrected himself. "Nessa and Jenni would have my head for that. Few *people* are possessed of your mettle. Actually, the majority of the ones I can think of are women. My mother was scaling cliffs into her fifties."

At that, he grinned. White teeth against tanned skin. Heaven help her, there was nothing ordinary about that grin. How had she,

Lavinia Yardley, who had always considered herself an excellent judge of gentlemen, assigned him such middling marks? Was it because he wasn't a gentleman? Or was it because she was no longer Lavinia Yardley?

And what if she wasn't? Wasn't Lavinia Yardley, or the Duchess of Cranbrook, but someone else?

Dear God, if she could only *be* the redoubtable woman this man so admired. She'd prefer the Tapa Shan mountains to Cranbrook's estate in Fowey.

Her heart accelerated.

His smile widened. She could see quite a bit of his neck above that ludicrous kerchief. Inexcusable, really. But this was Cornwall, not Rotten Row. And his neck was not exactly an eyesore.

"You're a legend, Mrs. Pendrake." He shook his head, lips still quirked. "I don't know that *I* would have continued into Mongolia if wolves had eaten my donkey."

She snorted. Mrs. Pendrake sounded more like a lunatic than a legend.

"Very sensible," she said. "I hope your indomitable mother, too, would think twice."

"Doubtful." He laughed, then sobered.

"You and your husband both." He held himself straighter as he said it. "Legends. I mean that sincerely." He did. She couldn't doubt his sincerity. His face was like an open book. An open book with slightly foxed pages. The sun-browned skin, the lines around his eyes. He'd grown into that face, and it reflected his thoughts, his emotions. The moment felt *too* sincere.

"Well," she said. This had all gotten rather out of hand. The train was chugging now. She smelled coal smoke. And something else, some green, heathery scent the man had brought with him through the trees.

"Was it the first time?"

"What?" She blinked at him.

"The strawberries." His gaze had sharpened again, roving across her forehead, cheeks, chin. "They never disagreed with you before?"

She stiffened, resisted the urge to scratch. "Once before. I was very young." She'd been given a strong purgative, then put into a soda bath, and afterward her father rewarded her for her bravery by reading to her from her favorite book of fairy tales. "I'd avoided them since."

"They were incorporated into something, then?"

He liked to ask questions, this man, to get to the bottom of things. But her honesty had hit a hard limit. She gave a one-shouldered shrug. She wasn't about to tell him more.

That she'd marched from the balcony to the breakfast table in her wedding dress and forced herself to eat one chilled red strawberry, then another, even as her lips began to prickle. The information would make for a pretty speech.

*I poisoned myself deliberately. It was unpleasant, yes. However, I had no choice but to become intensely, rapidly indisposed. Nothing else would have kept my bridegroom from consummating our marriage. I acted to prevent that consummation. You see, another man has already made his mark, a reality to which said groom will prove less amenable than I'd hoped.*

"A syrup, I think." The train belched more smoke as it began to pull out of the station. "I'm much better now," she said firmly, closing the subject. A pause, while the man seemed to consider something. Then he nodded.

"Good," he said. "We have a busy week. Tomorrow, we'll botanize on the moor. In the evening, we're off to Kyncastle. Then down to Great Peth, and on to the Lizard and back up to Truro. A grand tour of Cornish flora."

The moment had come. She must disabuse him. *Thank you, but I prefer flowers in arrangements on mantelpieces where they belong. When your happily married legendary Mrs. Pendrake shows up, I'm sure you'll have a splendid time.*

His look had turned rueful as he watched her.

"We're similar, you and I. For years, I was addicted to the danger, and the challenge," he said. "Succeeding where others failed. The plants of the British Isles bored me to tears. Then . . . things changed. I don't even miss the old days." He grinned. "Well, not much. Now that I'm head of Varnham Nurseries, I can always commission myself if I'm suddenly pining to reacquaint myself with frostbite, seasickness, and electric eels."

She opened her mouth.

*We are not similar. I am not Mrs. Pendrake.*

It was slipping away, the moment. It had come and gone. She was in the pull of something rare and powerful. Her whole body had tipped subtly forward.

Could it be so easy? Step out of one life and into another?

"Trust me," he said. "Cornwall won't disappoint you. Shall we?"

One station fly remained, horse cropping the grass. At the man's gesture, the driver hopped down to help him load her trunk.

The last car of the train had pulled away from the station. Sight lines opened between the two platforms. Glancing over her shoulder, she could see the liveried figures milling about, and behind, the row of shining black carriages. Cranbrook was stepping out of one, the watch in his hand catching the sunlight. His hand focused her attention. In the train compartment, he'd kneaded her thigh, as he had at that long-ago dinner party, but this time those puffy white fingers had probed her flesh hard enough to hurt. She'd made a small, anguished noise, and he'd laughed and twisted his fingers, panting as she gasped. He liked to hurt. Her distress excited him.

Revulsion overpowered, strong enough to make her retch. She didn't retch. She hurled herself across the wet grass, diving into the fly, scrambling across the seat. *Madness.* This was going to end in disaster.

*Doom-doom. Doom-doom.* Her heart gave her the reminder. She was already living a disaster.

The man swung up after her. Everything about him was warm, confident, relaxed. *Head of Varnham Nurseries.* He was an enterprising gardener, one who'd gotten his start as a plant hunter. A peculiar, risky pastime. She remembered the year that a blossom like a golden bell won all the medals at the flower show. Everyone had traded stories of the plant hunter who'd carried it out of the jungle, and of the tiger who'd pursued him.

If you wanted to risk life and limb abroad, surely the army provided more respectable opportunities, not to mention attractive uniforms.

And Mrs. Pendrake. A plant *huntress*? She'd never heard of such a thing. She herself had gone plant collecting once when ferns were at their smartest. Part of a group of giggling debutantes who'd had to turn back when they reached the field because their crinolines didn't fit through the stiles.

Tapa Shan mountains. Mongolia. Mrs. Pendrake and husband—legends among plant hunters. And where was this husband? With any luck, chasing after a rare rhododendron in Borrioboola-Gha. If he planned to meet them in Cornwall . . . the game would be up before it began. But what was the game? Where would this ruse lead her? She'd have to flee to Mongolia herself to escape Cranbrook's reach.

When news of her disappearance reached London . . .

"It's not far to the inn." The man interrupted her racing thoughts and she tried to smile. A fearless, legendary smile. Her face felt stiff and tight. She'd borrowed—no, stolen—a life. It might be taken back at any moment.

The fly jostled as they drove in a wide circle over the grass. They tilted onto a rutted dirt lane. *There.* She saw it as they rolled past. The privy. It stood in the shade of a large tree. Unsurprisingly, a brown one.

"Brown oak," she muttered.

"I should have suspected." The man leaned back against the seat, throwing a boot up on one knee. *"Complete ignorance regarding British trees and shrubs? I quote you."*

He sounded delighted and clapped his hand on his knee, which was bouncing. Even sitting, he gave the impression of boundless physical energy. No wonder he had to trot around and around the globe. "Tell me. How did you identify it?"

"Oh. Well." She craned her neck for another look. Too late. "Anyone could spot a brown oak."

"No, indeed," he said. "You have a remarkable eye. Anyone could spot it's half-dead and likely to topple on the privy, I won't argue there. But it's a damn good trick to gauge that the wood within is stained when you can't see any fruiting bodies of the *Fistulina hepatica*. I only know it's brown oak because I've been here in August."

Ah. Brown oak referred to some quality *within* the tree. Her cheeks burned, a flush spreading beneath the hives. *Damned good trick.* He'd attributed her idiotic statement to a deeper understanding. Why, how unexpectedly marvelous, this presumption of intelligence. No one had ever thought her intelligent. Pretty, yes. Quick-witted, perhaps. Intelligent? No. Somehow she had never thought to mind. A little burst of retrospective anger was quenched by a sweet rush of gratification. *Unearned* gratification, a voice whispered, but she silenced it, settling in beside him on the seat.

"I suppose you'll keep surprising me," the man said. Her instinct was to respond with a saucy smile. Instead, she returned his look, direct, on the level.

"I suppose I will," she said.

# CHAPTER TWO

MRS. PENDRAKE DID not appear to be enjoying the ride. She sat rigidly, arm braced against the door. Her eyes were enormous. Blue eyes. The color of the forget-me-nots threading the hedges.

A bump sent them both a few inches up into the air.

Neal rapped the roof with his knuckles, just for show. Cornish drivers were all madmen.

If the devil himself tried to slow them, they'd run him off his feet. Which made for great good fun. He'd always liked a breakneck pace. Well, not *always*. Not during that lightning storm in Argentina. His horse had spooked as he mounted and dragged him half a mile dangling from the stirrup. The episode had been a bit too painful, and a bit too on the nose. He'd very nearly been sliced to ribbons by the variety of pampas grass he'd been sent to collect. But in every other circumstance, the faster the better. Improved the circulation.

The road curved dramatically, and the driver cracked the whip, accelerating into the turn. Mrs. Pendrake gasped. Her hives looked livid. The color had drained from her face, accentuating the patches of inflammation.

There could be no doubt. Faster was *not* better in the mind of his future wife. An amusing divergence. He could tease her about it into their dotage. The exception that proved the rule. They were, after all, eerily compatible.

*She* is *you*. That was what his friend Simon Hitchens had told him after hearing her lecture on *Lilium regale*, the regal lily of the Chinese Empire, at the Royal Botanic Society. *But prettier, and in petticoats.*

The cab tipped, eliciting a cry from Mrs. Pendrake, high-pitched and feminine. She covered her eyes. Had she covered her eyes while boating over the Yeh-Tan rapids? Or clattering down snowy ravines in that donkey cart? Her manuscript never mentioned mortal terror, and her encyclopedic observations of the terrain indicated obsessive, unabating attention. She left so little out a reader could be excused for asking himself if she so much as blinked.

A *thunk* as the left wheel returned to earth.

"Dear Lord," she whispered, and he realized she'd begun to pray.

Might she be overly pious, then? The cab swerved again and Mrs. Pendrake yelped in a new register.

"*Christ*," she swore, revealing—to his relief—a healthy eclecticism in relationship to ecclesiastical propriety.

"*Do something*," she hissed, and he rapped again on the roof. The driver didn't slack the pace but neither did he increase it.

"We'll be quite all right." Neal smiled. To no effect, as her face remained buried in her hands. "There are hardly ever any bang-ups."

He put the toe of his boot on his tin specimen box, which was rattling against his portfolio on the cabin floor. Doing damage to the loosely packed plants. A shame, but no tremendous loss. He'd walked to the train station on a lark, and the area of the moor he'd explored on the way was already well botanized. Reverend John Jenkins, of St. Neot, maintained excellent records as far west as Kilmar Tor.

He'd wanted to wait for Mrs. Pendrake before venturing into less-trammeled territory.

And now she was here, in the flesh. Expiring with terror.

"Can you smell the lady's bedstraw?" He inhaled deeply, through his nose and his mouth. The evening air had a honied taste.

She lifted her head, bracing herself again against the door, but made no response. She seemed to be holding her breath.

Perhaps it wasn't the speed that troubled her. She might suffer from claustrophobia. His brother Perran, newly appointed to the faculty of the medical college at the London Hospital, was co-writing a paper with a French professor on the subject of extreme dread of enclosed spaces. At Christmas, he'd expounded on the topic to Neal as they roved the family home in Penzance looking for the children, whose zealotry in hide-and-seek made it abundantly clear that they were not among the afflicted. Indeed, Perran's youngest son—the winner— had to be sawed out of a cupboard. Neal did think he'd experienced a touch of claustrophobia himself, during stormy transatlantic voyages, and during afternoon teas in those sealed-up London sitting rooms stuffed with marble bric-a-brac.

They weren't enclosed per se on this country lane. But the towering hedges leaned so close to the sides of the cab that ferns and foxgloves slapped the windows. Sometimes a stone clattered audibly against the fender. He could see how it wasn't *unlike* plunging down the long green gullet of a sea monster.

"This will open up soon," he said. "Any moment now."

Mrs. Pendrake remained silent. Her shoulders slid up around her ears. He felt the muscles in his forehead tightening.

"These aren't your springy Midlands hedgerows." He tried to draw her attention to the window. "They're solid, filled with stone. Proof perfect that our driver has never, in his long career, made the slightest miscalculation."

*Nicely done, Traymayne.* He suppressed a wince. Not the most assuring line of reasoning. Her grimace confirmed it.

"Are the crashes always fatal?" The question emerged like an accusation.

"When they do happen . . ." He abandoned the sentence and began again. "Our driver hasn't ever crashed and won't ever crash. That was my point. There now, look."

The hedges fell away from the road and they were bowling along the crest of a hill, the land undulating into the distance, green fields striped by the flowering hedges. The setting sun sent ruddy light slanting through the clouds. The lane unspooled smoothly before them.

She slumped forward, her whole body relaxing. He, too, relaxed, scrubbing a hand through his hair. There was something communicable about anxiety. His awareness of her agitation had coiled him tight as a spring. He made a mental note to ask Perran if he knew the Greek for *that* phenomenon.

She heaved a breath and cast her eyes about.

"Much better," she said, and turned to look out the window. "Are those sheep?"

He tilted his head, peering over her shoulder. "Cows."

"Hmm. On the small side, then." She pressed closer to the glass. He refrained from comment. The creatures were far away, pale dots on the pastures. But, well, they were very cowlike all the same. British Whites and Jerseys. A zoologist she was not.

"And which way is the sea?"

"That way." He had to reach over her to point. As he did so, he glanced down at her hair, blond, elaborately coiled and curled. The locks that had tumbled down were pin straight. His mother had always claimed there was an inverse relationship between the outside and inside of a woman's head. The more overdeveloped the hairstyle, the more underdeveloped the cognitive powers.

"We're not heading toward Fowey?" She remained turned toward the window and spoke with studied casualness. Yet he saw her shoulders tense.

"No," he replied slowly. "We're heading north. Fowey is south. Why? Do you have some reason to go there?"

"No!" She turned abruptly and pressed back into her seat. Her gloved fingers skimmed her reddened cheeks, then she folded her hands tightly in her lap. "Just a point of reference. Do you think we'll get more rain?"

He hesitated. There was something deadly and familiar about that tone of voice, about that exact question. Usually, it presaged prattle. Or else an uninspired dialogue punctuated by increasingly awkward silences. Rarely did it indicate interest in natural conditions and their effects on human, plant, or animal behavior. But perhaps he should take her at her word.

"Rain?" He studied the clouds—billowing, a bit dirtied by their fierce transit over the heights of the moor—and shrugged. "My mother always says the weather in Cornwall is good in a novel, bad for a picnic. It's a windswept, wild place, or it is in this district, at any rate."

Mrs. Pendrake spoke with an odd quaver in her voice. "I like novels *and* picnics."

To his immense surprise, her lower lip bumped out. A localized swelling. But no, it couldn't be attributed to a sudden intensification of her symptoms.

Mrs. Pendrake was pouting.

He stared, aghast. She didn't notice. The tension that had gripped her when she'd mentioned Fowey seemed to have dissipated into girlish sadness, drooping head and all. "It will be a long time, I fear, before I'm reacquainted with either, novel reading or picnicking."

"I don't know about that," he said, at a loss. Was he meant to comfort her? Or was her sulk some devilish prank?

He had thought himself ready for this encounter. He had prepared by ruthlessly uprooting any expectation. By opening his mind to every possibility. What if her voice grated? What if he didn't find her *pretty*, as Simon had? If there was no physical rapport whatsoever? Secondary issues. The relationship he desired rested on a foundation of intellectual affinity and common interests. Everything else would grow in time.

His parents' relationship presented the model. Their profound mutual understanding had strengthened each of them in their pursuits while also nourishing their decades-long union. Whereas *he* had always let impulse and attraction guide him, with disastrous results. He was planning the antithesis of seduction. With Mrs. Pendrake, he would establish a reasonable, affable, equable, *equitable* connection.

Conversation, of course, formed the cornerstone. They'd already laid it together. Not in person, no, but on paper. When he'd first written to her in April, she'd been five weeks back in London from Hong Kong. Their letters, while growing friendlier over the past two months, less strictly professional, remained focused on botany. She wrote about the talks she was delivering at the Royal Botanic Society and at field clubs, about the botanical prizes she'd presented to schoolchildren in Newcastle upon Tyne. He wrote about the flora of Cornwall he was compiling, a massive undertaking, years from completion. She admitted that she, too, found herself fascinated by the native plants of the British Isles, which she'd long neglected in favor of faraway blooms. They'd shared few personal details, but the omissions told their own story. The omissions, and Hitchens, a trump when it came to digging things up. Dinosaur bones or Society secrets—he had a knack for uncovering both. Mrs. Pendrake, soon to enter the fourth year of her widowhood, remained romantically unattached.

At the end of May, she'd sent him her manuscript to read, "Recollections of a Plant Huntress in China, Mongolia, and the Malay Archipelago," and he'd reciprocated with an invitation, asking her to accompany him on an expedition across Cornwall, which would kill two birds with one stone. She'd have the opportunity to educate herself on native plants, and he'd gain the help of a masterful collector as he worked on his flora.

There was a third bird in this neat little scenario.

At the end of the expedition, he would propose. If she didn't accept, he'd present her with the evidence and wait for her to reconsider based on the merits of the case. Either way, they'd be engaged in time to surprise his mother at the midsummer festival and fulfill her dying wish. Perfect.

The plan, though, included no provision for pouting. He'd have to fall back on the rake's rule book. A promise was the conventional return on a pout, was it not?

"We'll pick a cove," he said. "There are dozens along the Lizard. One will serve as a site for a magnificent picnic."

At that, she smiled, a funny, lopsided smile that bent her nose to the left. A quirk of her features? Or had the strawberries particularly irritated the membranes of the sinuses?

"I didn't bring any novels." She sighed, then brightened. "But I have all my favorite issues of *The Queen*!"

His own smile faltered. But why shouldn't Mrs. Pendrake enjoy, in her leisure, the banalities of Society gossip, celebrity profiles, and fashion plates? Or dedicate hours to curling her hair and pinning bows all over her décolletage? True, he'd been taken aback when he'd first seen her waiting for him at the station. In fact, he'd even glanced up and down the platform to ensure there wasn't some other more sensible-looking woman standing alone by her luggage. If it weren't for the puffy eyelids and the rashes on her cheeks, Mrs. Pendrake wouldn't have seemed out of place at a garden party in Mayfair. Blond ringlets, pink silk—she resembled one of the Society butterflies with whom he'd been wont to entangle himself, back in the dark days before he'd come to his senses. In point of fact, she resembled Elizabeth. He hoped his mother wouldn't make too much of that unfortunate coincidence.

Her fingers rose again to her face, hovering, before she caught one hand with the other and forced them both down.

"Drat it," she muttered.

"Itching, is it? Hold on." He rummaged through his several coat pockets. Field notebook, pencil, tags and elastics, string, fishing twine, matches, seed and spore bottles, compass, knife, scissors, trowel. Glass clinked against glass, and metal clanked against metal. He'd worked out a credible filing system at Varnham and implemented it in both the London and the Truro offices, streamlining operations. And he could be meticulous when it came to selecting, collecting, and packing specimens. Also, pressing and drying them, taking notes. But organization had never been his strong suit. He rarely left one of his nurseries without an assistant running after him with his hat or the pruning shears.

"Aha," he said, fingers closing on a wide, shallow glass jar. That was the one. He passed it to her.

"Ointment," he explained. "I always keep a jar of it with me." *Somewhere.* "Helps when I nick myself or get into some nettles."

"Or give yourself boils." She frowned as she unscrewed the lid and sniffed. "What is it?"

He sat his elbow against the door, shifted his weight to the right. Difficult to face her in the tiny cab without crowding her with his body. Physical contact—*not* part of the plan. Passion was better as the graft than the stock.

"Aloe vera, beeswax, and olive oil." He'd tinkered with ratios and ingredients for years before he arrived at that simple formula. During their ill-fated courtship, he'd once mortified Elizabeth by offering a jar to Lady Phillifent. A servant setting down the bread sauce had knocked a candle and splashed her hand painfully with wax. Lady Phillifent, declining the salve, had inquired about the properties of aloe vera, and he'd doubled his offense by responding in earnest. Beginning with the plant's description by Carl Linnaeus.

His lips bent at the memory. For all her ribbons, Mrs. Pendrake was a woman of substance. A woman who had bucked convention to travel the world. A woman who appreciated the consistency of the Linnaean system. He did her a disservice. Not all intellectual women wore pince-nez. For the love of God, he'd read her manuscript! She was *nothing* like Elizabeth.

She tugged off her gloves and dipped a fingertip into the jar. Ungloved, her fingers were slim and tapered. His eye snagged on her rings. Gold, with diamonds and sapphires. Clearly, Mr. Pendrake had been wealthier, and flashier, than the average plant collector.

He averted his gaze as she rubbed the ointment into her skin.

"Thank you," she said. "Mr. . . ." He looked back at her. She arched her eyebrows, performing the pause. "Don't you think . . ."

"Yes." He rushed to answer. "Yes, of course. Call me Neal."

"Wonderful." She handed him the jar, and for a moment his palm tingled, cool glass and warm fingers.

"You do the same," she said.

He grinned at that.

"Very well," he said. "Neal."

"Call me by *my* first name, if you please." She tossed her head, extending her long throat, lifting her chin. He felt his forehead knotting once again, this time with the intensity of his befuddlement.

She had the coiffure, couture, and even the *mannerisms* of a London butterfly. But . . . perhaps she did *not* have the mannerisms of a London butterfly. Perhaps he was only ascribing her such mannerisms due to her beauty. She *was* a beauty. Why not admit it? A rash didn't disguise the obvious. Mrs. Pendrake, due to heritable variety within the species, happened to be possessed of a swan-like neck and a saucy, pointed little chin—what really could she do about it? She had to move her head sometimes. It wasn't fair to categorize the movement as a *tossing* of the head. Mrs. Pendrake didn't *toss* her head the way Elizabeth tossed her head.

She'd begun to rub her thumb along her cheekbone.

"Aloe vera," she murmured.

He handed the jar back to her.

"Keep it," he said. "I recommend putting it on again before you go to sleep. We've begun selling it, actually. At the nurseries, and mail order, out of the London office. It softens the skin in addition to soothing minor injuries." Gardeners were buying it, and amateur botanists, but his managing director in London had also reported wider sales as word of mouth spread. "I've half a mind to advertise it as a cosmetic. Make Varnham a household name."

He'd been thinking aloud. His sisters often told him doing so was a negative trait. Many males were predisposed to it. Thinking aloud. Also, overexplaining. Whistling.

She was looking at him thoughtfully.

"What do you call it?" she asked.

"Varnham's Ointment."

"Dreadful. I wouldn't buy it." She made a moue of distaste. "It sounds like something you'd rub on a pig."

Opinionated. *That* wasn't a surprise. He cleared his throat. "Do you have a better suggestion?"

"Dozens I'm sure." She considered, finger tapping her lower lip. "Varnham's Natural Beauty Balm. Varnham's Floral Face Cream. Varnham's Bloom of Youth. Varnham's Cool and Lasting Aloe Lotion."

The cab began a broad turn and she broke off to look out the window. The hills had flattened as they'd approached the edge of the moor, and in the graying light, scattered trees, bent by wind, cast black shadows on the otherwise unbroken landscape.

"What are you doing?" she asked, glancing back at the sound of his pencil scratching the page.

"Making a note. Varnham's Bloom of Youth, did you say?" He jotted it down inside the cover of his notebook. This was promising. A first, albeit minor, collaboration. He remembered sneaking out of his bed, sitting in the hallway, listening to the murmur of his parents' voices. His father reading aloud from one of his papers in progress, his mother interrupting with comments, or vice versa.

*Cool and Lasting Aloe Lotion.* Another fine phrase. He jotted that one down as well. Interesting—she had shown more consideration for euphony, more verbal flair, in that brief recitation than she had in four hundred manuscript pages.

She was watching him write with undisguised satisfaction.

"You'll need to perfume it," she said when he lifted his pencil. "Gardenia. No! *Azalea.*"

"One of the varieties you brought back from China?" He grinned and dropped notebook and pencil into his pocket. No need to make a note. The Pendrakes had introduced an exquisite collection of azaleas to England. It was due to those azaleas that he'd first taken notice of the couple, wondered at the rarity and rightness of such a partnership, and begun to follow their career. Husband and wife—a plant-collecting team. And that was before they'd sent seeds and samples of *Davidia involucrata*, succeeding where Varnham's plant collector had failed.

"The most fragrant one," she said. She was suddenly lit up, radiant, her swollen nose pulled by her smile into that piquant, adorable slant. Maybe she was remembering halcyon days on the temperate island of Chusan, wandering azalea-covered hills.

"So," he said, tilting his head, forming the phrase. "We'll call it . . . Muriel's All-Natural Aloe and Azalea Lotion for a Radiant Complexion?"

"Muriel's?" She blinked at him. "Oh, I see. *Muriel.* Pendrake. Well." She resettled herself on the seat, flustered. "You should keep the Varnham, if you want to become a household name."

"Let's decide over dinner." The inn had come into view, rising from the moor, lonely and beautiful behind its low stone wall. It was exactly the sort of place that most appealed to the wayfaring botanist, almost a part of the countryside itself, the slate walls covered with mosses and liverworts.

He hid his grin, waiting to see her face reflect the pleasure he'd felt when he'd first discovered it.

Blue eyes swung toward him.

"We're not staying *there*. It's a pile of rocks!"

Multiple exceptions, then, were to prove the rule of their immense compatibility.

"Just for a night." His grin strained. "Inside it's rather cozy." Cats prowled in and out of the kitchen, and last night he'd crunched a fish skeleton under his boot going up the stairs. The dark, rambling rooms wouldn't have passed muster with a well-heeled holidaymaker accustomed to gas jets and Chippendale furniture. But for those with adventuresome spirits, those who knew how to take their rest on damp bedrolls under the stars, the charm of the place was bound to outweigh any minor discomfort. Wind howled all night on the moor, but the inn stood stoutly against it, impermeable, thanks to the spleenwort, yarrow, and rue vegetating in the crevices. Should he mention the yarrow? Which detail would beguile her?

"It's warm and dry," he said at last, deciding upon a more basic recommendation, because she'd begun to shiver slightly, and he realized that the light had dimmed dramatically, chilling the air. The clouds lay thickly atop the inn's roof tiles, swallowing the chimney stacks. If you looked at it with the wrong eyes, well. A grimmer establishment didn't exist on earth.

"There's an enormous hearth," he added hopefully. "Very cheerful. The turf fires do smoke a bit."

The radiance had fled from her face. Whatever joy she'd found putting her imagination to work, improving upon Varnham's Ointment—it had withered. Too brief a bloom. Her shivering grew more violent and she hugged herself, leaning her forehead against the window.

"Muriel?"

"It's only . . ." Her voice wobbled. "Never mind. It's only . . . It has been an exceedingly long day."

As he watched in horror, his future wife began to cry.

# CHAPTER THREE

NEAL STOOD THE miners at the bar a drink as he waited for Muriel. It was still a novelty, having so much ready coin in his pocket. He'd tried to negotiate for a lower salary, but Charles Varnham wouldn't even hear him out.

"Not a penny less, and you're worth twice as much," he'd said. Neal had wanted to speak from the fullness of his heart. *I'd give anything for things to be different.* But he'd only nodded and gripped Varnham's arm. The older man knew what was in Neal's heart. That was why he'd chosen him to run the company in the first place. Neal didn't flatter himself that it was for his knowledge of the industry, or even for his skill as a plant collector. Varnham was a family business, had been headed by Varnhams for generations. Charles Varnham wanted a son for his successor, and Neal was the closest thing he had left.

The scrape of stools across the raw floorboards alerted him to her presence. He'd been leaning against the bar, and he straightened as the other men stood or tipped their glasses. As though a woman had never stepped foot in Crawthevyn Inn.

Maybe it was the tulle.

Muriel had changed into a low-cut evening gown, a gauzy shawl wrapped around her shoulders. As she crossed the room, she took small, deliberate steps, circling the puddles. Beer, he hoped. Should he rush forward and throw down a handkerchief? Good God, but he'd arranged things poorly.

Muriel had made it clear in that first letter that she had no intention of working for Varnham. Not because she was renewing her contract with Edevane & Fernsby. On the contrary. She was done with China, done with long journeys and perilous searches. She'd accepted his invitation to botanize in Cornwall, but clearly she'd been operating under some misapprehension as to what that entailed. She'd imagined an expedition on British soil was like a walk in Hyde Park.

What he should have done—too late now—was secure them lodging at a less ruinous hostelry, one of the shipshape little inns on the High Street in Camelford.

He pulled out a chair at the table farthest from the hearth. Nonetheless, she gave a dry, reprimanding cough as she lowered, straight-backed, into her seat. His heart sank by inches, and he batted at a cinder—had chivalry ever taken such an absurd aspect?—as he folded himself into the chair across from her. Wisps of peat smoke curled toward the rafters. The light was so low he couldn't gauge the color of her dress—gray, blue, lilac?—or distinguish on her face the shadowy marks. What blotch was the rash, and what blotch the sign of her recent storm of weeping?

Mary, the innkeeper's wife, emerged from the kitchen, scooting a cat with her shoe. "Greedy guts," she muttered. "Out with you." She caught sight of Neal and approached, smiling broadly. She wore a cap on her white hair, and her apron, dimness notwithstanding, looked none too clean.

"Neal Traymayne," she said in a round, rich voice. "What can I do you?"

Last evening, once she'd connected him with the Kyncastle Traymaynes, Mary had plopped down at his table, subjecting him to a lynx-eyed interrogation. With unflagging interest, she'd moved methodically from bud to root of his family tree, getting up from time to time to bring another pasty. She didn't release him to his bed until he'd eaten three and tucked into a suet pudding.

"Pasties." He grinned at her. "Four. I worked up a powerful appetite." He had at that. He'd walked easily twenty miles on his roundabout route to Bodmin Station, with only a few hard biscuits for his lunch. "Another ale, as well." He raised his empty glass. "Thank you kindly, Mary."

"And the lady?" Mary's quick, sharp gaze ricocheted between them before settling on Muriel. Neal had explained that his expected traveling companion was a woman of science, a respectable widow come to assist him with his botanical fieldwork. Whatever image Mary had called up at the words *woman of science* and *respectable widow*, Neal would wager by her expression it misaligned point by point with the reality.

"To drink?" Muriel licked her lips. She seemed distracted by the entrance of a small, ragged figure who tottered as he approached the bar, dwarfed by his rucksack. A peddler, Neal guessed.

"Ah . . ." Muriel didn't so much as look toward Mary. "Möet?"

*Christ.* She'd answered automatically, Neal felt certain, and meant no insult. He waited a beat for her to hear her blunder, but she continued to watch the peddler with a faint scowl.

Crawthevyn Inn catered to poor colliers and furnace men, farmers, vagrants, horse dealers, cabmen, families in rickety coaches breaking up the journey between coasts. French champagne was not on offer.

"Oh, aye," Mary shouted above the din. The miners had begun ragging the peddler for a song, a dozen boots stamping in rhythm. "And to eat?"

The stamping ceased, and a miner handed the peddler a foaming glass. Muriel looked away, giving Mary her full attention.

"To eat?" she echoed. "Why—I haven't seen the menu."

"You're looking at the menu." Mary opened her arms and bobbled a mock curtsey. "Fish and chips or pasties. What will it be, dearie?"

For a moment, Muriel stared, a mutinous expression playing across her features. Was she about to demand lobster salad and asparagus with Montpellier butter? Neal bit the inside of his cheek. In China, she had mingled with Europeans, attended state dinners at the British Legation. But she had also ventured into rural precincts. Her manuscript included words of praise for the kind souls she'd encountered in the villages and described their foods as "delicious" and "more interesting than the knife-and-fork fare" she'd eaten in cities at the consulates. Would she now rebel against a Cornish pasty?

"I don't know." She frowned at Mary. "What's in the pasties?"

"Everything but the devil," said Mary. "And we'd throw the devil in too, if ever he came to Cornwall." She threw a wink at Neal, who'd heard, throughout his nigh on thirty years of life, more than several variations on this saying. Muriel opened her mouth, then closed it.

"Well then, pasties it is," said Mary. "And I don't envy you, Neal Traymayne."

She marched for the kitchen, already shouting to the cook. Muriel played with the ends of her hair, such shining, pale hair it looked nearly as white as the smoke.

"Women never like me." She flicked the strands behind her shoulders. Her eyes seemed suspiciously full, and she dabbed at them with a tuft of tulle.

"You must think I'm being a ninny." She dropped the tulle and smoothed it, fingers moving with nervous excitement. "The strawberries did something to my brain, I fear." Her laugh partook of that same nervousness. Her gaze met his, then flicked away.

"I'm typically very strong-minded," she continued, eyes lowered.

"Intrepid. You know, very *extraordinary*. I've done all sorts of amazing things, haven't I? But all I've done since meeting you is shake with premonitions of death and *cry*. You must be horribly let down."

"No. No, not in the least," he said, but she looked up at him through her lashes, shaking her head.

"It's true, I've been *wretched*. I'm too sick and too tired to make sense, and if we sit across from each other, you have to spend your meal looking at my *face*. I don't know how you'll abide it."

Before he could protest, Mary's arms reached between them.

"Your ale," she said to Neal. She pursed her lips at Muriel. "Your Möet."

Muriel followed Mary's retreat with her eyes, then looked at the glasses on the table.

"They're both ale," she said.

"Yes." Neal cleared his throat. "So they are. Well then. Cheers." He lifted his glass. She stared at him for a long moment.

"*À votre santé*," she said at last, and clinked her glass against his. He couldn't help but laugh at the way she screwed up her face as she drank. He'd never seen a pint of ale met with such determination. As she set down the glass, she caught his smile, and suddenly she was laughing too.

"How is it?" he asked.

"The worst Möet I've ever had in my life." She took another sip, fanning smoke with her free hand. The room, he noted with chagrin, was growing smokier, and so warm that more than one miner had stripped to his shirtsleeves. Best to fall back on some safe subject, familiar to them both.

"In your last letter," he began, but she cut him off, her fanning hand making a sudden chop.

"Please," she said. "Let's talk about something we *didn't* discuss in our letters. It will be so much more entertaining."

The bar erupted in laughter, as if the spirit of Crawthevyn Inn had declared its agreement.

He tipped the cool ale down his throat, considering.

"How did you first come by your interest in plants?" he asked.

"Oh, I don't know. Flower shows. Same as any girl." She traced a finger up and down her glass. Maybe it was too predictable a question, too impersonal. She'd meant she didn't want to talk about *plants*. Another question pushed against his teeth.

*Why did you agree to meet me?* If this were a simple flirtation with a pretty widow, he would ask her exactly that, among other things, his eyes communicating possibilities. *What do you most hope to discover on our excursion?* But he'd had too many summer flings. This would be different. He would take care preparing the ground. This would last for all seasons.

"I do know." She looked up, looked straight at him. Her eyes were darker by candlelight. Delphinium blue.

"My friend's mother kept a glasshouse in the garden when I was very young. It's one of my first memories, standing inside looking up at trees stuck all over with tiny glowing yellow suns."

"Lemons." He smiled.

"Tiny suns." She shrugged. "It felt like magic. I'm sure that sounds silly."

"It doesn't," he said, and meant it. His father had studied the chemistry—the capture of light in carbon bonds, the production of starches by green cells. He had one way of describing a lemon. But there were other ways.

"Tell me," he said. "Did you get to taste any of that sunlight? Did this friend's mother show you other wonders?"

She dropped her eyes. "She died soon after." A pause as she drew her finger around the rim of her glass.

"And you?" she asked. "How did you first come by your interest in plants?" She made her lips a little bow of smiling interest.

She didn't want to linger in that glasshouse. Very well, then.

"My father was a professor of botany." He could talk easily about his father now. For years, his grief and guilt hadn't permitted it.

Digory Traymayne had died of a long illness, but not so long that Neal returned from South America in time.

"A professor of botany," she repeated, as though it were a foreign phrase.

He had been so much more than a professor of botany—a doctor, a writer, a gentle and loving spirit.

"He was on the faculty at the University of London. We moved from Cornwall so he could take the post." It had seemed at the time, to him, the death knell of his merry boyhood. A dramatic reduction in gaiety and freedom. Life contracted. No more running along the tops of hedges. No more riding in hay wagons or chasing turkeys through the orchard. And worst of all, no more splashing in the sea, bathing in deep pools accessible only by sheep tracks through the rock and heather.

"As a toddler, I used to sit on Loudon's *Encyclopaedia of Plants* to reach the breakfast table." He swallowed more ale. "Perran's first word was *Cruciferae*, Nessa's was *Caryophyllaceae*, Jory's was *Leguminosae*, Jenni's was *Rosacea*, mine was *Umbelliferae*. I'm not serious, of course. But you get the idea." He shrugged. It was only barely an exaggeration.

"A big family." She sounded thoughtful, maybe even wistful. "Those are your siblings? Perran, Nessa, Jory, Jenni."

He nodded. "I'm the youngest. The one who gave our parents a world of trouble."

"Trouble? What sort of trouble?" The corner of her mouth lifted, the bow of her small, perfect smile loosening. *Trouble.* That was what entertained Muriel Pendrake. Good. He liked a woman who liked a bit of trouble.

"I didn't sit for my examinations at Oxford. Instead, I entered Varnham's service and shipped for the Americas. My mother claimed that her hair turned stark white the day I left, same as happened to Thomas More the night before his execution."

"And to Marie Antoinette, poor darling." Her hand floated up to adjust the tulle. He blinked away the discomfiting vision of an enormous bunch of plumes sticking up from behind her head.

Muriel wouldn't wear feathers, surely. She was sensible of the havoc the feather trade wreaked on wild birds.

"My mother prefers Thomas More," he said. Something stroked his leg. Not Muriel's foot? *Ah.* One of the kitchen cats rubbing against him. He held his upper body still and tried to hook the cat behind his calf and push it back, away from Muriel.

"Someone had better prefer Thomas More." She was looking at him dubiously. "If not Thomas More's mother, then your mother. No one is *ever* Thomas More at a fancy-dress ball, and every year there are a dozen Marie Antoinettes."

He blinked again. She spent her nights in London at fancy-dress balls? Amid all that feathered millinery?

He responded slowly, following the thread. *Thomas More.*

"My mother loves More's idea of Utopia," he said. "I think it's the part about digging a trench and making your own island."

"Digging trenches!" She leaned forward, and he smelled otto of roses, the fragrance overpowering the fug of smoke and grease and fire-warmed flesh. "I'd rather join her in scaling cliffs."

"She enjoys both. Or did." He and his siblings had been shocked by her gaunt appearance at Christmas. The lilac shadows beneath her eyes. Many days pain had kept her indoors, she who had always been the picture of health, robust, with high color and windblown hair. "My mother is a geologist, a paleontologist, and a fossilist. Self-taught." His father was far more well-known in scientific circles. On those occasions when Heddie Traymayne *had* received credit for her specimens, Digory was usually behind the scenes, applying the necessary pressure. Same, too, with her publications, a slow drip of them, making—every handful of years—a small ripple in some geological journal. Neal knew it rankled his mother, to be considered an amateur, a mere enthusiast. It had rankled his father, too. He had always introduced her as Hedra Traymayne, *my wife and fellow scientist.*

"When she talks about my sisters, she looks like the cat that got the cream." Surreptitiously, he pushed the cat again and felt the tiny pricks of its claws through his trousers. Too bad he'd removed his gaiters. "Nessa attended Bedford College, and Jenni went to Cambridge, to Girton."

He couldn't keep the pride out of his voice. He'd always looked up to his siblings. Along with his parents, they were the giants of his childhood. Perran, serious with his books of anatomy, his forehead tall and white as though it had been starched with learning. Nessa, kind and jolly, never without her umbrella, which she used exclusively for catching insects. She would pop it open, flip it upside down, and position it under a plant, a plant that—if he was lucky—she'd let him shake until beetles rained down. Then there was Jory, a colorful liar, finding fun in everything and everyone, particularly Perran, whom he'd pip in every subject, just for the laugh. And Jenni, the closest to Neal in age, the ringleader of all their games, a mathematical prodigy and a terror at chess, at whist, really anything at all. A glorious terror, his Jenni.

Muriel wore a strange expression.

"Fancy," she said. "My mother would not be so delighted if her daughter grew into a bluestocking."

"No?" He propped his chin on his hand and studied her.

"I am an only child." She lifted her glass, lowered it without drinking. "And marriage was my mother's one and only goal for me. It would be different if I were a spinster."

"Of course," he said, lifting his own glass. She had fulfilled her first two plant-collecting contracts with her husband. But the third—the third she had fulfilled alone. It must have been difficult for her, returning to China by herself.

She furrowed her brow. "I believe there's a cat under the table."

"You don't say." He reached out an exploratory foot and brushed her skirts. She swept her legs back.

"This is a Worth gown. It shouldn't be climbed on by cats."

"Certainly," he agreed, sighing. After tonight, her gown was going to reek of peat smoke, even if it wasn't tattered by Greedy Guts or some other feline denizen of Crawthevyn Inn. He pushed his glass a few inches with his fingertips. He'd drained the ale and needed another. "My sisters, by the way, are not spinsters."

"Did they have a Season?" She seemed to forget the cat in an instant, leaning forward again, curious.

"Good God, no." He laughed. "A Season? My parents believe in women's education. And a Season . . ." He shook his head. "It's a head-emptying program."

"Is it?" she asked. He heard sudden frost in her voice. Her eyes narrowed. "That must be what's wrong with my brain, then, not some passing indisposition, but permanent damage I sustained as a debutante. I had a Season. More than one, in fact."

Now he'd done it. She was in a state of high dudgeon, lips a thin line.

"I wouldn't ever suggest that your head, or any woman's head, had actually *been* emptied." He looked to the rafters for help. None forthcoming. "It's that Society is so much rubbish. Granted, the rituals are somewhat interesting, from an ethnological perspective. If you went to a ballroom thinking of it as a human zoo, you might . . ."

Christ, he was the one now digging a trench. He changed tack.

"I did not grow up in Society," he said. "Or, my father *was* a member of the Linnean Society, and the Royal Society, and the Royal Botanic Society, a fair number of societies . . ."

He laughed. She did not.

"But we were very much outsiders to *Society.*" Outsiders, but sometimes a bit too close for comfort. He'd had to wallop blue bloods daily as a charity case at Eton. Still, the friends he'd made at

Eton, and Oxford, the glimpses they'd provided into their world, proved useful when he interacted with wealthy clients. His smooth manners, his attitude of drawling indifference to the prospect of a given sale, played enormously well. Useful. But damned tedious.

"I gather you did grow up in Society," he continued.

She inclined her head at this statement of the obvious. Her smirk looked familiar. It was Elizabeth's smirk. He'd seen it on the faces of other lovers as well, those with West End addresses. As though they got fitted with them at the same modiste.

"But given what you've achieved, how much you've seen of the world, we must be in agreement."

"About what?" She folded her arms beneath her breasts. She would not make this easy. But *of course* they shared this common ground, despite her prickliness around her Season. He smiled.

"Why, women's education."

"Women's education!" She laughed and shrugged out of her shawl, letting it drape the chair back behind her. He wished he could follow suit and take off his damned wool jacket. The room was stifling. Her neckline dipped below her collarbones, in which the shadows pooled. A man's gaze could drown there. He caught himself and found her eyes. She was glaring daggers.

"Of what use is an education?" she demanded. "Of what use, when the single most important factor in your future is who you marry? I've never met a man who asked me to work a sum or find the Cape of Good Hope on a globe. Do you propose to educate men to seek out education in women?"

He had the unpleasant suspicion that he was gaping.

"No? In that case, an educated woman risks making herself unmarriageable for what? A position as a schoolmistress educating other girls until they reach the same pass? What will happen when there are as many schoolmistresses as female pupils?"

"Surely," he said, regrouping, "new kinds of opportunities—"

"And in the meantime?" She didn't let him finish. "Head emptying as the Season may be, you'd have to be empty-headed not to see that it provides a woman with the very best *opportunity* that presently exists." She drooped a bit, those graceful shoulders turning inward.

"Not that it's any guarantee," she said in a softer voice. Then she shrugged. "You can *believe* in women's education, like children *believe* in Father Christmas. Your sisters were lucky if they married and married well."

Oh, she was *rare*. Not a variety of Society butterfly or woman intellectual, despite shared traits with both. She belonged to her own genus.

"I have often thought . . ." He hesitated. "That you and your husband were the luckiest of all."

For a moment, he wondered if she hadn't heard. As he'd spoken, a low din had erupted. Commotion at the bar. A glass shattering, a few cheers, curses. Then he saw that her eyes were wide, fixed upon him.

"I'm sorry. It was cruel to speak of good fortune when you lost him so young." Another blunder. Now she looked stricken.

"But when I first heard of the Pendrakes, they—you—caught fire in my imagination. A husband and wife, traveling together, sharing every discovery . . ."

"Pasties." Mary banged two plates down in front of them, four pasties for him, two for Muriel. No cutlery. She took in Muriel's flushed face and raised her eyebrows at Neal. "Another round?"

Neal glanced at Muriel's glass, nearly empty, as he passed his glass to Mary. Muriel finished her ale with a gulp.

"Please," she said.


Muriel Pendrake was a widow. Lavinia let the information sink in, watching Neal break apart his pasty, the steam billowing from the hot meat and potatoes. Why hadn't that possibility occurred to her? No Mr. Pendrake. The only husband threatening to pop out of the shadows was her own.

Impossible that the Duke of Cranbrook would look for her here, in this godforsaken heap. Still, she jumped every time the men at the bar raised their voices.

"I'll ask Mary to fetch a fork." Neal twisted in his chair, flagging down the nasty old baggage, who was already making her approach, pints in hand.

"Your pasties?" Mary beamed at Neal as she set down the glasses. He beamed back.

"Even better than yesterday's," he declared, laying a hand on his heart. Lavinia resisted the urge to snort. They *were* yesterday's, she'd be willing to wager. Nothing fresh could emerge from that kitchen. The batch of pasties was probably baked during the Interregnum. None of the other patrons seemed the dining type. Wise of them. Gin didn't go off.

"And yours?" Mary trained her beady eyes on Lavinia's untouched plate.

"Heavenly." Lavinia folded her arms.

"Mary." Neal assumed a conspiratorial air. "We're well content and only wanting a pair of forks."

Mary wasn't fooled. She looked straight at Lavinia.

"What kind of forks would you be wanting? Certain folks are particular. Do you need separate forks for the onions, the swedes, the potatoes, and the beef?"

"Any forks will do excepting that one." Neal gestured, grinning, and Lavinia squinted. A fire-blackened toasting fork hung over the hearth.

Mary laughed.

"You're a good lad," she said. Lavinia did snort at that. The slattern! She was *simpering*. Neal had changed for dinner, changed into a collared shirt and black jacket. She probably took him for a lord. Lavinia cast a critical eye over his person. Nothing objectionable in the tailoring. And it did offset his natural advantages. Absent the bulk of that ridiculous canvas coat with its overflowing pockets, his body looked long and lean. What a divine injustice—that *he* should have those eyelashes! If she were his sister, she'd scream with envy, Girton or no Girton. He wasn't a *pretty* man, eyelashes aside. But his blunt face, with its large nose and square jaw, was undeniably attractive. This Mary seemed to think so. Her wrinkled face was tense with calculation. She was like that awful Mrs. Pickering who did Swedish exercises before every ball, the better to chase down bachelors for her daughters. Did Mary harbor designs on behalf of some great big galumphing girl out in the milk shed? Or was she just a sop for male attention? And Neal! He was shameless. Had he *winked*?

*Drat it.* She was *not* too missish to eat with her fingers. She gripped the greasy pasty in both hands and took a bite. Crust, thank God. She might have conceded defeat if a human finger or ossified rat tail slid out onto her skirts. She swallowed and raised her head. They were both looking at her. She gave Mary a bright smile.

"Heavenly," she said again. "Like God himself came to Cornwall."

Neal shook his head, laughing. Mary shook her head too, but she was muttering to herself.

"Never mind, then, Mary," Neal called after her as she marched away, snatching up bottles. He was still laughing as he fell upon his own plate. He ate vigorously, devouring the first pasty, then the second. For a moment, Lavinia stared. When had she last seen someone take so much pleasure in a meal? Fashionable people were far more disinterested, far more languid at their tables. She never allowed herself more than a few mouthfuls of soup, a morsel of quail, a glass of champagne, a glass of madeira, perhaps an ice. She tried another bite of pasty. If it had been baked during the Interregnum, it had kept fairly well. Or maybe the Interregnum wasn't as long ago as she thought. She'd know if she'd gone to Girton.

The pasty was, in fact, rather heavenly. The soft, flaky dough, the juicy meat. Corseted for a ball, she'd never dream of ingesting a particle of such heavy food. Tonight, in such a barbarous place, with such an uninhibited companion, she surrendered to her hunger. She ate quickly, washing down larger and larger bites with ale. She caught Neal looking his approval, that unordinary smile making her breath catch. She choked on pasty, swallowing yet more ale to dislodge the crumb, blushing furiously.

What was wrong with her? Handsome men were ubiquitous in the West End. Ballrooms came furnished with them. Their smiles never made her gasp. Only George had ever had that effect. The humiliations of this past year must have left her newly vulnerable. She'd been cut from every Society function. Received no invitations. Unless you counted the Duke of Cranbrook's wedding. To which she would *not* have been invited if she wasn't the bride.

The heat, the smoke, the alcohol—she could feel them going to her head. A rising giddiness. But wasn't she always light-headed, *empty*-headed, a giddy girl, so different from Neal's mother and sisters, from the legendary Mrs. Pendrake? What would it be like to have a head filled up with the names of plants and Chinese mountain ranges? She moved her head experimentally on her shoulders, imagining it. A widow. An intelligent widow. Free to board a train alone and meet a man and lodge with him at the edge of the world, or at least the edge of England. What *were* Muriel Pendrake's intentions? What were Neal Traymayne's?

He raised his ale, eyes meeting hers over the rim of the glass as he tipped his head back. She didn't even know if he was a bachelor, a widower, a married man. Perhaps, though, Mrs. Pendrake knew. She couldn't give herself away by asking the question directly. He started in on his third pasty.

"Are you . . ." She rubbed her fingertips against her palms, feeling the glide of the grease and the grit of the salt. "Have you been . . . lucky? You said, your imagination caught fire . . . have you found, for yourself . . ." Dear God, she must be delirious.

He chewed his pasty, then wiped his fingers on his napkin. For a moment, he looked at her. His nose and cheekbones were like crags interrupting the plane of his face. That bump on his nose, its crookedness, emphasized his unswerving gaze.

"Alas, no." He tilted his head. "I'm a bachelor. I looked, but I looked in the wrong places. The most obvious mistake you can make as a plant hunter. You'd think I'd have known better."

The giddiness spread. Her body tingled with new awareness. A bachelor. So this was to be a seduction. Suddenly, she stood on firmer ground. She knew a thing or two about seduction. She'd given her heart—more than her heart—to London's most notorious seducer.

She could manage a seduction far more handily than she could manage the flora of Cornwall. *Thank heavens.* And to think she'd been worrying that he was serious about the botanizing!

*Be careful*, a voice inside her whispered. *He's likely serious about both. He might even think they're the same thing.*

"We all make mistakes," she said, then lifted her glass and drained it. Had Mrs. Pendrake made a mistake when she failed to board that train to Bodmin Station? Had she missed her destiny? But Lavinia didn't have time to spare tears on Mrs. Pendrake's account. She doubted Mrs. Pendrake would have much use for them anyway.

Neal pushed his hair back from his forehead and a thick lock sprang back instantly. His hair tended toward disorder, was just long enough for its natural curl to make a show of its resistance to the comb. He needed pomade, vats of it. Probably he made his own pomade out of some viscous plant material and honey. *Varnham's Pomade.* God save ladies and gentlemen from ambitious gardeners.

"Where did you find Mr. Pendrake? If you don't mind my asking."

It seemed that Neal and Mrs. Pendrake had not shared much in the way of confidences. An exchange of unscented, sober, intelligent letters about *specimens*. Good thing. Their restraint gave her freer rein for invention.

"Our fathers were friends." She broke the corner off her second pasty and nibbled it. "I knew him from a child." George would laugh if he could see her, playacting the part of an eccentric, plant-obsessed widow. He wouldn't mind a bit if she cast him as that lucky unfortunate Mr. Pendrake.

"Did he always have a love of the outdoors?" Between those starry black lashes, Neal's irises shone a warm brown. Something had gentled in his gaze.

She laughed. "No indeed. He loved clubs, theaters, gaming dens, public houses, gin palaces. I think he only saw the sun during horse races. A scapegrace you could call him. Ran up enormous debts. Got hauled in front of magistrates."

Neal's eyebrows shot up. "And you knew?"

"Everyone knew." That and much more. George had been linked to all sorts of women. Actresses, singers. Demimondaines. A Polish countess. The Princess of Wales. She'd let him cajole her into discounting those particular stories.

*Vinnie*, he'd purr against her ear, against her lips. *My Vinnie. Lies are always loudest. The truth is you and me. The truth is* this.

"I loved him regardless," she said. "We loved each other."

Neal leaned back in his chair. One hand cupped his elbow, the other his chin. He was lean but well-muscled, broad across the shoulders. Bent, his arms bulged. George had been taller, thinner, more finely modeled, with that straight nose, that golden hair. Perfectly beautiful. A wicked angel.

"So," she said on a breath. "We eloped." Here the story would depart from reality. "We eloped and went to France. After that he changed completely. Abandoned his old ways. Started picking flowers." She'd often dreamed such foolishness. George transformed by married life, waking up early enough to take her shopping on Regent Street, to host stylish luncheons, to star in all of London's most glamorous daytime activities. The heir apparent to a dukedom and his lady promenading. Turning heads. Setting trends.

She managed a weak smile. "And that's that. Before we knew it, we were legendary plant collectors."

Neal stirred in his chair, some thought tilting the corner of his mouth. She couldn't read his expression.

"What?"

"Nothing." He shook his head. "Only—you defended the Season so staunchly. But you yourself didn't give a fig for the protocols. Eloping with a childhood friend . . . France, then the Far East . . . multiple commissions from Edevane & Fernsby . . ." He shrugged. "You made your own opportunity."

"What of it?" She looked at a spot above his head. The spiral of smoke looked almost blue. Belched from the very bowels of that hellacious hearth. "We both know that I am exceptional."

"Hmm." The low sound he made might have been affirming or disbelieving. Her eyes flew to him. He had a firm mouth, but his lips knew how to curve just so. He *was* a flirt. A flirt trying so hard to fool himself about his better nature, he'd fooled her too.

"*I* never thought to meet my future husband at a musical evening or lawn tennis match," she said. "I always knew who I was going to marry."

She'd even delayed her Season by a year because her *future husband* had tempted her with a wilder, far more alluring proposition. George had helped her orchestrate the lie to her parents, supplying her with the name of the elite finishing school where she was to refine her manners and her French, as well as the name of the genteel friend with whom she'd share her room. He'd even sent the friend's "mother" to call on her own. To this day, Lavinia had no idea from whence this woman came, a dignified woman, well-bred and solemn, diamonds in her hair, armed with stupefying minutia about the operations of the Parisian school, the charms of its aristocratic headmistress, whom she claimed as a near relation. George could be thoughtless, but he could also be *thorough*.

The weeks they had spent together on the French coast remained the happiest of her life. She'd learned *everything* about love, about being in love. Some nights George went out gambling and didn't come back to the hotel until the early morning, long after she'd cried herself to sleep. But those agonizing absences made his embraces, his kisses, all the sweeter.

The following spring, when she'd debuted, danced in lacy white, sipped lemonade with the other girls, she'd burned with memories, with her secret knowledge. Her *wickedness*. George had made her flesh of his flesh. She was like him, a beautiful, damned, gorgeous creature, wildly, wickedly alive. Everyone else was stuffed with straw and clockworks. Of course he was going to marry her. *As soon as my damned sire stops acting so feudal. As soon as I've dispatched his latest mortally plain matrimonial candidate. After Ascot week. After I've fixed a few bad tallies. Soon, my darling, my Vinnie. I'll paint our names on the dome of St. Paul's Cathedral, you'll see.* She'd never doubted. She'd turned down a dozen other offers, doling out rejections haughty or enigmatic, depending on the suitor.

She had considered herself engaged to George until the day he died.

How could everything solid melt into air? How could every truth be a falsehood? Her life had reversed, as though she'd passed through the looking glass.

Her heart began to pound that dark rhythm. *Doom-doom. Doom-doom.*

"You must miss him very much." Neal spoke softly. She realized, with a small jolt, that he had observed the changes in her expression, mapped the longing, confusion, and despair.

"I thought I would die too," she replied, fisting her hands. She'd never been able to speak her pain aloud. She'd never had the right.

She hadn't been George's wife, his fiancée. She hadn't even been one of his acknowledged conquests. She hadn't been anything to him at all, not that anyone knew. "I couldn't bear that the hours kept passing. It made no sense, that the clock hands hadn't stopped. I felt as though I were going mad."

Effie had wept openly at the funeral. She and George had never been close, but she was his sister, and very much alone, with Anthony stationed halfway around the world. Lavinia had wept too. No one had looked askance. A pretty, sentimental young girl always had leave to weep in a church. And she had been a childhood friend of the deceased, who was himself a beautiful young man gone before his time. Tears became her.

She had wanted to howl, to gnash her teeth, to burn the church to the ground.

"But the hours did keep passing." She dug her nails in her palms and took a quick, sharp breath. "I survived it."

Talking thus, with Neal watching her, his eyes so warm and kind, burst something small and hard inside her. The pain was more, and then, it was less.

He leaned forward, reaching out. She froze as his thumb and forefinger closed on a curl that lay close upon her temple. She felt a slight tug and then he withdrew.

"Ash," he said wryly, showing her the gray flake, then pressing it to powder.

"*Did* your mother's hair turn white in one day?" she asked, touching her curls gingerly. "You never said."

"I don't know." He smiled. "I was three years in South America. Her hair was white enough when I returned, but if it happened in an instant or over months, I'll never know. My siblings wouldn't dare contradict her."

"Why did you leave for so long?" The thick, hot air and the murmur of voices seemed to form a cocoon around them. She felt tired but disinclined to push back her chair, to say good night. The dark stone passages of the inn were empty and foreboding. This room, for better or worse, held all the life.

"Varnham gives three-year contracts, same as Edevane & Fernsby. Why did I leave in the first place, is that the question?"

"Of course," she said quickly. "Of course that's what I meant." Edevane & Fernsby. That would be the nursery that had employed the Pendrakes.

"I went on three collecting missions, in fact. The same as you." Another flake of ash floated over the table. This one he didn't catch. He blew upon it, and it looped up and was lost to view against the dark rafters. She tore her gaze from his lips.

*Three collecting missions?* That made nine years. How old was Mrs. Pendrake? *Thirty?* A blow, if she could pass for a woman at such a stage of life!

"Perhaps I'll write about them someday," he continued. "Your manuscript has inspired me."

*Manuscript?* She made a noncommittal noise, and he tipped his head back, a thoughtful angle.

"Why did I leave?" He mused for a brief moment as her eyes traced the strong line of his neck.

"Because I knew it would be hard." He straightened and looked at her. "In my life up until that point, it was as though . . . as though my parents had put everything they had on a low shelf for me. Love, knowledge. Everything, right there, within reach. I was grateful. But I also wanted to stretch out. To find things for myself."

She nodded, but she could scarcely give it credence. Such wholesomeness! So many of her acquaintances had grown up with every luxury, but so few talked of their parents with gratitude or love. *She* had been one of the exceptions, with her doting papa. The criminal. What a farce it turned out to be, her happy childhood.

Neal was speaking again, and she nodded again, listening. Or, wasn't she listening? Her papa was giving her a sweet from his pocket. Not a low shelf, but yes, she understood what Neal was saying. About the need to break free. To discover something on your own. She nodded again. Oh, dear. Her head jerked back. She was falling asleep at the table. Her cheeks flamed with mortification. Neal rose at once.

"That's enough of that," he said, considering her. "You're exhausted." Suddenly, he grinned. "Let's sneak out before Mary brings the pudding. It's not their specialty."

He produced a bill, wedged it beneath his plate. Overpaying thoughtlessly, as though he didn't count out his own earnings. George's noblesse oblige had manifested as a cynical extravagance, a way of putting others in their place. *Worship me. Worship me, so I can despise you more than I despise myself.* Neal was simpler. Too simple. It disconcerted.

As they made their way out into the hall, she tried not to look at the half-naked men slouched on stools or, God Almighty, sprawled on benches. Neal, though, stopped to exchange indecipherable phrases with several. One of the lot, a giant, gripped Neal by the shoulder and grinned. He was missing several teeth.

"You're popular." She couldn't help but remark it. Stepping into the dark hall was like plunging into cold water. She could feel him close behind her, feel the air displaced by his shrug.

"Theirs is a hard life," he said. "I remember the food riots when copper collapsed. Now the tin mines are closing. More and more Cornishmen are becoming Cousin Jacks, emigrating to work the mines in Australia, North America, South Africa. Then there are the ones like those, who hold on tight to what they know and are broken for it."

He wasn't Cornish. That was what she'd thought when she'd first heard him speak. His accent didn't place him in the West Country. The edges of his words had been polished by education, or by his years in London. Now she realized herself deceived.

"You think of yourself as one of them," she said. "A Cornishman."

His laugh was soft. "If I do, I might be the only one here. But I moved back, for better or worse. Watch yourself."

She promptly barked her shin on a settee. Something leapt down, hit the flagstones with a thud, and shot away. Neal maneuvered around her.

"Cat," he said, but she wasn't so certain. "I should have taken a candle."

She heard him feeling along the wall.

"This way."

She rested her hand on his forearm and let him guide her.

"Neal," she said, emboldened by the darkness. "You mentioned my manuscript . . ."

"Here's the first step." His arm moved over hers until he held her tightly. Together they mounted the stair.

"I read every word," he said. "The detail is most remarkable. If you dropped me in China I'd recognize the hillsides by the configurations of the trees."

*Jolly.* Her body felt warm where it pressed his. She tried again. "You don't have it with you?"

They reached the landing, chilly, with a damp odor, and moved along the passageway.

"I do," he said. "Of course I do. I promised we'd discuss it."

"I need it." The words burst from her. "I can't tell you how many errors came to mind as I sat on that train. They're plaguing me. I won't let them stand. Whole hillsides, completely misrepresented. You'll give it back to me?"

"Now?" He had a deep voice and it sounded deeper in the hushed darkness. They had stopped walking, but he still held her arm.

"*Now.*" She didn't care if she sounded desperate. That manuscript— it contained Mrs. Pendrake's thoughts, thoughts *she* needed to think if she were to continue her performance.

"As you like," he said, and pushed open a door. When he lit the candle, she could see that his room was the same as hers, the floorboards rough, the walls unpapered, the bed narrow. A single bare table stood in the corner. He'd pushed his trunk against the wall under the window and now he knelt beside it.

"Here." He handed her the fat sheaf of papers. The candlelight flickered over his face. His eyelashes cast spiky shadows on his cheeks, barred his brown eyes with impenetrable darkness. His lips were slightly open, shadows bracketing the corners, which had a humorous tilt. She held the manuscript against her chest. It wasn't the chill making her skin shiver.

A bachelor and a widow, unobserved together in the night. The bed was close enough to touch.

She wasn't a widow, of course. She was a married woman. If she hadn't fled Bodmin Station, she'd be in Fowey with the Duke of Cranbrook. She'd be lying on a mattress as soft as a cloud in an elegant bedroom. Lying beside—lying *under*—that foul old goat. A miracle that she was here instead. That she would sleep undisturbed, alone.

She didn't want to sleep alone. The admission widened her eyes. She wanted the warmth of this man pressed against her, the protection of his body, a shield against the terrors of the night. When she closed her eyes, the painful memories would crowd out pleasant dreams. The abyss of the future would open and swallow her. Neal looked strong. He looked *safe*. A bulwark. Dear God, she wanted to curl against him until morning. To take comfort in his solidity. She sensed that he would hold her if that was what she asked. That he would hold her without making demands of his own. How odd that he inspired such trust and so quickly.

Did the candle cause her face to flicker as well? What did he see when he looked at her? Her dry throat cracked as she drew breath.

"Let's get you to your room," he said.

When she'd shut her door behind her, she listened for his footsteps. They began after a pause—giving her time to wonder if he stood, as she did, with fingers on the door handle—then faded down the hall. She put Mrs. Pendrake's manuscript on the little table and tore through the contents of her trunk, lifting out the newest notebook, only a few pages covered with her scribbles, romantic stories begun and just as quickly abandoned. She used to entertain herself for hours, writing romances at her well-appointed, cunning little desk, thinly veiled fantasies of her life with George. First, these fantasies concerned their life to come. Later, their life that might have been.

At the Rossell Hotel, she'd stopped. Even fantasy had felt fragile. It couldn't support the weight of her attention but disintegrated into so much fairy dust.

The wind moaned outside the window and rain pattered the glass. Her fingers trembled as she undressed and they trembled as they closed on the pencil. She drew up her knees on the bed, curled on her side, notebook open, trying to write the line that would help her imagination take flight, lift her out of this desperate predicament.

*One fateful day*, she wrote, *the duchess decided she'd get on so much better as a pirate.*

She closed her eyes. There, she could see her, the beautiful blond duchess stealing away from her boor of a husband, running into the trees, where brigands had made their camp, a turf fire burning, their leader with his wild locks and craggy nose keeping lookout.

She'd expected to cry herself to sleep, but before the first tear could fall, she was falling herself and knew nothing until the sun rose red above the moor.

# CHAPTER FOUR

CORNWALL, LIKE ANY affliction, simply took some getting used to. When the fleas chased Lavinia from the bedroom, she repaired to the bar. When Mary harried her away, she found a seat in the back garden. When rain threatened, she ducked around the building, sheltered in the entranceway, then repeated the cycle. By late afternoon, she'd found her rhythm. The sun had become more certain, and she'd established herself in a corner of the back garden under an arch of flowering vines. Such delicate clusters of blossoms, white and palest purple. Why not let them alone, let them stay innocent and nameless? Scientists were horrible busybodies, sticking their noses into everything, imposing Latin where it didn't belong.

Sighing, she bent her head over Mrs. Pendrake's interminable "Recollections." The woman had marched the Roman alphabet all over China, giving no quarter.

*Focus.* A bird hopped along a water trough beside an outbuilding. Poor little bird. It, too, had probably had some Latin slapped all over it.

*Focus.* She bent her head lower, but her straw bonnet cast a shadow on the type, which strained her eyes. She angled her head this way and that. Sighed again. Her skin had finally calmed. She couldn't remove the bonnet and risk exchanging hives for freckles.

Varnham's Ointment soothed well enough, but it didn't lighten spots. She looked up and saw, with a start, that Neal was returning across the great expanse of moorland. His figure was still a dot in the green vastness, almost as distant as the black hills with their sinister rocky peaks.

She attacked "Recollections" with new vigor. Neal had not exaggerated about the detail. Mrs. Pendrake was launched on an exhaustive catalogue of the trees and shrubs of northwest Hupeh. Lavinia found the prose as wooden as the subject. She thumbed through a dozen pages. More shrubs. She flipped to the middle. A chapter on the latest techniques of bulb collection and carriage. *Lethal* book! She slammed it down beside her on the bench. She should bury it in the garden. Let it mingle with the roots and the seeds and the soil. Clearly, humans formed no part of the intended audience. Hardly a human received mention! And when humans did appear—the occasional diplomat, servant, villager, French missionary, fellow collector—did they receive the same consideration as the *Berberis verruculosa*? No, they did not. Mrs. Pendrake, so copious in her description of flora, fauna, and geology, couldn't conjure more than a solitary adjective for the "friendly" members of a mountain tribe or the "charming" wife of the British consul. Even the dearly departed Esmé Pendrake remained a colorless outline.

What kind of *people* were they, the Pendrakes? What was their provenance and breeding? What were the conditions of the soil from which *they* sprang? Mrs. Pendrake wrote nothing of interest, nothing relevant.

Exasperated, she pulled off her gloves and dropped them on the manuscript, a makeshift paperweight. *No more.* Tying the velvet ribbon more tightly beneath her chin, she struck off down the grass bank to meet Neal. The turf looked dry enough. It wasn't. As the ground leveled and began its slow, immense roll toward the oddly shaped hills, water seeped up over her slippers with every step.

"Hallo!" Neal called a greeting that the moors stretched so it sounded mournful. Dark birds lurched into flight between them. Ravens, or buzzards. Crows. Did it matter? She decided to wait, the wind shuddering her skirts. She'd dressed in her plainest gown but she'd no intention of letting the hem drag through weeds and slime.

"Couldn't resist after all." He drew near, offered her an impish grin. He wore the same brown canvas coat and gaiters, but framed against the sea of rock and heather, the rough outfit seemed less laughable. He himself was composed of rough features and natural tones, as though meant to blend with hills, forest, or field. George had startled the senses. Eyes of unlikely jewel blue. Hair like beaten gold. Striking pallor. But an untrained gaze could sweep over Neal Traymayne, all shades of brown. Bark-brown hair, honey-brown eyes, sun-browned skin. Humble as a hummock.

Her gaze clung to him as his stride halved, then quartered the yards between them. He didn't look *humble*. He looked a ruffian, of the moor but not bound by it, entirely unowned, as free as the wind.

"I wish I'd time to show you the marsh, and the tor," he said, pausing before her. "But I saw Tomas's carriage on the road. He stopped at the Jenkinses' farm is my guess, but he won't be long."

She turned to look at the ribbon of road running past the big gray inn, winding through the patchwork of fields.

"You can't mistake Tomas's carriage. It's cream colored, for one thing. Cream with sky-blue. No one wants a doctor rolling up in a black coach like Death himself come calling. Or that's what Tomas says. My theory? He likes a bit of flash. I sometimes think *those* Traymaynes would have done better in London than our branch."

He started walking again, more slowly, inviting her to fall into step.

"He's taking us to Kyncastle?" she asked. "Where you're from?"

"Where my father was from." He shaded his eyes, looking down the road. No cream-colored carriage as yet. She could make out a house on a ridge and dozens of pale specks ranging up the slope. If she were a betting girl, this time she'd go with cows. "We lived in

Penzance, near my mother's family. But we visited the Kyncastle cousins every summer when the pilchards started running. We children were meant to help, bringing buckets of fish and salt to the women in the cellar, but all we did was add to the confusion."

He laughed. What a talent he had for gaiety. Mirth without malice. There was always something a bit cold, a bit cutting, about laughter in London, at least among her set. *Former* set. Oh, they'd smiled her half to death during Papa's trial.

This morning, Neal had not looked quite so gay. She'd descended the stairs at half ten to discover him leaning against the wall by the inn's massive front door, arms folded, brow cocked. Everything about his posture communicated restlessness. At that moment, half-asleep, stiff from a night of myriad discomforts, she could have stamped her foot at the injustice. She hadn't known plant collectors kept such shocking hours! In London, she'd just be ringing for the breakfast tray. How dare he make her feel that she'd delayed! The certainty that Mrs. Pendrake would have bounded out of bed at dawn sharpened her tongue.

"Why do you stand there like that?" she'd snapped. "I'm not a cat to be herded out the door. If you want to go, go, but don't tap your foot at me. I won't be rushed along. Besides, I've better things to do than botanize a blasted heath!"

As she'd swept past him into the bar, his expression had registered shock, and something else. Why, he'd rather resembled a jilted lover. She'd almost whirled around and thrown down the gauntlet. *If you want to make love to Mrs. Pendrake, say so and do let's stay inside. No need to muddy ourselves digging up violets.* Luckily, she'd mastered herself. Better not to talk about making love. Or, for that matter, to talk about "Mrs. Pendrake" in the third person. She hadn't whirled. She'd processed grandly through the empty room and sat at the largest table, where she was served a lowering meal of hard bread and ripe cheese.

Neal certainly didn't mope like a jilted lover. The pique he'd seemed to feel at her behavior had blown by. His smile was open and his step undeniably jaunty. She wondered if he might be the least broody soul she'd ever encountered. In *her* world, everyone made a game of nursing grudges. Maybe as a nurseryman, he was too busy watering the plants.

"How was it? The botanizing?" She pointed at the long metal box that hung at his hip. "Did you fill your vasculum?" She felt a strange thrill as she said the word. At least she'd gleaned *something* from "Recollections." Vasculum. And that cloth-wrapped rectangle hanging from his other shoulder—that was a portfolio.

"Not bad for a blasted heath," he said, grinning as color flooded her cheeks. "I did get lashed by rain. But I found a few decent samples for the herbarium."

"Of course, I normally wake much earlier." She looked straight ahead so the curve of her bonnet hid her eyes. "On other occasions, I will be eager to join you."

*Oh, stuff.* She didn't have much experience with apologies. She could only hope she'd landed in the general vicinity.

"Teasing," he said. "It's one of my many bad habits. Easy to acquire if you're the youngest of five, and I never even bothered to resist. Impatience is another of my faults. I'm sorry I was waiting for you this morning with such obvious ill grace."

She blinked, angling her head to look at him. *He* apologized very neatly.

"When you asked for your manuscript last night . . ." He shrugged, adjusting the strap of the vasculum with long, skillful fingers. "I should have inferred you'd want to spend the day correcting those errors you mentioned."

*About that manuscript.*

"What do you think of my 'Recollections'?" The ground was sloping up now, a gradual rise that would lead them to the back garden. She slowed their pace. His smile shifted, became a touch more complex.

"It's wonderful," he said smoothly. "Brilliant. A milestone in botanical literature. You'd asked me about possible publishers. I thought I might put you in touch with my friend Alan De'Ath. He's an art critic, not an editor, but he knows all the literary people. He's also—"

She interrupted. "You do think it should be published, then? You don't find it irredeemably dull?"

She stopped, catching her breath. She wasn't hardened to all this tramping over varied terrain. He stopped too. The clouds shifted overhead and a beam of sun slanted across his face. He could afford to go hatless. He didn't freckle but tanned evenly. When they caught the light, his irises looked warm, bright. She hadn't realized brown eyes could *be* so bright.

"I don't know what you mean." He gave her a quizzical glance. "The book is comprehensive, but—"

"I mean the writing," she said. "The sentences! They go on and on and on. I found one that ran across three pages and half of it was Latin. You said you read every word. You didn't once cry for mercy?"

"Cry for mercy?" He laughed, realized she was serious, and sobered, eyes narrow. "Of course I didn't. Writers are always severe with their own work. When we were at Oxford, Alan drew a pistol and *shot* one of his manuscripts. He might have been rusticated, or even expelled, but during the disciplinary proceedings, the manuscript came before the dean, who was so impressed he gave Alan a prize."

She rolled her eyes. "Bullets aren't known for handily dispatching paper. I think your friend Alan *wanted* to get his manuscript in front of the dean. Otherwise he would have thrown it into the fire." Lord knew she'd burned stories, poems, and love letters enough to heat a country home through a year of Januarys. "That is the preferred method."

Neal whistled through his teeth. "Just like Alan too. I never thought of it." He shook his head, sunstruck eyes glinting. "Aren't you clever."

She looked away. Devious was more like it.

"Teasing again," he said. "You're more than clever. As for your 'Recollections,' I respect the erudition."

"Blast the erudition!" She glared at him. "I say very explicitly in the preface that my intention in writing is *to capture the bold and energizing spirit of the age of botanical discovery.*" She was quoting now. "It's not meant to be an erudite book but an energizing one. Something to *thrill readers and inspire new enterprises.* Were you thrilled?"

"*I* was thrilled, yes." He rubbed the bridge of his nose. He was a big, strong man in a vast, open space, but suddenly he looked cornered. "Perhaps it's a bit technical for the nonprofessional reader."

"The chapter on how to pack bulbs?"

"Not the strongest of the chapters," he murmured.

"The hundred-page list of shrubs?"

"Several of them invaluable introductions." He frowned. "Encountering them in print, all together, does require a certain fortitude."

"You promised to discuss it with me." Now that she saw weakness, she bore down with all her might. "Was your idea of discussion a few blandishments? I set out to write an adventure. The book is a patent failure on its own terms! Were you not going to tell me? Is that the measure of your respect?"

"Christ." His brow knotted. Eyes narrowed, he cut a look at her through his lashes. She ignored the flutter in her stomach. Bizarre. She'd begun her line of questioning in an attempt to validate her own struggle with the manuscript. She'd wanted to enlist Neal *against* Mrs. Pendrake for the secret gratification of her own sensibility. But suddenly, she seemed to be arguing for Mrs. Pendrake, *as* Mrs. Pendrake. A woman who deserved honesty from her colleagues. Not mollycoddling.

"You're right." Neal made the admission, a curious expression on his face. "About the book, you're perhaps too harsh. I won't let you burn it, or even shoot it. But you're right to demand more from me than flattery."

She stared at him. "I'm often right," she said. "And often demanding."

She let her lips curve and saw his eyes flick to her mouth. What *would* she demand from Neal Traymayne? Last night, she'd wanted him to hold her. Now, in the light of day, the wind blowing against her, cool and scented with herbs, she suddenly felt bolder and more playful. She was a vagabond, after all, capable of anything. A pirate of lives. She'd captured the *Mrs. Pendrake* and could steer her in any direction, full sail.

Not a bachelor and a widow. A ruffian and a vagabond. The way forward more perilous and more delicious.

The wind changed direction, and she gathered her skirts and ran with the strong gust at her back. He was at her side in an instant, and together they crested the long, low hill. The inn rose before them. She didn't care that her feet were wet, that she had fleabites on her ankles. This feeling was worth anything. She turned to look back at the moor, that strange, earthen ocean, the shadows of the quick-moving clouds streaming over the grass.

"There's none of *this* in the book. The way it all makes you *feel*. That's what's missing." She turned her head. He was closer than she'd thought, below her on the hill so their faces were almost level.

"How does it make you feel?" His tone was light, amused, but his gaze had become speculative.

She laughed. What was the word? *Intoxicated?*

"Free," she said. When she smiled, she heard his breath hitch. He wasn't smiling. He was looking at her, the hollows standing out below the hard bumps of his cheekbones. His lower lip was full. You hardly noticed the fullness of that lip on a face so dominated by cheekbone and nose. Until you did. She decided a legend could refer to herself in the third person.

"How do you feel about Muriel Pendrake?"

Now he smiled. "I'm afraid you'll accuse me of flattery."

"Another of your faults." She shook her head, mocking him. He wasn't the only one adept at teasing. She had no siblings, but as children she and Effie and Anthony had twitted each other mercilessly.

"I was schooled to flattery in London. I didn't grow up in Society, but I'm not a stranger to it."

She hid her smirk. "You attended balls, then—pardon, *human zoos*—as an ethnographer?" She managed an innocent smile.

"Not exactly." The sun was behind him, his eyes in shadow. "Or if so, I took it too far. I engaged myself to an inmate."

"Engaged!" Amazement made her sputter. Amazement and displeasure. But . . . he was *her* discovery. A Cornish *gardener*, for the love of God. Yes, he'd lived in London, even gone to Oxford, albeit briefly, but he was refreshingly removed from the ton and its intrigues. Wasn't he? An unknown, like a hardy, inconspicuous weed no one had yet ruined with a string of pompous syllables. *Bachelor rusticus*. He couldn't have been engaged to a woman in Society! When? *Who?*

"I planted an avenue of monkey puzzle trees for her father." He shrugged. "It was not a good match. Ultimately, we agreed on that, if on nothing else."

Her eyes traced the lines of his naked neck. Had he shown himself to his fiancée without a collar? Had she tolerated canvas? Unbelievable. Granted, he cleaned up well, but nothing could be done about the fact that he *planted trees* for a living.

"Her parents couldn't have approved." She felt her frown deepen. Her own papa would never have indulged an attachment formed with a hireling who pushed a wheelbarrow, even if he was the head of his own nursery.

He pushed his hair off his forehead. His naked hand was broad and the sight of it did something queer to her insides.

"They made no objections." He moved his head and the sun glittered darkly along his jaw, the roughness there. He needed to shave. Badly. The rooms at the inn did not come equipped with basins. "On the contrary, my mother voiced her very strong displeasure."

She blinked. "But that's impossible." Was there something *wrong* with the girl?

"Why impossible? You haven't met my mother."

She didn't think she wanted to meet his mother. She pictured the woman in trousers, wielding a pickaxe and breathing fire. She let it pass.

"Your fiancée," she persisted. "She was a member of Society, and I assume not without the advantages a mother would wish for her son, particularly if that son had no certain prospects of his own."

"Are you asking if she was rich?" That bluntness couldn't have served him well at Society dinners. He sighed. "Quite rich. Beautiful too. But beauty fades. If you marry for beauty, you find your wife fades too."

"Wonderful line. Your mother's?" She folded her arms. The wind gusted but it didn't set her body to tingling or lend her feet wings. She felt heavier. "So, your fiancée was too beautiful for your mother's liking. How vexing for you. But some mothers are competitive with their daughters-in-law and prefer their sons marry dowdy women. Sons, however, tend to do what they please."

"My mother was right, though." He shook his head. "About Elizabeth and me. We would have made each other miserable."

He couldn't mean Elizabeth Fletcher? Her father owned a dozen factories. She'd have made Neal a fortune. She was rich enough, and frankly vulgar enough, to get away with marrying a gardener.

"It's a misery, yes, when you have too much money." She scoffed, even as images of her friends rose before her eyes, smiling cold smiles, dripping with jewels. George, sick with drink, clinging to the balcony railing, rings on every finger. You could *choose* to be miserable with too much money, certainly. But once your money was gone, you had no choice in the matter.

Neal had never been very rich, or very poor. He would never be able to understand her trajectory, the highs and lows, the aspirations and disappointments.

"Or doesn't your mother want you to stop digging holes? I recall she's fond of it herself."

She worried for a moment she'd gone too far. But Neal didn't bridle, simply raised a brow.

"She knows why I'm committed to Varnham." He drummed his fingers on his vasculum. "When I was with Elizabeth, I wasn't myself. I was trying to fit into the wrong mold. My mother saw that."

"So you ended it." She tugged at her bonnet strings with a touch too much force.

"Elizabeth ended it. She's thriving, I hear. Engaged to a baronet. Her father's monkey puzzle trees are thriving too. I had occasion to check when I was last in London."

There, a touch of irony. And she had doubted he had an ironic bone in his body. Another of his London acquisitions.

"But you wanted to know how I felt about Muriel Pendrake." He grinned, a crooked grin, most likely intended to charm. Was that his London grin? She gave the bonnet strings a final tug and dropped her hands.

"I've changed my mind," she said. She felt strangely humiliated, as though, in recounting the story of his engagement, he'd rejected *her*. She'd never been faulted for her beauty or her wealth. Quite the contrary. Beauty and wealth were her chief recommendations. Perhaps her only recommendations. To him they seemed no recommendation at all.

Despite herself, she had developed a fascination for his blunt gaze, the rough line of his outrageous nose, his smile, that tanned neck he exposed like he really *was* a king among outlaws. Why, she would *fall* in his estimation if he knew she was an absconded duchess. If he knew her only knowledge of plants derived from years of helping her mother spend the dahlia budget. He'd probably preferred her with her rashes. At least then he could keep priding himself on his colossal respect for her *mind*.

Mrs. Pendrake's mind. Mrs. Pendrake's courage. Mrs. Pendrake's insufferable erudition.

But his eyes *had* dropped to her mouth. His breath *had* caught when she smiled. He wasn't immune to her—the real her, Lavinia.

"I'll tell you anyway." His eyes glowed. The pause lengthened. Slowly, he raised a thick arm, and she thought for a heart-racing moment he was going to pull her against him. But his gaze tracked sideways, and he swung the arm back and forth, waving in greeting. His coat rattled and clanked. Flustered, she turned. A man in tartan trousers bounded toward them, waving his bowler hat. When he reached Neal, he let out an undoctorly whoop, caught him behind the neck with a hooked arm, and tried to wrestle him to the ground. Neal, with a powerful twist, rolled him across his broad back. The man landed neatly on his feet and seized Neal again, but this time they embraced, laughing.

"Muriel." Neal spun to grin down at her. "Meet my cousin Tomas."

# CHAPTER FIVE

MERRY CONFUSION REIGNED in the household of the Kyncastle Traymaynes. Neal smiled at the familiar commotion. There were new faces, but the tenor hadn't changed over the decades. In the large, bright dining room, children tumbled underfoot. Dogs barked hopefully as platters of chops passed over their heads.

*Boiling* was what his mother called it when family came together. *The house scarcely holds the whole boiling of us.*

Muriel didn't seem to know what to make of the boiling. Nor did his cousins know what to make of Muriel. His letter describing a female botanist joining him for a bit of collecting hadn't prepared them. How could it have? He hadn't been prepared himself.

*Pretty as an apple blossom* was Tomas's murmured pronouncement once Muriel had been swept up in the whirl of introductions. Neal had smiled at the saying, even as he bristled at the implication. Muriel Pendrake's prettiness was neither here nor there.

But pretty she was. Her pale blond hair was only a few shades more golden than apple-blossom white, and her eyes startled with their crystalline blueness. Now that the swelling had subsided, her nose appeared thin and straight as a pin. Its fineness emphasized the full and rosy lips, cut along the lines of a cupid's bow. Gone, the sweet, off-kilter quality to her features, the disarming imperfections. Her loveliness overwhelmed.

He tried to stay beside her so she wasn't boiled alive. Soon, though, he was corralled, first by Tomas's sisters, Alice, Loveday, and Emmeline, and then by Kelyn, Tomas's wife. Kelyn fired questions as their twins—crawling when he'd seen them last—clung to his legs. One of them gnawed his shin. A man always had a reason for gaiters. If this expedition had taught him anything thus far, it was that.

"Hold tight," he warned as he walked the length of the dining room table to where Tomas knelt, arms stretched out. Gleefully, the twins released Neal's legs and began to climb their father.

"And how is Nessa?" Kelyn had followed. "And Jenni?"

"Both thriving," said Neal. "Eager for news of you and the children."

Kelyn set a dish of fried potatoes on the table, which was already groaning beneath the weight of the repast. Family meant everything to the Traymaynes. Alice, the eldest, had long ago married and moved across the valley, but her siblings still celebrated her return to the house, a near weekly occurrence, with elaborate, exuberant meals. For Neal's less frequent visits, they outdid themselves.

"What a feast," he said, admiring the spread of steaming dishes.

"And how is your mother?" The question coincided with a small lull in the noisy preparations. Neal had been waiting for it. He looked at Kelyn, then at Tomas, who dislodged the twins and came to stand at Kelyn's side. Tomas's face had grown uncommonly grave.

"Sharp as ever." Neal took a breath. "And hoping you all come to Penzance for the Golowan Festival." After a moment's hesitation, he continued in a lower voice. "She says it will be her last."

He suddenly felt Muriel's eyes on him. She was standing nearby, against the wall, keeping out of the path of the children, the dogs, and the bustling women. She didn't approach, but as his gaze brushed hers, he saw that she was listening. He acknowledged her presence with a small nod. He didn't want her to feel she was intruding. He'd brought her into the thick of it all. She could hear anything he had to say.

Kelyn took his hand. "That might not be so, Neal."

"I told Perran." Tomas caught their old lurcher by the scruff of her neck before she could nose Muriel's skirts. "I've extirpated tumors myself. I'm no homicidal vivisectionist, you know that. Operative treatments are yielding encouraging results."

"Thank you for those letters." Neal smiled at his cousin. "She trusts your medical opinion more than she does that of her own sons in this instance." It was true. She'd refused to listen to Perran or Jory, both well-respected doctors, convinced they'd let desperation override their reason. But in the end, Tomas, too, had failed to bring her around.

Neal released Kelyn's hand and pressed his fist into his thigh. The muscle in his arm went rigid. "If anyone could have convinced her, it would have been you."

"Stubborn woman." Tomas shook his head. "God love her."

Heddie Traymayne had always been stubborn. She'd ignored her symptoms for months. Neal suspected she'd seen signs even earlier than she admitted, that her illness was well advanced before she sought advice, and that, as a result, she was correct in her assessment.

Surgery was not an option.

Tomas took the hand Neal had released and kissed his wife's knuckles. "Well, my treasure, what say you to midsummer in Penzance?"

Kelyn dimpled. She had a round, sweet face and a steadfastness that acted as an anchor for her more mercurial husband. "As long as you keep the twins out of the fires."

"Might have to truss them like chickens," Tomas grumbled. "The scamps."

At that moment, they'd set their sights on Muriel and were waddling toward her at full speed, grubby hands outstretched. She drew back against the wall with a gasp.

"Do you have children of your own?" Kelyn addressed Muriel kindly, as Neal scooped a twin and held him kicking under his arm. Davy Strout, Loveday's fiancé, a strapping fishermen with a shoal of siblings, seized twin number two and turned him upside down. His squeals of delight were piercing. Muriel made a face.

"I am not so fortunate," she said.

"But you do like children?" asked Emmeline. She was the youngest of the sisters and, with her slim figure, brown ringlets, and lively green eyes, the acknowledged beauty of the family. She'd emerged from the kitchen with several manchet loaves on a board and was watching Muriel with her lips pursed.

"Of course I like children." Muriel smoothed her skirts and Emmeline's eyes followed the gesture, although whether it was the rings sparkling on Muriel's hand or the vivid blue silk that caught her eye, Neal couldn't guess. "And I adore babies. They're lovely tucked into wickerwork prams on the Champs-Élysées."

Emmeline goggled. *Dear God.* Neal hoisted his twin onto his shoulder. The boy immediately grabbed a fistful of his hair. Davy still dandled the other upside down and his face had turned red as a tomato.

"These two are a menace." Neal unwound his hair from the tugging hand and tweaked the boy's nose. "They'd do better in a wicker hamper." He glanced at Muriel, but she was staring dreamily into space. Her eyes seemed larger and more luminous. She'd been speaking completely in earnest. She *did* adore babies, just not the two in front of her. She adored perfectly composed, picturesque babies, babies presented at opportune moments by the nursemaids and governesses who cleaned them, petted them, and dried their tears.

His future wife, so untypical in so many ways, typified her social class in others. He had a feeling he could break his brain trying to figure it out. He sighed, depositing his twin gently on the threadbare carpet.

"We could sail to France, would you like that, Kitto?" Davy flipped the boy and set him on his feet. Kitto turned a dizzy circle and sat hard on his bum.

"Why, have you a sailing ship?" Muriel's head snapped toward Davy, the mist clearing from her eyes. She stared, lips parted. Davy cocked a brow, not above a bit of grandstanding.

"I captain a fine fishing boat," he said, grinning madly. "Will that do you?"

Davy was a good chap, Neal had always thought, and devoted to Loveday, but, regardless, a bit of a jackanapes. If he didn't watch himself, Emmeline would give him a wallop with the breadboard. Her pursed lips had compressed into a hard line, and the bread was in danger of sliding off the board. She'd tilted it like a cricket bat. She was a high-spirited girl and fiercely protective of her older sister. Neal stepped between Emmeline and Davy to offer Muriel a wink.

"Leave Davy to the pilchards," he said. *And to Loveday*, he thought, but added only: "We'll sail to France from the Lizard, how's that? It's a shorter trip."

The words ignited something within her. Her eyes burned his.

"You mean it?" she asked, oddly breathless. His jaw tensed. Oh, he would break his brain for sure. He'd intended to jape, not proffer a real possibility.

"You truly want to sail to France?" He said it with barely contained disbelief. "Like a smuggler?"

"Exactly," she cried. "Yes, that's it." Her color had heightened. Ferocity of expression ill befitted such a doll-like countenance, but by God, she managed. All she wanted was the cutlass. He touched a thumb to his forehead and laughed his perplexity. What in bloody hell had happened to Muriel Pendrake between today and the date of her last letter?

*You asked what I would most like to see on our venture*, she had written. *I find I cannot rank my various enthusiasms. Certainly the rare clovers, and the rushes, and that unusual heather you've described with the pink flowers tipped with crimson anthers. As eager as I am to explore the cliffs, coves, and valleys—the whole of Cornwall—and learn every one of her native plants, I confess I have a keen interest, too, in touring your hothouses in Truro, particularly to see the pitcher plants from Borneo. Perhaps I'm being greedy trying to fit it all in. We haven't yet begun and already I fear the time will fly by!*

That was then. Now, she didn't seem moved by moorland or heathland, by native species, or for that matter to remember her keen interest in his hothouses, in the pitcher plants and hybridized orchids. Far from fearing her time in Cornwall would fly too quickly, she couldn't fly to France quickly enough.

"In that case, you *are* better off with Davy," he said, with a slight bow to the younger man, who puffed out his chest, then frowned as Emmeline ground his toe with her heel. What Emmeline muttered sounded to Neal very like *sail to the dickens.*

Kelyn seemed to think so. She cleared her throat and took the breadboard carefully from Emmeline's hands.

"The lot of you can sail wherever you please," she said. Her voice was severe but she couldn't hide the twinkle in her eye. "But not now. Now it's time to eat."

Tomas sat at the head of the table as his family ranged down the sides. When Aunt Joan and Uncle Kitto were still alive, Uncle Kitto had been the one to preside over meals, making them all laugh with tales of his mishaps on the road. Washed-out bridges. An impassable stretch of sleeping sheep. As a family doctor, he'd spent dawn to dusk on horseback visiting far-flung patients. No flashy equipage. Not even a dog cart. Tomas was a different kind of doctor, with a thoroughly modern sensibility. Nonetheless, Neal could see how much it pleased him, taking on his father's role in the family, and in the county at large.

Tomas had never fought against the tide of his life, as Neal had. He hadn't lost time in mad, dangerous endeavors. Lost friends.

"The Jenkins girl has come round." Tomas was recounting his news from the day while Kelyn poured the beer. "Cobbe fell off the church wall and bruised his head, the rascal."

As Tomas spoke, the rest of the family interrupted with questions and sallies. Laughter rang out. Neal's thoughts drifted.

*You can't wander the world forever, my boy, like an anointed rogue.* That was what his father had said when Neal returned from his first commission with Varnham and contracted at once for the second.

*There's too much Traymayne in you. You'll see. Your roots are too deep.*

His eyes found Muriel. She sat catty-corner to him, between Davy and Alice's husband, William. William was a great bear of a man, as gentle in nature as one of his Jersey cows. He'd been married to Alice for the better part of a decade, but, at that moment, Muriel was smiling up at him and he looked as besotted as a schoolboy. He served her half the dish of fried potatoes before he realized what he was doing. Alice didn't seem to mind, or even notice. She was calling to their three children, who'd decided to play a game of libbety-lat on the stairs.

"Libbety-lat, libbety-lat." Their voices chorused as their feet pounded the step. "Who can do this and who can do that?"

"I tried," Alice said comfortably, abandoning her efforts and forking a chop onto her plate. "By sunset, they'll be hungry as the grave, and I'll remind them they chose libbety-lat for dinner."

"We'll send you home with whatever you like," said Kelyn, laughing. "We can't let the children go hungry. They're thin as lathes."

"Oh, don't mind that. The more they eat, the thinner they get." Alice sighed. "I can't say they feature me in that respect."

"So you're not wanting me to pass you this gravy?" Kelyn made to put down the gravy boat, and Alice reached for it, dimples flashing.

"That I never said."

"Leave a drop for our guest." Tomas grinned at Muriel as Alice doused her chop. "I hope you like potatoes."

Muriel looked down at the mountain on her plate.

"Oh, I'm sure I'll like these," she said. She picked up her fork and took a tiny bite. "Exquisite," she said, treating the table at large to a dazzling smile. "You don't know how difficult it is to find a decent cook in London."

She looked to Neal for confirmation. He smiled back, teeth aching where the molars ground together. Elizabeth herself couldn't have chosen a less apposite line. He registered the unfairness of his irritation even as it flared. There was a pause before Kelyn spoke up.

"I am the cook," she said mildly. "But William grew the potatoes, so I don't dare take the credit. They come flavorful from the ground."

Muriel blushed furiously.

"I've often thought it would be charming to cook," she said to Kelyn. "A soufflé, for example. It could become all the rage. *Cooking*. You could make an evening of it."

His cousins exchanged little glances. Muriel straightened her shoulders, her face bright with embarrassment. But she *would* be a success. Neal could see the determination stamped on her features. Irritation aside, he had to hand it to her. She didn't give up easily. You could admire the tenacity, if you ignored the technique. Eyes wide, she turned to William.

"And you!" She shook her head. "I would never have known you for a farmer. I thought one distinguished farmers by their smocks."

Emmeline made a choking sound. William tugged the lapels of his dark jacket and smiled uncertainly. Muriel bit her lip, eyes narrowing as she refined her strategy.

"You could pass for a man in town, is what I meant to say." She delivered this last with the air of a woman bestowing a considerable compliment and sat back in her chair, pleased.

"You do look well, William." Neal speared one of the last fried potatoes from the dish as he came to Muriel's rescue. "How is the herd?"

Unfortunately, William had always been a man of few words. The presence of a raving beauty at his elbow batting her eyes as she insulted him with the highest praise she could muster did nothing to loosen his tongue.

"Doing keenly," he said.

"Glad to hear it," said Neal after a pause.

"Summering on the moor," William added, with a touch of desperation. He turned his attention abruptly to his plate and began to masticate an overlarge bite of chicken.

For several minutes, silverware clinked, silvery notes against the background of pounding feet. Davy bumped Muriel as they reached for their glasses.

"It's my curse," he said with a grin. "Click-handed." He waggled the fingers of his left hand. Muriel looked at him blankly.

"Left-handed," hissed Emmeline. "Click-handed means left-handed."

Tomas laughed, leaning forward. "Mrs. Pendrake, you can settle my mind on something. Are the Chinese as deuced difficult to understand as the Cornish?"

"I should say not." Muriel reached again for her glass. "I spent years in China, however, and I've only just come to Cornwall."

"You speak Chinese, then?" Tomas lifted his eyebrows at Neal.

"Perfectly," said Muriel, sipping. "I speak Mongolian as well. And the languages of the Malay archipelago. Oh, and Latin of course, but only with plants."

Neal felt his own eyebrows lift. She'd mentioned her facility with language in her "Recollections," but he hadn't realized the extent of it. No doubt it had given her and her husband the edge over the collectors who had to rely exclusively on translators.

Impressive. A welcome reminder of what he already knew: the

pampered-miss routine belied her depths. It was the showy, quivering high note. Distracting from the lower, richer, more resonant music that swelled beneath.

Tomas shook his head admiringly. "That puts the rest of us to shame. Even Neal. What did you learn over there in the Argentine?"

"Some Spanish." Neal smiled. "Some Mapuche."

Tomas shrugged, dismissing the relatively partial accomplishment. He raised his glass to Muriel. "How do you say *to your health* in Chinese?"

"Oh, you don't. It's considered bad luck." Muriel put down her glass. Her eyes met Neal's. Their expression could have meant anything.

"Well then, we'll do it in Cornish," Tomas said. All around the table, glasses lifted and clanked together.

"Fish, tin, and copper!" Davy crowed, and swilled his beer.

"We're so happy to have you here." Kelyn beamed at Neal before turning to include Muriel in her warm regard. Muriel paled, her throat working. Then a new kind of smile crept across her face, tentative and impossibly beautiful. Neal felt some subtle, answering movement inside his chest. He'd have to remember to ask Perran if the heart was capable of smiling. Of course, Perran, overserious, would denounce him as a dunce and drag out an anatomy book. He never tired of lecturing his chuckleheaded younger brother. And Neal never tired of giving him cause.

"Tell us, Mrs. Pendrake, do you have brothers and sisters?" asked Loveday.

"Not a one." Muriel glanced at her, the smile still playing over her features.

"Neal must have told you about *his* sisters," said Loveday. "Nessa and Jenni. They're also intellectual women."

"When we were growing up, I thought their house was built of books," Alice interjected as she spooned peas from a tureen. "You couldn't see the walls. That's what I always noticed, the books, and those horrible stuffed seagulls and owls in Uncle Digory's study."

Fascinating, what caught in other people's memories.

"You thought Julius the owl was horrible?" Neal asked with interest.

Alice groaned. "You didn't name the thing!"

"Oh, Aunt Heddie's collection of skulls put the taxidermy to shame." Tomas sawed at a chop, grinning hugely.

Loveday turned back to Muriel. "Did your parents encourage your scientific pursuits?"

"My mother prefers hats to skulls," said Muriel with a dryness that increased the general mirth. Only Emmeline scowled. Neal leaned back in his chair, grinning. Society had supplied Muriel with the affectations of a spoiled girl, but it hadn't spoiled her.

When his mother had looked him in the eye on Christmas Day and said she wanted nothing more than to see him settled down at last, she had meant with a woman like Muriel Pendrake.

"The hats did sometimes incorporate gull wings." Muriel was smiling around the table. "Although birds of paradise were the favorite ornament."

"*Truly* horrible." Loveday's eyes had widened. "Scientific taxidermy is one thing. But the slaughter of thousands upon thousands of birds of paradise for their skins, *millions* of birds murdered yearly for *accessories* . . ." She shuddered. "Jenni formed a society, the Society for the Protection of Plumage. She campaigns against bird hats."

"She's winning in Cornwall," said Davy. "I've never seen a bird on a hat, not a dead one anyway."

William guffawed loudly.

"It's hardly a joking matter." Loveday gave Davy a troubled look. Neal doubted she'd ever seen a bird hat either, but Jenni had considerable powers of persuasion. What was more, Jenni was right. He cleared his throat.

"There are plenty of bird hats in London," he said. "I can attest to it. I know an ornithologist who keeps a log of birds he sees atop women's heads in the parks. Dead birds," he clarified, shooting a glance at Davy, who pulled a face to keep from laughing. "He has logged hummingbirds, bluebirds, robins, parakeets, starlings. It's not millions of birds, it's hundreds of millions. From North and South America. Africa. India, too. New Guinea."

He met Muriel's eyes. Her expression was as troubled as Loveday's. It must have cost her incalculably, defying family expectation, her entire upbringing, to follow her own path.

"Please," groaned Tomas. "We're all members of the Society for the Protection of Plumage in this house. Jenni made us sign pledges. You can spare us the statistics."

"Your mother doesn't still wear birds of paradise on her hats?" Loveday returned her attention to Muriel.

"Of course not." Muriel straightened. "I put a stop to that."

"Oh, well done!" cried Loveday. "Jenni will love to meet you."

"I look forward to it," said Muriel, and began to cut a potato wedge into fourths.

"A good thing fish don't go on hats," said Davy under his breath to William. This time William's guffaw clogged. His face purpled. Tomas rose to slap his broad back, and at last, he sputtered and collected himself. Emmeline was hiding her face in her hands.

Alice sighed. "Gravy, please."

Neal's grin lasted all the way through the whortleberry pie.

Later, as he walked with Muriel along the cliff path, he saw that her eyes kept wandering away from the wildflowers to fix on the sea. Kyncastle was nestled in a narrow ravine, a few whitewashed cottages scattered on the slopes, additional cottages and several shops lining the cobblestone streets that fronted the harbor. The water, lapping gently around the quay, whirled and crashed just beyond the cliffs, kingfisher blue waves shattering into foam on the rocks.

"Did they meet Elizabeth?" she asked suddenly, turning. He'd knelt to examine the wild thyme carpeting the edge of the path and sat back on his heels. The vantage was unusual. He had to slant a look up at her. She'd taken off her bonnet and hung it about her wrist. The setting sun gave her hair and skin an apricot glow.

"Good Lord, no." He picked bluebells as he rose, newly aware of his size. He was shorter than Jory, taller than Perran. Not a towering figure in the grand scheme of things. But she was a small woman, delicately built. He shifted around her, interposing his body between hers and the cliff's edge.

*Male vanity.* That was what Jenni would call it. *No one is going to fall off this cliff unless you dunderheads knock each other over trying to guard the damned edge.*

Ah well. He couldn't help himself. At least he didn't have to compete for the outermost track with Davy, William, and Tomas. They started walking again, up toward the old parish church on the brow of the hill.

"Elizabeth thought Cornwall the preserve of savages," he said. "I suggested a wedding in Penzance and she showed me the door."

"What was she supposed to do?" Muriel laughed her disbelief. "Marry you in Penzance?"

"I didn't suggest she sprout pig trotters and fly," he said. "People *do* get married in Penzance from time to time."

"Not Society people." She arched a brow at him. "Now I see that you misrepresented your engagement. *You* ended it. She only made it official."

He blinked at her. "That's not how I saw it at the time." There was, though, a certain truth to it. He'd dug in his heels at exactly the moments when he knew Elizabeth wouldn't budge herself.

"Avoiding responsibility." She shrugged. "Do you know what?"

They circled a boulder and she put out her hand, letting it brush the blooming sea pink that clung to the rock.

"You're a snob." She lifted her chin. "Cornwall is better than

London. Science is better than Society. Girton is better than a Season." She fluttered her lashes at him.

"Snobbery," she said.

"*I'm* a snob." His startled laugh was returned by a seagull wheeling overhead. "That's a first."

"Because your snobbery favors the inverse of what's commonly approved among snobs." She looked pleased with herself. "That makes it trickier to identify. However, I am an expert and nothing escapes me."

"An expert on snobs?" he asked. "Or an expert snob?"

"Both." She stopped short, and as his stride carried him forward she crossed behind him. "You were blocking my view of the sea," she said, stepping off the path onto the carpet of wild thyme. A few feet away the slope dropped off, the fescue and bristle bent giving way to bald rock.

"I was raised around more snobs than books," she said. "A few stuffed birds, yes, but many more stuffed cravats."

He came up beside her. The wind sent a few loose strands of hair streaming over her shoulder. The ends tickled his cheek like spider silk. She took the inflorescence from his hand and considered it narrowly, the individual flowers drooping, each a blue-purple bell, petals curled back to reveal pale yellow anthers.

"Poor Elizabeth didn't know the Latin for this plant, so you feared to introduce her to your intellectual sisters." She mocked him. With the sea as her backdrop, her eyes seemed to draw and concentrate the very essence of blue.

The bluebell in her hand looked washed out in comparison.

"*Hyacinthoides non-scripta.*" He took it back, twirling the stem between his fingers. "I did introduce her to my sisters. It was all very . . . amiable."

Muriel snorted. "And your mother? How did that introduction go? You must have dreaded the day."

He hooked the tickling strands of her hair with his finger and pushed them against the wind. "My mother was in London to see her specimens in the exhibit at the new Natural History Museum. And to see me, of course."

"Of course." She was watching him with unnerving attention.

"A tea was arranged." It had not gone well. And yes, dammit, he had dreaded it.

As the wind gusted, he took a deep breath, filling his lungs. Otto of rose mingled with the briny scent of the sea, and the subtler scents of the wild grasses and sunbaked stones. He usually walked along this cliff alone. Muriel's presence somehow shifted his perceptions. Intensified the contrasts of the terrain, the clarity of the airy fathoms overhead, the density of the ancient cliff walls, the dizzy fall to the waves that folded blue upon blue upon blue. His senses felt *awake*. So awake his brain seemed to be lagging behind.

"And?" she prompted.

The blasted tea. She was damned curious about his engagement. He cleared his throat. What he needed was to rest his eyes. Blue sky, blue sea, blue silk, those spellbinding irises. No respite anywhere.

"And," he said. "And, we drank tea. Discussed the Boat Race." It was the one event on the Society calendar that his mother couldn't do without. She made a special trip every year so she could shout at the top of her lungs for Cambridge and proclaim to anyone who even looked in her direction that her daughter went to Girton.

"That was that." He shook his head. "No one quizzed Elizabeth on the morphology of the *Plesiosaurus*."

She laughed. "Nonetheless you sat in judgment, you and your mother, noting the shortage of scientific facts stored in her mind, as Society snobs might note the shortage of crustless sandwiches and good silver."

"I am not a moralist," he said, irked by the satisfaction in her voice, then doubly irked that she'd goaded him into protest. God, she could be provoking when she tried.

"I don't find inherent virtue in science." Now he sounded like his adolescent self, ready to hold forth in a Traymayne family debate. Her brows were arched at a wicked angle. *Blast it.*

"If two people want a marriage based on crustless sandwiches, I wish them every joy." He lifted a shoulder in a lopsided shrug.

"But you want a marriage based on dinosaur bones," she murmured, in that dry tone she'd used at dinner. Now he was triply irked. Because he found he liked her provocations, her irreverence, and heaven help him, his positive response was not strictly cerebral.

"What if I did?" He grinned. "Is it snobbery to know what's important to you and what isn't? My parents agreed on the importance of dinosaur bones, bryophytes, and children, and on the unimportance of most everything else. If they were snobs, they were the same kind of snob and as happy as the day they married thirty years on."

The corners of her rosy mouth wilted slightly.

"Perhaps they were happy," she said, turning back to look at the water. The wind molded her dress to her thighs. He glimpsed the rounded contours, the shadowed blue valley between them. "Perhaps they weren't. Things are seldom what they seem."

Her head tilted and her features blurred. Suddenly, the scene before him lost its saturation, seemed to gray. It became the picture of loneliness. A woman of ageless sorrow posed on a cliff in the dying day.

He knew only the barest outlines of her married life. The professional triumphs that yielded cultivars sold in every nursery in Britain. The few private details she'd shared about her elopement. The accounts he'd read in horticultural journals about Esmé Pendrake's death in Hong Kong, a fever that came on as he and Muriel prepared to ship home.

*Things are seldom what they seem.*

She'd been lied to, he realized. Misled and mistreated. Of course Pendrake hadn't changed completely. There were no bonified reformed rakes in the fossil record. Those only existed in novels. Romantic fiddle-faddle. Once a scapegrace, always a scapegrace. Pendrake had hurt her, and badly. He could read it in her face, her posture. He should have read it between the lines in her manuscript, in what she *didn't* say.

Christ, she must have found his idealization of her marriage hopelessly naive.

*We'll never make a proper cynic of you*, Alan had lamented over him on more than one occasion. *Too bloody healthy. Get a canker, won't you, Neal, and let it fester?* It had been a while since Alan had made that particular gibe. Not since Neal had come back from Argentina, and James hadn't.

She shifted to look at him. Her eyelids had tightened and her eyes seemed longer and thinner, their expression worldly, weary, older than her years.

"Your mother is not well, is she?" she asked.

"No." He held up the bluebell and watched the wind move the bells, almost heard their soundless chime. "She's dying. Cancer of the breast."

On a breath, she folded her arms across her chest, then slowly, she lowered them. He continued before she could speak.

"She hates fuss," he said. "Anything that smacks of pity. Also, she's rarely amenable to doctor's orders. My brothers think she may be the worst patient in the history of the profession."

She accepted his attempt at humor, mouth tugging into a smile.

"If she were here, and well, would she scale this cliff?" She tipped her head, peering down. The top of her ear peeked through her hair.

"You seem ready to scale that cliff," he observed. "You've no fear of heights?"

"I've no fear of anything after that cab ride." She took another step toward the edge. The sunset had begun to streak the sky, to tip the frayed edges of the windblown clouds with rosy pink. The deeper blue of the sea was ripening to violet near the horizon. The cliffs across the harbor towered, their tops mantled in emerald green. She sighed. "I can see why you're snobbish about Cornwall."

One more step toward the giddy edge. She opened her arms to the wind.

Her bonnet sailed wide of her, ribbons fluttering.

"Oh please, no," she cried. "It's a Virot!" And she lunged after it. Everything seemed to happen at once. The bonnet vanished over the edge and she reached it a second later, snatching at nothing, swaying forward as he leapt toward her. Something—not her bonnet—shot up in front of them. A kestrel riding a current of air. It set the gulls to screaming.

Muriel flung her weight backward and whirled, ducked her head, and barreled into him, her skull connecting with his chest. He stepped back, pulling them back onto the path, arms coming instinctively around her. They stood unmoving.

*Good God.* He'd tried not to anticipate the feel of her, the fit of her against him. Her soft, curved flesh radiated the fading heat of the summer day and, pressed close, smelled salty as well as sweet, the light sweat of her exertions mingling with the rose, and some other fragrance—gardenia, variety unknown—diffused by the slippery mass of her hair.

He'd tried not to anticipate, to fantasize, to *act* . . . but why exactly? Bloody hard to remember. He didn't want desire to dictate his decisions. Lord knew, his instincts hadn't always guided him well. His infatuations had flared and faded, flared and faded. The hotter the spark, the quicker the affair burned out. But this time, he'd already done everything differently. He'd met Muriel Pendrake on the page—on over four hundred pages—months before he'd met her in person. He'd reversed his priorities. Laid groundwork. No matter what he did now, this couldn't flare and fade.

The intensity of the heat he felt did not bode well.

He rested his hands lightly on the fine bones of her shoulders, which pulled back as she straightened, breasts sliding up along his shirtfront. As her head lifted, her eyes fixed on his, violet in the last light, twin mirrors of the sunset on the Celtic Sea. The dratted seagulls were diving now, and he threw up his arm to wave them off. With a little cry, she pressed her face into his neck. He felt the softness of her skin, the moisture of her lips, the shape they made as she smiled. For she *was* smiling. Laughing at her fear. Or else . . . *not* so afraid at all.

Every muscle in his body had tightened. If the wind blew at this moment, he'd vibrate like an Aeolian harp.

When she stepped back, she cupped her hands above her face and hunched. He kept his arm raised as the seagulls veered and shrieked. The kestrel had risen higher and hovered. She peeked between her fingers and gasped.

"He's watching me!"

He wouldn't blame the kestrel if he was.

"This reminds me of Chile," he said, still waving his arm, hand fisted. *More male vanity.* He grimaced. *Come on, man, are you going to punch a seagull?* The Society for the Preservation of Plumage would put him on probation.

He was laughing at himself as he continued. "James, James Varnham, and I brought his fox terrier with us to South America. Idiotic idea, by the way. In the Andes, condors fancied her for luncheon. We developed a whole gymnastics routine to keep her safe."

"Are you comparing me to a fox terrier?" A seagull swooped and she doubled over.

"I don't know." He grinned at her, boxing the air, uppercut, jab, uppercut, jab. It felt good. "Should I pick you up and run for shelter?"

"We'll both run," she said grimly, and was several lengths away before he could command his legs to give chase.

LAVINIA HAD A stitch in her side by the time they'd reached the church. Neal suffered no such malady and bounded at once over the stone stile into the churchyard, a far wilder churchyard than any she'd ever seen. The graves were mounded with tangled grasses and the gravestones tilted every which way.

"Dwarf thistle and adder's tongue," called Neal, shaking back his hair as he rose and came toward her. He'd draped his coat over a rock down on the path and now she saw that he'd rolled up his sleeves. *And* soiled the knees of his trousers kneeling on damp earth. He seemed blissfully unaware of the impropriety. As an expert snob, she wanted to wrinkle her nose. But part of her envied him his unselfconsciousness. She was painfully aware that she must look a fright. Sweaty, lank-haired. And her only bonnet—lost!

She gathered herself. Mrs. Pendrake wouldn't care one jot about a lost bonnet.

Thank heavens she hadn't been wearing her hat with Brazilian hummingbirds at the station.

"Dwarf thistle and adder's tongue," she called back in her jauntiest Pendrakean voice. "I see some eye of newt right behind you. Shall I fetch the cauldron?"

Given that he was botanizing the ingredients for a hellbroth, it might not matter that she'd developed witch locks and a stoop.

He laughed. "There's plenty of bloody cranesbill as well, and navelwort. But let's leave it all be for now. I was actually hoping to find something else."

She filled her lungs as he approached, easing the stitch, until the pain sharpened and burst. She straightened. *Thank God.* This regimen of stuffing oneself with potatoes and marching felt like murder. For her, anyway. Nothing seemed to strain Neal physically. Walking, running, brawling with birds, jumping walls. He had an unusually lithe tread. Most men, however graceful in the ballroom, kept their hips stiff when they walked. Neal's body moved sinuously as he took rolling, irregular steps. For him, the ground wasn't something to stomp. It was something to study and cultivate. He took care as he placed his feet.

"At first, I thought you might be paying your respects." She didn't clamber over the stile but stopped when she reached the low stone wall. Farther down its length, the stones had loosened and lay in a tumble, so that the churchyard merged with the wild hillside. The funereal order of the grand cemeteries she'd visited made death seem so formal and tiring. Here, life and death observed no discernible boundary. All was *natural*, and somehow less fearsome. She had to acknowledge the strange appeal.

"There are Traymaynes aplenty in this ground." The wall reached as high as Neal's upper thigh and he gave it a critical look as he leaned against it, testing it with his weight. "I always greet my grandparents."

"The churchyard—it's so peaceful," she said. He heard the appreciation in her voice and smiled.

"As good a place for eternal rest as any. The church itself is in a sore state. See those?" He pointed at shadowy depressions in the dimming heath.

"Those are slates," he said. "Blown from the roof."

Slates didn't interest her. She looked instead at his extended hand. A blade of grass stuck to his knuckle and dirt caked his nails. He lowered the hand, brushed it absently against his trousers. She swallowed.

If the fact that she'd fled the Duke of Cranbrook didn't prove she'd gone mad, her reactions to this unwashed gardener removed all doubt. She admired pretty men in suits, with gloves and top hats. Dirty nails, thick wrists, muscled forearms, that wide, hot, salty neck—her pulse wouldn't race if she were in her right mind. Elizabeth, at least, had gotten him scrubbed for tea.

"No one has been buried in the churchyard for years. Services, weddings, funerals—everything has moved to St. Symphorian down in the valley. I come up here for the dandelions."

Did he? That was a bit of luck. "Look no further."

She bent, broke off a stem from the plant at the base of the wall, flourished it. "Voilà!"

Triumph was sweet. Muriel Pendrake herself couldn't have acted with more swift decision. She grinned. As it turned out, she quite excelled as a plant huntress, so long as dandelions were the quarry.

She did wish the stem wouldn't ooze that milky sap onto her fingers.

He glanced at the dandelion in her hand, then leaned over the wall, studying the plant, its cluster of fuzzy yellow heads. "Pick me a leaf?"

She complied, removing the leaf neatly, a scientific cut through the base of the leaf with her fingernail. She passed it to him, arranging her face into an impassive yet intellectual expression.

"See the rough hairs?" he asked, stroking up the leaf with his thumb. She moved closer, stretching her neck.

"The one I want has glabrous leaves, flecked with purple."

Alas, as enjoyable as it was to play scientist, to be taken seriously, dandelion leaves interested her less than slates.

She studied the lids of his downcast eyes instead. No need to plead insanity when it came to those eyelashes. They were thick as wings. The lashes swung up. His gaze focused.

"Hmm," she said, pulling back slightly. "Yes, I see."

She stroked the tip of her nose with the dandelion head, before she realized that the gesture didn't suit her. She wasn't a girl on a stroll through Hampstead. She was a woman of science.

*Stuff it all.*

The tiny, fuzzy petals tickled like feathers and were about as fragrant. She tried to keep her voice impassive.

"So," she said. "This dandelion won't do?"

It was vexing, to surrender her triumph, and also her illusions about dandelions. Wasn't their homely charm based on their *lack* of variety? They popped up everywhere, and they were all the same.

Oh well. Not the rudest of her various awakenings.

She moved her fingers down the stem and lifted the dandelion higher so its head nodded agreement.

"I found a new species." Neal grinned, flashing his white teeth. Another objectively attractive feature. She was only *half*-mad, perhaps. Except, she found his strong, unshaven jaw equally attractive, with its wide angle balancing his cheekbones and the dramatic hollows of his cheeks. Even the bump on his large nose. She liked the crude *firmness* of his face. His lips, too, were firm—not pillowy like George's— but precisely cut, the bottom lip almost squared off. She watched his lips as he spoke.

"I first noticed it growing there, beneath the chancel window," he said. "My father's herbarium includes hundreds of dandelions, none with those shiny, flecked leaves."

He lay the rejected leaf, hairy and plain green, atop the wall, as though in illustration. "I thought it might be a European species. But I've gone through the monograph of the genus."

His brown eyes were bright with excitement, glowing in contrast with those raven's wing lashes. "I sent the description and a specimen to Kew. It's official. I've written up a paper. More of a note, really."

He hesitated. "What I can't figure out is how my father missed it. He didn't miss anything."

Lavinia could hear something like reverence in his voice. He revered his father. Revered *both* his parents, and his siblings. He brimmed over when he spoke of them. Neal Traymayne had never suffered a rude awakening. Did he live in willful ignorance, or had he experienced unfathomable good fortune?

"I've never named a native plant." His smile widened. "I've introduced species to England, but it feels different, identifying something at home, more or less underfoot, but overlooked. Not properly seen."

Mrs. Pendrake would have shared his excitement. "And what are you calling it?" She mustered a smile.

"*Taraxacum hedrae.*" He said it with such delight that, suddenly, despite the Latin, her smile became real.

"After my mother, Hedra," he added, glancing back into the churchyard, lashes slanting. "Something to give her at midsummer."

Her heart was beating queerly. A gift of dandelions. Utterly worthless. She'd only ever received costly tokens, from her papa, from George, from Cranbrook, ill-gotten or tied with invisible strings, binding her. How precious, the worthlessness of weeds, presented as a way of honoring this wild place, connecting his mother to these cliffs. Cliffs she might not see again.

Neal Traymayne knew how to love differently from anyone she'd ever known. His love wasn't angry, or destroying, or rotten, or gilded. It was sunny as a dandelion. Proximity to such brightness could make stunted things grow. Was that the source of this feeling? Some crushed part of her, sealed off since George's death, stirring, ready to unfurl.

The last man to kiss her had been Cranbrook. He'd polluted her mouth.

"What will we do with this one?" She held up her dandelion. "This non–*Taraxacum hedrae.*"

He raised his brows. "We could press it if you like."

She shook her head, leaned closer to the stone wall. His eyes narrowed, gaze hot. Too hot for a man well and truly preoccupied with dandelions. *Good.*

"I'd rather blow on it and make a wish, like I did when I was girl. Before I became too practical." She smiled. "Didn't you ever make wishes on dandelions?"

"I've seen it done." Now his look was sardonic. "It works better once they've gone to seed."

"True." Her eyes dropped to the yellow head, all the bright, fresh petals tightly lodged. "We'll have to try together." Her eyes fixed his. "Combine our efforts."

He understood. How could he not? The dandelion bobbed between them. He rubbed his firm, stubbled chin, the smile on his lips amused. Surprised. Wary.

"Are you thinking of a wish?" The toes of her slippers climbed the stone. She couldn't get any closer.

They looked at each other across the wall.

She wasn't the blushing maid she'd been with George. No, she would never be that innocent again. With Neal, though, she didn't have to be innocent. He hadn't contracted for her virginity. On the contrary, he thought her a brilliant, liberated, adventuresome widow. A woman who broke every mold. Who did what she pleased.

She leaned forward. Lavinia flirted, but Mrs. Pendrake took charge.

"You're not thinking of a wish," she said. "You're trying to decide whether or not to kiss me." She put her hands on the flat, gritty stone, smearing the dandelion stem, hoisting herself higher. She spoke briskly. "In that case, let me put your mind at ease."

As she lifted her mouth to his, he laughed, his breath warm against her lips. For a stomach-plunging moment, she thought he'd pull back, and she opened her eyes. His lashes swept down as he studied her face, shading his eyes, turning them black.

"But I *was* thinking of a wish," he murmured, fingers brushing over her knuckles, touching the ravaged dandelion.

"No matter." He rolled his shoulders, a movement that brought his body forward, closer to hers. Shaded by those heavy lashes, his eyes seemed to hold some secret. He raised his hand, traced a finger down her jaw, along her chin, up to her lips.

"It wasn't unrelated," he said, and slowly, he lowered his face. His lower lip came between hers, nudged them gently apart. Cranbrook had attacked her mouth, teeth mashing, tongue darting in and out.

George had been more languid, plying her with champagne, his dizzying kisses tasting of smoke and whiskey. Neal wasn't languid, not like George. His body was thicker and harder, contained more raw vitality. She shivered as his palm skated across her shoulder, calluses scraping lightly at her skin. She pressed forward, the stone cutting into her waist, and he pulled at her lip, suckling and plumping it, licking the delicate underside, his fingers wrapping the back of her neck.

A kiss to cleanse her of her husband. And of her doomed lover too.

He didn't seem inclined to stop. It was to be kisses, then. Many of them, deep and lush. She opened her mouth, inviting him in. Why not? She was never going back to Cranbrook. She would sail to France in a pirate ship, and Neal Traymayne would turn the captain's wheel.

She reached up to wind her hand in his thick, rough hair, cupping the back of his skull. His tongue pressed inside her open mouth and she felt a corresponding pulse in her belly, a fullness, a hot tug. Ah. *This.* She remembered it. With George, it had made her gasp and writhe, do things she'd never dreamed. She moved her tongue beneath his, the hot slide of it making her shift her weight, drive her hip bones into the stone. He had the rhythm and taste of waves. The sensation kept breaking over her. His lips were salty with both of their sweat. With a ragged breath, he dragged his mouth from hers. They pressed forehead to forehead, his eyelashes beating against her brows, her eyelids. His hair smelled faintly of peat.

At that horrible inn, she'd imagined curling up against him, being held, nothing demanded. Giving to George had left her empty and craving. Left her with less of herself. Neal made her feel bigger. Larger than life. Intelligent. *Legendary.*

He laid his fingertips on her cheekbones and bent his head to kiss up her jawline. The wall seemed designed to maximize their torture. Uneven corners of stone bruised her thighs. The thickness meant their torsos couldn't touch. Space became tantalizing, wind stirring around and between them, the skin around her nipples tightening.

It was a torture she could endure forever.

Kisses were as different from each other as dandelions. His lips grazed hers, their pressure light, and then his breathing changed and he was drawing her lower lip between his teeth, and her hands molded his incorrigible neck, so tanned and muscled, audacious and unfashionable, palms recording the flex of the tendons. Oh, to kiss, and kiss, and kiss. Mouths should always be wet and warm and open and stroked inside and out. His hands found her spine, moved to her waist. Her thighs burned against the stone.

Something groaned. Not her. Not him. Her eyes flew open at the thud. He stepped back, arm bent behind his head as he surveyed the destruction. The wall had slumped at the corner, spilling out onto the grass in a mass of loose stones. His chest rose and fell on quickened breath. Kissing her hadn't *strained* him, of course. But he looked . . . stirred. She drank in the cool air, her heart pounding in her ears like surf.

He cleared his throat, flipped a stone with his toe. "Bound to happen sooner or later." He didn't sound breathless. He sounded amused. Balancing on the balls of his feet, he clambered over the ruins to join her outside the churchyard.

He grinned down at her. "Don't blame yourself."

"Me?" She crossed her arms, indignant, but he tugged them, laughing, and took her elbow, swinging her around so they faced down the path. She gasped as they pivoted, a gasp that converted to laughter. She liked his rough-and-tumble physicality. He seemed careless of his strength, but every gesture evinced control. She leaned her shoulder into his upper arm.

"This will give Cobbe something to do," he said, as they began to walk arm in arm back toward the village. Oh, contact was delicious. Barring spare moments during those weeks in France, she'd never gotten to walk abroad with George, to hold on to him. In London, their encounters were furtive, liaisons in empty libraries while the band played in the ballroom. In public, he scarcely ever glanced in her direction.

This happiness was too green and bruisable. *Caution.* Caution was required.

Her lips were wet and felt particularly cool as the wind moved over them. Tingling. The wind—an extension of their kiss.

"Cobbe?" she asked, trying to follow the thread.

"The master mason." Neal held her so close that his stride seemed to carry both of them, a rambling gait, her hip swinging in rhythm with his thigh. "He falls off walls with frequency and only builds them on the rarest of occasions. He's angry as a badger that the architect brought his own masons with him from London. They're the ones that will take down the church tower stone by stone."

She looked back at the church, the square black tower rising against the graying sky, shockingly primitive and pagan. Her papa would never have approved.

"Why bother to repair the wall?" she asked. "Ruins improve the scene. They're in fashion, you know. Once the tower is gone, the church will match the wall. More ruined, less ugly."

"I'd love to hear you share these ideas with Tomas." He started walking again. "He was the layman lobbying with the vicar for an architect to restore the church. The old tower is coming down, but a new tower is going up. Less ugly, I think, by your lights. The architect designed it. You can meet him if you like. Discuss the latest trends in follies, ruins, and those little houses for hermits that aristocrats like to stick in their gardens."

Neal was laughing.

The enormity of it hit her. A London architect. Her hands went clammy.

"He's in Kyncastle?" Her voice strangled in her throat. "The architect?"

"He's been in Kyncastle for months, doing a survey, making drawings. He stays at the vicarage."

"Ah." A croak. She tried again. "His name?"

"Don't recall it." *His* voice was easy. A small, pacific bird perched on a ledge of rock sang out. Neal whistled to it, a passable imitation. His warm hand cupped her elbow.

How many architects in London? How many who knew her? Nothing to worry about. The odds were so slim.

But her old life suddenly cast its shadow upon the new, and that darkness blended with the coming night as she descended the path.

# CHAPTER SIX

"Squally weather," sighed Loveday as wind rattled the parlor window.

"Not as I know by." Emmeline's response sounded sour.

Lavinia made a noncommittal noise and continued writing. She'd been perched for hours in a wretched stick-back armchair, but in her story, the dauntless duchess was enduring worse discomforts, pulling the oars of the pinnace as shots whistled overhead.

Courageous lady! She'd just sacked her husband's estate and the pinnace rode low in the water, weighed down by the ancestral jewels.

A small thump made Lavinia glance up. Emmeline had thrown down her sewing.

"I'm going out," she announced, rising. "I told the vicar I'd bring round his bread."

"Infamous." Loveday dropped her own sewing into her lap and addressed her sister with exasperation. "You told Kelyn you'd finish up that pelisse. At this rate, the boys will be breeched before you're done."

"All the more reason to stop now." Emmeline sashayed to the window and craned her neck to peer up at the sky. "It's not even raining."

"It's raining all sorts!" Loveday's chair creaked with the force of her protest. Lavinia bent again over her notebook. Rain wasn't a bad idea. The men firing from the shore would lose sight of their target in the mist.

"I'm not sugar that I'll melt," Emmeline grumbled, dragging back to her chair.

"That you're not," agreed her sister tartly. But there was no strong acid in her voice.

"Finish up the pelisse," she said. "Then you can run around wet-shod and dripping, and I won't say a word. Although you'd do better to follow Mrs. Pendrake's example. She knows how to take advantage of a slaggy day. She must have written a dozen pages!"

Oh, why involve her in it? Lavinia laid down her pencil and tried to match Loveday's sweet smile. She was far more convivial than Emmeline, the chit. Plainer too, although her looks would be vastly improved if she didn't tie up her hair in that matronly bun and wear such dismal dresses—dull brown and gathered all wrong for her figure.

"I'm only writing notes." Lavinia adopted a modest tone, covering the exposed page with the palm of her hand. "A few additions for my little book on the shrubs of China."

"I don't know how she saw any shrubs in China," muttered Emmeline, stabbing her needle into her sewing, an unpromising wad of red flannel. "This morning it was fine and she couldn't be stirred."

Lavinia froze her smile on her lips. Emmeline wasn't a chit. She was a minx. Did she truly insist on war?

"Hush." Loveday attempted to shush her sister. "Her work is important, and we must let her attend to it."

Lavinia picked up her pencil with a gracious nod. Good of Loveday to champion intellectual women. But she found she couldn't write another word. Emmeline's barb had gotten under skin.

The day *had* dawned bright and clear. Lavinia had woken with the household—the roosters could have roused the dead—but she'd stayed in the small upstairs bedroom until the murmur of voices in the kitchen quieted. Only when she felt assured that Neal was well on his way did she creep down the stairs for her tea.

For all that she'd longed to accompany him, she *couldn't* botanize all day in the sun without a bonnet. If she'd known clouds would blow in, she might have risked it.

Emmeline sniffed. In certain instances, such a sniff registered as a comment in itself. In other instances, it proved the opening salvo.

"She could work on her book anywhere, anytime," said Emmeline.

So. The minx persisted. Well, Lavinia could handle a minx. They abounded in Society. Time-tested processes existed for establishing precedence among them. Here in Kyncastle, Lavinia would have to cut corners and establish dominance by any means necessary.

As an intellectual woman, she elected to take the high ground.

"Are you addressing your sewing?" she asked, looking up. "For you are not addressing me, and I do not think you address your sister. She has too much good sense to listen."

A dignified reproach, one that enlisted Loveday, isolating Emmeline across the battle line with only her maltreated flannel as an ally. Emmeline, however, did not raise the white flag. She eyed Lavinia boldly.

"Neal brought you all the way here," she said, her voice every bit as dignified as Lavinia's, and equally reproving. "I should think you'd want to see what he had to show you."

Vexing. The minx had a point. And Lavinia *did* want to see what Neal had to show her. If it weren't for that cursed bonnet, she'd be by his side at this very moment, soaked and uncomplaining, checking every dandelion leaf in the parish for purple specks.

She felt her chin pucker as she repressed a frown. Emmeline noticed and pressed her advantage.

"Instead, off he went *alone* to Juliot woods." She shook her head sadly and gave her curls a consoling pat. They were exactly the kind of curls Lavinia had always desired, fat and glossy. A very average shade, though. Mouse brown. "He looked disappointed," she continued. "You think highly of yourself, and you don't think of anyone else at all."

"Emmeline!" Loveday gasped.

Lavinia's instinct was to flinch, but instead she pressed her lips into a smile. "I cannot work on my book *anywhere, anytime*, as you suggest. In London, I am run off my feet. There's always something to do. Parties, bazaars, dances, plays—so much stimulation! Every moment, a new engagement. I don't think you've *been* to London?"

Loveday answered for Emmeline.

"Not since she was a little girl," she said. Loveday was decidedly not a minx. She was more of a lamb, or a dove. She wanted to keep the peace between her sister and their guest.

"We all went when Uncle Digory and Aunt Heddie lived in Croydon," she explained. "But Emmeline had lately pinned her hopes on Neal. He was living in full fig. A very nice part of London. What was it called?"

"South Kensington." Emmeline scowled.

"Very nice," Lavinia murmured. And then before she could stop herself: "A bit out of the way of things."

"Is it?" Loveday began to sew again. "He moved to Truro before she could make her visit. Poor dear. She was inconsolable."

Loveday wanted to keep the peace, but her talents lay elsewhere. Sewing, for example. Her needle flashed steadily. Emmeline narrowed her eyes.

"I was meant to be there for the whole Season," she hissed, skewering her flannel, then giving it a twist. "Tomas and Neal had agreed, and then Neal *left*."

This was *too* good. Lavinia showed her teeth, smile widening.

"The Season is the worst, for women intellectuals," she said. "You think you're going to spend a dull day doing your work, and then, the next thing you know, the Prince of Wales is entertaining, and Sarah Bernhardt is going to be there, and you simply cannot refuse the call. The distractions are endless. I'm sure it's hard to believe in a place like this, where the hours stretch on forever because there's so little to fill them."

"I should hate it," said Loveday placidly. "Large crowds make me short of breath. There's not enough air in London. Who is Sarah Bernhardt? A friend of yours?"

"She's an actress," snapped Emmeline. "A terrifically famous one. Really, Loveday, she'll think we live under a rock."

"But you do live under a rock." Lavinia smiled brightly. "These tall cliffs rising all around are so striking. It's the charm of Kyncastle, isn't it? And Sarah Bernhardt *is* a friend." Lavinia had to bite the inside of her cheek to keep from laughing at Emmeline's expression. Certainly, *friend* stretched the truth. She had met her idol, though, on two occasions, once in London and once in Paris. The second time, they'd exchanged a full sentence. "It was a perfectly reasonable question. You don't give your sister nearly enough credit."

"You have no siblings." Emmeline glared. "Perhaps you should reserve judgment."

"I always wished for an elder sister." Lavinia smiled at Loveday before resting her gaze on Emmeline. For a moment, she considered her, that English rose prettiness, which Emmeline clearly thought wasted on fishermen and farmers. Then she moved in for the kill.

"Elder sisters always seemed to me a great boon," she said. "Except . . ." She let her gaze roam slowly down from Emmeline's face before meeting her eyes again. "I could not abide the hand-me-down clothes."

Emmeline went white and she clutched her sewing to her breast, an attempt to cover up her printed cotton frock. The frock was childishly simple and more than a little faded, with telltale darts where the fabric had been taken in. Emmeline bent her head, but not before Lavinia saw the shimmer in her eyes.

*Tears.* Lavinia bit her lip. Vain, silly girls were always the most sensitive.

No one moved. Finally, Emmeline turned, her torso rigid. Lavinia recognized that stiff, brittle posture. It had been hers this twelvemonth in London.

*I am armored against your insults.*

She wondered if she had been as unconvincing.

"Is that Kelyn calling?" Emmeline said to her sister. "I might be needed in the kitchen."

She stood, still clutching her sewing, and walked from the room. Loveday looked after her, then looked at Lavinia, surprise and hurt in her eyes.

"I do think I hear Kelyn," she said quietly. "If you'll excuse me."

Lavinia rose with Loveday but stood stock-still in the modest parlor. The room suddenly seemed colder, and deathly quiet. This pang in her stomach—an unwelcome mix of contrition and shame.

Victory was hers. *Queen of the Kyncastle minxes.* A worthless title. It did her as much good as *Duchess of Cranbrook.*

She walked to the window. A view of the neighboring cottage, smaller than the Traymaynes', potted geraniums on the windowsills splashing the gray afternoon with color. She shut her eyes, leaned her forehead against the cool glass.

How old was Emmeline? Eighteen? The youngest daughter of the household, a girl who read gossip columns, collected the pictures of the beauties advertised in the illustrated papers, followed the career of Sarah Bernhardt. A girl who dreamed—like so many pretty girls before her—that her face would someday make palace doors swing open.

A lifetime separated eighteen and twenty-four.

Suddenly, Lavinia felt old, old as time itself. In London, she'd kept accounts, kept track of the social ledger—girls scoring off one another, their relative positions weighted at the outset by factors beyond their control—birth, wealth, beauty. She'd enjoyed tallying her points. What a prize had awaited her!

George's face swam in the darkness. She opened her eyes, lifted her hands, cooled her wrists against the glass.

Debutantes favored temporary self-serving alliances over friendship. Close competitors formed sets, each pleased to see her own sparkle increased by her radiant company. Each ready to claw her confidantes when the moment came to distinguish herself. That was the law of the jungle. Not the jungle. High Society's *human zoo*.

Cora, Agnes, Elise—they'd tittered after her broken engagement. After her papa went to jail, they'd turned their backs. Showed her their hard, jutting backsides.

This Season, bustles were de rigueur. And for the very first time, she hadn't been able to afford a visit to the dressmaker. The other girls grew larger, built out with cushions and steel hoops, and she diminished in contrast. Her silhouette advertised her sudden, mortifying poverty.

If Cora had been the unfortunate instead, or Agnes, or Elise, Lavinia would have been the one to titter, to sweep past, backside swaying like the hindquarters of a horse.

Those were the rules. Winners rarely questioned them.

She could remember—barely—days when she didn't calculate, when the world wasn't divided into rivals and conquests. And she could remember with stark clarity the day she'd scraped her palms swinging in the linden trees with Effie.

Her mother had confined her to the nursery for an entire month. *You're not to think of playing outdoors until your hands are white and smooth and you can prove to me they will stay in that condition. A duke's daughter can run about like an urchin because her breeding is in her blood. You, Lavinia, must always remember that you are only as well-bred as you appear. Show me that you can be prettier than Effie, and I will take you to the milliner's to pick out whatever you like.*

How she'd missed clambering in the garden with her favorite playmate! It wasn't the same afterward, hanging back, watching Effie exert herself fiendishly. Hoping she'd tear her stockings or smudge her face, so she, Lavinia, could parade past the adults. Pretty. Perfect.

Where had being the prettiest gotten her?

She turned from the window and surveyed the empty room. If she were alone *here*, it wasn't because of her silhouette, or her papa's theft. She needed to figure out how to relate differently.

She tucked her notebook under her arm and walked slowly toward the kitchen. She'd not spent much time in kitchens. This one was cavernous and warm with a good, savory smell. Steam and smoke mingled. She entered tentatively, stubbing her toe on the uneven slates. An enormous chimney rose over an oven topped by a great stone slab on which pots bubbled. Dried beef and herbs hung from a ceiling rack. Oak sideboards filled with cups and willow-patterned dishes flanked the long table.

The three Traymayne women stood by the fire, where Tomas's wife, Kelyn, was stirring curdled milk in a brass pan. They fell silent as Lavinia approached.

Lavinia came up to them and cleared her throat. What to say?

*I'm sorry* might be a good start. *I'm sorry, Emmeline, that I taunted you about your dress. If I still could, I would take you to hobnob with the nobility in Belgrave Square, and you should see for yourself how it compares to your country pastimes.*

Suddenly, she ached to tell them the truth, to tell them who she was, the whole story of all she'd had and all she'd lost. She didn't want to be excused but understood.

No words came. She forced open her lips.

"I thought I'd see if I could help with anything," she said, surprising herself. And, from the looks of it, the other women as well. They exchanged glances. Emmeline responded first.

"Soufflé isn't on the menu." She folded her arms. Lavinia saw that she'd cast her sewing on top of the wood in the wood bin. Kelyn stepped away from the fire, face flushed, and fanned herself.

"I've no need of help," she said. "Though I thank you for asking."

"Oh," said Lavinia. She looked from woman to woman. Loveday and Emmeline resembled each other strongly at that moment, with their straight backs and the fire picking out the tawny lights in their brown hair. Kelyn was round and dark, cut from a different cloth. But all three shared something, an intimacy that manifested in the way they stood, an easiness among them.

A lump rose in Lavinia's throat. "Well," she managed. "In that case." She couldn't go on.

As she turned away, Kelyn spoke again.

"I don't need the help," she said. "But if you've an *interest* in Cornish baking . . ."

Lavinia turned back eagerly. Kelyn was smiling. Her dimples made sweet dents in her cheeks. Kitchen work hadn't spoiled her looks or her disposition, or depreciated her innate quality, which was undeniable, and refreshingly distinct from her consequence.

"A great interest." Lavinia made the affirmation with such fervor that she believed it herself. Which made it almost true.

"When I'm finished with the cheese, then." Kelyn nodded. "You and I will bake the saffron buns. We'll find a spare apron."

"She can use mine." Emmeline piped up with suspicious enthusiasm.

Lavinia smiled. She'd have to check the pockets for hornets.

"Thank you," she said, to all three of them.

"In return, you'll tell us about China," said Kelyn. "I have so many questions."

"I'll describe every hillside," Lavinia promised, and pressed her notebook more tightly to her side.

Sheltering beneath an outcropping of rock with Reverend Henry Curnow, Neal watched the rain fall in sheets. Thick mist blanketed the sea, and the dark jagged cliffs across the harbor poked out like the turrets of a ruined castle. Impossible not to imagine gazing upon them with a fairer companion than the good reverend.

He could *feel* Muriel's hair tickling under his chin as she nestled against him, *feel* the warmth and pressure of her body. Imagination conjured sensation—the two of them standing front to back, dry in the slate alcove as the storm crescendoed in the theater of the sky.

Rain slapped him in the face.

"Chr—" He wiped his streaming brow, biting off the word. Curnow was an old friend of the family, a passionate rambler and botanist in his own right, given to quoting Bishop Newton in his sermons.

*True philosophy is the handmaid of true religion and the knowledge of the works of nature will lead us to the knowledge of the God of nature.*

Even so, churchmen of all stripes frowned on blasphemy.

"Curses," Neal finished, and Curnow laughed his deep laugh. A big man, he sent his voice up from the center of his frame, where it resonated wonderfully. His parishioners were touchingly vain of him.

*Fit for a cathedral* was what they said. Didn't stop the farmers from falling asleep in the back pews. Or the gentry from grumbling about the cost of restoring the parish church.

"A bad gale this is." Curnow shook his head. "I know you don't mind a drenching, Neal, but I won't have your skull cleaved in two by flying slates. The church will be going to pieces in this wind."

Neal leaned out from the alcove, squinting up the cliff path. He could see a thin sliver of the church between the rocks, the black tower holding fast against the racing clouds. Still standing. Curnow wanted to tour him through the nave so he could see the plants growing beneath the holes in the roof.

"If it's not *Elatine hexandra* sprouted in the font, I'll eat my hat," said Curnow, touching the wide brim. "And you might find your dandelion in the aisle." He sighed. "Not today, though. Will you stay a spell?"

"Through tomorrow." Neal angled himself behind a projection of rock. "Then we head west."

Curnow's broad face looked suddenly bland. Too bland. He was trying not to smile. It was the *we* that had done it.

When Neal had dropped in at the vicarage after the deluge drove him from Juliot woods, he'd spoken of Muriel in neutral tones, but the old man's ear had pricked at once. Just as quickly, he'd tried to mask his interest, bringing out his notes and a medal-worthy collection of *Hepaticae*.

Curnow was one of dozens of local botanists contributing invaluable lists for Neal's flora. He also belonged, covertly, to another group—no less sizable, it seemed, in number. Neal thought he might call it the Neal Traymayne Bachelor Relief Society. His mother was the president, of course. Neal wouldn't put it past her to have written to Curnow, asking him to scour the parish for well-read young women with established aptitudes in fields including, but not limited to, geology, entomology, zoology, and botany.

"Tomorrow, then." Curnow rubbed his damp whiskers. "We'll walk up together, with this Mrs. Pendrake if she's amenable."

He produced a pipe, but another wet gust seemed to make him rethink the plausibility of a satisfactory smoke. Sighing, he returned it to his pocket. "I hope that by your next visit the church is no longer the site of botanical interest."

"I'd drink to that," said Neal, grinning. His father and Curnow used to meet for pints in Kyncastle's only pub and talk long past closing, standing in the street and projecting their voices—as only drunken professors and parsons could—so that the whole village was privy to their conversations. As a boy, Neal would hang out the window to listen. Even then, the topics included the parish church's various dilapidations. "It's been a long time coming."

Curnow's thoughts seemed to have hewed to Neal's.

"Your father knew how to tip a glass." He looked at Neal. His eyes were close and deeply set under heavy gray brows.

"He rejoices with us now," he added, in a lower register. "But on a farther shore."

Neal let the back of his head rest on the rock. Platitudes. They occurred in speech and in thought and let the mind paper over any manner of unpleasant truths.

"I can accept a god as first cause." The rock bit into his skull, just hard enough to hurt. "But I cannot believe my father's drinking ale in heaven."

"What do you believe?" Curnow's voice held only gentle curiosity. Neal studied the rain. It had slowed to a patter, the sheets disaggregating into drops.

"That he's soil. That he's mixed with quartz and serpentine and carbonate of lime and foraminifera and sedges and grasses, and fresh and salt water."

The words scraped a little in his throat. If what he said was truth, he didn't know how to feel about it. Death was both more and less final than he'd learned on Sundays.

Scripture inspired Curnow, but time and again he'd demonstrated his willingness to entertain ways of thinking that deviated from chapter and verse. His reply had a musing quality.

"He's Cornwall, then." He spoke slowly. "Is that what you mean? He's not away or above or beyond. He's the shore itself, this one, right here."

"Essentially." Neal rolled his head on his neck and the rock bit harder. "But materially, he's more Penzance, where they put his body in the ground." Neal could feel Curnow's gaze. Perhaps he'd gone too far. The pause lengthened.

"You're not going to argue?" Neal said at last. "Tell me about the difference between the body and the soul?"

Curnow laughed and the sound reverberated. "As the Lord as my witness, I don't argue with Traymaynes. I only pray for them."

Neal's lips quirked. "Blue sky," he said, and pointed.

Curnow was still looking at him. "I always thought your father would prepare a flora," he said. "He knew every inch of the county."

"He didn't have a long enough retirement." Again, the tightening in his throat. Two years to the day after he'd moved back to Penzance, Digory Traymayne was dead. "The project will take a decade." Neal would be lucky if it took *only* a decade. He had to collect material, visit libraries and herbaria, confirm records. Almost every botanist he'd written in the county had written back offering to help. Even so, the compiling and organizing alone would be a massive undertaking, and he'd have to fit it in around his work for Varnham.

"That's why you're doing it." Curnow struck a match. He puffed his pipe, the richly scented smoke welling around them. "For him. Though you don't believe he's looking down on you from one of those clouds and smiling."

Neal lifted his head and stepped out from the alcove, holding his hands palm up. Coolness sprinkled his palms. Light poured through a black-rimmed hole in the clouds directly overhead. Curnow joined him on the path. Did he want an answer?

About why he was preparing the flora.

About whether or not he thought the sun sparkling on the feldspar in the cliffs was a sign of his father's approval.

Neal stretched his cramped shoulders. Motives were twisty things that grew in shade. He made decisions for a whole tangle of reasons.

"This won't hold," said Curnow, surveying the sky.

"I might risk it." Neal tapped his thumb against his specimen box. Perhaps he would go a bit farther up the path, collect some bluebells to dry for Muriel. But not if Curnow was going to labor and slide back to the village.

"Shall I put you home?" he asked Curnow, politely and in his very best dialect. Curnow rewarded him with a chuckle.

"I can put myself home well enough," he said. Despite his years, and his size, he walked miles and miles in a given week, collecting plants, birding.

"More's the pity," he added, and Neal remembered with a jolt that his wife had died the winter before last. Whatever look passed across his face, Curnow caught it and shook his head, smiling, to banish it.

"Tomorrow to the church," he said. "With Mrs. Pendrake."

When Neal reached the patch of flowers, he couldn't help but step off the path, spread his arms, and try to feel what Muriel felt as she first beheld the magnificence of the harbor, ultramarine water framed by those steep, crenellated cliffs. He stepped right to the very verge, and that was when he let his eyes sweep down and saw, on a little jutting ledge, Muriel's straw bonnet.

He saw it, and at the same time, he apprehended a way to reach it. Where he stood, the cliff dropped with sheer verticality a hundred feet down to the churning waves. Not even a raven could find purchase. But the ledge was several yards to his right, nearer to the bend in the path, the level elbow that marked the spot where the steep climb to the church began in earnest. The cliff was lower there, stepping down in stages.

The rocks would be wet. He jogged down the path, stood his specimen box against the boulder, folded his coat on top, and walked carefully to the cliff edge across slippery turf. He dropped into a crouch and lowered his legs over the side.

This was why his mother's hair turned white overnight. It wasn't South America, per se, that she feared, but the impulse that sent him there. That had always sent him up or down cliffs, trees, even buildings. The gatehouse at Eton. Tom Tower at Oxford.

He'd joked about his mother scaling cliffs. She did have long experience scrambling to difficult-to-access places, sometimes using fixed ropes. She was considered and bold. He was impulsive and *too* bold. Raving mad.

Risking his life for a bloody bonnet. Probably ruined already by rain.

His knuckles cracked and strained as he descended, gripping the small bulges of rock. His toes sought the cracks in the slate. At any moment, the clouds could burst again, wash him off the face of the cliff. Quickly, then. The muscles in his shoulders burned and seemed to separate from the bones. He reached a portion where the cliff became less perpendicular and he could sidle along a narrow ridge, catching his breath, before he lowered himself again into space, clinging to the corner of a slab, tensing his stomach, pedaling his legs in slow circles until he found his holds. When he came level with the ledge, he braced himself and worked his arm through the knotted loop of ribbon. He kept climbing down, bonnet batting the cliff, until he could rest both feet on a wider brow of rock. It became an even wider shelf, projecting backward under a low arch. A cave, formed as a vein of some softer mineral eroded over the years. He stood beneath the archway, swung the bonnet around on his arm, whooping. His heart was bashing itself against his sternum.

*Raving mad.* James used to say it of both of them, and they'd whoop together, frozen or half-naked, on whatever improbable promontory.

Gulls mewed faintly. The eeriness of their calls brought to mind all the legends he'd been told as a child, of witches, ghosts, and pixies. They sounded almost human. He whooped again and tested his nerves by looking down. He was perhaps twenty-five feet from the base of the cliff. The water swirled, mesmerizing. A gull shrilled, just as faintly, but this time something about the sustained, hopeless note made him search for the source. Nothing. The wind and rain had chased the birds to their roosts. He looked again, down at the water, and then back at the harbor with its moored fishing boats, at the white cottages. His eye had snagged. *There.* He squinted. Farther out than the moorings, a small vessel bobbed on the waves. Upside down.

*Dear God.* He saw them now, two dark heads and beating arms. Fool boys, thinking they could best it, rowing out in dirty weather for a lark.

You were raving mad, until you were a corpse.

How long would it take to climb back to the path, run through the village to the harbor? Too long.

Down was always faster. Could he spring far enough out into the water to avoid getting sucked down and smashed on the rocks? Some questions weren't worth asking. He let the bonnet drop from his arm. Down he went.

LAVINIA WAS EXPERIENCING a sublime pleasure, the idea of which would once have made her peal with incredulous laughter. She was biting into a warm golden-yellow bun that she'd baked with her own two hands. What unparalleled satisfaction.

Granted, Kelyn had started the process in the wee hours of the morning, steeping the saffron in milk, mixing the dough, setting it to rise, but she'd explained the stages so thoroughly as they kneaded that Lavinia could imagine she'd participated from the onset. Anyway, who cared to make such fine distinctions?

She had worked the springy dough and watched the buns burnish, and now the crust was squeaking between her teeth and the butter was dripping over her lips, and it was simply *divine*.

She'd never have guessed. In a kitchen, you combined dry things and wet things and added labor and heat and the things metamorphosed before your eyes. *Magic.* More likely science, but again, who cared?

Loveday was telling an amusing story about Neal as a boy. They'd been off to a cove with marvelous sands stippled with shells and deep pools for bathing, and as they rode in the wagon on the long journey home, Neal had taken a caraway seed off her biscuit and told her that if she planted it she'd have a whole crop of biscuits come September.

"Did you plant it?" Lavinia's laughter came out of her nose. Snorting wasn't ladylike. And snorting in a kitchen with flour in your hair, eating standing up, straight off a tray?

*Who cares, who cares, who cares.*

"Of course I believed him." Loveday had halved her bun and was spreading it thickly with clotted cream. "He's very convincing. Perhaps you don't know that yet."

"Perhaps she does," said Kelyn. Lavinia thought the dimple in her round cheek looked delicious, like a currant in a cake. *Everything* was delicious. "She's here, after all."

"I'm glad that I'm here," said Lavinia, adding a spoonful of cream to her bun. Loveday paced to the window.

"I don't know why Emmeline *isn't* here," she said. "It doesn't take an hour to walk a loaf of bread down the lane."

"She's attentive to the vicar." Kelyn stacked dirty bowls on the table. "I only hope she brought the umbrella. It sounds like Bedlam broke loose."

Indeed, the wind had started howling and the house gave a great shudder. They all jumped as the front door banged.

"That'll be the storm," said Kelyn, but a moment later, Emmeline burst into the kitchen, hair plastered to her cheeks, eyes wild.

"Yestin and Tristan," she gasped. "In the harbor."

"And Davy?" Loveday started forward.

"He's there, he's taking the boat out after them." Emmeline gulped air. "And Neal, he saw them first. He jumped—he jumped from the cliff."

"God protect us!" Kelyn's hands pressed her heart.

"The vicar watched him go in, but the waves were so high." Emmeline's voice rose in pitch. "He doesn't know . . . He didn't see . . ."

Loveday was already brushing by her, hurtling down the hall, and Lavinia realized she was running too. The wind knocked her breath away as she stepped out into the gale. The little stretch of midafternoon calm had allowed the storm to regroup, to double its force. She was half-blinded by rain, tripping behind Loveday, who seemed to fly over the cobbles. Other villagers had come to their doors, and some were already out, ahead of them, feet pounding the winding streets. A shout had gone up, become general.

"The Strout boys!"

"The harbor!"

The shore was thronged with men, and Loveday shoved her way between them, Lavinia insinuating herself into the gaps, stumbling as her feet sank in the sand. Fishing boats were tossing in the water, tilting so far to left and right that their masts splashed the waves. Beyond the headlands, the sea was roaring, breakers dashing themselves to vapor, so the spray rising and the rain falling became a single frothy veil. Again and again, the veil was rent by a surge of dark water. The day itself was drowning. Here and there in the bay, black rocks broke the surface of the water, collared by foam. Was that Davy's boat tumbling over the billows? And Neal—where was Neal?

"Tide's running in." A woman moaned near Lavinia's ear. Lavinia spun and bumped Emmeline, who gripped her arm like a vise. Her face was stark. Around them, the crowd expanded, became a damp mass of elbows, shoulders, and hips. Lavinia was knocked this way and that. She could no longer see the water. Voices merged with the explosive thunder of the sea. Emmeline pulled her forward, and they struggled closer to the pier. There was Loveday, clasped in the arms of an enormous black-clad man. Her sobs were harsh as the wind.

"More boats are going out." The man's deep, carrying baritone reached them. "Fear not, child. God is with them."

"What's happened?" Emmeline cried, and a woman at her side answered.

"He's been run into the reef, poor Davy Strout."

"Smashed? The boat?" Emmeline's fingernails cut into Lavinia's skin. The woman drew up her shawl, shaking her head.

It couldn't be borne. Lavinia broke Emmeline's grip and clambered up onto a piling. She had to see. The wind almost bowled her over, but she held herself upright. The rain had slowed and more of the sea was visible, the agitated surface striped with foam. The man—the vicar—he hadn't misled. Two boats were halfway to the headlands, their crews pulling hard on the oars. She realized her fingers had twisted together with brutalizing force. The bending bones would snap. Her rings would slice her pinky in half. Men were leaning from the first boat, straining to pull something from the water. A boy. They had him under the arms and then he was over the side. She searched the bay, sweeping her eyes from left to right

"Davy!" The name burst from her. "He's there. He's there!" It didn't matter what she said. No one out on the water could hear her. But the second boat was approaching the rock to which Davy clung. They'd seen him.

*Neal.* She tottered as the wind slacked. Where was Neal? In her nightmares, she found herself often on the Thames embankment, watching as George was fished from the river. He was wearing the charcoal-gray lounge suit he'd worn on the ferry to Dieppe. His eyes stared through her.

In those nightmares, she couldn't speak, couldn't move. The horror unfolded again and again. The man she loved, whose warm body had been her delight, cold and stiff.

Now, she watched from the shore as Neal floundered somewhere in that crushing volume of water.

*Where?* As the sea rocked, she saw debris in the trough between waves. A plank of the shattered boat. Two figures holding on to it.

"There!" She was yelling for all she was worth. "There!" And, as before, no one could hear. But the men in the boats *didn't* see the plank, its human burden. They were moving in the wrong direction.

The horror unfolded. She changed nothing. Couldn't speak, couldn't move. *No. No. No.* Fate's witness. Fate's victim. *No.* She jumped from the piling, fell forward onto her knees.

"There!" She *could* speak even if no one heard. She would keep speaking until they did. She would scream until her throat ran with blood. And she *could* move. She had control of her limbs. She could act, would act. She ran through the crowd to the edge of the water and then she was wading. The sea lapped her shins, cold as ice. She waded parallel to the harbor, toward the cliffs, pointing, her voice ripping out of her.

"There! He's there!" A swell lifted the water to the height of her waist, and she flinched but didn't stop, didn't let it carry her over. Another swell pushed harder, tugged her skirts so she staggered. Oh God, if she fell, if the water rolled her, rolled over her . . . She found her footing.

The crowd on the shore had taken notice. She could hear the shouts, a tumult of voices, and then, as more and more people understood, as they tracked her movement, her extended arm, a collective call rang out.

"There! He's there!"

The whole village was chorusing, the chant rising, equal to the gale. And the second boat, it was turning, beating toward the cliffs. She was shaking violently. She couldn't feel her legs, her feet. The waves pushed and dragged, tireless, wearing her down. She tucked her arms, hands fisted under her chin. The first boat shot past, its grim crew leaping out into the shallows, tugging it up onto the sand. Lavinia turned and saw Davy holding his brother in his arms, splashing to shore. Tomas and the vicar ran to him, and together they lowered him onto the vicar's black coat. When she turned back to the sea, the second boat was only yards away. Neal sat among the men, hair black and dripping, shirt plastered to his broad shoulders.

He didn't stare through her. He stared at her. And then that boat, too, had passed. She heaved her legs to change course, her skirts tangling. She could move faster now, back to the pier along the water's margin. Ahead, the other boy was being carried from the boat, coughing and twisting. Tomas knelt by the first, lifting and bending his arms and legs. Loveday and Davy stood pressed together.

"He's breathing." Tomas looked up at them as a woman broke

vigorously through the crowd. She gathered the boy into her arms and rocked him with unspeakable tenderness, then widened her arms so the second boy could lean into them. She never stopped murmuring, and as Lavinia approached she made out the words, a steady stream of threats and dire warnings.

That would be their mother.

"Get them home to the fire." Tomas stood, hand on his forehead, expression haggard.

"Muriel!" Loveday caught sight of her and held out her hands.

At what moment had the transition taken place, formality giving way to familiarity? It had begun in the kitchen, with shared endeavor, and then, the tempest, the crisis, had stripped all of them down, not only her and the Traymaynes, but the whole village. They were joined by fear, hope, common purpose.

She grasped Loveday's hands and Loveday gasped. "You're cold as ice."

"Bloody hell," Tomas growled. "What's this I hear about you diving off a cliff?"

Neal had come up behind her. She turned as Davy charged, clapping him in an embrace. "God love you for a maniac." Davy let go abruptly, pivoting to expel water. He'd swallowed a fair quantity.

Neal shook wet hair from his eyes. "I was most of the way down already."

"Bird's nest? Or was it some blasted rare moss that caught your eye?" Tomas's gruffness made poor cover. He'd been well and truly frightened. It was written in the lines of his face.

"A bonnet, in fact. On a ledge." Neal's gaze slid over and found hers. She was too cold to laugh. She blinked at him. She didn't doubt that he'd gamble with his life for a bit of vegetation. But for her *bonnet*?

"Tomas, don't keep them talking," Loveday touched her brother's sleeve. "They'll catch their death of cold. All three of you need to get out of those wet clothes."

Bad luck that Lavinia was still looking at Neal. Had her face betrayed her at the phrase? *Get out of those wet clothes.* He might as well take his shirt off now. The wet cotton molded to the muscles of his arms and chest. His trousers seemed suctioned to his thighs. Her throat felt very tight.

The crowd was dispersing. Everyone was cold and wet, even those who hadn't dunked in the sea.

"And I need to go lock the twins in their room until they're forty-five, so they never make such damnable mischief." Tomas shook his head. Imagining his own sons out on that boat. "What were those boys thinking?"

Davy coughed. "Thinking it'd be fun, I'd wager. They'll catch it from Mum, you'd better believe. I should help get them home."

He joined the small knot of people clustered around the boys. Most of the men, like Davy, were thatched with straw-colored hair, and the women and reedy girls sported blond braids. Strouts. They began to walk up to the village, still in a huddle. Loveday and Tomas followed. Families took care of each other here.

None of Lavinia's relatives had written her or her mother during or after the trial. They maintained what Lavinia had once thought a necessary and universal distinction.

There was family, and then there were *poor relations*.

"Why were *you* in the water?" Neal's voice was husky. They fell into step behind the others. She slanted a look up at him.

"They were going in the wrong direction, the boats." She glanced back at the bay. The wind had calmed and the water looked dark and glassy. "I saw you, you and that boy, but I couldn't make myself heard."

"So you strode into the sea to save us." Neal smiled faintly.

"You make it sound dramatic." She swallowed and stopped short. He was teasing her, but his eyes shone with peculiar intensity.

And it was real. This moment. She had stridden into the sea, just as he said. *She* had. Not Muriel Pendrake. That intense look was for her alone. Her chest expanded.

"I suppose you do have me to thank for your life," she conceded, as her heart—given more space to soar—fluttered wildly against her ribs.

He laughed, gave an admiring shake of his head. Admiring but also . . . negating.

"You were magnificent," he said. "But I was paddling us toward the Cow Tooth. It's what they call that round flat rock. There." He pointed. "You can barely see it. It disappears at high tide, but even then if you climb atop, the water doesn't reach your knees."

Unbelievable.

"So you had everything under control." She stared at him. "Cliffs, storms, inaccessible bonnets, drowning boys—all fun and games to Neal Traymayne."

"About your bonnet." He pushed back his hair. "It was the one casualty. I might be able to retrieve it tomorrow, although I can't vouch for its condition."

"Retrieve it?" Now she gaped. He was joking, yes. She knew him well enough to recognize the glint in his eye. But he meant it. He'd go down the cliff again. "Have you a death wish?"

"Not at all." He shrugged. "Or—not anymore."

She understood then. He was so kind, so straightforward, so admiring, so different from other men she'd known, that she hadn't realized until now.

"You are atrociously arrogant." She couldn't help but look again at the jagged cliffs, the drop down to the sea. What a good opinion he had of his own physical prowess! She shifted her gaze to scowl at him, at the wide neck, broad shoulders, and thick arms he esteemed so highly. "What would your sisters say?"

"They've known me to climb worse." He was grinning. He really hadn't experienced a moment of fear, getting spun about in that crushing water, with his life and the lives of those two boys hanging in the balance.

Perhaps it wasn't arrogance, but a mental infirmity. But of course, plant hunters were lunatics. She'd lost sight of that essential fact because Muriel Pendrake made it all seem so mortally dull in her manuscript. Why, just the other day he'd laughed about battling condors in the Andes!

"Also, I am a member of the Swimming Association of Great Britain." As he uttered this ridiculous line—with a breeziness that indicated perfect awareness of its absurdity—he pushed up his sleeves, and she saw that the hairs on his arms were standing on end. How long had he been in the water? He must be congealing with cold. But he seemed completely unconcerned. He was enjoying himself. The danger had passed and now he relished the aftereffects. Any scrapes or bruises would be his to wear as badges of honor. Fool man.

"My friend Alan—who fought the one-sided duel with his writing—we joined together," he continued. "We're passionate advocates of the sport. I sponsor a club in Truro, or rather Varnham sponsors it. Alan edits a weekly swimming paper, *The Swimming Record*. He's won dozens of quarter-mile championships himself. Timed races in artificial pools. He can't get enough of them. I prefer tidal swimming myself, rivers and ocean, the long-distance challenges. Shorter races too. Jump from a boat at London Bridge and swim to Greenwich."

*The Thames.* Her breath stuttered. How casually he said it. *Jump from a boat.*

"This wasn't the day I'd have picked for a diving competition." A water droplet running down his forehead rolled off the bump on his nose, fell, and divided at the corner of his mouth. He licked it away with the tip of his tongue. "But I beat my personal record."

He stood there, dripping with brine, large, confident, casual, *joking* about everything that had happened. It *wasn't* a joke, what they'd all just experienced. It had been a harrowingly close call. A reminder. So what if he was skillful, strong, young, thought himself bloody invincible.

Fate didn't care what he thought.

He turned, started walking again toward the village, but she didn't move. She was rooted in place.

"What if you'd drowned?" The question came out with ugly force, a bark. "Who would care about your personal record then? *He broke his damned neck, but what a dive, forty feet.*"

Her heart had ceased to flutter and beat thickly. *Doom-doom. Doom-doom.*

"You could have drowned," she said. "Anyone can drown."

George in his charcoal-gray suit, eyes staring, flopped onto the shore by rivermen. Shivers moved up her spine.

He'd turned back around, and he watched as her mouth worked. His face became grave. Slowly, he reached out, cupped her elbows, exerting just enough pressure for her to know she could choose.

They were in public. But no one else lingered so close to the shore. Lights were twinkling above them in the village, signs that the villagers had returned to their houses, their fires. Her breath grated in her throat and her weight tipped toward her heels. Resisting him.

"Anyone can drown. Anyone can die in any number of ways." He said it in a low voice. All his sunniness—suddenly clouded. He was looking not at her but at a point over her shoulder. He, too, saw someone's blank face, staring eyes. With a jolt, she recognized his haunted expression.

But he blinked away the apparition, focused. On her. Wet, his lashes were more winglike than ever, black and curved.

"The miracle is—we're alive."

His hands on her elbows felt warm and steadying. Between those dark, beating wings, his eyes beckoned. She didn't realize her weight had pressed forward into her toes until he was bending over her.

His face was cold. But his breath blew hot and sweet, and his tongue warmed the curves of her lips. She swayed closer, twitched at the contact with his clammy shirt. Her soaked skirt made an upside-down funnel and the cold traveled up from it, against gravity. He drew back a fraction of an inch, fingers massaging along her jawline, and then he settled his mouth on hers. A lingering kiss. The heat they built there, at that junction—it flickered through her. Her lips were *vibrating*.

She pulled away. "Your teeth," she said. "They're chattering."

"Are they?" He sounded bemused. "I hadn't noticed." He chafed his biceps, stamped his feet. Literally. His *feet*. She stared.

He was barefoot.

He grinned at her with clenched teeth, grinding them together.

"Careful," she muttered. "You'll chatter your thick skull."

He laughed as though he weren't about to freeze solid.

The moment had been real. But it couldn't last.

He was an unshod *arrogant* lunatic gardener, and she was a flibbertigibbet who didn't know a Chinese shrub from a hill of potatoes.

A *married* flibbertigibbet.

What she'd felt in the Traymaynes' kitchen—that had been real too, the warmth of the fire, of Loveday and Kelyn's laughter, of the dough in her hands.

If only she could *be* who everyone thought she was.

She took Neal's hand, his broad palm stretching hers.

"Toasted saffron buns," she said. "That's the answer. We must make haste."

Toasted saffron buns. A delicious, temporary solution to all life's woes. He tugged her forward and they set off across the sand.

# CHAPTER SEVEN

No bonnet. Four hours of morning sun. Lavinia examined her face from every angle in the mirror mounted atop the oak dresser. All things considered, the damage had been minimal. She tolerated sun, it seemed, in larger doses than she tolerated strawberries. She looked blooming, rosy. The rosy *nose* was not optimal, of course. Rosiness, if it had to occur, should be of mild degree and confined to the upper cheeks. But at least her skin remained smooth.

She'd spent ages in the dim chancel of the church wrapping lichens in paper while Neal and the vicar alternately hammered and chiseled them off the rock wall. Maybe that sunless interlude had been her saving grace.

Before she left the well-appointed bedroom, she applied a thin coat of Varnham's Ointment. A woman should be pictured on the advertisements, all dewiness. She'd tell Neal that this was an essential stratagem. Not her, of course. She'd suggest Emmeline.

Which reminded her.

She found Emmeline in the kitchen preparing lunch for the twins, milk pudding and soft-boiled eggs. *Now or never.* She plunged ahead without even a greeting. Their track record with pleasantries being what it was.

"Upstairs, in my trunk," she began, "I have a gown, a *lovely* gown, lace and pale pink silk, from Paris."

"How nice for you." Emmeline dealt a severe blow to the egg in her hand and flicked shell at the table.

Lavinia could tell she'd best hurry to the point.

"It's the perfect color for your complexion, and it would fit you perfectly, I know it would." She had an eye for such things. The gown was unforgiving, cut in the slender style, the tight bodice extending all the way down to the hem, but Emmeline was slim and small breasted, within an inch of her height.

She took a deep breath. "I want to give it to you."

Emmeline dropped the half-peeled egg onto a plate. Shocked. But not pleased. She crossed her arms. "I should wear *your* hand-me-down clothes, is that it?"

Lavinia sighed. After last night's long, genial dinner, at which the near tragedy had been recounted for Kelyn—with lavish attention paid to each person's role in averting it—she'd hoped that she and Emmeline might put their spat behind them. Hadn't they united, albeit briefly, at the harbor?

Clearly, the girl still prickled at her slight.

"It was a beastly thing to say, and I'm sorry." Well, that wasn't so hard. But neither was it effective. Emmeline slid the remaining shell from the egg and began to savage the white blob with the back of a fork. Lavinia watched her for a moment.

Without looking up, Emmeline spoke in a voice as dry as sand.

"A gown from Paris. I could wear it to the Kyncastle opera."

Lavinia flushed. Hadn't she herself put on her most supercilious air and pointed out that Kyncastle offered *nothing* in the way of entertainments? On what occasion was Emmeline to put on Parisian finery?

"Well, you could wear it to a musical evening, a dance . . ." She trailed off. Neal had mentioned a midsummer festival in Penzance,

but from Tomas and Kelyn's response she'd gleaned it involved bonfires, which didn't seem quite the thing.

Did all Cornish dancing occur at barbarous ceremonies for the
blessing of hayricks or barrels of fish? There had to be gouty noble-
men who hosted country balls somewhere on the northern coast.
Why wasn't Tomas leveraging his liniments, collecting invitations
for his sisters?

Oh, bother. Emmeline really would look wonderful in that pink
silk.

"You could wear it tonight," she said, slowly, as the notion took
shape. "If we arranged a little party."

The fork stopped moving. Emmeline was staring at her. Here it
was, the chink in her armor.

"Not a dinner party, of course." She pressed a finger to her lips,
making rapid calculations. "It would be after dinner, an evening
entertainment."

As she spoke, she felt her own eagerness mounting. Finally, she
could draw on her own expertise. Why, she knew *everything* about
parties. One didn't plan them the day *of*, obviously, and certainly
they were never attempted without a generous budget, and servants,
and a grand house for hosting, but hadn't she learned to adapt to
unfavorable conditions?

First things first: scale down.

She began to pace. "We'd only need light refreshments."

Cakes, biscuits, ices, bonbons, little sandwiches of cold tongue or
watercress, tea, coffee, lemonade, wine, champagne. How she missed
champagne!

She looked around the kitchen and bit her lip.

Scale down. And then: scale down further.

"Beer and biscuits," she declared. "That will do nicely. Wine if it's
available."

There must be a few bottles in the cellar. Doctors were almost
gentlemen.

"And we don't need four musicians. Two are adequate. There's not time to print programs, but I can write cards by hand with the order of the dances so ladies can keep track of their engagements. Perhaps it should be on the shorter side, as everyone keeps such early hours. Eighteen dances. Better fourteen."

She and Neal had to catch a morning train in Bodmin.

"The parlor is far too small. We could move the dining room table against the wall and roll up the carpet." She felt her brow pucker. How many guests could the dining room hold? And what would the master and mistress of the house have to say about it?

"I don't suppose Tomas or Kelyn would mind," she murmured doubtfully.

"The guildhall," breathed Emmeline, eyes shining. "There's a piano."

Lavinia's heart lifted. She'd seen the guildhall. It was on Fore Street around the corner from the pub and letter office, a grim, medieval structure, all gray stone and slate. Probably the main room had low ceilings and smelled like a cave.

Scale down. Adapt.

She nodded. "We can bring in flowers," she said. "To liven it up." Not cut flowers from the florist, wildflowers she would gather herself. Foxglove and daisies and heather, and others that Neal had pointed out on their walk along the stream into the valley and up into Juliot woods. Willow herb, toadflax, sea carrot, yellow iris, pennywort.

"Kelyn could make her ginger biscuits." Emmeline was pacing too. "Loveday's the best on piano. Or I could ask Emily Polwhele. She's even better. Mr. Hichens plays the hornpipe."

*Hornpipe.* Lavinia stopped short. How to object without giving insult? One didn't put on a Worth gown and dance to *hornpipe.*

"Perhaps a violinist?" she said. Emmeline snapped her fingers.

"Mr. Barnett!" she exclaimed. "He fiddles."

Fiddle. She shrugged. *Good enough.* They had all the pieces. Location, musicians, refreshments, decorations. Now they needed to get to work. There were only so many hours.

"Let's go find this Mr. Barnett, and Emily Polwhele." Lavinia made to spin on her heel but Emmeline spread her arms, looking down at the table.

"Lunch," she said glumly. "Kit's in a choking phase. I have to watch him like a hawk."

She set two bowls of milk pudding on a lacquered tray.

"Oh." Lavinia frowned. *Lunch.* She squared her shoulders, stepped up to the table, and selected an egg from the basket. "I'll give the twins lunch, then."

More hands made light work. Wasn't that the saying?

She examined the egg. One had to break the shell, then peel it off. She picked up a spoon and rapped the egg sharply. To her gratification, a wide crack spread halfway around the egg's circumference.

Clear slime welled and slid onto her fingers. She dropped the egg with a cry and it split open on the table.

Emmeline pursed her lips. "Those ones aren't boiled." She took an egg from a black-bottomed pot and passed it to her. "Try this one."

Lavinia didn't meet Emmeline's eyes. She focused on rolling the new egg back and forth on the table so the shell crinkled beneath her palm.

*Anyone could have made that mistake.*

Let Emmeline poke fun at her.

But when she looked up, she saw that Emmeline had clasped her hands to her chest and was staring dreamily into space. She glanced at Lavinia and lowered her hands, a blush mantling her cheeks.

Lavinia returned her attention to the egg. She didn't want to embarrass the girl in the midst of some romantic reverie. The egg was spiderwebbed with cracks. Shouldn't all the tiny pieces of shell fall off?

"Do you think—" Emmeline clattered two spoons on the tray,

then leaned forward, unable to contain her nervous excitement. "Do you truly think people will come?"

Lavinia's gaze shot up. "Of course people will come."

There wouldn't be a line of carriages, and dozens of glittering aristocrats spilling out of them, but there would be people. The whole village, if Emmeline wanted. Exclusivity wasn't an option. Not at the guildhall. Besides, best not to leave out any potential partygoers, given the size of the total pool.

"We'll tell everyone," she said. No guest list. No invitations. They'd spread the news by word of mouth. Shout it from the cliff tops.

"People will come." Emmeline nodded. "People will come," she assured herself, and traced a circle on her cheek with the tip of a loose curl.

*People.* Lavinia hid her smile.

"You could invite him personally," she said, picking at her egg with as innocent an expression as she could muster. The shell was somehow still stuck together.

Emmeline stood bolt upright, blushing furiously.

Ah. Just as she'd suspected.

Did Kelyn and Loveday know that Emmeline had a sweetheart?

His jaw would drop when he saw her in the pink silk.

Lavinia scooped the peeled egg onto a plate. A sorry, mangled-looking blob, yolk peeping through where the white had come away with the shell.

The twins would have to make do.

Lavinia and Emmeline had a party to plan. The first and last ball of the Kyncastle Season.

"WHAT DO YOU reckon they've been doing?" Davy sat back on his heels and wiped his forehead with his shirt cuff. Neal threw his rag onto the dock and shook his head slowly.

"I haven't the faintest idea." He rolled his left shoulder, easing the tight muscle, then crossed his arms behind his head and flopped onto his back.

Not a cloud in the periwinkle sky. Yesterday's storm had blown by and taken with it every scrap of moisture. The air over the bay was still and bone-dry.

He'd pay a pound sterling for a breeze.

It was hot work, repairing the hole in the hull of the Strouts' battered seiner. He and Davy had been at it for hours. The sun had crept west and come down from its heights, beams slanting with diminished intensity. But that was only a small mercy. He pulled damp cloth away from his chest, used his shirtfront to fan himself.

*Sweating like a furze bush on a dewy morning.* That was what his father would say. What else would his father say if he *could* look down from heaven, as Curnow had suggested?

*Tell me, my boy, are those my father's Hessians you're wearing?*

*They are. Tomas brought them down from the attic. Maybe you missed it—I had to kick off my own boots yesterday to facilitate an unexpected swim.*

*Missed it? Bollocks! I interceded on your behalf. Why do you think it stopped raining?*

*Why—what a Romish idea. You can't be serious.*

*Of course I'm not serious. The dead mustn't have a sense of humor?*

*What I hear the dead have is a bird's-eye view. If that's the case, you might help me find that dandelion, the one I'm naming for Mother.*

*Your mother wants you to settle down, do you know that?*

*She told me.*

*I want it too. You're too reckless. You need to keep your feet on the ground.*

*Well, you'll both be happy to hear I've found my future wife.*

*Is she happy to hear it? Your future wife?*

*I don't know. I haven't told her yet.*

*Reckless and presumptuous. What will I ever do with you?*

*Watch over me, I suppose. Rejoice but on a farther shore.*

*You always had a smart mouth. I'll rejoice on your wedding day if you find a woman who can get the upper hand of you.*

Neal sighed and lifted a leg to inspect the big black boot, a Regency relic, the sound of his father's deep, amused voice echoing in his ears. The memory of his voice was stronger, clearer somehow than the memory of his face. Enough daydreaming.

He sat up. "There they are again."

Muriel and Emmeline were coming along the street that fronted the harbor with their heads together, apparently locked in conference.

Davy grunted. He'd returned to his labors, using pitch to fill in the seams between planks in the boat's hull.

The seiner would be as good as new. Not so the smaller boat, the dinghy Davy's brothers had rode into the storm. Fragments were still washing up onshore, and the boys had been tasked with collecting the wreckage. They'd spent the afternoon scouting excitedly up and down the shoreline, dragging what they found across the sand to Davy, who'd eyed each splintered board, assessing its usefulness, before tossing it in one of two piles.

High-spirited lads that they were, they'd taken the day's work more as a reward than a punishment.

Neal rose to help Davy with the last of it. As he did so, he looked again toward the young women. Emmeline saw him looking and nudged Muriel, who turned her head and gave him a cool wave. Then she marched into the pub, Emmeline on her heels.

Neal whistled. "I think they're having a pint."

Davy banged the bottom of the boat so hard it slid an inch on the blocks, and laughed. "Are they, now?"

The small panes of the pub windows were dark. No seeing through to the scene inside. Neal returned his attention to the boat.

"It's anyone's guess."

Muriel and Emmeline had been popping up at every turn. When Neal had loped back up through the terraced houses of the village—for a stouter saw, a second caulking iron, more pitch—he'd passed them each time, coming *and* going. Once he'd seen them through the open door of the bakery, Muriel with her hands on her hips haggling loudly with Mrs. Wilmot. Once he'd seen them coming out of Mr. Barnett's house, Mr. Barnett following with a grin as wide as a griddle, a spring in his step to match his springy gray hair. Once he'd seen them emerging from the footpath behind the vicarage, their arms filled with flowers.

Whenever they spotted him, they raised their eyebrows, smiled, waved, or shot each other mischievous glances, but they never stopped what they were doing long enough to exchange a greeting.

Thick as thieves, tearing about hell-for-leather. It could mean anything.

"That's more than a pint they've got there." Davy directed Neal's attention.

Muriel and Emmeline had reappeared, each holding a jug of beer. They ducked into the alley.

Neal leaned his elbows on the boat, squinting after them. At last he gave up, reconciled himself to the mystery.

"We'll figure it out when they want us to," he said, and Davy laughed.

"That's what I'm learning." He grinned happily. "I'll be prepared come September."

When he married Loveday.

Neal grinned back at him. "I wouldn't count on it, coz."

A recalcitrant plank monopolized the next hour. When they finally started up to the quayside, Tomas halloed, bounding down to them.

"The house has been bewitched," he called. "Come help a man disenchant his kingdom."

The sight that greeted them in the Traymayne dining room was certainly a strange one.

"Where are the chairs?" asked Davy, circling the table.

"With the women, perhaps?" Tomas scratched his brow.

"Cold," Davy pronounced, leaning over the table to squeeze a wedge of potato in a serving dish. He felt the tureens. "Everything's cold."

Neal poked his head into the kitchen. The empty kitchen. The air smelled sweet and gingery. The cups and dishes were missing from the sideboards.

"Kelyn?" Davy looked at Neal as he returned to the dining room. Neal shook his head.

"You can see why I turned around at once and went in search of reinforcements." Tomas popped a wedge of potato into his mouth.

"You've done it now," said Davy. "What if the pixies stole away your wife and children and put a spell on the food? You're under their power."

"In for a penny," said Tomas, and filched a second potato.

"Footsteps." Neal prowled to the staircase, Davy and Tomas behind him. Muriel was sailing down the stairs in a low-cut gown of red silk and white lace, making ushering gestures with her hands.

"Don't stand there woolgathering," she said. "You need to dress and dine and help carry the refreshments down to the guildhall. The ball starts promptly at nine."

*Ball?* His frown was automatic. Muriel had turned the whole house, no, the whole village, upside down for a *ball?* And now she was issuing commands?

Christ, he'd have to apologize to Tomas. What must his cousin be thinking? His houseguest was the pixie.

She stopped halfway down the staircase.

"You look so consternated," she said to them all. "I should have made it more clear—you are most certainly invited."

Loveday appeared at the top of the stairs.

"Muriel, do you think *this* shawl . . ." She trailed off, spotting the men on the landing.

"I think so!" Davy burst out heartily. A jackanapes, perhaps, but an endearing jackanapes.

Neal's frown smoothed at Davy's dazzled expression and Loveday's answering blush. She did look uncommonly well. Something different about her hair. It was loose, that was it. A few pieces twisted back over her ears, but aside from that, curls tumbling on her shoulders. The lavender wrap brought out the green in her hazel eyes.

Muriel was surveying Davy and Loveday, the hint of a smile curving the bow of her lips. Loveday's hair was her handiwork, of course, and that lavender tulle had been magicked out of her massive trunk.

Neal turned to Tomas, who'd put his foot up on the bottom stair and was leaning against the banister. Consternation was giving way to mirth. Neal could see that no apology would be necessary.

"What shall I wear?" Tomas asked Neal, then broke into laughter. "The better question is—what shall you wear? Grandpa's Hessians will pair strangely with your London kit."

"I didn't pack much in the way of London kit." Neal's gaze wandered back to Muriel. She'd done up her own hair into a bright crown. "Do you have a pair of Grandpa's pantaloons and a frock coat? I'll go as a historical figure."

He addressed Muriel. "Is it a fancy-dress ball, by any chance?"

Smiling, she descended to the bottom stair. "It's eclectic, really. Wear what you like. Within limits, of course." She swept him with her eyes to make sure he understood that his present pitch-stained attire was thoroughly out-of-bounds.

Did she think him that much of a boor? He preferred mountaintops to mansions, yes, but had no trouble navigating either. If Muriel Pendrake wanted a man who could dance, she didn't need to take herself back to London, or Paris. He would suffice. More than suffice.

"All right, lads," he said to Davy and Tomas. "We've got our marching orders. Let's fall to it."

He bowed to Muriel. "I, for one, wouldn't dream of missing the first quadrille."

# CHAPTER EIGHT

By the fourth dance, Lavinia had ceased to fret about the depressing venue. More and more people were crushing into the assembly room, calling out greetings, depositing coats and hats higgledy-piggledy, undaunted by the lack of a proper cloakroom. Some newcomers joined the dancers, while others leaned against the walls and heckled them good-naturedly, tapping their feet and tipping back bottles of beer and spirits. Thank God so many young men had thought to bring their own refreshment. The first wave of partygoers had drained the jugs. Everywhere Lavinia looked: people enjoying themselves. No one complained about the crooked floor, or about the unpleasant humidity that, along with the smoke from the lamps, produced a visible fug. The musicians played with a lively tempo, more often than not, the same lively tempo.

The ball was a success.

And Neal—Neal waltzed like a prince. Or not precisely like a prince. He glissaded smoothly as any peer of the realm, but his revolutions and counterrevolutions seemed designed to dizzy her. Also, his facial expression wasn't royal. No fixed little smile or lordly sneer. He laughed as they turned, as though his supreme gracefulness made him the victor in some riotous contest. She wanted to feel annoyed, but he never missed a step, never hopped, or kicked up his heels, or made a brusque or jerky movement. He was waltzing perfection, if waltzing was compatible with that uninhibited glee, the sort of glee one expected on the sports field, not in the ballroom.

Of course, this wasn't a ballroom. Maybe his boisterous, muscular approach modulated brilliantly for an evening in a guildhall. Certainly, he was getting his share of appreciative heckles.

Spinning in Neal's arms, Lavinia glimpsed a row of girls on the room's perimeter. They wore garishly bright dresses and hardly seemed forlorn in regard to their unpartnered states. Forward was more like it.

"You're a brave, fine man, Neal Traymayne," one called out as they swept past, a buxom girl with thick dark braids and a daring smile. Her friends giggled and hid their faces.

But of course, Neal *was* a kind of prince in Kyncastle, one of the London Traymaynes. For the ball, he'd donned a dark coat—the same he'd worn at that horrid inn—and his cravat was fresh, white, and passably knotted. With those hundred-year-old boots, and that raffish grin, he looked a rough-hewn cavalier. Every girl in the valley no doubt hovered in her doorway and sighed when he came to visit, hoping he'd happen along.

She and Neal should dance with other partners. Appalling etiquette this, the two of them, coupled for the quadrille, waltzing every waltz.

It wasn't that she wanted to keep him from the rustic maidens. Of course not. It was that *she* was also perfection at the dance. She'd languished a whole Season, denied access to the spheres in which she used to shine. Now she'd entered a separate sphere—small and a bit dingy, but vibrant all the same—and she could feel her blood humming, just as it had before. She couldn't bear to bumble about with a lesser partner. It was too lovely, how she and Neal twirled together, his hand light on her waist, her torso arched back from his, everything about their position, their movements, elegant and exquisitely balanced.

She wanted to dance with him forever.

Just then, he swung them deftly into the center of the room, out of the path of a careening duo with flapping arms. From the shout that went up, she guessed they'd careened on to endanger a less-agile couple.

Neal laughed down at her, steering without seeming to calculate, relying on his impressive physical intuition. The same physical intuition that made it possible for him to descend sheer rock walls and skim the tops of waves.

"It's like dancing on the deck of a ship." He'd bent his head to murmur by her ear. He meant the floor, the rough, wide planks, the steep pitch. Even so, her whole body felt flush with the possibility of escape, of a future.

The two of them on a ship to France.

The duchess and her paramour.

Unlike the duchess in her story, she'd have to set sail without the plunder from her husband's estate. She'd be penniless, depending on Neal, as she'd once depended on her papa, on George, on Cranbrook.

But no, she'd never even get that far.

Unlike the duchess's paramour, Neal, for all his princely grace and piratical swagger, was *not* a ruffian king, a fugitive beholden to no one and nothing. He wouldn't spirit her across the sea, live with her in Paris.

*Unless.*

She kept her eyes trained straight ahead, studied his cravat, the top of his tanned neck, the hard angle of his jaw.

Unless he fell in love with her. Fell senselessly, torrentially in love with her, the kind of love that permitted no reason, no moderation.

Then he would do anything.

The waltz ended abruptly, a scuffle by the piano causing Emily Polwhele to bang an off chord on the keys.

Neal tightened his hold, pulled her a fraction closer than perfect form allowed, then released her and scanned the room. A group of lanky young men with tankards had surrounded Mr. Barnett, demanding . . . *something*. The ringleader had an enormous Adam's apple and the loudest voice. Volume was not clarifying.

"Crowdy so we'll dance!"

Lavinia wrinkled her nose at Neal, who translated.

"The boys are wanting a jig," he said as the fiddle struck up. Mr. Barnett began leaping about—*he* didn't suffer from rheumatism for all he had to be nearing a hundred—and a portly man unceremoniously displaced an old woman from one of the Traymaynes' chairs, settled a drum on his lap, and beat it for all he was worth with the palm of his hand.

Unsurprisingly, he wore a smock.

The old woman lifted her feet in rhythm, circling the piano as the young men cheered.

Neal raised a brow and gave Lavinia an appraising look. She shook her head. Jigs were not in her repertoire.

"You disapprove?" he asked as they drifted away from the uproarious skipping and kicking toward a gap in the spectators arrayed along the far wall.

"Of Emmeline's ball becoming a barn dance?" She stopped by the window, where the wildflowers had wilted in their bottle on the sill. Had she forgotten to add water? With all the preparations, the afternoon had gone by in a blur.

*No green thumb here.*

She sighed. "The inevitability of the blow has somehow softened the impact."

He smiled at the wryness in her voice. She'd hoped he would smile.

"*Emmeline's* ball?" He watched her closely. The floor thundered as dancers stamped along to Mr. Barnett's wild bowing. "Is this what it took to win her over? She wasn't convinced by yesterday's heroics, so today you arranged for her coming out?"

"More or less." She smiled. *Heroics.* He wouldn't admit that she'd saved his life, but he had just called her a hero. Not quite. But still.

"Bravo." His eyes looked almost black in the low lamplight. "Every Kyncastle Traymayne is now in your power."

"Are they?" She turned to fuss with the blossoms, so she could slant a look at him over her shoulder. "Only the Kyncastle Traymaynes?"

Balls—barn dances—they existed to facilitate flirtations.

George had liked to see her flirt.

*Fills me with pity for my fellow man, who otherwise I'm inclined to despise. There but for the grace of God go I, that's what I say to myself. Because those poor pups will never have you, not my Vinnie. My very own. Mine.*

Neal wasn't a pup. And George—George was dead.

She would silence him.

Neal's smile stretched. "All the Traymaynes in Kyncastle," he amended, and came closer with an idle step, peering over her shoulder.

He said in a changed voice, "You picked the orchids by the vicarage." He touched the pink lip of a flower, bending it with a gloved finger.

Was he scandalized? She'd learned on their walk to Juliot woods that he didn't dig up every wild plant he saw, and when he did choose a specimen, he took pains to leave everything around it intact.

"You didn't pick all of them?" he said. The other bottles of wildflower arrangements stood on windowsills obscured by the crowd, and on the table in the makeshift refreshment room. Orchids featured prominently in each bouquet.

"For a good cause." She couldn't help but touch the same flower. Her gloved hand brushed his as she ran her fingers over the delicate lobes. The muted sensation maddened her, and she bent over to inhale the faint scent of vanilla diffusing from the petals before she withdrew. The white leather at her fingertips was smeared with pollen, a golden stain.

"For Emmeline," he agreed, and then his brows knitted together. "But—this bittersweet might have contented her."

He *was* scandalized. Chagrin changed to indignation.

"You grudge her the orchids? After you reneged on your promise?" she said. "I spent all afternoon organizing a dance because *you* went hieing off to Cornwall before you could show her a proper good time in London. It wasn't very cousinly."

Now he raised his eyebrows. Would he question what she knew about *cousinly* behavior? She had no siblings, but she *did* have cousins. A few of them. Whom she'd lorded over as a wealthy young beauty destined for a duchy.

Those cousins, it was safe to assume, had very much enjoyed her comeuppance following her papa's reversal of fortune.

He didn't, though, quiz her on her own family feeling, or failure thereof. The lines in his forehead smoothed and his eyes hooded.

"How fortunate she is, then, in her friends," he said, and she was relieved to hear the teasing note in his voice. He wasn't going to belabor his point about the orchids.

As he leaned against the wall, a lock of hair fell across his brow, and she itched to push it away from his forehead.

"The guildhall hasn't seen such numbers since Joan Traymayne was tried for a witch at the court of assizes." He pushed the lock back himself, mahogany brown hair against the fawn-colored leather.

"When was that?" She glanced around the room, imagining a bench of black-clad justices, a woman in rags, old and bent but with Loveday's face. "They didn't find her guilty?"

"They did indeed," said Neal. "It was 1646, the only year the assizes were ever held in Kyncastle."

"So she was hanged," breathed Lavinia. Neal claimed an executed witch among his ancestors. Perhaps a jailed father wouldn't shock him.

"That was the sentence. But the good people of Kyncastle decided instead to string up the judges." Neal grinned with pride. "Just to teach them a lesson. They lived to tell the tale."

She stared at him. Certainly, those judges would have recounted their version with considerably less relish.

"Did you note that iron hook with the wooden handle on the nail over the mantelpiece in the parlor? Legend has it, that's the gaff my several-times-removed grandfather used to whack the chief justice of the Prince's Council. Knocked his wig off." He laughed. "I don't think my mother would have married my father if his forebears had let a woman of the family go to her death for witchcraft."

*His having a witch in the bloodline wouldn't have been enough to win her over?* Lavinia bit her tongue.

"Emmeline didn't share that bit of history," she said. Where *was* the girl? She seemed to have a penchant for disappearing, but at her own ball? The last time Lavinia had caught a glimpse of her, she was standing by the piano with a look of utter desolation on her face.

The ball was a success. But the right *people* hadn't yet arrived.

Neal shrugged. "I'm surprised someone didn't tell you about Mistress Joan, as we call her. She's a beloved figure in our family. Emmeline had other things on her mind, I'm sure. The two of you could have walked to Devon, what with all the back-and-forth."

"I'm well aware," she said. She had a keen sense of how much she'd walked. Her feet had been blistered *before* she started dancing.

He fixed her with that direct regard of his, so different from that of other men she'd known.

"I did regret the timing of the move, for her sake." He said it in a low voice, difficult to hear over the music. "But I couldn't delay any longer."

Did he leave London out of delicacy, to spare Elizabeth Fletcher's feelings? Or out of disgust after he spied—while planting rhododendrons in a garden square—a flock of ladies in bustled gowns with swansdown trim? Realization hit a moment after these pettier possibilities surfaced.

His mother's illness.

The thumping of feet grew louder as Mr. Barnett bowed with

even more vigor. The room was crowded enough that dancers kept colliding. Tomas might find his services in higher demand tonight than yesterday, when those little boys had nearly drowned themselves.

"Come along!" That forward girl—she'd danced close enough to catch Neal's eye, thick braids bouncing. *Those* could whack a man and knock his wig off. "Come along, co!" she cried.

Neal tossed her a smile, made a small regretful gesture.

Lavinia frowned. "Why did you settle in London in the first place? You weren't there very long."

"A year," he said absently. "January to January." His gaze tracked the dancing now, and his fingers drummed his thigh in time to the music. "I went for Varnham," he added, almost an afterthought.

His gardening business. He was the head of the nurseries, not a jobbing gardener. She should stop thinking of him as such, despite his brown neck and dirty fingernails.

Maybe he'd been engaged not to Elizabeth Fletcher but to Elizabeth Davenport. Not out of the question if one emphasized the *business* rather than the *gardening* side of things. A businessman would have just cleared the threshold of eligibility for Elizabeth Davenport.

Pointless considerations.

His foot was tapping. The music had gotten inside him. He was bursting with it. She should release him from his agony.

*Go on*, she should say. *You want to dance, dance.*

Maybe it wasn't the music, though. Maybe it was that girl.

"But you live in Truro now," she said, plowing on with the conversation. "And you're still running Varnham."

"We have several branches, but the main branch is in London." With seeming effort, he refocused his attention on her. "I couldn't have taken over the business without first spending significant time there. But that wasn't my intention in going. I went to London for *Charles* Varnham, James's father. The rest followed."

She didn't understand and must have looked her question, but the jig ended with a roar that made utterance a wasted effort. The crowd shifted, couples rearranging, more people herding toward the center of the room. Another jig started up, the tempo faster. Red-faced, Tomas emerged from the dense center of the crowd, beckoning.

*Say it.*

"Go on." She turned to Neal, smiling brightly. "You want to dance."

He observed only a moment of perfunctory hesitation.

She watched with a sinking heart as he joined the dance, stamping the rhythm on the floor in those old boots, his long, muscled legs swinging as he pivoted to give Davy a deliberate bump with his shoulder. Davy spun around, grinning, and cut a mad caper that Neal mimicked but with an added flurry of steps that proved impossible for Davy to replicate. He tried, gamely, tripping as he did so, to the groans of onlookers. What a funny style of dance it was. Far too loud and frenetic and *leggy* for London. High knees not being encouraged in the best circles.

Lavinia studied the dancers, picked out Loveday and Kelyn and the reedy blond Strout girls from the harbor, all smiling as they twirled, hands on their hips.

Suddenly, she felt as though she were standing outside it all, behind a thick wall of glass. She didn't belong among these revelers, nor did she belong anywhere else. If Cranbrook found her, he'd soon discover he didn't want her. Her mother might take her back, but back to what? Two poor relations were double the inconvenience. Returning, she'd only make things worse.

She'd belonged with George. His Vinnie. But even George hadn't wanted to keep her.

She'd spent two years in hiding already, hiding from the truth.

George would never have married her. He'd made her feel so special. The golden god of her childhood looking upon her at last, *seeing* her.

*You, Vinnie. It's always been you.*

But he'd let her dangle. He'd toyed with her. She'd been his play-thing, nothing more.

The music sounded distant in her ears. She had to brace herself against the windowsill. No one knew who she really was. Not Neal Traymayne, certainly. But not her mother, either. Her papa. They'd both believed her to be a pretty, silly, capricious, but ultimately bid-dable young girl, their innocent daughter. They'd be appalled if they knew of her deceit. She'd lied to them, and to herself, for George, for love. Or rather, for dazzlement and delusion. For a fairy tale.

Now she was running from Cranbrook, and her parents would never understand what drove her. Visceral repulsion, yes. But she *couldn't* sacrifice herself, even if she had the stomach to suffer the old goat's caresses. For Cranbrook, only a virgin sacrifice would do. *Fresh ingredients.*

She felt a wave of nausea.

The air smelled of beer and mildew, damp wool and warmed flesh. Her breath came shorter. She should push her way to the door, keep running, this time down to the harbor, where she'd climb aboard one of the boats. Sail north, all the way to the north pole, present herself to the polar bears as a long-lost cub. Forget human-kind.

Or sink.

A final madness to cap this mad week.

As she started forward, she saw the flash of rich pink silk out of the corner of her eye. Emmeline, crossing to the corner of the room. At first, she didn't make out her companion, so absorbed was she in the study of her protégée. Emmeline couldn't dance a jig in that form-fitting dress, but she could promenade like the best of them. Lavinia hadn't seen finer mincing and slinking in all the beau monde. Her curls framed her face, which was luminous, soft and ravishingly pretty as a petal. She was smiling up at the tall, hand-some man on her arm.

She was smiling up at Derwent Druce.

Lavinia's breath stuttered. Druce had been an assistant in her papa's architecture firm, a particular favorite, trumpeted for his talent as a draftsman and expected to one day accede to the partnership. He'd come often to the house with his drawings and would pass a mannerly quarter hour with her and her mother in the drawing room before he and her papa closed themselves in his study.

He would recognize her anywhere.

Heart hammering, she slid along the wall, head down, making for the antechamber, where hours ago she'd dusted a wooden table and arranged the bottle of wildflowers, the plates of ginger biscuits, the jugs of beer, the cups. It was a small, stuffy room, used for storage, with crates and barrels lining the walls. Mercifully, it was empty. She stood by the table, staring at the crumbs on a willow-pattern plate, listening to the sounds of fiddle and drum, of stamping feet and pealing voices.

It would all end here, now.

Emmeline's sweetheart was the London architect. She should have guessed.

*Attentive to the vicar.* A girl like Emmeline was never attentive to a vicar.

But she couldn't have guessed that the man tasked with restoring the parish church was Druce. Or could she have? Was that why she'd tried so hard to squelch her misgivings, to put the thought of the architect out of her mind?

Derwent Druce hadn't been directly implicated in any of her father's wrongdoing, but he had been tarnished by association.

He was exactly the London architect ready to leap at the chance to linger in a backwater. The fiddling stopped. Mr. Barnett had exhausted himself, perhaps, or taken pity on Emily Polwhele, who began to pound the piano keys, launching into a *valse à deux temps.*

"Muriel." Tomas and Neal had appeared in the doorway. Absurdly, she stepped behind the table, as though she'd be less vulnerable—less visible—with the wildflowers and empty jugs between them. Neither man seemed to register the oddness of the motion. Both entered the room, Neal sitting casually on a barrel, Tomas coming right up to the table to address her.

"Has Emmeline confided in you?" he asked, brows knotted. "I have just observed a familiarity between her and a certain gentleman that made me wonder . . ."

"If she had, it would be a confidence." To her surprise, she formed the words easily. No matter how vanquished she felt, it seemed her instinct for self-preservation would not desert her. "I'd hardly tell you."

Neal laughed. "What did I say?"

Tomas shot him a look. "She is my youngest sister and charge," he said, with unnecessary bluster, given the audience. Perhaps he imagined the gentleman in question already before him.

"I should know if she has developed an attachment," he said. "And to *Druce*." He shook his head. "Seems a decent chap, but he'll go back to London and break her heart."

Neal lifted a shoulder. "Maybe he's serious." He glanced at Lavinia. "She might end up in London with him."

"And break her sisters' hearts." Tomas frowned. The idea of Emmeline taking up permanent residence in London didn't sit well with him. They were more than close, the Traymaynes. They were downright clannish.

How stifling—and how comforting—it must be.

"You pay his salary." Tomas tipped a jug of beer, verifying its emptiness. "Maybe you should talk to him *seriously* about the seriousness of his intentions."

"What?" Lavinia blinked. Tomas returned to the doorway, poked his head out, then turned back to them.

"Derwent Druce," he said, "the man who at this moment is hugging my sister and passing it off as a waltz, is an architect come from London to restore the church. The parties most directly concerned refused to contribute the requisite funds in full, and so my dear cousin stepped in with an offer of financial support."

"An investment in conversation." Neal kicked one heel against the barrel, two kicks per three-note bar of music. "Once the church is restored, no one will talk about how the church needs restoring. A new topic will have to be discovered."

"He'd like to pass it off as self-interest." Tomas grinned. "He's embarrassed by his own generosity."

"Stop it." Neal closed his eyes, rested the back of his head on the wall.

"Embarrassed by his wealth, then." Tomas watched Neal for a reaction and when none manifested, he sighed. "In any event, he'll have suasion with young Druce."

Lavinia studied Neal's rugged profile, the black satin lashes against his cheeks the only frill. Perhaps plant nurseries could earn a man a better living than she'd imagined.

"Curnow hired him," said Neal, eyes still closed. "What's more, he's in the suasion business. He'll talk to Druce if that's what you want. I've barely met the man."

"He might stay in Kyncastle." Tomas hung on to the doorframe, seemingly undecided as to whether he'd rather continue on in the antechamber or dash into the dance to pry apart the couple in question. "He had some trouble in London. You must have heard about it. You were still in town. Architect caught fleecing a duke. That was Druce's firm."

Neal opened his eyes. Lavinia's hands were clenched into fists at her sides. She prayed that he wouldn't look at her.

"Doesn't ring a bell," he said, and she could have kissed him.

"The plight of dukes, even the fleeced ones, has yet to keep me up at night," he added dryly.

"Aren't you the very daps of your mother when you make that

face," said Tomas, letting go of the doorframe and committing to the antechamber. "The architect, Yardley—he wasn't playing Robin Hood. He starved the duke's tenants and was selling jobs on the side, abusing his public office."

Lavinia's cheeks were burning. HUNGRY BABIES IN HAMPSHIRE. Her father had raised the rents in the villages on Anthony's estates without reporting the increase and pocketed the difference. The heart-wrenching accounts of the affected tenants had run in all the papers.

"Remind me how an architect starves a duke's tenants?" Neal sat up on the barrel. "I thought a duke starved a duke's tenants."

Would they not stop? She wanted the floor to open, wanted to drop down a black chute.

Tomas put a boot on a crate and leaned forward, bending his knee. "This Yardley was a friend of the late duke and acted as his trustee. The son and heir brought the charges. He'd been engaged to Yardley's daughter, so at first the attack savored of sour grapes. Then the evidence came to light."

"The whole thing has a bad savor." Neal's heel had yet to miss a beat. "But Druce isn't to blame."

"No." Tomas sank lower, then straightened his bent leg. "And he talked about it frankly at the church ale. We'd all had a bit to drink. Said the news had shocked him. Yardley was kindness itself, generous to a fault, he said."

Lavinia's eyes pricked. Her papa always had a smile and a good word. Everyone who knew him liked him. George, Anthony, Effie—they'd preferred him to their own father. Anthony and Effie—especially Effie—had suffered for it.

"Easy to be generous with someone else's money," observed Neal, with a hint of a sneer.

Tomas pushed off the crate. "He lavished it on his daughter, according to Druce."

She couldn't listen to another word of this. But she was penned in the room. Her skin crawled and she felt light-headed. Her papa stole food from babies so she could eat French chocolates. Was that how Druce imagined it? Was that how it had been?

"He's a good fellow, I think. Druce," mused Tomas, and went again to the doorway.

"They're still dancing," he reported. "But my wife is not. If you'll excuse me, I'm going to ask if she'll honor me with her hand for the next waltz."

Lavinia heard Neal's feet hit the flagstones. She looked over as he approached.

"Will you honor me with *your* hand for the next waltz?" His grin faded. "What's wrong?"

"Nothing." She shook her head. Were the tears still standing in her eyes? She had to blink carefully. "Nothing. The ginger biscuits are all gone."

He laced his gloved fingers together, searching her face. Concerned.

He was in her power. He'd said so, jokingly, and he showed his respect, his attraction, his esteem, his consideration, in so many small ways.

But he hadn't fallen in love with her. Fallen so deeply in love that it wouldn't matter if she were named Muriel, or Lavinia, if she were someone's widow or someone's wife, if she wanted him to follow her to Paris or the north pole.

"Cowslips are edible." He plucked a stem from the bouquet, a thin green stem from which many yellow trumpet-like flowers depended. He held it out to her. Her blinking became less careful, more quizzical, as she put out her palm. She hadn't realized the bouquet was part of the refreshment.

"The orchids look more delicious," she said.

"They do, but they're not." He laughed. "You can take my word for it."

She wouldn't wonder how many plants he'd sampled, and about the resultant hives, boils, and blisters.

She separated one yellow trumpet and put it between her lips, drew it into her mouth.

"It tastes bright." She let her eyelids drift down. For a moment, she was back in the glasshouse with the beautiful duchess, the first she'd ever known, George's mother, and that large, vibrant woman was pulling a tiny sun down from the dark green leaves, holding it out to her, so she could sniff the cool rind, sharply sweet and clean. The cowslip tasted like citrus and morning light. When she opened her eyes, she saw that Neal was staring.

"Here." She handed him a flower. "Do you know—if we plant one of these crumbs—" She gestured toward a plate. "We can grow a new crop of ginger biscuits?"

For a moment, he looked puzzled, then comprehension flared.

"Loveday." He sighed, dropping the flower into his mouth. "She planted that caraway seed in a pot and watered it every day for a month."

"You can't pretend you weren't pleased with yourself," she said, because he was trying to hide a smile.

"You have to understand, I'm the youngest of five." He pinched a crumb from the plate. "I was always getting told everything. I never got to do the telling."

"So you told tales to your younger cousin?" She ate another flower, dry on her tongue and then that sudden tang.

"I taught her all I knew," he protested. "But my stock of knowledge was small. When I ran out of facts, I had to rely on invention."

She laughed and the breath rushed back into her chest. She liked laughing with Neal Traymayne. She wouldn't mind staying in this dusty cobwebbed room with him. If she could keep him here, until the dance ended, until Derwent Druce was fast asleep in the vicarage, until dawn, when Tomas woke to harness the horses and drive them to Bodmin Station, they could continue a little longer as they were, mutually enticed, dreaming the same dream.

It was a dream, not a lie, this idyll as Muriel Pendrake. It was a tale she told because she'd run out of facts, or at any rate, facts that didn't hurt. It was a last chance, and she wouldn't feel guilty for taking it.

"I wish I could plant this crumb so it yielded a dozen ginger biscuits." He threw the crumb back onto the plate, looked at her through his lashes. "But such a feat is beyond even Varnham. Are you still too hungry to dance?"

"I want to dance," she said, coming around the table. "But not out there. Here."

He hadn't expected that, but he was equal to it. He gave a mock bow and reached for her, then cocked his head. "Ah, but Mr. Hichens has arrived. The night will go on in jigs."

Out in the assembly hall, the hornpipe shrilled along with the fiddle, and the raucous shouts and thumps sifted dust down from the ceiling. Lavinia coughed. This was her proposition, though. She couldn't back down.

A jig. Bother.

Slowly, she gathered her skirt and lifted it well above her ankles. She kicked up one white satin slipper and turned on the other, skipping in place. That was as far as memory served and space allowed. She looked up at Neal expectantly.

"Not bad." He folded his arms, amused, tapping the fingers of one hand on his elbow. "But we can't dance a jig in this clutter."

Without warning, he leaned forward and gripped her around the hips, raising her clear off the ground. He set her on top of a barrel and stepped back, grinning his satisfaction. The gasp she'd been too startled to emit exploded as a laugh.

"We're to dance on these barrels, then?" Better not to tell him she'd feared all Cornish festivities led to exactly this.

He sprang up onto the adjacent barrel. His head brushed the ceiling, and he flicked several times at his hair.

"Spider," he explained, catching her look. "Never mind. I'll have to stoop a little." He began to strike his heels and toes on the barrel in time with the music, feet flying back and forth, and side to side, faster and faster, until he stopped with a stamp and grabbed her hands.

"We used to practice on hogsheads of pilchards." He said, chest heaving. "We'd stink aloud of fish at the end of it, but we worked out dozens of steps, Jenni and Tomas and Loveday and I."

"I will learn them all," she vowed. *That should take a while.*

"We'd leap from hogshead to hogshead," he said. "If you touched the ground, you lost."

"I played a game like that." She held his hands more tightly. "We were only safe on stone or wood, so we had to run between the fountains and the trees."

"We?" His thumb found her palm and pressed.

"Effie, my friend. She and I." The tension in her fingers relaxed. "We'd play all day in the garden whenever we could."

Which was less and less often, until it was never. They'd grown apart, even as their fathers became more entwined. Effie had eloped, without a word. She hadn't confided in Lavinia. But then, Lavinia had never confided in her, about George. Effie had been abandoned by her husband. Instead of welcoming her home, her father had locked her away in an asylum, or Lavinia's papa had done it, or they both had. Competing stories circulated.

Fact: she'd remained there even after her father died, until Anthony had found and freed her.

Lavinia remembered every moment of that dreadful morning when Anthony stormed into the breakfast room to confront Papa. She'd listened, aghast, to the accusations before her mother forced her from the room. That morning ended her engagement. Toppled Papa from his pedestal. Life accelerated on its downward spiral.

Small wonder Effie hadn't flown to her, eager to renew their friendship.

"This is your friend whose mother grew lemon trees," Neal spoke quietly, both thumbs making small circles.

His memory was keen.

Talking to him was dangerous. She wanted to share more of herself than was wise. Maybe she was through with talking.

She took a breath and jumped to his barrel. He swayed backward and clasped her against his chest, but he didn't lose his footing. He wouldn't. He was the lithest man alive.

"We have to leap from barrel to barrel," she said, mouth muffled by his cravat.

"Mmm," he said. "Those were hogsheads we leapt between, twice the size of these barrels. And we weren't full-grown."

He was full-grown now. Hard and tall and *full*. Held close, she rose and fell with his breaths.

"I'll return to my barrel, then," she said, her reluctance an invitation, and tipped her head to look at him. His mouth met hers, that bright taste on his lips, his tongue stroking into her, the feeling inside her sweet and then sharp, an urgency that made her twine her arms around his neck, crush her breasts against his broad chest.

He felt it too. He deepened the kiss, one hand tracing down the side of her body, the swell of her breast, the dip of her waist, the flare of her hip, before he caught her beneath the buttocks and gathered her more fully into him. Oh, he was gorgeously thick and firm and strong, and *safe*. The barrel might splinter beneath their feet and send them crashing to the flagstones, but she'd leapt to *him*. She couldn't be hurt, not in his arms.

Now his teeth were running lightly down her neck, and he was licking the curve of her shoulder, lingering there before kissing back up the front of her throat, burning kisses. His chin rasped skin warmed and wetted by his mouth. He bit the lobe of her ear and she moaned aloud, felt his smile on the soft underside of her chin as he nuzzled her, forcing her head back. As her back arched, her breasts pushed up, and his hand wandered over her collarbones, cool leather sliding down the slopes of her breast, then tangling in lace.

This, too, this could take a good while.

Provided Neal's strength held.

And the barrel.

In fact, the situation was rather precarious. Physically. Not to mention that a few feet away, beyond the open door, the whole village of Kyncastle was assembled.

She opened her eyes as he dragged his mouth from her neck. His eyes were gleaming, lids heavy with desire, but that glint—his teasing look.

"This barrel is going to go the way of that stone wall," he predicted.

"I won't bear all the responsibility." Her voice shivered only slightly. And he couldn't hear the wild pounding of her heart. She sounded almost as teasing, as collected, as he did.

"Everything is ancient here and near to crumbling," she said. "And you outweigh me by five stone."

Gently, he put her from him, lifting and shifting her again without any apparent strain until her heels came down on her own barrel.

He wasn't senselessly, torrentially in love with her. But the desiring, teasing, burning-hot look in his eyes was encouraging, to say the least.

If they weren't in a musty, dusty, spider-filled storage room from the Middle Ages, he wouldn't be heaving that sigh, crossing his arms. He'd be doing something else. To her. With her.

"Shall we join the dance?" he asked.

She stared at him, that blunt, rough face spangled with those luxuriant eyes, and considered her course of action.

Was it better to wait it out in the antechamber or make a dash through the crowd for the door? Both had their risks.

"We'll stay right here," she said. "If I'm to learn to jig, I prefer a private lesson."

"Snob," he murmured.

"What kind of snob kicks up her skirts on a barrel?" she demanded, crossing her left foot over her right, then her right over her left, adding a little hop once she had the way of it. Not a jig, exactly, but he couldn't discount the effort.

He didn't. He clapped his hands along with the music, grinning his admiration.

"My kind of snob," he said.

# CHAPTER NINE

MURIEL FELL ASLEEP on the train to Falmouth, her head on his shoulder. Neal rested his cheek on her hair, enjoying the feel of it against his skin. He was drowsy too, and the light streaming through the windows heated the compartment, pressed down his eyelids.

They'd all gone late to their beds.

She stirred against him, and he sat up, gazing out at the country-side. Green fields dotted with cows. Some sheep. Come midsummer the green would deepen leaf by leaf.

Come midsummer.

He drifted. Drifted to Golowan, Muriel's first. The long day giving over to night, the paths dark, glowworms in the hedges. He was walking with Muriel, her hand in his, walking up to the bonfires on the hills, and then to the orchard, where the air was tart with swelling fruit. He lifted Muriel up onto a barrel, slid his hands up her legs, rolled down her stockings, and she bunched her skirt in her fists, held it higher and higher, exposing her bare calves, her sweet kneecaps, the tops of her thighs, which he kissed, so she gasped, jumping at his touch. He reached to steady her, one arm deep inside her skirts, palming the fullness of her backside. She lifted her skirt higher, and he licked to the apex of her thighs, to the split in the linen, the dark damp gold of her peeking out, and Christ, how he wanted to taste, to lower her over his mouth, and . . .

Ahem.

The discomfort of flesh bunched inside trousers grown suddenly tight alerted him to his . . . state.

*Think of* Blumenbachia chuquitensis.

He made a furtive adjustment. Like he was a bloody schoolboy. Except as a schoolboy he'd never slipped into daydreams about a woman on a barrel. It had taken Muriel to unlock the erotic potential of your basic English cask.

They'd barely gotten to explore the possibilities.

Last night, he'd have liked to hop off his own barrel and show her more exciting ways of positioning herself. A knee hooked over his shoulder, perhaps, or—once he removed the satin slipper she'd shredded on the nail heads in the floor—her instep flexing in his hand as he nestled between her legs, his tongue working a slow rhythm. Jigging could involve any part of the body, provided the practitioner had the agility and the endurance.

Unfortunately, it wasn't the time or the place for such an intimate performance.

She'd rehearsed the steps he taught her as she stared at his feet, the pink tip of her tongue at the corner of her mouth. Utterly, adorably concentrated. She'd proved a quick study.

Tomas's eyes had started when he'd charged back into the room and glimpsed the two of them atop the barrels, tapping out one of their childhood routines. Neal hadn't been able to let the opportunity pass.

"You've been edged out," he'd called. "You're no longer the second-best barrel-top dancer in Kyncastle. She is."

"*Second*-best?" Tomas and Muriel had sputtered their indignation in unison.

Muriel fit right in with the Traymaynes, in terms of competitive spirit.

"You haven't seen Emmeline?" Tomas had peered into the dim corners of the room. "She and Druce seem to have vanished. I'd hoped to find them here, eating ginger biscuits." He'd stared moodily at the crumbs on the plate.

"It's a nice night." Neal had bit back a smile. "Perhaps they went to look at the stars."

"My worry exactly." Tomas's frown had deepened. What a bear he was with Emmeline. Neal's protectiveness as a younger brother had always taken on a more doglike quality. He was at the ready to attack should his sisters bid him, but he didn't lumber about, nosing for trouble.

"Let's ourselves go look at the stars," Muriel had suggested, and he'd returned to earth, swinging her down from her barrel. Arm in arm, they'd breezed past Tomas and through the crowded assembly room, out into the clear, cool evening air.

They'd walked along the harbor, pressed close, the moonlight silvering the ripples on the bay. Luckily, neither of them cared overmuch for stars. When they stopped walking, they found their attention equally fixed on the closest—rather than the farthest—points of interest.

Eyes. Lips.

He glanced down at her, the dark gold lashes against her smooth cheek, mouth slightly open.

Should he propose in Great Peth? Or wait until they reached the Lizard? Yes, wait until the Lizard, when they'd walked over heath and down cliff paths fringed by honeysuckle to a quiet, sandy cove, picnic basket in hand, in fulfillment of his first promise.

Suddenly, Muriel bolted upright, the crown of her head knocking his cheekbone, elbow driving into his side. Her eyes were wide open, unseeing and terrified.

"A dream," he murmured, a strange bubble forming in his chest.

When she had bad dreams, *he* would be the one to soothe her. He would come to know her moods, waking *and* sleeping, to know what visions played out behind her eyelids, her most secret fears—and desires.

Slowly, she relaxed her posture, muscles loosening, as her gaze focused.

"What was it?" he asked.

"One of those dreams where you're being chased," she said simply, and with her smile seemed to dispel the last shadow of it.

He bent to retrieve her notebook, which had slid off her lap onto the floor. She wrote in it diligently, what he wasn't quite sure. Maybe she described the Cornish landscape, or recorded her thoughts for a future volume of her "Recollections." He resisted the urge to open it, passed it to her. A card slipped from beneath the cover, fell into the narrow space between their bodies. He fished it out.

"Useless," she sighed, taking it from him. "I wrote out a dozen of them before I realized we wouldn't have little pencils for the ladies to fill in the names of their partners." She turned the card over. Instead of numbers and blank lines, this side listed dances. "It's just as well. The musicians didn't follow the order anyway. And it was a marvelous ball regardless." Her voice purred, and she leaned back against the seat, head tipped up, eyes closing again, that full, rosy, tempting mouth slightly curved with satisfaction.

He looked at her.

She was beautiful.

No, she was achingly beautiful.

She was not Muriel Pendrake.

He worked the square of thick white paper out from between the thumb and forefinger of the woman who sat beside him, studied the black script. Muriel Pendrake wrote on the whole a clearer hand, less ornamented, the letters upright and narrow. Even allowing for the more decorative style of calligraphy a woman might adopt for a dance card rather than correspondence, he could not reconcile the *W*s, nor, most saliently, the *P*s.

The *P* of that *Polka* was never the *P* of *Pendrake*.

He drew in his breath as the woman listed toward him, her weight settling again on his arm, his shoulder.

She was not Muriel Pendrake.

But perhaps he made too much of the inconsistency. An errant *P* wasn't enough to prove a person was someone else entirely.

And yet, the certainty lay against his mind like a knife blade. As soon as his thoughts began to take shape, the certainty cut.

Thinking hurt.

The past days scrolled through his head, rife with vague suspicions he'd been quick to dismiss, so powerful was his ruling misconception. Now, in light of his discovery, the sum of inconsistencies indicted him as a fool. The little blank looks that punctuated her claims to some knowledge she never demonstrated . . . her aversion to dirt, to sun . . . her unwillingness to discuss any of the topics they'd introduced in their letters . . .

His throat felt dry, his eyes hot.

She'd asked immediately for "Recollections of a Plant Huntress." A manuscript densely informative as to the topography of little-visited Chinese provinces. *Christ.* Was she a spy? A beautiful player of the Great Game, posing as Muriel Pendrake so she could get her hands on that manuscript, send it to Russia?

Nonsense. If she were a spy, she'd have done a *better* job at the impersonation, packed her trunk with specimen boxes instead of silk dresses.

Unless . . . ah, another twist of the knife. Unless she packed the silk dresses not to convince, but to distract, to overwhelm his judgment and appeal to his idiot vanity, his proven lust for pretty blond women, knowing he'd make allowances because he'd *wish* to believe his attraction was mature, intellectual, destined to deepen and endure.

But then . . . it seemed unlikely that Russian intelligence had made a study of his foibles.

*You're not so special that they would have needed to make a study.* An unflattering voice in his head pointed out the embarrassing truth. *Your self-delusions and attractions are the common sort.*

Even so. There had to be another explanation. He couldn't quite believe that this deception—however disquieting—rose to the level of international intrigue.

Perhaps she was a tart hired by a rival firm.

His brain worked better when he was moving. Walking, riding, swimming. If he had to sit still, he tended to jiggle his foot, tap his fingers. He needed a physical counterpoint for his mental activity. The wonderful thing about choosing a life as a plant hunter, and then finding himself the proprietor of the most successful plant nursery in England, was that, by and large, he avoided sitting still altogether.

That had been his goal when he went down from Oxford. An existence in which chairs played only a supporting role. A bad pun, but a sound principle. These days, he could dictate his business correspondence, delegate sedentary tasks, sit when and for how long he chose.

At the moment, fool that he was, he sat trapped, motionless, supporting the weight of this slumbering woman. Her soft, even breathing taunted him. His muscles were tense, but he didn't twitch. His own breathing made no sound.

Despite everything, he couldn't allow himself sudden movement. Something kept him frozen. He didn't want to disturb her.

A tart. He tested the idea. A tart sent to glean information. Every year, the *Varnham Plant Catalogue* came out advertising new cultivars, and orders poured in. Certificates and medals from the Royal Horticultural Society and the Royal Botanic Society followed. This spring, his best gardeners had been breeding a hardy winter-flowering begonia.

If Edevane & Fernsby discovered which dwarf Andean species

Varnham's gardeners had crossed before the information was made public, they could experiment with their own winter-flowering begonia, try to get it to market first, claiming the credit and capturing the sales.

Muriel Pendrake—the real Muriel Pendrake—might have told old Edevane that Neal had tried to poach her for Varnham. That might have raised his ire, allowed him to justify to himself an unscrupulous plan.

Good God, maybe the real Muriel was *in* on it. That would explain her failure to appear at Bodmin Station. She'd given her blessing to the whole operation. Let a girl willing to exploit her charms—adept at bartering her kisses—act in her stead. The real Muriel never had any intention of coming to meet him. Or if she had, she'd let someone dissuade her. She'd listened to tales, perhaps, of his broken engagement. Of the widows he'd dallied with in the past. Decided he was a bad prospect as a friend, lover, or husband. She might have listened to darker tales—old Edevane would know them all—of James Varnham's death in the Argentine. Certain versions of that tale painted Neal in a very bad light indeed. If she believed the rankest speculations, she'd have no reason to feel protective of his business interests.

He wouldn't vibrate his legs, so instead his organs shook. He'd be sick if he didn't still this ripple, which he felt in his liver, his kidneys.

It didn't square with the facts as he understood them, this new hypothesis. Muriel—the false Muriel, the achingly beautiful untrustworthy woman sleeping trustingly on his shoulder—had hardly tried to pry from him the secrets of his hybridists. She'd seemed from the beginning—he could see it in retrospect—more preoccupied with guarding secrets of her own.

That flash of fear when she'd asked if they were heading toward Fowey.

The way she'd blazed at the prospect of sailing for France.

The sinews in his neck were so tight a headache had formed, low at the back of his skull. He couldn't work it out. She'd been calculating, certainly. But was it all calculation?

When she'd waded out into the frigid bay to point the boats in his direction. When she'd organized a dance to please his dear young Druce-besotted cousin.

Every time she'd kissed him.

All part of her plan. Furthering her purpose. False.

*His future wife.*

His instincts hadn't gotten better. They'd gotten worse. He'd decided he was ready to marry for the right reasons. Picked out the woman who looked perfect on paper, the kind of woman he wanted to want. Then he'd let himself fall swiftly under the spell of a lovely fraud who'd barely bothered to fake an interest in botany, so confident was she in the recommendations of her other assets.

She saw him much more clearly than he could see himself.

He burned with the humiliation of it.

He couldn't sit still another moment. As if sensing his intention, the woman turned in her sleep, snuggling into him, so that he felt the curve of her breast against his arm, the warmth of her thigh. Her head grew heavier on his shoulder.

He should fling her off.

An impostor. A false Muriel.

He should shake her awake.

*Whatever you're after,* he'd say, *you won't get it from me.*

He'd woken this morning to the sound of roosters, the smell of bacon frying, hoping they were after the same thing. Love, family. He'd lain for a moment in the bed, wishing she were there beside him, feeling relieved—grateful—that desire had a place after all in the well-reasoned partnership he'd plotted at a distance. Desire wasn't the whole of the bond between them, but it was its boon. Not a jeopardy, a joy. He could admit that he wanted her.

He'd believed, this morning, that he would have her, all of her.

He'd slept little but had sprung down the stairs, gone out in the pale morning light and collected the eggs, as he'd done with Tomas as a boy.

He'd have to say goodbye to that particular delusion. What he wanted so badly had never existed.

The false Muriel would not be joining him in Penzance at midsummer.

He would take her past Great Peth, straight to tiny, remote, inconvenient Mawbyn, and there he would leave her. Out in a field if he had his druthers.

For now, though, he kept his body immobile, and Muriel—the false Muriel—rocked with him gently as the train picked up speed, wrapping her arms around his biceps and hugging it, smiling as she dreamed sweeter dreams.

THIS INN WAS more promising than the last. For one, it wasn't situated on the edge of a bleak, howling moor. The hansom had rolled along through wooded green hills and stopped in a picturesque village square lined prettily with cottages climbed over with roses. The frontage of the inn was likewise bright with roses, and the man who greeted the cab, old and half-deaf, with a shock of white hair standing straight up from his head, had a twinkling eye and wore a spotless white flannel suit. He looked like a benevolent grandfather presiding over an afternoon lawn party with a full tea and the promise of a cricket match.

"Come along of me," he said to Neal with charming simplicity. "I'll send the boy to fetch the trunk for the missus."

He thought Neal was her husband. So had the passengers on the train, all smiling their approval. They did look well together. And throughout the many legs of the journey, she'd clung to Neal like a newlywed. She'd needed his strength.

What if her flight from Cranbrook had been reported in the papers? If they pulled into a crowded station and she saw a reproduction of her own face staring back at her from beneath a lurid headline?

Her fears had proven baseless. *The Cornishman* listed rooms to be let, situations wanted, the produce and value of copper ores sold last Thursday at Truro. She'd scanned the dense type every time someone in her vicinity turned a page.

Advertisements for sulfur hair restorers. Wine of phosphates. Wholesale coals and potatoes. "The Tale of the Cat-Hammed Cow," a humorous skit for sale at the undermentioned booksellers for sixpence.

Nothing about a missing duchess.

Cranbrook had kept things quiet. She didn't have to worry that every farmer in the West Country had been mobilized to flush her from the hedges.

A wan sorrow mixed with her relief. Her mother had been expecting her to write from Fowey. Cranbrook would have to have told her. Shouldn't her mother have forced Cranbrook's hand, gone to the police herself, scandal be damned? For all she knew, her only daughter was dead in a ditch.

It helped Lavinia, of course, the lack of public outcry. She didn't want to be found.

But it also hurt.

By the time she and Neal had boarded the second train, she'd managed to let go of her sorrow *and* her fear. In part, because she hadn't let go of Neal. Touch bolstered her. She began to feel a bit giddy with him at her side. His presence comforted and excited her at once.

He wasn't hers. He couldn't be. She'd have to let go eventually.

*Unless.*

She watched as he followed the grandfatherly ostler into the inn. He hadn't kissed her in the cab, as she'd imagined he might. He'd seemed preoccupied, distant. Something weighed on his mind.

His mother's illness, perhaps. He would move heaven and earth for his mother, it was obvious. And if *he* had gone missing at Bodmin Station, that mother would doubtless be out scouring the hills herself, no matter how sick she was.

Lavinia stood in the sun, not caring that it warmed her cheeks. Birds were twittering. Her sorrow returned, stole up on her. She missed her old life in London, before everything fell apart. But no, it wasn't so simple. The seeds of destruction had been sown long before they bore fruit, long before George's death and her papa's imprisonment. What she missed was a fiction, the belief that hers was, would always be, a charmed existence.

Two small boys went pelting past. An even smaller girl ran after them, but she tripped and went sprawling, the half-eaten bun in her hand rolling across the cobbles. The cab horse stretched its neck, plucked at the bun delicately with its lips, and devoured it in two bites. The little girl sat up, eyes filled with angry tears.

"Mean old horse," she said. Lavinia walked the few steps to the girl and crouched down beside her. Princess gowns didn't permit such indelicate postures. But Lavinia wore a blue cotton dress, with forgiving pleats, one of Emmeline's, which she'd traded for her lilac silk with the Swiss waist. Not in the least fashionable, but tremendously comfortable, lightweight, permitting ease of movement. With her hair in a simple twist, she blended.

"That looked like a very good bun," she said. "Was it cinnamon?"

The girl's sticky mouth showed definite signs that it was cinnamon. Her brow furrowed.

"It's all gone," she said accusingly, still glaring at the horse.

"Well then, let's get another," said Lavinia, and put out her hand. "We can share it. Would you like that?"

The little girl's hot fingers closed around Lavinia's thumb.

The bakery door tinkled as they pushed it open, and the woman behind the counter looked up from the tray of buns she was sliding into place. She had the same wide-set hazel eyes as the girl, the same heart-shaped face.

"I told you not to go running off after your brothers." She sighed. "Look at your poor elbows." She sounded more amused than angry. The little girl went up on her tiptoes and flung an arm onto the counter, feeling for a bun.

"You'll burn yourself on the tray," said the woman, slapping the little girl's hand lightly with a floury rag. "Leave over, now. You already had your sugar bun."

"Horse ate it," said the little girl, looking to Lavinia for confirmation.

"It's true," said Lavinia, stepping forward. "A mean old horse. I told her I'd buy her another."

"If there's one thing this child doesn't want for, it's sugar buns. Thank you all the same." The woman smiled a broad, gap-toothed smile. She was pretty, and young, and female, but she wasn't looking at Lavinia with antipathy. In fact, she wore a decidedly friendly expression.

"I saw you and your husband drive past," she said, and Lavinia tried to ignore the flutter in her stomach. Neal. Her husband. What if that were the truth of it?

Mrs. Traymayne. Happily married. Easily befriended by wayward children and women who worked in bakeries.

Mrs. Traymayne would never feel this odd loneliness, this sense that she belonged nowhere.

"You've just arrived, and already you're scraping my Annie off the ground." The woman shook her head. "Usually a newcomer can expect an hour of peace before she steps on one of my children." She sighed. "Welcome to Mawbyn."

Lavinia left the bakery with a package of two sugar buns, Annie gripping her thumb in one hand, a bun of her own in the other. Neal was standing outside the inn looking down the street. He turned and she saw the moment he saw her. How his body stilled. Then he folded his arms across his chest. The cabdriver had climbed back up to his seat and chirruped to the horse, which began clopping toward them.

"Bad!" scolded Annie, pointing her bun at the horse, before hugging it close, a protective posture that very much did *not* protect the cotton of her dress.

Skinned elbows, buttery bodice.

If Lavinia were married to Neal, they might have *this* kind of daughter—grubby, disheveled, irrepressible—and maybe they would let her be, valuing her happiness over her presentability, letting her play without self-consciousness or shame. Letting her climb and tumble and shout, come what may.

Lavinia held Annie's hand tighter, but the girl had glimpsed her brothers and went off like a shot, running toward the green, where a game of leapfrog was underway between towering trees.

Oaks. Or elms, perhaps. Hang it.

"Lovely village," Lavinia observed as she drew up to Neal. She held up the package. "Sugar buns," she said. "I doubt they compare to Kelyn's pastry, but the bakery did smell divine. And the horse approved his portion heartily, so there's that recommendation, if a horse's taste can be relied upon."

Something about the strange look in his eyes made her prattle.

"I like all these roses," she added brightly.

Her husband. Everyone assumed it. She could touch him, she could lean into him, even in the center of the village. Why these misgivings? His mood in the cab had been just that—a mood, a fleeting indisposition.

But it hadn't fled.

They stood close together, but his erect posture seemed to repel any overture, to communicate unbridgeable reserve. He'd never been reserved with her. He'd always been warm, easy, quick to laugh. Surely she was mistaken.

She put her hand on his arm, and they both looked at it.

Embarrassment and confusion flared.

She withdrew her hand, a sour taste pooling in her mouth.

"There's a botanist, Laura Odgers." He cleared his throat. "Classified the British mosses. Also published a very good volume of botanical watercolors. We've been exchanging specimens." He shoved his hands in his pockets, eyes fixed on the treetops. "I'm going to pay her a visit."

*Her.*

Comprehension was slow in coming. He meant—he was going to pay a visit to a lady botanist.

"Now?" She couldn't muffle it, her surprise and disappointment.

He shrugged, glancing at her coldly, before his eyes slid past her again, looking down the lane. "I can't pass up the opportunity to see her in person. She lives at Rock House, just up the hill, and keeps an extraordinary garden. I always drop in when I come through Mawbyn. You don't mind dining without me?"

She blinked at her package of sugar buns, and he continued.

"Not on sugar buns, of course. Or pasties." The words might have been teasing, but his tone was anything but. "It's a common table, but what the fare lacks in Frenchness, you'll find well-compensated in freshness. Duck. New potatoes. Gooseberry tart."

He looked at her without seeming to see her. "Your room is on the second floor. Mr. Phillips will show you up."

The final blow.

She sucked in her breath. He hadn't let a single room for them both.

Mr. and Mrs. Traymayne, signed in the register. An old-fashioned four-poster bed with sachets of dried rose petals between the linens. His naked limbs, thick and tensed against their own power, so that he could handle her gently.

The glow of expectation that had softened her harder feelings—the loneliness, the dread—extinguished itself.

Tears gathered hotly behind her eyes. He watched her blankly. If he noticed her distress, he gave no sign.

Should she abase herself utterly, ask one of the questions that threatened to slip from her lips?

Was he passing the night at the inn himself?

Was he staying instead with this Laura Odgers?

Why hadn't he mentioned Laura Odgers before? Why had he let her assume . . . what exactly? What had he let her assume?

*Everything.* It wasn't assumption. A man didn't invite a woman on an excursion to let her dine alone.

Except men did. Or they did with her.

In Cannes, she'd spent much of her time drifting alone through the grand hotel, reading novels at little tables, drinking chocolate that always tasted slightly bitter. Sometimes she'd glimpse George from the terrace as he sauntered down the Croisette.

But he *couldn't* have invited her to the yacht races, or to the parties. Acquaintances from London might have turned up, might have recognized her, asked questions. It had made sense, his leaving her behind. It had even seemed loving, this consideration for her reputation. Protective.

Recently, she'd begun to change the story. To fault George for not loving her, not considering her, enough.

But Neal? If Neal, too, wanted to flee her company, maybe the fault lay with her.

She wasn't worth loving.

"Is something the matter?" He put it to her casually, as though the answer couldn't possibly be of his concern. A faint smile curved his lips.

"Of course nothing is the matter." She said it with composure. In days gone by, she would have cried and stormed. "Confer with your colleague, by all means. I'm sure you have much to discuss."

He had the grace to look chagrined.

"Pertaining to the flora," he said stiffly, and the insistence made her heart sink further. He wasn't being honest with her. She had no right to demand his honesty, of course. But she'd come to take it for granted.

Honest, steady, blunt, kind Neal Traymayne. He *had* had designs on Muriel Pendrake, she was sure of it.

Something inside *her* had leaked out, had worked this transformation.

*My sweet Vinnie.* George had liked to stroke her hair, rubbing the pale blond strands between his fingers, kissing her white shoulder. *You're like a meringue.*

Meringues stirred the appetite. They didn't satisfy.

She'd squeezed the package of buns too hard. She felt the oil through the paper.

Neal brushed a thick lock of hair from his forehead with the back of his large hand.

"You and I will go collecting in the morning," he said. "In your last letter, you mentioned you were particularly looking forward to rambling in this part of the county."

"I did." She kept her voice level. Not a question.

"I am," she said, and felt a small rush of hope.

Tomorrow might bring another reversal.

She lifted her chin. "Even more so now that I've seen the hills. They remind me of China."

His lips curved again, a mocking light replacing the chagrin in his eyes.

"How fascinating it will be for both of us, then," he said. "We'll cover every inch of the terrain. Miles and miles. Starting at first light."

She swallowed. "Good."

"Good," he said.

She wouldn't watch him walk away. She gazed at the green, the laughing children rolling now down the slope.

She hadn't thought she would truly escape Cranbrook. But his lust had its limits. As did her mother's love. Her papa's love. George's love.

No one was searching for her. That realization was worse than anything.

She swallowed hard, looked down at the cobbles.

When she looked up, Neal was gone.

# CHAPTER TEN

WHEN NEAL DESCENDED the narrow, crooked stairs, the lamps were still lit and the walls held the night's chill. The world was hushed. Outside, the birds slept—the nightjars returned to their nests, the skylarks and thrushes not yet risen.

This morning he wouldn't wait. If Muriel did not appear before he'd finished his tea, he'd bloody well rouse her and *not* with a breakfast tray.

Let her try to maintain her ruse now that he'd decided to put it to the test.

She was already awake, sitting out in the little tea garden with Mr. Phillips. He hid his surprise, stood for a moment in the back doorway, watching. The golden flowers of the laburnum tree seemed the sole source of light in that dim courtyard. Muriel and Mr. Phillips had chosen the table directly beneath the hanging bunches of blossoms. Their heads were tipped together, hair pale as moth wings.

He would have given a small fortune to know what they said.

Who was she when she wasn't playing a part? When she refilled an old man's teacup, listening intently to some tale of travelers past, or when she ducked out of a bakery with a grinning little girl clinging to her hand . . .

He turned away, slipped down the hall, bolted tea, frizzled bacon, and eggs with butter by the window in the sitting room. His eyes felt sandy from a sleepless night. The dreams that had beckoned were all rose-scented softness, delphinium-blue eyes, sighs of pleasure. Asleep, he was defenseless, always on the verge of surrendering to some sweet treachery, so he'd fought off slumber.

Outside, in some farmyard, the roosters began to crow.

He pushed back his chair.

He would not surrender.

HE REACHED THE top of the hill and looked down to where Muriel still struggled upward, snatching at branches as her thin-soled city shoes slid in the fallen leaves. He'd set a brutal pace, up the woodland's steepest slope. A footpath wound around the hill—the footpath he'd followed last night to Mrs. Odgers's—but that gradual ascent was entirely too pleasant for what he had in mind.

Not a ramble. An ordeal.

Muriel would cry for mercy before the sun had time to climb above the trees.

Except . . .

She did not.

As he led her, whistling, along the needlessly tortuous route, she fell farther and farther behind. But whenever he paused, she caught up to him, sweaty and smiling.

Once she disappeared amid thick trees, and at last he scrambled back down the muddy track, expecting to discover her doubled over, vanquished, begging for him to put an end to their march.

She was crouching beside a rotted log, uncovering the base of a dandelion plant so she could inspect the rosette of toothed leaves.

"They're smooth." She looked up at him, big-eyed, hopeful. "And spotted."

"Wrong species," he said shortly. "This way."

He was off again, climbing the embankment with long strides. Putting distance between them before he could soften.

She'd stopped to root around in the muck for his mother's dandelions.

The variety she'd been inspecting wasn't even close to the one he'd described. She had no eye for leaf margins, or surfaces.

But she'd made an attempt to help him. She'd muddied her hands making it.

*Not because she cared.* He had to remind himself. Because she knew it would move him, this display of thoughtfulness. She manipulated shamelessly.

Finally—the sun shone directly overhead—*he* had to rest. His heels were bleeding—damn Hessians—and he felt bedeviled by thirst. He tossed his empty specimen box onto the carpet of bluebells and boosted himself up onto a boulder. There he stood, drinking from his water flask, gazing between the trees toward the headlands, waves of green turf brightly spangled with tormentils.

He couldn't hear the sea, but he could smell it. The salt on the air.

A sound alerted him that she'd reached the high ground.

She crashed through the ferns, staggering as her skirt snagged on a thorny blackberry, and then she swayed, a scant yard away, hand pressing her ribs, wincing as she breathed. She thought herself unobserved. Didn't bother trying to hide her exhaustion. Her dress was filthy at the hem, with threads unraveled from tiny tears in the skirt and bodice. She had twigs in her hair, and a red line across her cheek where she'd been whipped by a thin elastic branch. Her eyes seemed to glow.

He'd never seen her look so discomposed.

She looked like less of a beauty in that moment.

And more beautiful.

He sat down on the boulder, swinging his legs over the edge. She startled at the sight of his boots, hand flying from ribs to throat.

"There you are," she said, all cheeriness, craning her neck. The smile returned to her face. "Such a pretty spot." She circled the boulder, unable to disguise a slight limp. Her heels fared worse than his, he'd wager. But she made a good enough show of admiring the blackthorn trees and the bluebells.

"Enjoying yourself?" he asked.

"Immensely." She answered without hesitation. "Are we going to walk out to those cliffs?"

Were they going to saunter across the flat, grassy heath?

He smiled.

No, they were not. They were going to plunge headlong into ravines and labor through swamps until one or both of them collapsed.

"We're going to the river," he said. "A branch of it runs through the valley to the estuary."

Her eyes had locked on the water flask in his hand. Slowly, he lifted it to his lips, drank deeply.

"The terrain is a bit rough, and a bit prickly," he said, wiping his mouth with the back of his hand. "The brambles grow in thickets. But you've an interest in the genus, so you won't mind the tangle."

Her smile wobbled. After too long a beat, she nodded.

"Shrubs." She said the word grimly, plucking ineffectively at the twig in her hair. "I can't seem to get enough of them."

At this, he laughed despite himself. She wouldn't give up easily. Fine. He was willing to dedicate hours to the project.

"Here." He handed down the flask, watched as she gulped water like a child. Kneeling to pick bluebells in Kyncastle, he'd looked up at her as the sun burnished her hair and skin, made her gleam like some goddess of the cliffs. Now he perched above her, and she appeared small and breakable, utterly within his power.

He'd trained himself to tend to fragile things. Specimens. Seedlings.

His impulse was to jump down from the rock, settle her on a dry tussock, remove her shoes, rub ointment onto her blistered heels, refill his flask at the spring, and bring it back to her, dripping with sweet, cool water.

This situation required a different approach. Rougher handling.

"I almost forgot," he said. "I have a treat for you."

He lowered himself to the ground, lifted the flask from her hands, and dropped it in a pocket, then reached inside his coat.

Her brow smoothed. She was ready for a treat, a kind gesture that restored the balance between them.

He would *not* feel guilty.

He fetched up a silver cigarette case. It had belonged to James. Whenever he flipped it open, he *felt* like James, like he was physically inhabiting a memory.

He'd watched James make the gesture he made now a thousand times.

"Mugwort," he said, extracting a cigarette and offering the case. "Or mostly. I blend it with mullein, tobacco, and a bit of mint. In one of your letters—"

Every time he used the phrase, he saw her tense.

He lit his cigarette, sent smoke spiraling toward the treetops. "In one of your letters," he repeated, "you said you smoked Turkish cigarettes. You'll prefer these, I promise you."

"Smoke?" She laughed. She saw the look on his face and a thin line appeared between her brows. "I was joking, of course."

"Not at all." He pressed the case into her hand. "You picked up the habit on those long ocean voyages and keenly regret that London's social mores don't permit a lady to indulge. Why would you deny it now?"

She bit her lip, staring at the neat row of slender cylinders.

"Tobacco appeals to me less these days," he continued, beginning to find the fun of the situation. "It's poison in large quantities. We use it to fumigate the nurseries, or make it into a wash to kill greenfly on the bushes. But a pinch mixed judiciously with herbs . . ." He shrugged, took a long draw, and blew a lazy ring that twisted slowly in the motionless air. "You told me you were eager to try it."

"Of course," she murmured, shoulders sagging. Then she pushed them back, took a cigarette between her fingers, and set it between lips pursed as for a kiss. For a moment, he admired the absurdity, then he struck the match.

The coughing fit was instantaneous. Her eyes watered as she caught her breath.

"Very nice," she wheezed, and puffed again, letting the smoke fill her open mouth and roll out.

"Mmm," he said. "Hold on to the case, then. They're all for you. Shall we?"

She was coughing as she followed him along the edge of the heath and then down into the valley.

They reached the river at a narrow bend, disturbing a heron that ran a few steps on its long, thin legs, then opened its wings, flying over them, awkward and magnificent. Muriel gasped as its shadow swept her face. The look she gave him was pure wonderment.

*Dammit.* He didn't want to share such moments with her, such looks.

She should have broken hours ago.

He clenched his jaw against an answering smile. They'd keep walking. Over mudflats exposed by the ebb tide, along creeks that split off the main river, cutting channels through the mossy banks.

It was cooler by the river, refreshing, and he redoubled the pace, skirting the bracken, ignoring the little white flowers that rose from downy stems, likely catchfly, rare enough to merit a second glance in other circumstances.

He'd given up even the pretense of collecting.

The river turned sharply, and the trees drew closer together. He took the bend and accelerated. Muriel had fallen behind once more, and so he heard, rather than saw, her protest.

He turned at the cry. She'd thrown herself down on a thick bed of moss and lay with her hands beneath her head, looking up at the green canopy.

"We're rambling too fast," she said, propping herself on an elbow as he picked his way back to her. "I want to appreciate the mosses. Like Laura Odgers does," she added, with a touch of asperity.

He dropped down beside her, stretching out his legs.

"Laura Odgers studies moss. She doesn't sleep in it."

"I suppose you would know how she sleeps." She looked away. "I didn't hear you come back last night."

Ah. So she'd lain in her dark room listening for his return.

Because she was jealous? Or . . . because he'd frustrated her plan to dig her claws into him more deeply?

Mrs. Odgers, plump, vigorous, and voluble, had kept him late, first rehanging the henhouse door and nailing together new nest boxes, then chatting over several courses—garden vegetables, chicken, fresh berries—and only afterward displaying her specimens, saving the one in which he'd indicated the most interest, the *Bryum roseum* in fruit, for last.

He hadn't minded her delaying tactics in the least. An old family friend, she was like an aunt to him, and besides, he'd wanted to linger elsewhere, anywhere but at the inn with Muriel.

On the way back into the village, he'd stopped at the Three Crowns for a pint and stayed for two.

He pressed his fingertips into the moss, rose moss, the tiny green whorls intricate as lace.

"It was a long night," he said. Was his smile fittingly sphinxlike? He maintained it until she flicked her eyes to him. She'd been getting sun these last days. He couldn't tell if she'd colored. She was certainly frowning.

Good.

"So, does it still remind you of China?" He waved at the alders, at the river glinting as it curved along the bottom of the valley.

"Tremendously." At once, she assumed her specialist air, gave their surroundings a once-over, and nodded sagely.

*Nice try.*

"What in particular?" he prodded her, noting the pulse in her eyelid as she gazed down at the moss.

"The woody plants," she said, and sat up, tucking her legs beneath her. "But also—"

She met his eyes. "Looking at someone's back as I walk. It's a very particular sensation."

He inhaled. Not the squirming evasion he'd expected. No, she'd mounted a flank attack. He'd been behaving badly. He knew that as well as she did. But for just cause.

He'd apologized needlessly to this woman before. She wouldn't startle him into begging her pardon.

"You don't mention that sensation in your book." He lifted a leg, rotated his ankle, which exacerbated the pinch of the cracked leather.

"I don't mention any sensations in the blasted book." She scowled. "I told you, that's the problem with it."

"A literary problem. But perhaps better for your departed husband's reputation." He raised his brows. "It doesn't sound as though your additions would be complimentary."

He couldn't help but glance at her fisted hands, the rings on her fingers. Had she borrowed them—stolen them—to complete her costume, a pretty picture of enticing widowhood? Were they *her* jewels, relics of her own ill-fated marriage?

She was thinking of a particular man when she spoke about love. She couldn't have conjured ex nihilo the emotion he'd glimpsed, for example, that night at Crawthevyn Inn, or that evening in Kyncastle.

"I can be scientific about it." She tossed her head, and a thin lock of hair snaked down around her shoulder. She pushed it behind her ear, lips thinned. "I will replace the chapter on how to pack bulbs with a chapter on how to classify men. Discuss the varieties in terms of characteristics and uses. I'll have to provide basic descriptions as well. My husband was a showy specimen. You, less so."

He blinked. Why—she'd insulted his appearance. Good thing he didn't harbor any illusions in that regard. He'd polished his manners enough to move between worlds, but a man couldn't do much about his face.

"But it turns out you've more similarities than differences," she continued, then broke off, ripping up a handful of moss.

"We walk too fast," he offered, and at this bit of glibness, she glanced at him sharply and scrambled to her feet.

"Never mind," she said, brushing off her skirt.

He stood. "What *do* we have in common, Mr. Pendrake and myself?"

Surrounded by so much green, her blue eyes looked pure and clear as rainwater.

"You can't be trusted," she said.

It was too much. Coming from her, it went beyond boldness. It was insanity. *He* could not be trusted?

"Clearly, your new chapter is aimed at experts," he said, biting off the words. "I'm afraid you'll need to explain your criteria for the benefit of the layman."

"You lie to yourselves." She tugged fiercely at a thread dangling near her waist, but her gaze did not leave his. "Which permits you to believe you're not lying to others. Which means that women end up cruelly deceived, and you think nothing of it."

"I can't speak for your husband." Before he could stop himself, he reached out, stilled and lowered her fingers, snapped the offending thread. "But I've never deceived you. If this is about last night, about Laura Odgers, I—"

"I couldn't care less about Laura Odgers." Her lips turned down. Not a pout.

Not *not* a pout.

"Maybe you care for Laura Odgers, maybe you don't." She narrowed her eyes. "What matters to you is whether your *mother* cares for her. Isn't that what Elizabeth discovered?"

His jaw dropped. He closed his mouth with effort. Closed it hard.

"Let's leave my mother out of it." He said it through gritted teeth.

"Easy enough for me." She shrugged. Her gaze wavered, and she looked down the bank, at the river. Her voice dropped, murmured like the slow current. "I wanted the man I loved to put me first. I put him first, before everything."

He swallowed. The blue thread had wrapped around his fingers, and he shook it off.

"And what did he put first?" He spoke softly too, unsure how she'd led him into this conversation, which, for all the trappings of falsity, contained some raw kernel of truth.

She meant what she said. He'd stake his life on it. God help him that he wanted to know about this other man, this man who'd hurt her so badly.

But she didn't answer. Instead, she gave herself a shake.

"I'm hungry," she said.

"How unfortunate." He stared at her lovely profile, the straight line of her nose, the curve of her lips, the defiant tilt of her chin. He was the one hurting her now.

*Different.* It was different. *He* was different. Completely.

He shook his empty specimen box, patted his coat pockets, smiling slightly at the exaggerated theater.

She was watching him, mutinous.

"It seems I forgot to pack our lunch. Luckily, nature provides." He permitted himself a grin.

"In one of your letters . . ." he began, and she drew a sharp breath. Oh, she was close, very close, to breaking.

"You described catching your meals in the Min River." He peered down at the river, but he could see her startled, displeased movement out of the corner of his eye. "Wait until you gut a Cornish trout and cook it on a stick over an open fire. Nothing like it. You'll never go back."

"Go back?" She made a strange sound, not quite a laugh. Some wildness had overthrown her. She reached out blindly to steady herself, pressed her fist into a tree trunk.

"No," she said. "No, I won't. You're right about that, at least."

Again, this impulse to soothe her, to sweep her into his arms.

*You're right*, she'd said. There was no going back.

They'd soon see what else he was right about.

A gull cried, and he started forward, catching her hand and tugging her after him, so that they bounded together, a breathless, exhilarating descent to the river's edge. She tripped on a root and would have fallen, but he pulled her close to his side, bearing her weight as the bank crumbled into soft clay. He lurched to keep their balance and laughed, her wildness doubling within him.

Maybe he'd leave her *here*, on this riverbank, hot and hungry, to fend for herself.

As soon as the ground leveled, she jerked away and darted ahead of him, so that, for a time, he followed her as she clambered over stones. She had to bend her slim back as she went, scrambling over logs.

"That's a promising pool," he said, and she pivoted with a gasp, startled to find him so close behind her. She'd gone quickly, but nowhere near quickly enough.

If she'd thought to prove a point by outstripping him . . . well. What a disappointment for her.

"And . . . there's some succulent mud." He stepped around her and squatted at the base of a willow. They'd taken a fork, and the river had narrowed, trees crowding in, the shadowy banks thick with moss. Reluctantly, she came to him and stood while he turned over the damp soil. When he rose, he took her wrist and placed the writhing knot of worms into her palm.

Elizabeth would have screamed. At which scream he would have winced, remembering his mother's exasperation at displays of daintiness.

The fair woman before him—blotchy with exertion, sweat darkening the hair at her temples—she didn't flinch. She kept her arm rigid, lowering her face to inspect the worms, nose wrinkled with distaste.

He produced the line, and the hook, from his pocket, handed them to her.

"Bait the worm on the hook," he said. "I'll find a spot for us. The fish will rise from that eddy, and we'll want to stay behind it."

He turned, walked a few steps, glanced over his shoulder. She was standing perfectly still, looking down at her outstretched hands, a bleak expression on her face. She felt his gaze and slowly raised her head.

"Muriel Pendrake." He purred it, and she tried—valiantly—to smile. But she knew, already she knew. Her throat moved convulsively.

"The worms aren't cooperating," she said, with a lightness that jarred with the fear he read plainly in her eyes. "In China, they leap onto the hook."

Her struggling smile suddenly widened. She hoped to dazzle him with that heart-clutching prettiness. To stave off the inevitable.

The time had come.

He prowled back to her. The light filtering through the leaves dappled her with gold.

He'd always been susceptible to dappled things. Fawns. Finches. Foxgloves. He'd avoided noticing the sweet freckles forming across the bridge of her nose.

"Muriel Pendrake," he repeated. Silky. Threatening.

"Yes?" Her smile faded. She was shaken. Exhausted and shaken. He was the immediate cause of that troubled expression, but she had created the situation. She was to blame, she and her lies.

"I like the sound of it, that's all." He looked down at her. "Don't you?"

She made an uncertain motion and more slippery hair fell down to frame her face. She couldn't push it back, not with her hands filled with mud, worms, the hook and length of line. She was helpless, stippled with light, rather like a trout herself.

He'd caught her. Now what would he do with her?

He laced his fingers together, settled his chin on them, to keep from touching the shining lock, rubbing his fingertip over her cheek.

"Muriel. Pendrake."

Her eyes begged him to end her torment. He could clasp her to his chest, taste the sun and the shadow on her skin, put it off—this reckoning—for another hour, another day.

That was a reprieve, though, not a resolution.

"What's your real name?" he asked.

## Chapter Eleven

WITH HER EYES shut, she could pretend she didn't exist, had winked out. And hadn't she? She wasn't Muriel to him. She wasn't anything. How much easier if she could disappear entirely. Leave no trace.

She felt the dig of his fingertips as he took her face in his hands. "Look at me." His voice grated.

She wouldn't, tried to shake her head, but his fingers dug deeper. She didn't want to see the transformation she'd noted in him across the past two days completed, irrevocable. Neither of them existed anymore, not for each other. Better to sink into darkness.

"Look at me." Distinct menace in his voice. Her gentle, teasing gardener—no more. Her chest *creaked*, the bony cage constricting, until it cut her heart. The soft red muscle inside her—sliced into ribbons. She screwed her eyelids more tightly together. Then his lips were at her ear, his breath burning.

"Muriel." It was a groan, a plea.

Her eyes snapped open. Neal filled her field of vision—blunt, squared-off face and broad shoulders—the whole of him big and thick and strong, and steeled against her.

"Dammit," he breathed. "Tell me what the hell else I should call you."

"Lavinia." Her own name clogged in her throat. She tasted the salt of hot tears, or blood.

"Lavinia what?"

Fair question. Tears slipped down her cheeks, wetting his fingers, his palms. He didn't loosen his grip. His brown eyes were banded with green and gold, striped as agate, and just as hard.

"Nothing." She heard her own whisper as she heard the river, the sifting of leaves, the flutter of bird's wings. She didn't exist but formed a part of this quiet green place, this moment in time.

He swore again and pulled back from her, flicking the tears from his fingers.

"You'll tell someone," he vowed. "If not me, you'll start with the justice in Mawbyn."

"And end up at the court of assizes, like Joan Traymayne?" She managed a bitter smile. No, she couldn't melt into the greenery. More shame awaited her.

"Lavinia what?" He repeated the question, and she blazed back at him, her sudden anger hot and welcome, a source of strength. Self-pity didn't stiffen her spine, not like rage. She needed this fit of temper.

"Just Lavinia." She let the clod of worms drop and balled her other hand, concentrating on the small sharp point of the hook pricking into her palm as she glared full in his face. "Or must a woman bear always the name of her father or her husband? What if the woman has come to regret both of those men with all her heart?"

Yardley. Cranbrook. Those names were bondage, brought her nothing but humiliation.

She twisted her lips. "You approve women rejecting all sorts of normal things if they're *intellectual* about it. How's this? I am *just* Lavinia, because that's my way of participating in the *querelle des femmes*. Are you satisfied? Does that meet the standard of your snobbery?"

"It does not." He sounded deadly calm, but she could see the bright fury in his eyes.

"You're a hypocrite, then," she muttered, but her gaze faltered under his.

His fury was justified. He'd discovered himself deceived, discovered the world to be other than what he'd imagined. She knew from experience how that felt.

Dizzying. Sickeningly so. It turned you inside out.

"And I am empty-headed as you please," she added, voice hoarse. "I didn't have an education that I could put to use. But I hardly made the most of marriage. In fact, I made the worst of it."

She turned from him abruptly. She didn't want him to see her expression.

"You have a husband."

Despite herself, she looked back in his direction. He stood motionless, a breeze riffling his hair. Behind him the river slipped by, water running toward the sea.

He exhaled. "Alive, I gather?"

This time, her silence was answer enough. He tipped his head, allowing the breeze access to his muscled throat, as though he needed cooling.

She was the one who'd been sweating like a pig, gasping, overheated by their deranged dashing up and down the countryside. He'd looked almost languorous in comparison, barely exercising his lean strength.

"Your husband." He lowered his chin, gave her an unpleasant smile. "The *showy specimen.*"

She stared. But of course, of course that was what he thought. Ah, what a muddle it was. She'd been a liar to him, but she couldn't make a clean breast of it now. The details were too damning.

*I am the daughter of that disgraced Robert Yardley, the warped Robin Hood who stole from a duke so he could live like a king. He kept me in egret-feather tiaras bought with his ill-gotten gains, and I never thought twice, not about the money or the egrets.*

*And that man I described? The showy specimen? He was my lover, not my husband.*

*As of last week, I do have a husband—I married him for his fortune—but he wants to deflower a virgin. You understand my dilemma.*

How sordid it sounded.

She slipped hook and line into the pocket of her skirt, rubbed the dirt from her fingers, and linked her hands at her waist. The posture steadied her. Until she remembered how she used to trip along beside her papa, clinging to his pinky. How she used to grasp George's hand whenever she sensed him stirring to slip away.

She had only her own hands to hold on to. Perhaps forever.

The loneliness she'd experienced in the village returned with such force she felt it like a physical sensation. Her skin prickled. The air was mellow, but clammy gooseflesh was breaking out along her arms.

"The scapegrace," Neal continued. "The rake with the penchant for gambling and gin."

She had thought his sharply cut lips fashioned for smiles, kisses. That was before she'd seen his sneers.

He narrowed his eyes. "Did his debts drive you to a life of crime?"

She made a small surprised movement of denial.

His jaw tensed and the tiny muscles of his face tightened, emphasizing its rugged planes.

"Let's forget *why* for the time being. *Who?* Who put you up to this charade? I've abandoned the hypothesis that you work for a foreign government. That conjecture—like my initial misbelief as to your identity—depended on an overestimation of your capacities."

"You're right." She averted her face. "A spy needs a brain."

"My conclusion exactly."

She mashed her lips together. Why should *this* hurt above all?

"We're agreed, then, that politics is beyond your range." He pressed on inexorably. "Unless—*do* you speak Chinese?"

She fought the urge to duck her head. Would he bring up each of her lies?

"No, you don't," he said with a mock sigh. Teasing without warmth. It was very close to ridicule. She opened her mouth to protest, but what could she say?

He clicked his tongue. "Tomas will be *so* disappointed."

"I speak French," she said, and winced at the inanity. Meeting his eyes was a mistake.

"*Enchanté.*" His voice was dry as sand. "French is preferable, I assume, if you make your living blowing into men's ears until they give up trade secrets. Out with it. Who hired you?" He took a step toward her. "Edevane?"

"No one." The words broke from her. "No one *hired* me. It just happened. That day in Bodmin . . ." She blinked rapidly against the rising tide, another surge of tears. "I crossed the platform to get away from him, my husband. I put the train and a few dozen yards between us, but it wasn't enough. I didn't know what to do. I couldn't go on, I couldn't go back. I felt hopeless."

All that, at least, was the truth. She trained her eyes on the river. Each droplet would drift until the end of time, might ripple into the Amazon, might rain down on Hong Kong.

She drew a breath.

"And then you were there," she said. "You came out of the trees, like in a fairy tale. *You* called to *me*. You wanted to believe I was someone else, your precious Mrs. Pendrake. I went along with it, that's all."

She knuckled her eyes, a childish gesture that made her scowl, self-conscious. Gone were the days when her tears worked miracles.

He gave an ironic laugh. "Christ. How perfect. It's all been a whim, then."

"It didn't feel like a whim. It felt like . . ."

He cocked a brow, and she had to force herself to keep going.

"It felt like fate." Her voice rasped. "I forgot that, for me, fate is nothing but disaster. I should have run into the woods, run from both of you."

"Indeed you should have." The sneer had become a snarl. "We wouldn't be together in these woods now, having this unpleasant conversation. I would have gone back to Truro to look for a letter from Muriel Pendrake explaining what detained her and advising me of her new date of arrival. She and I might this very moment be out on the moor making a study of the bog pimpernels in the hollows or the lichen turf on the high tors."

"I meant no harm." She said it quietly.

"What *did* you mean?" He considered her. "I'm curious. How on earth did you expect this to end?"

She swallowed. "In fairy tales, people transform."

Dear God, had she said it aloud? Retreat. Retreat for her sanity. Retreat before she spoke more nonsense.

She edged backward, the corner of a stone pressing her instep, causing her breath to catch. Too much walking, dancing, scrambling about, had rubbed her feet raw.

He slinked forward, closing the distance she'd opened. His eyes were hard, but those profuse, curling lashes—they were silken, soft. Gentling his gaze.

"I had this notion . . ." She went cold, then hot, but she couldn't stop the words. "I imagined . . . that *I* might transform. That I might become Muriel, if I wished hard enough."

"What then?" His look had altered subtly.

*Everything.*

"Whatever you had planned when you invited me to Cornwall." She bit her lip. "*Her.* When you invited her to Cornwall."

Both brows climbed his forehead. "Botanizing? It hardly seems to agree with you."

She flushed as he let his gaze travel from her limp, dispirited hair down to the filthy wreckage of her shoes. The old Neal Traymayne would never have treated her to such a mocking survey.

"Now who's lying." She saw his lips part in startlement and snorted. "Botanizing! You took her to meet your cousins. You pretended to like every page of her miserable, plodding *tome*. You kissed her."

"*You*," he corrected, eyelids lowering so the lashes shadowed his irises, made his expression dark and inscrutable. "I kissed you."

She ignored the flutter in her stomach. "You were trying to seduce her."

"And you wished to transform into Muriel." He wore a faint smile. "Why? If you're longing to be seduced, you might as well have stayed closer to home, and kept your own . . ."

He hesitated, sweeping her again with that sardonic gaze, attention lingering on her lips, her breasts.

"Identity," he finished.

"I don't want to be seduced. I want to be . . ." Horrified, she slammed her mouth shut.

*Loved.* Unsaid, the word seemed to hang between them.

She rushed to fill the air.

"I made the wish for all sorts of reasons. If I were truly Muriel, I wouldn't be lying, for one thing."

"Forget your objections to women's education and get thee to Girton," he murmured. "With logic like that, the sky's the limit. You might end up admitted to the Aristotelian Society."

She flushed at his withering tone. But she continued.

"If I were Muriel," she said, "I'd be fascinatedly fascinated by shrubs and fluent in Mongolian and I'd find your special dandelions with the purple dots and there wouldn't *be* an end. We'd have an unfashionable feather-free wedding in Penzance and give our children botanical names like Basil and Heath and Lily and Rose and live happily ever after."

"And the real Muriel? What happens to her in this fairy tale?

Does she transform into Lavinia?" He said it lazily, but he'd stilled every muscle, something inside him snapping to attention.

"I wouldn't wish that on her." She frowned. "I don't know what happens to the real Muriel. Lavinia . . . That's easy. She disappears."

She realized her knees were trembling with fatigue, but her vision had cleared. She no longer saw through a haze of tears.

"She won't be missed overmuch." It was a fact. She could say it without emotion. "Lavinia *was* empty-headed. Also, vain, spoiled, and a terrible snob, always making things more difficult for everyone around her. She had no friends to speak of and thought only of herself and—"

He interrupted her with a groan. "Stop. I'm *not* a judge on the court of assizes. I don't have a taste for self-flagellation. Besides, in my experience, it's simply the flipside of self-indulgence." His gaze was assessing. "You're not as thoroughly odious as you're making out."

"I'm not?" She blinked. His mouth tipped at one corner with derision, then he shook his head.

"I've certainly observed behaviors that support your claims." For a moment, she thought he might begin to list them, instances of her empty-headed, vain selfishness. Instead, he shrugged. "I've observed other behaviors as well, which contradict them. You did, after all, wade into frigid waters after a drowning child." He paused. "After *me*. Saving our lives made things significantly easier for the whole village."

"I thought you had the situation well in hand," she whispered. "Paddling toward the Cow Tooth, you said."

Something sparked behind his eyes, a hint of the old teasing friendliness.

"I might have been overstating the chances of a positive outcome, due to my atrocious arrogance." Now the quirk of his lips looked faintly humorous. "No one is without flaws. You've established yours." He grew serious again. "I'm not trying to defend you, or condemn you. I'm simply adding to the data. You got sunburned as an urchin picking wildflowers for a village party, which doesn't accord with vanity. You danced on a barrel in a spider-filled storeroom, uncommon for a terrible snob. I could go on."

She felt herself gaping at him. "But . . ." she said into the silence, throat working. "But I was trying to be someone else."

"You didn't succeed." He searched her face, his look penetrating, as though he could see through to her brain. As though he *wanted* to see her brain and suss out her thoughts.

"Every brave and generous act, every kindness . . . that sense of fun that I . . ." He rolled his shoulders uncomfortably.

"It was *you*," he said at last. "Lavinia. *Just* Lavinia. A woman neither all good, nor all bad."

Relief unwound within her. Her knees sagged, and she swayed toward him. How easy it would be for him to catch her elbows, to support her weight.

But no. With a muttered oath, he pulled back. She had to catch herself, take an awkward half step.

He wouldn't touch her. He'd prefer to let her collapse into a heap at his feet.

He didn't think she was all bad. He was too fair-minded for that. It didn't mean he wanted anything to do with her.

He thrust his long, tanned fingers into his hair, twisting the locks as though he'd rip them out by the roots. When he dropped his arms, she noted his hands were still clenched into fists.

"*Lavinia*," he said. "The laws that govern the physical universe will not permit you to transform into Muriel Pendrake. Nor will they permit you to vanish into thin air. That leaves you with two options."

A premonition made her shake her head.

"Live your life. *Your* life," he said. "Return to your husband . . ."

"Ha!" Rage again, jumping up into her throat. His eyes widened slightly but he continued in the same tone.

". . . or run into the woods, as you should have done in Bodmin."
He waved at the trees. "Avail yourself of this second chance."

She sucked in her breath. He thought to call her bluff. What
would she do in the woods? Sleep in the moss like a deer? Fish for her
supper?

It was none of his concern. He made that much clear.

Well, she wouldn't collapse at his feet. She would spare both of
them that final indignity. Without a word, she turned and stalked
away, head held high. Her ravaged feet made stalking a torture, but
she wouldn't hobble, no, not until she reached the next bend in the
river and was hidden from his sight.

She had just clambered inelegantly over a log and climbed up to
level ground when he fell into step beside her. His familiar tread, so
graceful, so at odds with his rawboned physique, summoned a
strange feeling, half pain, half longing.

She'd wanted him to fall in love with her. She'd thought less
about falling in love with him. How it might intensify her loneliness.
Make it feel fatal.

That didn't matter, though.

She hadn't fallen in love with him.

Of course she hadn't.

She batted at branches, not caring how they sprang back, if they
lashed her arms or his.

"What did he do to you?" he asked, and she walked faster.

"What do you care?" She loaded her voice with contempt to disguise the hurt. "Anyway, it's all over now."

Another truth. It was all over. With George. With Cranbrook.
With Neal himself.

They walked on silently, and she stole a glance at him. His hair
stuck up wildly, and his face was troubled. Framed by trees, he might
have been the fairy-tale huntsman, torn between duty and conscience. Should he cleave her breast in two, scoop out her heart? Or
should he help her escape the evil queen?

He had never looked more handsome.

She halted abruptly. "*Go.*" She flung out her arm, pointing downstream. "The village is *that* way."

He cleared his throat. "It's that way, in fact. Behind that hill." He indicated the correct direction with his finger, and she scowled at him. Damn him and his easy path through life. *He* was never lost.

"Fine." She began walking again. "You know best."

"Lavinia." Her name on his lips made the tears rise again to her eyes. He was still walking with her. "Where are you going?"

"The *woods*. Which means I can't get lost. They're everywhere."

This time, he made no comment on her logic. He caught her elbow and stilled her. He'd grown even more somber. His voice was low and urgent, the question emerging as a demand.

"What did he do?" His eyes glittered. "What did he do that you can't go back to him?"

*He died.* She wanted to scream it at him. She was stumbling muddy and hatless and blistered and scratched through the forest because the man she'd loved died. But that wasn't it, and she knew it. Her intake of breath felt strangely hard, bruising her lungs.

"Lavinia." Neal was staring. She could push back her straggling hair, but she couldn't wave a wand and restore her beauty. Her cheeks were burned red by sun and swollen by tears. The state of her dress would have embarrassed a fishwife. She looked ghastly.

His face, though, didn't register disgust. She couldn't decipher his emotions.

"Did he lift his hand to you?" At last, something identifiable. Neal's gaze had become dangerous.

"He betrayed me," she said on a breath.

Yes, that was it. Betrayal, not death, had parted them.

George hadn't been for her.

She hadn't been for him.

"He carried on with half the women of London, and I was too blind to see it. I thought we belonged with each other, to each other.

That was the first fairy tale I was stupid enough to believe. I should have learned something when that particular illusion shattered. Instead, I kept making wishes. I must be the stupidest woman you've ever met."

She could feel her mouth making an ugly shape as she fought to smile.

His hand was suddenly gripping hers. Her fingers stretched around his, a sweet ache that caused something hot to flare within her.

"Because you believe in fairy tales?"

She could scarcely bear the tenderness in his voice.

"It's hardly scientific." There, she'd pulled it off. Some sort of smile.

"Science isn't incompatible with faith." He shrugged, but his grip tightened. "The world would be a poorer place if everyone believed the same things in the same ways. We need scientists. But we also need dreamers."

"Is that what I am?" All at once her throat loosened and a sound slipped out, some mixture of a sigh, a sob, and a laugh.

How good it felt, the release of the pressure in her chest.

Not a snob. Not a ninny. A *dreamer*.

Suddenly, her foot throbbed so intensely she staggered sideways, free hand flying out, closing on his biceps.

"I need to sit down," she gasped. He nodded, frowning.

"As far as botanical rambles go . . ." He hesitated, and she realized his disapproval was all for himself.

"This one was rather on the agonizing end of the spectrum." He sounded grim. "To be frank, I didn't think you'd keep going. My intention wasn't to cripple you, but . . ."

"To teach me a lesson?" She pushed off his biceps, tugged her hand free, and started toward a clearing, the moss glowing emerald green in the sunshine.

"You should know I always keep going," she muttered. "Lavinia is appallingly stubborn."

He laughed as he used to laugh, the sound rich and warming. Back at Crawthevyn Inn, she'd thought him the least broody of men. Again and again, she'd seen this initial impression borne out. He was ebullient, warmhearted. Quick to admit fault and apologize.

Quick to forgive.

*Thank God.* Thank God for his fundamental goodness.

The moss cushioned her feet, thickening beneath her as she walked.

"So she is," he said wryly, catching up to her. "I'll never forget how you stared down that handful of worms. The worms blinked first."

She stole a glance at him. His face didn't look so hard anymore, and he was joking, not jeering. Magnanimous man. His squall of anger was passing. She *could* win his forgiveness. Perhaps she already had. But the truth she'd shared—it was a half-truth. She'd spoken of George, indirectly, and of Cranbrook not at all.

She stopped.

"There's more," she said. "There's so much more. I've hardly begun to explain. About myself, about my marriage." She met his gaze, heart fluttering madly, a trapped bird inside her chest. "And all of it is shameful, beyond anything *you* could ever dream, with your happy family."

To tell *him*, to tell good Neal Traymayne—what deeper shame could she know in this life? She would do it, though. She would tell him.

"My family. I—" She was breathing too fast.

"Shhh," he said, and touched her wrist, a gentle touch. "Take your time. You don't have to tell me now."

His touch, his tone of voice—they soothed her. She felt her heart steady, and took a slow breath. Her nod was grateful. Could he see how grateful?

She might say *thank you.* But before she could speak, he was steering them toward the top of the slope. He wasn't tugging her, yanking her along. He matched their steps. A pace that didn't punish. He was done with punishing her.

"We'll sit under that willow," he said. "We could both use a rest."

She did need to rest. But when she reached the willow, she didn't sit right away. The view was too lovely. She stood and gazed down the bank to the river, which cut a deep and narrow channel, the sides tightly hemmed with green. And then she saw it, tucked close to the shoreline.

The ship.

# CHAPTER TWELVE

IT WASN'T A miracle, her safe passage to France. The ship was a ruin, no longer lying at anchor, but slumped at the edge of what must once have been a deep pool, its hull half-buried in mud. No sails, no ropes. Those were long decayed.

Nonetheless, the blood roared in her ears.

"Ah." Neal threw an arm around a nearby tree trunk, swung his body around to get a better look.

"I haven't seen her in years." He gave a low whistle. "She's a beauty."

"You knew of this?" She stared, rapt, at the ship's tall, naked spars, at the enormous captain's wheel with the broken spokes. How thrilling it must have been, to grip that wheel and to feel the ship responding, lifting and turning, surging through the waves.

"One of the wonders of these woods." Neal pointed. "And there's our old friend."

Long and thin, the heron stood motionless on the poop deck, blending with the rails.

"Hello, Captain Heron," she called out, and heard Neal's low laughter.

"The ship is centuries old," he said. "Or that's what I recall.

Mrs. Odgers took me to see it with my mother when I was a boy. She's been rambling this river for sixty years and knows every legend."

He was squinting down at the ship, unconscious that her attention had shifted suddenly to him.

Laura Odgers was his mother's contemporary. Perhaps older than his mother.

Her face warmed. The sun shone stronger where they stood, but the warmth originated inside her.

Dear God, what *hadn't* she pictured last night? She'd imagined—vividly—Neal passing those dark hours in every position, except sitting upright, sharing reminiscences with an elderly friend of the family.

Could he read her thoughts? Just in case, she shaded her eyes with her hand. The sun provided all the excuse she needed.

"It was a pirate ship, wasn't it?" she asked throatily. "In the story I'm writing—a novel, really—the heroine flees her husband and becomes a pirate and harries the Cornish coast."

"That's what you're writing in your notebook?"

She stiffened at the amusement in his voice. Yes, he'd overestimated her on that front as well. Would he mock her?

*A novel*, he'd say. *I thought you were writing something of more consequence.*

He intercepted her look and grinned the grin that made her breath catch.

"A novel," he said, and shook his head. "I should have known that a novelist was naming my ointment, not a botanist."

*A dreamer. A novelist.* How smoothly those words had rolled off his tongue. What possibilities he saw in her. For her.

If only she'd met Neal Traymayne years ago. But no, years ago, she didn't have the eyes to see him.

"It wasn't a pirate ship, not in the story I was told." He leaned a shoulder into the willow. "Legend has it that ship was hidden there when the tide of the civil war turned and the west fell to the Parliamentarians. Members of the Prince's Council were to be spirited to the Scillies. But something went wrong, obviously. The ship is still there."

"A traitor," she suggested. "He revealed the plan to the enemy. Instead of Cavaliers, Roundheads burst through these trees and slaughtered the crew."

"Are all novelists so bloodthirsty?" Again, he flashed that grin. "I read too many horticulture journals."

"How dull. I couldn't tolerate reading any." She responded automatically, tensed, and then, just like that, the tension dissipated. She could say what she pleased without worrying if it matched up with Neal's image of Muriel Pendrake. Hiding her smile, she turned to the river.

"Still, it *might* have been a pirate ship." She sighed as a breeze rustled the willow fronds, looked up at the tiny green leaves fluttering down around them. A leaf settled on a dark wave of Neal's hair.

She knew how his hair would feel between her fingers if she plucked at that leaf.

She closed her eyes, blocking him out. She imagined the ship in its prime, bows and decks painted red and gold, white sails bellying in the wind. She could see it rigged for speed and racing downriver, past the headlands to the open sea.

"I'll claim it for you."

Her eyes flew open. "What are you talking about?" Even as she laughed, she was frowning. His voice held that same cocksure note she remembered from when they stood soaked to the skin in the Kyncastle harbor.

He was already unwinding the lightweight green scarf from around his collar.

"Red or black would be more piratical. But this ensign is at least distinctive." He shrugged out of his coat. Without the scarf holding his collar together, his shirt gaped at the neck, exposing a triangle of bronzed skin.

Why did this man's neck overwhelm her? She shouldn't stare at it, but staring was better than the alternative. She wanted to taste it, to put her lips and teeth to that muscular curve.

"By your leave."

Mortified, she jerked her head up. His expression was all politeness, but his eyes were glinting.

*Has my lady looked her fill?*

She made an unintelligible noise and he was off, vaulting logs and rocks, then skidding down to the mud. He circled around the ship's hull and vanished from sight, and the next thing she knew he was up on the deck, weaving around ancient blocks, springing over weather-rotted boards.

"You'll break your fool neck!" she shouted as he shimmied up the mast, which was nearly certain to splinter, to send him crashing through the deck, and Lord, if he wasn't laughing, legs wrapping the ancient timber as he knotted his scarf to the pinnacle.

"What shall we call her?" he shouted down. "*Lavinia's Revenge?*"

She put her hands on her hips. "Is *Neal's Inglorious and Untimely and Entirely Unnecessary Demise* too much of a mouthful?"

"You're the wordsmith." He shrugged—shrugged!—as though maintaining his hold on the mast required no special concessions. "I'm thinking *The Bluebell* has a nicer ring."

"Thinking! That's a laugh." She ended with a mutter. She wasn't going to shout herself hoarse while he monkeyed around twenty feet in the air. What kind of natural scientist didn't understand gravity?

She couldn't help it. She shouted again. "I hope you and Captain Heron there enjoy yourselves!"

She'd leave them to it, the birdbrains.

She moved swiftly behind the willow and sat, setting her back to it. She tried not to interpret the sounds floating from the river. A particularly loud thud made her wince. But Neal's arrival was only delayed by a few moments more, and she heard him coming, whistling as he climbed the bank. She stood hastily, feet protesting, and met him as he crested the rise. Instinctively she fisted her hands on her hips, but her remonstrances caught in her throat.

He looked, if possible, even more disheveled than before. Even more raffishly attractive. A light sheen of sweat made his cheekbones gleam. She could smell him, clean sweat and aromatic smoke.

"You look proud of yourself," she managed.

"There wasn't any danger," he said, then checked himself. "Or— just enough. And now, behold!"

The wind had kicked up and the green scarf streamed out from the ship's mast like a pennant.

Glancing between his wide white smile and the green scarf, she felt an answering ripple within her. Hot and red.

"Your ship," he said. "*The Bluebell.*"

She couldn't resist his good humor, not when she'd lately feared he'd shuttered himself to her forever.

"*The Bluebell,*" she repeated, more breathlessly than she'd intended, then nodded. "I'll put it in the novel. My pirate is French, though. So his ship will be *La Jacinthe de Bois.*"

"Not very fearsome, for a pirate." He tipped his head. "I liked it as a name when I imagined you the ship's mistress, with your eyes like bluebells."

She flushed. A high compliment, coming from a botanist. "He's not a fearsome pirate."

"No?" He laid a finger across his lips, regarding her. "He doesn't pillage and murder? Why is he a pirate?"

"Freedom." She shrugged. "Danger."

"In that case, I understand." He lowered his hand, rubbed his thumb absently along a red weal on his palm.

Another man might have torn his palms open on that mast, but Neal had calluses. She remembered their roughness.

"I wish . . ." she began, ignoring the wary light that came into his eyes. "I wish we were in my novel. I wish that ship were the brigantine *La Jacinthe de Bois*, and I was the heroine and you were the pirate she'd met in the woods, the one who offered to share with her the freedom of the high seas."

"I don't speak French," he said, his tone light.

"I'll rewrite it," she said. "He's a Cornish pirate and his ship is *The Bluebell*. He sacks estates for the fun of it, and he always tempts fate by taking the time to dig up flowers, which he keeps alive in glass cases in his cabin."

"The deck," he murmured. "He should put the cases on the deck. Not much light in the cabin, I'd wager. Never mind. Go on."

"The deck, then." She exhaled. "The *deck* of his ship is bursting with plants and flowers, bow covered with bluebells. And his parrot speaks in slogans on behalf of the Society for the Protection of Plumage. Now do you approve?"

He laughed, and she felt a sudden surge of power. *She* had the ability to elicit that grin. They got on well together, despite everything. She couldn't define exactly what they shared, but their connection was real.

"'Outlaw the market hunting of birds,'" he quoted. "That's their slogan, if I remember correctly. You'll come up with something catchier."

"Certainly," she retorted, pleased at the implication. He believed she might improve upon something thought up by one of his brilliant sisters!

"And when we're pursued by aggrieved landowners, or the authorities," she continued, "we'll retreat to our hideaway on the French coast. Maybe we'll like the life there so much we give up piracy altogether."

Other men indulged her when she spoke. Neal listened. He was listening now, too intently. She sensed it coming, some negation. Some rejection. One of his rolled-up sleeves had slipped down and he pushed it back as he folded his arms.

She reached out then, watched her hand close on his forearm as if her hand belonged to someone else. It was so much paler than his forearm and looked flimsy against its bulk. He could break her grip just by flexing.

She closed her eyes, and when she opened them, he was staring at her.

"It didn't come true." She formed her lips into a smile. "We're not in my novel. We're not sailing for the French coast."

Slowly, he shook his head. The humor went from his face. He, too, seemed to understand that their ill-defined rapprochement had come to an end.

"If France is still your destination . . ." As he slanted his gaze toward the river, she noticed the shadows on his eyelids, smudges of fatigue.

Into the lengthening pause, without looking back at her, he said, "I'll take you to Plymouth. You can get on one of the steamers to Roscoff."

She loosed a shuddering breath. It was more than she deserved from him.

It wasn't enough.

*Come with me.* She couldn't say the words. Neal had Varnham, his family, the Cornish flora . . . Muriel Pendrake. He had everything to lose.

He would refuse. And she would crumple.

She said simply: "Thank you."

"What will you do in France?" His brows knitted together. He worried for her.

How decent he was.

If only he were *slightly* less decent. If he had knocked on her door last night, she would have opened it. And now he wouldn't be looking worried at the prospect of abandoning her at the port. He would be looking implicated, entangled, trapped, bewitched—knowing he couldn't let her go.

He was waiting for her answer.

"I'll take a post at a school in Paris." She said it calmly, a sharp pain in her chest. "A friend of a friend knows the headmistress."

That woman with diamonds in her hair had described Le Manoir down to the stone angels flanking the entrance, the grotto built of Fontainebleau rock in the park. Surely, all that description had some basis in reality.

She'd lied to her parents about attending Le Manoir. Now, years later, she would walk between those stone angels, impoverished and humbled, begging to be taken on as a member of the staff.

Pity Justice if she were truly blind, unable to enjoy her ringside seat to all this comeuppance.

She laughed and Neal's darkening expression told her that the laughter sounded hollow. She tightened her grip on his forearm. It befitted a pirate, so wide and so tan.

*Come with me.*

Her feet screamed, but she rose onto her toes and pressed her mouth to his. His lips were warm but unyielding.

She felt his fingers close on her wrist and he lifted her hand, pressing a kiss into her palm before pushing her arm into her chest until she stepped back.

"This goes nowhere," he said gently, and she saw the color leaching out of the sky, the leaves, the river, the waving green flag. The heat in her core turned ashy.

But she tilted her head at a defiant angle. "So? We're here, now." She licked her lips. "Together."

His fingers still encircled her wrist, his thumb tight to her leaping pulse.

"You said I planned to seduce Muriel Pendrake." His smile was crooked. "In fact, I planned to marry her. Hell, maybe I still plan to marry her, I don't know. But . . ."

"But you want to marry. Someone. I see." She worked hard to swallow. "Maybe Muriel Pendrake." Her voice was fraying. "Maybe a different woman so long as she's unattached, scientific, and amenable to your schedule."

"Don't," he said, his thumb moving up her wrist, sliding into the hollow of her palm, still burning from his kiss.

Now her laughter sounded unraveled. "Your mother's hair won't turn back because you marry the right woman. She's dying and so you want to rush to her with your bride and show her you're all grown up, exactly the man she wants you to be, when there's nothing more *childish*, more—"

He yanked her wrist, dragging her into him, and she gasped as her breasts crushed against his chest. But she wouldn't be silenced. She raised her chin higher, glaring up at him.

"Maybe there's nothing about *this* that goes anywhere, that gets you to Penzance in time for the wedding you think will make your mother so happy, and maybe I don't compare to Muriel Pendrake, with her knowledge of plants and languages and birds and dinosaur bones and who knows what else, but you can't deny there's *something*—" She broke off as the breath he heaved caused his chest to expand, increasing the pressure, the heat. Sensation gathered in her nipples.

"Something," she whispered. The ashes within her had gone molten. She couldn't explain. He felt it too, or he didn't.

She wormed her free arm up between them, touched his high, angled cheekbone, skated her fingers over the concavity of his cheek, settled them on his jaw.

She directed his head downward. His chin rasped the sensitive skin of her lower lip, and then their mouths hovered a breath apart.

"Don't go, then." His growl warmed her lips. "Stay. Sue for divorce."

"Impossible." She went to lick her lower lip and the tip of her tongue stroked the curve of his. He hissed. She didn't even realize he'd moved them both forward until her shoulder blades bumped the trunk of the willow. The fronds fountained around them, cool and green, but she felt hot flickers traveling through her, wild as runaway flame.

He felt it too. The jut of his arousal pressed her lower belly. His eyes were hooded, but the irises were clear. They bored into her.

She couldn't face Cranbrook. Sailing to France would be easier.

*If Neal came with her.*

Lies and wishes. They'd been the source of so much trouble in her life. Her next utterance would be both.

"I wish we had today, just today," she whispered.

"For what?" He was so close now that his eyes twinned in her vision, and the beating of his lashes tickled her skin.

"Something." She shifted her hips and he groaned into her mouth. "Everything."

He moved his lips to speak, but her own lips were between them, and his answer became their kiss, sweet and then deep, deeper—shattering.

# Chapter Thirteen

HER BREATH CAME faster, but he worked his tongue slowly over her lips, planting his forearms on either side of her head, pinning her.

He planned to linger.

*Everything*, she'd said.

One day wasn't enough, not for everything he wanted to do to her. Damned if one lifetime was enough.

Her husband was a cad and a simpleton. Why would he seek other women when the one who shared his table, his bed, offered endless delights, endless challenges, provoked the mind and inflamed the body, irritated and enticed and . . .

*Christ.*

She was undulating against him, sighing into his mouth, so he stilled her, pushed his tongue inside as his thigh nudged her legs apart. Her mouth opened to receive him, tasted sweet, with a slight savor of mint, of mugwort, and he stroked a wicked rhythm that she interrupted with gasps, tangling her tongue with his, catching at his lower lip with her teeth. He broke the kiss, ran his lips down her throat. Her skin was smooth as silk but salted with her sweat. It stung him. Oh, but he liked the *burn* of her. He licked away the salts, flicking with his tongue, then sucking the lobe of her ear into his mouth, twisting his fingers in her damp hair until she hissed.

He was already so hard it hurt. He slowed his breathing, eased his lower body away.

The madness of the situation struck him. He *had* surrendered. He'd let Lavinia goad him into defying reason.

He opened his eyes. She'd opened hers. Bluebell blue.

"You're stopping," she said, softly, without surprise. As though rejection and disappointment were her constant companions. Betrayed, and alone in the world, she made wishes knowing they wouldn't come true.

He hated that resigned note in her voice. But he wasn't a magician, had no power to banish past hurts.

That last wish she'd made, though. *That* he could grant. No magic required. Only desire. Desire, and a willingness to suspend his own better judgment.

They had no future together.

But they could have today.

"I'm not stopping," he said. "I haven't begun."

He lifted her into his arms, carried her from the willow into the sun-dazzled clearing. Her mouth was wet on his neck, and her fingers threaded into his hair. As he lowered to his knees, he had to detach her gently, laying her down where the moss made a thick bed.

"You said you wanted to appreciate the mosses," he murmured, sitting back on his heels. She propped herself up on her elbow, made a face.

"What if I don't, though?" she asked. "Could you appreciate a woman who *doesn't* appreciate the mosses?"

She taunted him. But he detected an odd quaver in her voice, an unexpected vulnerability in her eyes.

"It depends." He brought her muddy shoes onto his thighs, tugged at the laces, worked them off one by one. Her stockings were wet at the toe and the heel. He scooted her closer, drew her calves onto his thighs, and pushed up her skirt.

"She doesn't *object* to moss, does she?" His hands slid up to her garters. "It's comfortable, cool, fragrant . . . one of the great luxuries of the forest." He dropped her stockings behind him and set her bare calves on the green mat. "Fit for a queen. A pirate queen, at any rate."

"Nature's settee." She arched a brow but the trouble still lurked at the corners of her mouth. "I haven't the foggiest notion, though, of the Latin."

He stared, cursing himself. He'd called her empty-headed. Made it clear he didn't think her capable of being a spy, let alone a scientist. That she was less than she'd pretended to be.

"You'd learn easily." He tried to push with his eyes, to bring forward all his certainty. "If you put half a mind to it, you could memorize the Latin name for that tree, and that bush, those flowers. I could teach you in no time."

She was biting her lip.

*He* wanted to bite her lip. But it was more important to speak. "The Latin doesn't matter. You already know how to describe the world, and you do it more vividly than most. And you know how to imagine other worlds."

The look on her face made his heart swell in his chest. Damn her husband. Damn everyone who had kept her so starved for recognition.

"I could label dinosaur bones all day long, sort through dusty boxes." He took her bare feet into his hands, comparing them like two fossils so that she laughed and kicked at him, but he tightened his grip, looked at her seriously. "Anyone can say *that's the tooth of an iguanodon.* I'd want *you* to help me picture the living beast."

She snorted, but her eyes were bright. "I wouldn't be surprised if an iguanodon lurched out from between the trees. These are the woods that time forgot."

He kept fondling her feet, avoiding the blisters on her heels, rubbing his thumbs into her soles.

"That's it," he said, grinning. "I became a plant hunter instead of a professor because I wanted that feeling. The sense that anything could happen. I feel it in places like this."

"I know," she said dryly. "Or on mountaintops, or better, ledges. You'd be thrilled if a massive purple iguanodon charged right at us, crowing like that sinister rooster."

He blinked. She *did* have a knack for imagery. It had never occurred to him—an iguanodon *crowing*.

"The rooster in Kyncastle," she clarified. "I'd never heard such an ear-splitting sound! I'm certain dinosaurs couldn't sound worse. So just imagine. He's thundering toward us, the iguanodon, with a horn on his nose and making the most hideous racket. You're happy about it, aren't you? You don't mind one bit that he might gobble us up."

He laughed. She watched him, mouth curving. Holding back her own laughter. Still, she wanted an answer.

He'd never met anyone like her, of *that* he was certain. Should he tell her that iguanodons were herbivores? No. It was entirely beside the point.

"I'm happy about you," he said at last. She'd deceived him, yes. But she'd told him why, and he believed her. The raw suffering in her eyes had been real. And now he had a chance, here, now, to discover more about the real Lavinia. Not just what she suffered, but what brought her joy. Pleasure.

She made him feel the very excitement he'd pledged to sacrifice for a relationship based on conversation.

But he *could* talk to her. They didn't have the kinds of conversations he'd imagined—two people upholding each other's points of view. No, they vexed and surprised each other. That was part of it.

"I prefer you to an iguanodon," she said, primly, as though she were perched on a chintz settee in a drawing room, instead of sprawled on nature's settee, letting him manipulate her plump little toes.

"Do tell," he said. "I want to know all your preferences."

"I don't know what you mean."

"You do, though." He smiled at her. Freckles dusted her nose, and her cheekbones were rosy with sun. Her hair straggled from its pins. She looked wild. Skittish, but also bold.

"For example, you prefer Moët to ale, saffron buns to scones, novels to horticulture journals, late nights to early mornings, London to Cornwall—"

"I'm coming around on Cornwall," she interrupted.

"Mmm," he said. "I'm glad to hear it."

His fingertips stroked up from her ankle to her knee. She had soft pale hairs on her shinbones, like on the undersides of young sycamore leaves.

"How do you prefer to be touched?"

Her shock was almost comical. Her jaw dropped, and her chest, throat, and face turned a deep, blooming red.

Clearly, no one had ever put the question to her.

He lowered his voice as he pushed her skirt higher. "You're so good with words. I want every detail."

She shook her head, emphatic. Almost frantic.

"Let me . . . I can touch *you*." She spoke in a strangled voice and sat up, pressing her palm to the bulge in his trousers.

He felt himself straining against the fabric. She swallowed, moving her hand, her expression concentrated. He sucked in his breath.

"The question isn't what you can do." He bent his torso over her, pulling her against him. "I don't doubt you can do anything."

If she kept touching him, that adorable, determined look on her face, she'd find out one thing she could do, quite a bit sooner than he'd like.

He couldn't remember a time a woman's hand had worked him to this state.

His voice was rough. "The question is what do you want."

He cupped the back of her head, claiming her mouth as he bore her slowly down onto the moss. Her arm snaked between them—she was trying to release him from the trousers—but he slid down her body, kissing her throat, the swell of her breasts. Thank God she wasn't wearing one of her silk gowns with all the complicated panels and lace, the eyelets and hooks. He had her out of the thin cotton frock and ruffled knickers in a trice. For a moment he could only stare at her, her creamy body on a bed of green, breasts tipped with pink, dark curls glinting gold at the juncture of her thighs.

"You said everything." He studied her face as he unbuttoned his shirt, fingers trembling slightly. He wasn't nearly as calm as he sounded.

He wanted her. He shook with the force of it. "But we need to prioritize. There's so much." He took a deep breath as he let his shirt fall. The breeze felt deliciously cool, tickling his ribs. "Tell me."

"What?" She was up again on one elbow, brow furrowed in confused anger. "I said *everything*. That means . . ." She trailed off, eyes roaming down his chest. She caught her lower lip between her teeth. Then she met his gaze.

"Take me," she said hoarsely, and her eyes fell to his groin. Her look alone affected him like a finger stroke. The ache had become a torment.

An equal torment—his sudden knowledge of her innocence.

She knew nothing of the other pleasures he could offer her.

She'd been taught to give but not to take.

That husband of hers, he was an outright villain.

He came onto all fours beside her, nuzzling her breasts, flicking her nipples until they hardened against his tongue. His hand slid over her belly down the slope of her hip. He pulled his head from her breasts to take her mouth in a kiss as his hand slid further, and he teased the curls between her thighs. He burrowed into them with his first two fingers, felt the sudden shock of her moist heat. She cried out in his mouth, bucking, and her arm came around him, fingernails scratching down his spine, then her fingers hooked the band of his trousers. She tugged down.

He moved his fingers gently, feeling the soft wet edges and the hard knot of her, which swelled under his touch.

She still tugged helplessly at his trousers. Sighing, he removed his hand, plucked away her tugging arm and pinned it beside her. He stopped sipping at her lips to take her nipple between his teeth, to plant kisses on the undersides of her breasts and below her navel, and then he was hovering over her lower belly, admiring the fullness of her thighs, and everything that glistened between.

His touch had made her open like a crocus. He wanted to open her wider, to taste each ridge and fold, parting the lavender-rose of her, heavy with dew.

The stream of air he expelled with his groan made her squirm. He leaned in and licked the very center.

HER STOMACH CLENCHED as his mouth closed on her. Dear God, what kind of caress was this, the wet stroking of his tongue at the tip of her sensation? She gasped and wiggled, and his hand closed on her hip, pushing her into the moss, stilling her.

Her breath came ragged. Her legs butterflied around his wide upper body. He held her beating against his mouth, and her cheeks flamed with the near unbearable intimacy of it. She felt his fingers parting her, then the delicious, unsettling stretch as his knuckle churned against her inner flesh, his tongue sliding in rhythm.

Had George ever tried to position himself thus, propped between her thighs, spreading her? No, no, he'd kiss her mouth, her breasts, brush her down there with beringed fingers, then fit himself inside.

If he'd tried . . . she'd never have allowed it. She had wanted George to see her as a princess, an angel, wicked at times, but always irreproachably lovely. He would climb on top of her and she'd make sure her hair was fanned out like a golden halo on the pillow. She would run her hands down his smooth back, sigh prettily, let him take her, adoring his closeness, the flickers of pleasure in that secret place where he rubbed against her.

It wasn't secret now. She was open to Neal, to the woods, to the sky.

Neal had asked her what she wanted. She didn't know if she wanted this, this exposure.

"No." She bit back a cry as his lips, tongue, and teeth pulled and warmth flooded down her thighs. Louder. "*No.*"

At once, he was up beside her, the muscles in his arm bunching as he took her in a protective embrace. She shuddered against his hard chest.

"You don't like it," he murmured.

"No. Yes. I don't know." She was embarrassingly near tears, trying not to rub her legs together, to rekindle that desperate desire, almost a need. Sun filtered through the leaves, heating her bare shoulder, her brow. Some horrible insect had stung her cheek. She scratched at the lump. "I'm sorry. I look . . ."

He opened his mouth. He'd say *beautiful* and he'd be lying.

"Like you belong in these woods," he said, and gently untangled a leaf from her hair.

Her insides squeezed. "I don't belong anywhere."

"Today you belong here, with me." He pulled back so he could study her, and she was undone. *He* belonged in these woods, with his wild locks and bronze skin, his broad shoulders, his ribs knit with muscles, his body so lean and strong and *animal*.

"Unless you recant your wish," he said.

Recant? She was already shaking her head. She didn't want to recant her wish. That was the problem. She wanted to double, then quadruple it. She wanted today *and* tomorrow *and* the day after that. She was greedy and needful and ugly. She was dirty and bitten and throbbing with lewdness.

She was unpresentable. Unfit for polite company. Utterly unperfect, now and perhaps forevermore.

"It's not . . . nice . . . down there," she managed. His eyes seemed suddenly to darken as he understood her. She could fall into them forever.

"Oh, it's nice," he said, voice like velvet. His finger trailed over her collarbones, the callus scratching over her nipple, beneath the curve of her breast, lower and lower. "Like moss and lilies and riverbank and cloud."

She tried to laugh but it was trapped in her tightening chest.

"It's dirty." Her voice strangled.

"Mmm." His tongue moved over his bottom lip, and she realized with a start that he must be able to taste her there. "Like dirt too." He smiled. "Slippery mud. Seaweed. *Worms*."

Now she did laugh. "You're a lunatic."

"It's like everything," he said. His finger barely touched her, skimming the tuft of hair at the apex of her thighs. His face became hard, intent. His finger pressed down, found the spot that made her want to writhe and moan.

"You *do* like it," he said, watching her.

"Maybe too much." She gasped as he curled his finger. "What if I can't control how I . . ."

She couldn't finish. It wasn't just his touch but his face that took her breath away. She'd never seen him so purposeful.

"If you can't control how you look?" He inched his body closer to hers, stretched out to his full length, not on top of her, but beside her, staring into her eyes. Down there, his finger worked at her. "If you can't control how you sound?"

She couldn't help it. She groaned and rolled onto her side, wanting more contact. *Ah. There.* Her breasts bumped his hot, hard chest, flattened against his naked skin. He exhaled but didn't stop circling with his finger, didn't stop speaking . . .

"If you become completely *wild*, like a forest creature, or like a pirate queen who takes her pleasure without apology and gives no quarter . . ."

He pushed her onto her back and loomed over her, so his shadow quenched the light.

"God, I want it." He almost groaned the words. "I want to make you come and come apart and forget every goddamn thing but the feel of my mouth."

She quivered, legs loosening.

"Do you want it too? *Tell me.*" He waited, and she saw that he was vibrating with the effort, with his eagerness.

*She* had the power to decide.

"Yes." Her chest heaved. "Yes."

She shut her eyes against the sun as he nestled again between her thighs, spreading her even wider than before, tasting and tugging until she couldn't tell his tongue from his fingers. The fullness inside her pressed up through her belly, made harsh cries burst from her lips, but she didn't care.

This was no time for tidy, calculating prettiness. She clutched at his head, wrapped his hair round her fingers, tipping her hips, pushing herself into his mouth. Shameless.

The tension was going to make her split, make her shudder into pieces. Her back arched and her head went hard into the moss, which prickled the backs of her arms and her spine.

She was saying his name, saying words she'd never dreamed of uttering. She wanted him deep inside her, wanted his *cock*.

He gripped her hips, lifted her so he could fit more of her in his dark, hot, stroking mouth, and suddenly, she broke, releasing a guttural moan, pulses of pleasure rolling down her legs and cresting up into her belly, nothing like those delicate flickers she'd felt in the past, surface ripples that left her depths placid.

She was a whirlpool of pleasure. All of her was caught in the funnel of sensation. Now, at last, he settled over her and she felt the jolt of his weight, the delicious impact of his hot, hard chest. When she scrabbled at his breeches, he didn't bat her hand away, but let her push them down, helping her bare him.

In this, he differed, too, from George. He was thicker and longer, and she felt the dense, ironlike muscles in his thighs bruising her flesh as he rocked against her. *Yes.* She wanted this force, this urgency. She lifted her head and mashed her lips to his, tasting herself, and it *was* like everything, earthy and rich, sweet and sour.

His arm came under her, and she was clasped to his chest as he sank inside her, each slow inch reactivating the surges of pleasure.

With George, she'd tried not to move lest she do the wrong thing. She'd lain in his arms like a doll.

Now she gave herself over to the sweet wildness, digging her fingers into Neal's glorious backside, feeling the muscles flex and pushing with them, driving him deeper, angling her hips to create just the friction she needed. She was panting beneath him, sweat sliding between her breasts, moisture pumping between her thighs. And then she opened her eyes. His face was right there, jaw rigid, and those glittering eyes saw her, saw everything as she exploded, openmouthed, in his arms. He began to move quickly then, stroke harder, fingers threading hers, until shuddering, he jerked away and spent himself in the moss.

Later, after they'd dozed in the sun, limbs intertwined, *she* was the one who suggested they stay, stay all night, and he the one who laughed with surprise. They had no shelter, no dinner, no *water.* So ran his protests. But who needed shelter? She'd already ruined her complexion and glutted all the insects with her blood, and the woods were warm and nature's settee made a lovely bed if they only rolled his coat into a pillow. Though she *hadn't* ever caught a fish in the Min River, she did have a hook and a line in her dress pocket, and surely Laura Odgers, during her woodland tours, hadn't neglected the freshwater brooks and springs. So she insisted, and that was how they found themselves—hours later, after swimming and fishing, after dining on Cornish trout and pleasing each other more and even better—curled by a dying fire, her front to his back, in the mild summer night.

She turned her head, cheek pressing his shoulder blade, and looked up at the stars through the leaves—one wish fulfilled, so many out of reach.

# CHAPTER FOURTEEN

VARNHAM NURSERIES CONSISTED of thirty-seven acres, ten for ornamental trees and seven more for tree stock. Neal toured Lavinia around the remaining twenty acres, avoiding the botanic gardens, open to the public and always crowded in June, walking her through the hothouses and conservatories.

He was talking too much. She didn't really want to know about the boilers and ventilation systems, or about Varnham's patent superphosphate. But she kept asking questions, looking with interest, not only at the blue lobelia and scarlet geraniums, but at the glaziers installing new panes of glass and the garden boys laughing with one another as they sieved soil into pots.

In the third sweltering stove house of orchids, though, she began to fan herself vigorously and he had to hustle her out into the cooler, dryer air.

"That's enough orchids for one day," he said, leading her down the path toward the orange walk.

"There are *more* orchids?" She sounded almost scandalized.

He laughed and took her arm. It felt bizarrely comfortable, strolling with her on these grounds. It had felt bizarrely comfortable earlier in the day when they'd taken a cab from the train station to his town house in the center of Truro, surprising his housekeeper, Mrs.

Lampshire, who'd looked at Lavinia, polished her spectacles furiously on her apron, then looked again.

*Just passing through for the night on the way to Plymouth*, he'd explained, ignoring the tray in the hall piled with calling cards, refusing to think about the letters waiting on the desk in his study.

Mrs. Lampshire brought them tea and saffron buns with raised brows and a rigid step, but when Lavinia seized a bun with delight and inquired about the recipe, her demeanor changed in an instant. Before he could blink, they were all in the kitchen and Mrs. Lampshire was halving, toasting, and buttering the buns, the proper enjoyment of which, she claimed, was requisite to proper baking.

Clear butter had spilled over Lavinia's lip and she'd chased it with her tongue, and he'd chewed his own bun through a grin that hurt his cheeks, unable to tear his eyes from her.

If she hadn't asked to see the nursery, he might have proposed they take a turn in his own small garden, where the hornbeam hedge provided just enough privacy.

"More orchids," he confirmed, heart tripping as her hip bumped his thigh. "There's more everything. We trial more varieties of plants than they do anywhere else in Europe, excepting Kew."

Was he bragging? If he was, it wasn't on his own behalf. He couldn't take credit for Varnham's century of success. Nonetheless, he liked her wide eyes, her slightly dazzled smile.

"I hadn't quite realized," she murmured. "When you said you went about planting trees, I formed a different picture."

The path wound by the toolshed and the potting and packing houses, and he waved at the trainee gardeners trooping out with wicker baskets, the straw and mats protecting the delicate plants for shipment.

"That first year I planted plenty of trees. I weeded too. I mulched. I loaded coal with the stokers. Cleaned pumps. Treated blight. Propagated shrubs with the head gardener. I packed orders with the trainees." He shrugged. "I didn't want to come on hiring and firing, making decisions about the future of the business, without under-standing how it all works from the ground up. Some of the perma-nent staff are the sons and grandsons of Varnham employees. They weren't going to trust me so easily. Nor were our clients, for that matter."

"Because you're not a Varnham." She pulled away and stopped, facing him.

Why, she really was curious. About the nursery. About his role in it. He nodded slowly.

"That's right. Richard Varnham founded the nursery in 1790 and ever since, the proprietorship has passed father to son." Tight-ness in his throat made the words emerge like gravel. "I represent an unwelcome change."

Unwelcome to him above all.

"Look." He pointed. They'd reached the orange walk, a living wall of orange, citron, lime, and lemon trees. The fruits between the shiny leaves were green. No tiny suns yet. But he could see that she'd lost herself in memory. She hadn't lied about those childhood mo-ments in the glasshouse. Her blue eyes shone and she breathed deep, inhaling the sweet-sharp tang of the air.

*Stay.* He felt the urge to say it aloud, as he had in the woods at Mawbyn. *Forget France. Stay and fight.*

He didn't speak. She hadn't even trusted him with her surname. *Mrs. Stowe* was how she'd introduced herself to Mrs. Lampshire, cutting her eyes at him imploringly. A lie. She was hiding from her husband, yes. But she also hid from him.

Tomorrow she'd be gone.

She drifted to the fountain, perched on the marble lip. She wore one of her fussy silk gowns, gray trimmed with pink, but her hauteur had melted away. Her posture was relaxed, expression unguarded. She dipped her fingers in the water.

"How did it happen, then?" she asked, looking up. "How did you become the proprietor if no one wanted it . . . including you?"

She was perceptive. He stuffed his hands in his pockets, kicking away a pebble. Why was it still so bloody hard to talk about?

"It was supposed to be James, Charles Varnham's son. Only son." He didn't think he could manage more unless he sat. He joined her on the fountain.

"James," she said thoughtfully, and placed the name. "You fought the condors together in the Andes." The corner of her mouth lifted. Her eyes, though, her eyes were grave.

"Fought condors. Found orchids. Traveled to volcanic peaks and through hard-frozen snow and mosquito-filled jungles. Crossed the pampas." He returned her half smile. "He was three years older, a member of a Thames swimming club. We met at a race, nearly tied for first place. Or, that's how he liked to describe coming in second." He felt his smile twitch.

James never beat him once in competition, a fact Neal used to bring up as often as possible.

"Charles wouldn't have hired me as a plant hunter if it weren't for James. From my own father, I knew how to collect, make herbarium specimens, pack live plants, but I'd no commercial experience. James wanted to go to South America. Wanted it so badly he said he'd take a contract with Edevane & Fernsby if Charles wouldn't send him." He laughed. That had been a night. "Charles relented, of course. James wasn't finished, though. He wanted me to go with him." He paused. She was focused on him, lips parted.

"Charles said . . ." He'd never told anyone what Charles had said. He took a breath. "Charles said, *You'll either keep each other safe or get each other killed. I don't know which.*" He drilled his knuckles into the marble. "We know now."

She was shaking her head. "Charles didn't blame you. He made you the proprietor of Varnham. He knows it wasn't your fault."

Her chin had that stubborn tilt. She took his part without even knowing the story.

"He's fond of me." He looked away from the compassion in her eyes.

"James and I did well. We had good luck, and also good nerves, strong stomachs. Every expedition we sent back cases of specimens, plants, bulbs, seeds. We introduced new species of passion flower, lily, nasturtium, myrtle, cypress . . ."

A few of their discoveries had become commercial successes, and a few had excited interest among the botanists at Kew. Charles was never lavish with his praise, but he was proud. Both of them knew it.

He sighed. "Between expeditions, I spent much of the time at the Varnhams' town house in London. Especially after my father died. In part, it was so I could tend and study South American plants with the head gardener at the London nursery. But in part . . . I'd missed too much. Nessa's wedding. Jory's wedding. My father's illness, his—"

He broke off. He felt the old knot forming in his stomach.

"They welcomed me back, make no mistake. I was the one who avoided them. I couldn't bear to feel like an outsider."

"You're a Traymayne."

His heart thudded queerly in his chest. She'd said it with assurance, *as* assurance, like it meant something precious. "And?"

"And you stick by each other. You protect each other. You *love* each other. You join each other's ridiculous societies." She touched his hand. He stopped punishing his knuckles and grasped her fingers. "You share much more than a name. It's deeper. It's a whole way of being. You'll always have it, no matter how far you wander." She hesitated.

"No matter your disagreements with your mother," she said slowly. "When you're truly an outsider, like me, you start to see families for what they are. Yours is something special."

She glanced down, but not before he glimpsed envy and something else, some naked longing, in her eyes.

He exhaled. He *was* a Traymayne, in exactly the way that she meant. He'd known it once, forgotten, relearned the hard way.

But she was Lavinia, just Lavinia. Alone in a way he could

scarcely understand, especially if she didn't let him try. He lifted her hand to his lips, wishing he could bring her inside his circle of protection, which she was right in pointing out had never really broken.

"What happened next?" she asked softly.

He lowered her hand. "Charles was a bachelor for years, had James late in life. He wanted to step down, hand the business over. But I convinced James that we should go on one more expedition. Just one more."

Her fingers tightened on his. He stared over her shoulder at the orange walk and beyond, at the shining glasshouses in the distance, the gorgeously landscaped green acres that were James's birthright. Not his.

"We were in Misiones, in northern Argentina, camped for the night. We should have stayed by the fire, but it was hot, and we could hear the river, and I had one of my raving-mad impulses, jumped up, said I'd be the first one in the water."

He realized he'd gripped her back, too hard. He was mashing her fingers. He risked a glance at her, was staggered by the receptivity he saw in her eyes. She was ready to hear anything he had to say.

He turned his gaze back to the rolling green grounds. He'd lived with the regret, the remorse, for too long now.

"I said I'd race James to the bank. I knew he couldn't ever resist a challenge. I didn't know he'd taken off his boots. I started running, and he followed, and—

His throat closed and she kissed his bruised knuckles as he watched the sunlight dazzle on glass.

"He stepped on a viper." He tried to say it without transporting back to that night, but the memory was too vivid. He was there in the jungle, enclosed by dense vegetation that all but swallowed James's shout.

"It bit him on the foot. We were too far from Posadas. I knew it, but I got him on the horse anyway. We rode until he begged me to stop. I'd wrapped his ankle as tight as I could to slow the venom, but he tore off the wrapping. His leg was so swollen he couldn't bend his knee. He was bleeding from his gums. His nose."

"Neal," she whispered, and he realized she was calling him back to himself. He fixed his eyes on her face.

"I should have let him stay there, talked to him while he could still hear me. But I dragged him back onto the horse. He was in agony but we rode all night. For what? He wasn't breathing when we reached Posadas."

"You had to try." Her eyes were too bright. Her insistence moved him. He swallowed.

"He's buried there. All those cases of flowers I sent across the ocean to Varnham . . ." He could hear his voice getting huskier. "And I left James behind in that red dirt."

She pressed closer to him, pulling their clasped hands onto her lap, the silk cool against his skin. They listened for a moment to the fountain.

"It worked out well for me. That's what some people say." His shoulders tightened. Why was he telling her *this*? The rumors had salted the wound. Within two weeks of accepting Charles's offer, he'd tried to resign. "Here I am, head of Varnham. A usurper, if not a murderer."

She didn't gasp. Her gaze held steady. "People will say anything. You know the truth, and Charles knows the truth." She hesitated. "*I* know the truth."

Slowly, his muscles were loosening. Christ, he'd been maudlin. Embarrassment mingled with relief. As bizarre as anything else: the confidences she could elicit from him, and the easement she offered with a few words, a look from those bluebell-blue eyes. *Jacinthe de bois* eyes.

He almost smiled, managed a nod, dismissing the subject. "It was just idle talk." And it had been. Painful, but short-lived. He'd developed solid relationships with old and new clients, worked like a dog to prove himself to the gardeners, laid most, if not all, of the rumors to rest. But she was still looking steadily. Not fooled by his casual tone.

"Charles Varnham was right to trust you," she said, and smiled at him, a smile of such loveliness his breath caught. "You're devoted to this place, to his legacy. To James."

He itched to wrap his arms around her. Was he really going to put her on a steamer, wave once from the dock, and return to his life as though this whole episode had been a fairy-dusted dream?

"You said I can't be trusted," he reminded her.

Her hand turned in his, and her gaze wavered. He put a finger under her chin, tipped her head up.

"I should have said *I* can't trust you." She breathed the words, and they stared at each other. He'd seen her features blurred with pleasure, heard her breath break, felt her clutch around him, but this look was somehow more intimate. "You are different from . . ." Her voice dipped. "George."

He was holding his breath, willing her to say more.

"You're capable of the kind of love I used to dream about." The sadness in her eyes seemed to tinge the sunlight blue.

The growl in his chest escaped. Dammit, she denied him too much to speak of love. Every particular of her history.

"Tell me who you are." He forced her chin higher. "Give me more than *just Lavinia*, betrayed by George. What of your family? Your friends?"

He felt her chin trembling, caught her whole face in his hands.

"If you can trust me, if you can tell me the worst, I can face it with you, whatever *it* is."

She ducked her head, breaking his hold.

"Why are you running?" He spoke to her hair, the tip of her nose, the curve of her bottom lip.

Her chest heaved. At first, he thought it the prelude to a sob. Then he realized it heralded decision.

She looked up. Her expression arrowed through him.

She was illuminated, hope in her eyes, and fear. Her lips parted.

"I don't know where to begin," she said, voice tremulous but urgent. "I suppose it started—"

"Mr. Traymayne!"

Both of their heads jerked around.

"I didn't realize you were back." Robert Glendinning, one of Varnham's chief hybridists, was approaching along the path pushing a wheelbarrow of shell sand. He was a wide man, bearded, with a gleaming bald head, the perfect foil for his slender companion, a striking woman, with a strong jaw, a Roman nose, and a mass of coppery hair.

She froze, her garden knife pointed at Neal's heart.

"Mrs. Pendrake has been bored among the gladioli." Glendinning was all smiles. "So we spent yesterday with the fuchsias. We took cuttings from the Alba, and if I do say . . ."

He didn't. Neal was already on his feet, dimly aware that Lavinia hadn't moved. Muriel Pendrake, the real Muriel Pendrake, came right up to him, shifted the knife to her left hand, and gave his right a firm shake. Her gaze met his squarely.

"Neal," she said warmly. "I can call you Neal? What a ridiculous mix-up!"


HOURS LATER, NEAL sat in the dining room at the Red Lion Hotel, jerking his gaze between Muriel past and Muriel present, feeling more mixed-up than he'd ever felt in his life.

Muriel present—Muriel two—no, *the one and only* Muriel exhibited none of the reserve she'd demonstrated in her letters. Her prose might be airless, but she herself was a breath of fresh air. More than a breath. A rollicking gust.

At the moment, she was launched on an explanation of her side of the mix-up.

"It's an epic tale," she'd said at the nursery. "I'll need a pint to do it justice."

She had her pint now, and she narrated with singular vivacity. He could scarcely follow the twists and turns of the plot, not least because his swift glances at Lavinia broke his concentration.

Lavinia looked . . . not vivacious. She sat bolt upright, her posture rigid, watching Muriel with a fixed smile on her lips.

Neal glanced at Muriel, cut his eyes back to Lavinia, then rubbed his eyes with the heels of his hands. His divided focus was making his head pound.

Muriel *deserved* attention. He redoubled his effort, concentrating on her words.

Her story had begun at Paddington Station, when the cabbie had driven off before she could collect her portfolio. She'd hopped into another cab and started after him.

"We gave furious chase," she said, shaking her glass so that the ale lipped the rim. "Or rather, we tried to give furious chase, but the London traffic moves like treacle. We were furiously stuck behind an omnibus. I realized I was better off on foot . . ."

As she kept talking, with increasing animation, Neal felt dizzied by a possibility. What if this vivacious woman was also an imposter? What if the Muriels kept multiplying? His eyes slid to the front door. A third Muriel might fling it open at any moment.

Nonsense, of course. Lavinia's deceit had warped his mind.

His gaze returned to Lavinia and their eyes met. She'd been looking at *him*. She seemed to read his passing thought, or at least, the censure in it. Her smile faltered.

*Dammit.*

Muriel was laughing as she described her frenzied sprint down the street, how she'd dodged hooves and wheels, screaming blue murder.

"A Good Samaritan came to my aid, because he thought my *child* had been stolen. He went haring off, quick as lightning. When he reached the cab and recovered the portfolio, he was terribly out of sorts. Didn't think it worth the risk to life and limb. But *you* know differently. I have a new species of primula in there! Among other treasures." She grinned at Neal, and suddenly he found himself grinning back.

Yes, this was Muriel. The right one.

She wrapped up her account neatly as a potboy brought another round of beer.

In the end, she'd missed the train, returned home, waited for Neal's letter, received nothing, dispatched a missive to Truro, then followed on its heels.

"I like this hotel," Muriel commented, waving across the room at another party of diners just being seated. "The Mephams. I met them this morning. We walked the shoreline. It was beautiful, and *fascinating*. Glendinning says there's an algologist I should meet. Underton?"

"Underwood." Neal nodded. "Of course. I'll introduce you."

"Splendid!" Muriel beamed and turned to Lavinia. "And what do you think of the algae?"

LAVINIA MARSHALED HER forces and beamed back at Muriel.

"I've never thought of it." She kept her chin high. A few days ago, if she'd been quizzed about some woody, shrubby, soppy, or mucky thing, she would have put on her best Pendrakean expression and pretended knowledge.

Confronted with Muriel Pendrake herself, she had no such recourse. Nothing but her own ignorance to fall back on, her own empty head, decorated with a pretty smile.

Now Muriel would exchange a pained look with Neal, and they'd draw closer together and discourse about fascinating muck to their hearts' content.

Birds of a feather. A society of two perfectly suited plumes.

Muriel didn't look at Neal. She looked straight into Lavinia's eyes with unfeigned warmth.

"How was the botanizing in Mawbyn? Anything of interest?"

Lavinia's throat felt scratchy, so she took a small sip of ale.

*A friend.* That was how Neal had introduced her. *Lavinia Stowe. We've been out in the field.*

"Mosses," she managed.

"Tomorrow you'll have to show me what you collected." Muriel addressed Neal and Lavinia, smiling upon them both. "I adore bryophytes."

Her waving tresses gleamed in the light like beaten copper. She was so statuesque. So vivid. So *legendary*. And on top of it: so horridly likable. She'd accepted Lavinia's presence without batting an eye. She tried to include Lavinia in their discussion, as though they were all three fellows in science. Potential friends.

Lavinia hooked a lock of hair behind her ear. Her own tresses had seen better days. The ends were dry, and the roots had gone greasy.

"Is your husband joining us?"

Lavinia didn't startle. Too many years of sustaining flank attacks in Society. But the question stopped her breath.

Muriel hadn't meant to attack, of course. She'd asked the question with charming frankness.

Lavinia's eyes fell to her rings, which must have twinkled as she moved her hand, capturing Muriel's attention. The gold looked heavy, the jewels outsized. She wanted to make her hand into a fist and stuff it under the table. If someone could have told her that one day, she'd feel the impulse to hide her diamonds . . . that she'd long to flaunt instead some bit of arcane knowledge about iguanodon teeth, or the genus *Taraxacum* . . .

She'd have laughed. She and George would have laughed together.

"No, my husband isn't joining us." She lowered her hand in her lap, the movement slow and graceful. "I wish he were, though."

She looked down at her plate to avoid seeing if Neal reacted. If he didn't react.

How strange. After all her recent revelations and reversals, she suddenly wished that George sat beside her.

She and George had been birds of a feather, like Neal and Muriel. If he were here, she wouldn't feel the odd one out.

"Next time, then?" Muriel turned back to Neal. "I forgot to say, about the pitcher plants . . ."

Lavinia faded into the background. If George were here, he would arch his brow at Neal and Muriel, shake his head, drawl in her ear, his voice caressing and contemptuous, as familiar to her as her own.

*My Vinnie. A wallflower among the botanists.*

If George were here, he would turn Truro upside down until someone produced a bloody bottle of Möet.

She sipped her ale. When she looked at last to Neal, he was leaning on his elbow, head angled toward Muriel, talking easily. In Latin. Not entirely in Latin, of course. But Latin enough that Lavinia was shut out completely.

Eventually, they segued into English, so they could debate the theories of Charles Darwin.

Finally, Lavinia rose to make her exit. Neal and Muriel sat surrounded by empty glasses, locked in a heated exchange about intelligent design.

Neal broke off as she stood, looking up at her in confusion, almost as though he'd forgotten who she was. Or more accurately: as though he'd remembered he hadn't known in the first place.

"I'll accompany you," he said, but she shook her head. His house was around the corner from the hotel. And he'd been mid-sentence, eyes sparkling with enthusiasm. She could see how eager he was to express the idea forming behind them.

"You were about to make a point," she said. "Science isn't incompatible with faith because . . ."

She left them to it.

IT WAS WELL past midnight when she finally heard Neal's footsteps in the hall. She hadn't wished that he'd stop at her room, that he'd knock. That would only have made things harder.

He hadn't stopped.

He hadn't knocked.

She rose early, but not before Mrs. Lampshire. The kind housekeeper hurried about, spectacles winking in the gaslights. She was confused, clearly, that Lavinia was leaving so early. And leaving alone. But she packed saffron buns for her journey and roused the other members of Neal's small staff to see her safely off to the station.

Wrapped in her warmest shawl, Lavinia waited on the platform with her trunk.

The train wouldn't depart until nine. Under normal circumstances, Neal would wake long before.

But these weren't normal circumstances. He'd been out late, drinking deeply, communing with Muriel.

What a poor Mrs. Pendrake Lavinia had made! The contrast confirmed it.

She gave a small cough, pulling her shawl more tightly around her. A crumb of the saffron bun she'd been nibbling had lodged in her throat. That was why her eyes were watering.

Swallows swooped about. The sun was burning away the mist, but there was a chill in the air.

She'd traded her wedding ring to the clerk for the shillings he had in his pocket plus a first-class ticket, but not to Plymouth. To London.

The ticket's value was only a fraction of the ring's worth.

But already, she felt lighter.

With Cranbrook in Fowey, she could return to Harcott House. Take the chance and tell her mother the truth. The Yardleys weren't the Traymaynes. Her parents had failed her dreadfully. She'd failed them too. But it mightn't be too late. Perhaps she and her mother *could* unite. Figure something out. Her mother could face Cranbrook for her, and . . . what?

Her mind blanked. But she had no better hope, not really. Sailing to France with a pirate was one thing. Boarding an oniony steamer to Roscoff *alone* was quite another. She'd lain in bed before dawn, imagining Paris, the life she'd lead there, shut out of her favorite shops by penury, friendless and deplorable. She'd imagined arriving at Le Manoir, imagined those stone angels turning their backs to her.

At least her mother would give her a chance.

The thing was done now. Decided. Irreversible.

Even though she kept her gaze fastened on the east, in the direction of the city center, she *didn't* wish that Neal was climbing out of the next coach, or the next.

She *didn't* wish that he'd appear, that he'd sprint toward her. *Wait. Don't go.*

She was the last person on the platform. The last person to board the train.

# Chapter Fifteen

THE BUTLER HELD the tall front door open and stared, mustache twitching. He couldn't place her, rumpled and weary, half in shadow, and so Lavinia straightened her spine, stepped forward into the light, and announced herself.

"The Duchess of Cranbrook," she declared, yanking off her gloves as she strode past him into the entrance hall.

She paused beneath the chandelier. It felt as though years had passed since she'd crossed the threshold of Harcott House, a white-knuckled bride with a frozen smile.

Belatedly, the butler reached for her gloves, head retracted on his wrinkled neck. Before she could ask for Mrs. Yardley, she heard a cry from above.

Her mother stood on the second-floor landing, her mouth a perfect O of astonishment. She was dressed for going out, in her gray silk with the panels of brocade. The heron plumes mounted thickly on her hat bobbed as she started forward. Lavinia came to meet her, and they hesitated, face-to-face, at the base of the marble stair. Lavinia closed her eyes as her mother's familiar floral-amber perfume—Bouquet Suave—flooded her. She could be a child again, brought from the nursery to receive her mother's kiss.

Then she found her mother's gaze, the blue eyes a faded version of her own.

Those eyes were wide, not with shock, as Lavinia had supposed, but with horror.

"Your skin," her mother breathed. "What have you done? What were you thinking, running off? You worried me to half to death."

"You hide it beautifully." Bitterness twisted Lavinia lips. Her mother looked sleek, well nourished, and well rested. She'd darkened her eyebrows, put in her pearl tassel earrings.

*We're together, that's all that matters.*

As the train had sped through the countryside, Lavinia had imagined her mother saying those words, folding her into her arms. She'd imagined touching her mother's smooth hair, gone white with fear.

*Thank God, you're safe.*

"Don't let me keep you from your engagement." She stood aside, feeling a small, mean thrill as her mother flinched.

"It's a bit late for the theater," she continued in the same harsh tone. "You're going to a ball, then? How lovely that we could meet. Now your worry won't prevent you from enjoying it."

Her mother's gaze slid to the butler. She'd always hated scenes. Had always tried to make Lavinia quieter, softer, paler, sweeter. Unlike Papa, she'd never doted on Lavinia when she stormed and wept. She would withdraw coldly.

Lavinia wanted to cry now, if only to punish her. To rage in front of this slow-blinking turtle of a butler.

But her mother spun on her heel.

"Irving, I don't need the carriage after all," she said, already sweeping down the hall. "The duchess and I will take refreshment in the yellow sitting room."

In the yellow sitting room, Lavinia ignored the settees and walked to one of the three windows that looked out on the dark garden.

"You are fortunate your husband has kept this quiet."

She didn't turn at her mother's voice, only narrowed her eyes, trying to distinguish the statues from the topiary, the covered pavilion from the colonnade.

"*You* are fortunate," she replied. Cold air was leaking through the glass, and she suppressed a shiver. "Did Lady Chatwick invite you out this evening? Lady Sambourn? They didn't want you anywhere near their parties when you were the wife of a criminal. But now that you are the mother of a duchess, the old friendships have rekindled. It warms the heart."

"Lavinia."

Lavinia heard the rustle of her mother's skirts. Slowly, she turned from the window. Her mother had crossed the room.

"What in heaven's name has come over you?" She stood beside a round table topped with a Sèvres vase, finger trailing up and down the gilt handle. Her frown etched her face with sharp lines, aging her.

Lavinia used to feel her spirits rise and fall with the curve of her mother's lips. Her smiles were rewards, her frowns punishments. They allowed her to gauge her own successes and failures.

"Your marriage to the Duke of Cranbrook brought good fortune to each of us." Her mother tilted her head and the heron feathers swayed. "It is the perfect match. Exactly the kind of match I always expected for you."

"How can it be perfect?" Lavinia hugged herself, voice rising. "How can it be perfect if I loathe him?"

Her mother's frown lines deepened. She assumed the pained, disappointed expression Lavinia had so often provoked in the past, whenever she behaved unreasonably.

She *was* being unreasonable. When circumstances demanded, daughters married for titles, for money, for social acceptance, for the honor of their families, for a host of reasons other than love, or happiness.

Her circumstances spoke for themselves. She and her mother needed a proper roof over their heads. They needed to be allowed back into Society, however false their friends. It was the air they breathed.

So what if she loathed Cranbrook?

Her mother must have seen her sudden turmoil. Her face smoothed.

"I do hold the duke responsible for traveling with you too soon," she said, gentling her voice. "You needed more time to recover from your fever. You must have been delirious when you got off the train. That's what happened, is it not? You wandered off, in delirium. You collapsed and some passerby bundled you away to a doctor."

Despite the softness of her speech, her mother's tension was palpable. Her fingers had closed around the handle.

She didn't want to know how Lavinia had spent the week.

She wanted to know that Lavinia could recite the right story, a story that might convince Cranbrook that she hadn't bolted, humiliated him on the eve of his honeymoon.

She would act as Lavinia's accomplice, but only on behalf of the marriage.

Lavinia felt herself trembling. Her emotions were so many tight and tangled strings, and her mother had the knack for strumming them all at once. Guilt. Anger. Dread. Shame. Panic. They jangled together. She couldn't divide one from the other.

Even if she succeeded in explaining away her disappearance, there was no explaining away the underlying reason for it.

"I didn't have a fever," she whispered. "After the wedding . . . it wasn't . . ."

She hugged herself tighter so she wouldn't shake apart.

"What are you talking about?" Her mother's eyes went wide again. "I feared scarlet fever. You were red all over. You did seem better in the morning, but perhaps Dr. Barth was wrong. Perhaps it *was* scarlet fever, or something like. The strain of travel overcame you. You weren't yourself. The duke will understand, if we present it in the—"

Lavinia interrupted. "I ate the strawberries. At the wedding breakfast. I ate as many as I could."

She and her mother both startled as the Sèvres vase toppled. It rolled on the carpet, unbroken. Her mother's hands flew up, pressed her mouth. Her face was as white as her gloves.

"*Maman*." Lavinia stepped closer, stepped into the range of an embrace.

"They make you sick." Her mother spoke wonderingly, lowering her arms. She didn't reach out. She blinked at the vase. Blinked at Lavinia. Suddenly, she did look worried, cheeks hollowing as though she were gnawed from within.

Perhaps she was remembering that long-ago day, the fright of it, Lavinia struggling to breathe.

*Will it leave pocks?* That was what she'd asked the doctor in the hall outside the bedchamber.

Perhaps she understood, for the first time, the extent of Lavinia's desperation.

"Why? Why would you do such a thing?" She backed up until she bumped a sofa and sat down hard. "Why would you hurt yourself?"

"I was already hurt." Lavinia looked down at her. In the weeks leading up to the wedding, she'd been silent on the subject of hurt. Now she erupted.

"*You* hurt me," she said. "Papa hurt me."

"Hurt you? We gave you everything you ever wanted. Princesses have been raised with less." Her mother's voice throbbed. "And have been more grateful for it."

"You gave me everything you wanted me to want." Lavinia's heart pounded harder. "It's not the same thing."

All those years, she'd tried to meet impossible conditions.

"Is my dress perfect?" whispered Lavinia. "Is my posture perfect? Is my skin perfect? Will I be loved if I get too plump or too thin or if my hair won't hold a curl? I never had a chance to want anything besides *meaningless* perfection. Does it matter if your smile is pretty when you're dying inside?"

She smiled at her mother as tears slipped down her cheeks. "Maybe I could have been someone completely different. Someone *I* would have liked more."

"You do have a fever." Her mother turned her face to the painted ceiling, inhaling deeply. Lavinia watched the feathers on her hat trace a broad curve.

"Herons are incredible," she said softly. "Have you ever watched one fish? Or fly?"

Her mother didn't answer.

Lavinia's smile faded. "I feared my wedding night more than I feared sickness."

At that, her mother breathed in through her nose. As her nostrils pinched, her gaze remained fixed on the ceiling. She looked acutely uncomfortable.

"Brides are always nervous," she said. "It was my intention to tell you something of what to expect. But I didn't find the opportunity." Her head swung down and she sighed. "Really, Lavinia, is *that* what this is about?"

"No." Lavinia felt herself flush. "Yes. I was nervous, but . . . because I *knew* what to expect."

For a moment, her mother looked blankly. Then understanding sparked behind her eyes. She rose with a jerky motion.

"I thought of him as my husband." Lavinia's ears began to ring. Darkness streaked the edges of her vision. Her mother's face was her focal point. Her mother's white, frozen face.

"He was going to marry me. He *promised* he would marry me."

"Who?" Her mother's lips didn't move.

Lavinia gulped the air. "George. I loved him. I would have—"

The force of the slap made her stagger. Pain spread down from her cheekbone, a stinging sensation riding upon a deep ache that made her want to sneeze.

"The Marquess of Stowe." Her mother trembled. Her mouth made several ugly shapes.

"That family," she gasped. "That cursed family. They left me nothing. Nothing untouched by their vileness."

Lavinia stared, pressing her fingertips to her cheek. "Papa robbed *them*."

"Because he was obsessed with that madwoman!" Her mother spat the words. "That *slut*. She started it all."

Lavinia had never seen her mother's face twist with such violence.

George's mother, the Duchess of Weston, *had* been mad, famously so. George had refused to speak of her. Lavinia had sometimes wondered if *she* should have spoken, told him that she remembered his mother, remembered her standing in her glasshouse, picking fragrant, glowing fruit. Told him that, in her memory, his mother was beautiful and kind. Not mad. Magical.

Her papa had never spoken of her either.

"I was happy when she went to the asylum, when she died there." Hectic spots of color mottled her mother's face. "But it didn't end. Twenty years on and she's still blighting my life."

Slowly, Lavinia bent to pick up the vase, the porcelain cool against her palms.

She'd wanted to tell her mother the truth.

She hadn't thought what truths her mother might tell her in exchange.

Her papa . . . and the duchess. *God above.* A wave of horror crested inside her. Had Papa played a role in locking her away, as he had with Effie?

The close friendship between her family and George's family—a friendship that had predated her birth and lasted until her father's thefts came to light—it had been rotten from the beginning.

Her papa's love had been rotten. Had always been rotten.

Or maybe it hadn't been love at all.

She considered hurling the vase against the marble fireplace, then set it gently on the table.

Everything was different, but nothing was different.

How tired she felt.

She linked her hands at her waist. Managed to regard her mother calmly.

The older woman breathed strangely, as though sobbing without tears.

"I was happy, too, when you were engaged to Anthony." She broke off to draw more air. Continued. "My daughter, the new Duchess of Weston, banishing the old to *hell*. But he proved to be entirely his mother's spawn. And now I learn that you . . ." Her hands clenched into fists. "You played the whore to the other son."

It hit harder than the slap. Lavinia's mouth curved reflexively. Tears stung but didn't fall.

"Well then." She whispered through her ghastly smile. "We've both learned something."

She owed them nothing. Her mother. Her father. *Nothing.*

At that moment, the door flew open.

The maid who entered with the tray kept her head down. A pretty girl with a light step. She deposited the tray and skipped back to the door, disappearing with a twitch of her hips.

Beth. No, *Nan*. That was her name. The chit she'd dressed down on the platform in Bodmin. Lavinia stared after her.

"Darling."

She felt the air stir, and her mother was beside her.

"Forgive me." She took Lavinia's hands. "*Darling*, I . . ." She broke off with a soft cry, lifting Lavinia's hands higher.

A pause during which they both examined her rough knuckles, the dirt beneath her fingernails. Lavinia broke her mother's grip.

"Put these on." Her mother spoke urgently, tugging off her gloves.

"Why?" Lavinia took the gloves, tossed them on a love seat. She saw Nan again in her mind's eye. The girl should be in Cornwall, in Fowey. With Cranbrook.

Suddenly, Lavinia's body turned to lead. She watched as her mother sat, poured out two cups of tea.

"Sit," her mother urged. "Let's talk more calmly." She patted the cushion beside her.

"He's here," said Lavinia.

"Of course not." Her mother tsked. She added sugar to one of the cups and held it out.

Lavinia noticed how she cut her eyes at the door. What a liar she was. Like her papa. Like everyone. Except perhaps Neal. But with Neal, she'd lied enough for the both of them.

She wouldn't think of it.

"Sit," her mother said again, too sweetly.

"Cranbrook is back." Lavinia swallowed hard. "He's in London."

Her mother's laughter struck a false note. "Oh. Well, yes, he's in London." She returned the cup to the tray. "But he's not at *home*. He's at his club."

"You didn't tell me."

"I thought you knew. Isn't that why you came? To reconcile?"

"I came to find *you*." Lavinia looked at the door. At any moment, it might open, reveal her disgusting groom. "I believed him in Fowey."

"He returned to London at once." Her mother frowned. "To hire police detectives. He fears foul play. Kidnapping. It breaks my heart to see him. He is terribly concerned."

Now it was Lavinia's turn to laugh. "Poor man."

"He's not a man." Her mother struck the table with her bare hand and the service rattled. "He is a duke. He is your husband."

Lavinia looked at the pale, slender fingers, the gleam of the wedding ring, the soft glow of the polished nails.

"He won't be," she said, surprised by the strength of her relief.

"Darling."

Lavinia met her mother's eyes.

*Darling.*

*Whore.*

Neither word could reach her.

"It's not too late," her mother said, rising. "A man gauges his wife's innocence by her demeanor. It is 1883, after all. Wedding nights are not *biblical*. If you seem chaste, docile, timid . . . he need never suspect."

Lavinia realized she was shaking her head. "No."

"Come now." Her mother's voice lowered, became a hiss. "The appearance of modesty is not beyond you. You learned the trappings at that French finishing school, did you not?"

Lavinia laughed again, the sound deranged to her own ears. "Someday I'll tell you what I learned about modesty at Le Manoir." She heaved a breath. "Divorcée has a nice ring in French. *Divorcée.*"

Her mother's eyes were slits. "You have no grounds to sue for divorce."

"He does, though." Lavinia stepped around her mother, started for the door.

"He is friends with the lord chancellor. He has promised to appeal to him for your father's release. If he divorces you, your father will rot in jail." Her mother hurled the words at her back. "I'll be turned out into the street. And you? What will you do?"

When she reached the door, Lavinia turned. A mistake.

Her mother's face was livid. "Will you join the ranks of common prostitutes?" Her shoulders slumped but her eyes glittered. "The Marquess of Stowe preferred the company of prostitutes. Perhaps you should have done it sooner."

"I should have done any number of things sooner." Lavinia touched the door handle. "Goodbye, Mother," she said, but her mother started forward, walking with her down the hall, whispering frantically.

The whisper slithered after her even as she outpaced her mother, fled the house, climbed into the waiting cab. It burrowed deep into her brain.

*He might not divorce you, though. He might prefer to keep you. It's within his right. And it will go worse for you than you can imagine.*

Lavinia leaned back against the seat, breath shuddering.

She had always been very good at imagining. And she was getting better at imagining the worst.

Thick night pressed all around. Where could she go?

The glasshouse twinkled in her mind, the tiny suns glowing amid green boughs.

Finally, she gave the cabman an address.

She kept her eyes open as they rolled into the dark.

FOR THE SECOND time in one night, Lavinia found herself shoving her way into a ducal mansion. Thank God Anthony had sacked Collins. This new butler hadn't the same iron in his soul. He suggested, mildly, that the Duke of Weston wasn't to be disturbed, then surrendered the floor.

The third door she rapped on after mounting the stair swung open.

"Lucy, I'm—" Anthony began, and stopped short.

"Your Grace," he finished, a smile lifting the corner of his mouth. He leaned one shoulder on the doorframe and folded his arms, muscles swelling the white cotton of his nightshirt. It was short as nightshirts went, ending above the knee.

He wore no trousers.

Another man would look silly, disadvantaged, surprised in his pajamas.

Anthony looked like Achilles.

She hated him *and* George, hated them for their beauty, their money, their power, the devasting impact they'd had on her life.

"To what do I owe the pleasure of a midnight call from the il-
lustrious Duchess of Cranbrook?" Anthony's drawling coldness was
the opposite of Neal's frank, rough warmth. How enticing she had
once found such aristocratic airs. How hard to fathom now.

"Don't call me that." She glared. "I think I shall murder a duke
before I'm done, and it might as well be you."

"You've come to murder me?" Anthony sighed with mock resig-
nation, as though people were often turning up at his house on such
desperate missions.

Perhaps they were. Never so dissolute as George, Anthony possessed nonetheless his brother's knack for making enemies.

"Be quick about it, then, or Lucy will beat you to it." He looked
down his nose at her. "We were having a bit of a row, and she's run
off for a kitchen knife."

Lavinia blinked. He didn't seem upset about the row. His wife,
Lucy, was a prickly, outspoken East Ender, poor and not in the least
pretty or obliging, an artist with an inveterate streak of bohemi-
anism.

Now that she was Duchess of Weston, she probably quarreled
with her soft-boiled eggs. Anthony probably enjoyed it.

"I'm surprised she doesn't carry a knife," muttered Lavinia. "I
remember her lugging a bag that could have supplied sixteen junk
shops. There must be artillery clattering around between the vials of
acid."

When first they'd met, Lucy had produced such a vial from her
bag and deliberately stained Lavinia's gown. She'd done it for Lavinia's good, proving thereby that the green silk was dyed with arse-
nic. Still—a barbarous act of sartorial defacement.

Anthony laughed. He *did* enjoy his wife's eccentricity. She'd
never seen such a light in his eyes.

He stretched, threw an arm up on the doorframe, and regarded
her with better humor. They used to joke together, the three of them,
she, Effie, and Anthony.

"Lavinia," he said, and it sounded so normal she almost sagged to the ground.

*Duchess.*

*Darling.*

*Whore.*

He hesitated. "I will not apologize for my actions as regards your father."

"I didn't expect you would." She spoke with difficulty. "Revenge is sweet, as they say. It suits you."

He'd shorn his hair since she'd seen him last. The severe style emphasized the boldness and harmony of his Grecian features. And his green eyes, touched with that dreamy light.

His smile had faded. "Marriage suits me."

She snorted her incredulity, but it was so plainly true. Anthony had found happiness with his odd duck of a wife.

"As for revenge," he added. "If I could have spared you and your mother, I would have."

Despite herself, she didn't doubt it. Anthony had always tried to treat her decently, even during their farcical engagement. She *wanted* to hate him but she couldn't, not really.

God, though, she resented him. His good fortune.

He was waiting for some reply. She spread her hands wide. His prosecution of her father had completed her ruin. It didn't matter that the damage was incidental to the main objective.

"What is that worth?" she asked.

"Nothing, I suppose." He shrugged, expression hardening. "But, as you said, one duke is the same as another. I never thought you cared much for Cranbrook. Well played, Your Grace." He flashed white teeth. "You always land on your feet."

"My feet?" She laughed shrilly. "My feet are *bleeding.*"

Anthony straightened, seeming to take in her ravaged shoes and bedraggled dress for the first time.

"Aren't they, though." He said it slowly, letting his arms drop. A frown creased his brow. "Yes, in fact." Her blisters had rubbed open. She shifted her weight miserably, panic lancing through her as she imagined walking back out into the night.

"Lavinia." Anthony's voice was soft. "Why are you really here?"

"Destiny." She didn't look at him, tried to sneer, but her chin puckered. "I read it in the stars as a girl that I'd end up in Weston Hall."

"I don't believe it." Now his voice was flat. "I broke our engagement. But you won't convince me I broke your heart."

"Not you." She drew a ragged breath. "Your brother."

Perhaps Anthony, too, would call her a whore. She forced herself to meet his eyes. Their blaze almost frightened her.

"The stars were wrong," she said. "Or maybe my reading was wrong. Maybe you're meant to read the dark patches between the stars. The night before George died we met in the library at Lady Lytton's ball."

Anthony's face had become a mask.

"I thought I might be with child," she said, lifting her chin high, holding herself straight and tall against the shame of it. "He told me not to worry. We'd be married so soon the doctor himself wouldn't look askance at the dates. The next day he stole that yacht and drowned."

"Christ God." Anthony swore. He hit the doorframe hard with his fist. If she wasn't so light-headed, she would have jumped. She simply stared at him, motionless.

"The child?" he asked.

She shook her head, saw flashes at the corners of her vision. "A false alarm."

Anthony's look was dark, his beautiful mouth curving down sharply.

"Blind," he murmured, pressing his knuckles into his brow. "Christ, I was blind." She realized with a start that his disdain was for himself.

"What could you have seen?" She shrugged. "You were off rattling your saber."

Anthony had spent years soldiering, a few of them in the East, far from the intrigues hatched in London's ballrooms, the gnarled, clandestine goings-on that even the gossips nearest to hand inevitably got wrong.

"No one knew," she added.

"Your husband?" Anthony was still frowning, searching her face.

A shudder went through her before she could steel herself. Anthony's breath hissed.

She could see that he was already piecing the story together.

"Least of all him." She lowered her voice, as though to speak of Cranbrook might be to summon him. "He knows nothing of me. He doesn't even know where I am. I realized marriage doesn't suit *me* halfway through the wedding breakfast."

The muscles around Anthony's eyes and nose had contracted.

"There was no . . ." She fisted her hands. "*Consummation.* I ran off. It turns out, I'm still running." Her fingernails bit into the soft flesh of her palms. "Perhaps I can get an annulment."

"Does he want to be quit of you?" Anthony's tone was strained. "Badly enough that he would attest to his own permanent impotence?"

Lord, she was trembling. She could hear Cranbrook again, laughing away Lord Browning's tonic.

*No need.*

The old goat prided himself on his virility.

"Because if not . . ." Anthony shook his head. "You're the one in flagrant breach of your marriage contract. Your husband has his conjugal rights, and you have your conjugal duties. You can't withdraw your consent on a whim. That's how the court will see it."

"Surely your lawyers are good for something besides jailing my father." She summoned all her fear, all her dread, pushed with her eyes. "You will help me."

Waiting for his response was agony.

"Help you?" He pulled back slightly. "Legally, it all depends on your husband. There's nothing to be done."

"Nonsense. There's always something to be done," someone said in a husky voice, not a little bit reproving.

Lucy. *The Duchess of Weston.*

She stalked around Lavinia and stood glaring at Anthony, hair a loose tangle, cat clutched to her breast.

"But you won't figure it out tonight. Look at her. She's practically *extinguished.* Another minute and she'll topple over." She turned her sharp eyes on Lavinia. Many women—most women; all women that Lavinia had ever known—would unleash hell's furies if their husband's former fiancée showed up to his bedchamber in the dead of night. This one had jumped to defend the interloper.

Maybe she remembered that, not long ago, she'd been the interloper herself.

Or maybe she plotted her attack.

Suspicion made Lavinia bristle. "I'm hardly extinguished."

Lucy struggled as the cat turned a circle in her arms. "I've half a mind to extinguish this monster if he won't behave himself." She lifted him away but his claws caught in the embroidery on her silk wrapper. She sighed, working the claws free.

"What I meant to say is I've gone without food and rest myself. I can tell when someone's hungry and tired. *Ouch.*" She gave a tug and bent her knees to let the cat leap the short distance to the floor. Straightening, she focused on Lavinia. "You need hot soup and a good night's sleep."

"Hmph." Lavinia pursed her lips. *Hot soup.* To her mortification her stomach rumbled audibly. She clasped her hands at her waist and stood straighter. Lucy was watching her, watching her without pity or gratification. Simply waiting for Lavinia to agree with the obvious.

Lavinia exhaled. Why make things harder? If Lucy found it in

herself to offer hospitality, then she would find it in herself to accept it.

"I could do with a little supper." She nodded stiffly.

Accept it *graciously*.

"Thank you," she added.

"Excellent." Lucy smiled a wide, utterly disarming smile that
made her *almost* pretty. "Hot soup. And hotter water. I'll have a bath
drawn. Anthony, tell Mrs. Perkins to prepare a room."

"Also . . ." Lavinia hesitated. But she was beyond embarrassment.
She plunged on. "The cabman is waiting in the courtyard. He has
my trunk. It seems I lacked the money for the fare."

Anthony was frowning. Lucy gave a short nod and settled her
hands on her hips.

"You heard her," she said, turning to Anthony. "Go pay the cabman. And have the soup sent up. And tea."

Slowly, Anthony shook his head. Lavinia felt her heart plunge,
but he wasn't refusing his wife's command. He was conceding, a
bemused expression on his face.

"Unbelievable," he murmured, a hint of a growl in his low voice.
"You are unbelievable." The glance he and Lucy exchanged made
Lavinia drop her eyes.

The lump that rose in her throat was formed of equal parts relief
and envy.

After a long moment, Anthony heaved a dramatic sign. "Let me
put on my britches at least."

"Why?" Lavinia pulled a face as she looked up. "Everyone in
London has already gotten an eyeful."

Lucy snorted. The year before, she had painted a nude portrait of
Anthony that caused a stampede at the Royal Academy of Art's summer exhibition. The public couldn't get enough of it.

The cabman was likely to whip out his own print reproduction
and ask for a signature.

Anthony opened his mouth, then closed it with a pop. He glanced between Lucy and Lavinia, then shrugged and strolled, bare-legged, for the stairs.

"He doesn't need much encouragement," Lucy murmured, looking after him, and it was Lavinia's turn to snort.

Surely it was giddiness after a long, emotionally harrowing day that made her flood with warmth. Not fellow feeling. And yet . . . she and Lucy together in the hallway, shoulder to shoulder . . . it seemed something like camaraderie.

"He never did," Lavinia agreed, and a wave of tiredness caught her around the knees so she thought she really might topple.

An hour later, when she climbed into the soft, wide bed, she meant to write in her notebook. Instead, her weighted limbs carried her down, down into sleep.

She dreamed she was at Weston Hall, but not now, decades ago. A warm summer day. Both of her parents sat in the garden, taking tea with the duke and duchess, and George was there too, lounging by the fountain, and Anthony and Effie chased each other through the hedges.

She was peering down at them all from a secret perch in the trees, giggling as the game began.

*Where's Lavinia? Have you seen her?* All of them, up and roaming, calling out. *Lavinia! My Vinnie! Lavinia!*

She woke briefly when sun streamed through the gap in the curtains, but then, as no roosters crowed, she drifted off again and slept without dreams.

# CHAPTER SIXTEEN

"But by God, man—you'd never seen a picture of her?" Alan's ringing laugh rose to the rafters of the gardener's cottage. He'd listened to Neal's account—expurgated account—of the two Mrs. Pendrakes with transparent absorption. A rare occurrence. Alan tended to anticipate and interrupt, his thoughts running dizzying laps around his interlocutor's. It was a habit that had made him unpopular during their school days.

Neal was already regretting telling him anything.

"Of course I hadn't seen a picture." He leaned back in his chair, threw a boot onto his knee. A well-fitted, modern boot. With apologies to his grandfather, he'd tossed the Hessians in the dust cart.

Alan's eyes were glinting behind his pince-nez. Just like him to stick on the point that made a chap feel a bloody fool. But dammit, it wasn't Neal's fault that he'd been tricked. How was he to know his ignorance of Muriel Pendrake's appearance would be exploited by a deceitful debutante?

"Muriel is a *botanist*," he added, too testily. "Not a toothpaste model."

"Heaven forfend," murmured Alan with mock horror. His tone, and cocked brow, left no doubt he was remembering Neal's past entanglements. "Since when are you prejudicial to a pretty smile?"

"Since now." Neal scowled. "Wipe that Cheshire cat look off your face. It's bad for your image."

Alan flashed more of his teeth, a very fine set. None of them pointed and dripping venom as the caricaturists would have it.

"You remember Gareth Bidmead?" he asked. "I wrote the notice for his new opera—one-act musical comedy, absolute rubbish. Spare yourself a dire evening."

Neal grunted. "No danger there." His taste didn't incline toward light opera, but if it did, the name Gareth Bidmead was more than enough discouragement.

"If he ever talks to me again," continued Alan, "which I doubt, I'll have to tell him the whole story, to make it up to him. I won't use any names." He raised a hand as though to ward off objection. "Mrs. Pendrake will be protected. But it's too good to waste—a readymade libretto. Even Bidmead can't butcher it."

"Kind of you," said Neal dryly. "Make a tragedy of a man's career, then offer him a farce in compensation."

"Well." Alan leaned back in his chair. "He is a friend."

Now it was Neal's turn to laugh. "What of your own masterpiece?" He stood, stretching, and angled around the furniture to open the door. Sweet air rushed in. He propped his shoulder on the doorframe, reflexively patting his pockets.

His brain always caught up a moment too late.

No cigarette case. He'd given it to Lavinia.

"Finished." Alan stroked his side-whiskers with studied nonchalance. Even at Oxford, he'd insisted on styling himself like a septuagenarian wit from the Age of Reason.

Neal thought the *venerable man of letters* routine a tad overcooked. His was the minority opinion, based on more than a decade of friendship. The public took a different view.

"On to the next." Alan's voice flexed with its characteristic blend of arrogance and irony. He was gazing at Neal narrowly, all speculative intensity. Suddenly, he rose.

"So." He drew out the word to complement his saunter. "The first Mrs. Pendrake returned to her husband." He joined Neal in the doorway. "And the second—she's still in want of one."

Neal shrugged and looked away from Alan's smile at the vast garden: pink and white and green. Roses and poplars. "That's my understanding."

Lavinia had left only a brief note with Mrs. Lampshire.

*I'm wanted in London. Happy plant hunting.*

How he'd stared at those *P*s.

He and Muriel *had* plant hunted happily. They'd traveled to the very tip of the Lizard peninsula and all the way back to London in companionate tranquility. She was levelheaded and knowledgeable and continued to show herself a far livelier conversationalist than the dullest pages of her manuscript predicted. When they'd discussed that manuscript, and he'd shared—haltingly—his suggestions for revision, she'd thanked him warmly.

"The libretto requires one more reversal." Alan recalled his attention by rapping the doorframe with the top of his walking stick. "The amorous pairs must swap partners." He swung the stick to the right. "Mrs. Pendrake with the husband of the false Mrs. Pendrake. The false Mrs. Pendrake . . ." He swung the stick to the left so it thumped Neal's chest. "With you."

"Bloody hell." Neal knocked away the stick.

"She's the Pendrake I want to meet." Alan delivered two more raps to the doorframe. "I salute the intelligence that can improvise. She's wasted on that husband, clearly. But then, I expect she'd be wasted on you as well."

"How wasted?" Neal couldn't bite back the words in time.

*Christ.* Could he have sounded *more* like a jealous lover?

Alan grinned. He enjoyed setting traps. But when he spoke, his tone was almost gentle. "Your goal is to find a like-minded mate and settle down. You told me as much. That was the impetus for your little botanical junket."

Sunlight flashed on the lens of his pince-nez as he pivoted toward the garden. "In real life, old boy, you marry the imitable botanist, Mrs. Muriel Pendrake."

One last rap to the doorframe and he stepped out onto the path. He'd always had a penchant for dramatic exits.

Neal walked after him, and Alan slanted him an amused look. "What did you say her name was, the false Mrs. Pendrake?"

Neal glared. "Lavinia." As though Alan had forgotten it. He forgot nothing, the smug bastard.

"And you're convinced she returned to her husband?"

"Perfectly." Neal spoke through clenched jaws. The showy rogue had betrayed her, but clearly, she still cherished their attachment. At the Red Lion in Truro, he'd heard it in her voice. The wish she'd made had been for George.

"He's a libertine? Young and handsome?"

"Stop it already with the bloody Socratic method," Neal growled at him. "But yes, she gave me the distinct impression that he is a pretty, philandering blackguard who has many times over abused her trust."

"So they've been married a good while, or a bad while as the case may be." Alan said it musingly.

Neal hesitated. If Alan could figure out who she was . . . *Blast.* He did—and didn't—want to know. He bit his tongue, hoping *didn't want* would win.

"I believe his name is George." He supplied the last piece of information at his disposal, and, God help him, he hung on Alan's next words with bated breath.

Alan stopped walking. The sun licked up all the shadows, and the day baked with unseasonable heat. He didn't look uncomfortable despite his full-skirted frock coat. He considered Neal coolly, then slowly shook his head.

"The details don't correspond to any couple of my acquaintance." He seemed, though, to give it more thought, brows drawn together. Something had fired in his mind.

Neal flattened his lips. What did it matter if Alan identified her? She was married. She'd returned to her husband. What else was there to know?

Nonetheless, he couldn't tear his eyes from Alan's face.

A buzzing fly broke the spell. Alan batted it away, as though he were batting away the whole train of thought. He scowled down at a rosebush. "What's wrong with these blasted roses?"

Neal breathed out through his nose.

"Slugs," he said at last, drawing up to Alan and considering the leaves.

Alan picked one and held it up to the cloudless sky. Blue shone through the holes.

He brought the leaf closer to the lens of his pince-nez, then lowered it, sighing.

"Punctuality isn't Mrs. Pendrake's forte, is it?" He handed Neal the leaf. "You don't think she called at the house?"

Neal gazed across the lawn, at Umfreville House, the London seat of the Dukes of Umfreville. Alan had taken up residence when his elder brother, the current duke, went abroad with his family.

Neal shook his head. "I told her to meet us at the gardener's cottage." The cottage, a lovely little building, with an espaliered fig tree framing the door, had been standing empty, and so Alan had offered it to Neal for the duration of his stay in town.

"She'd rather see the grounds," he said, and knew it was true. "Like-minded." He sighed, and Alan raised a brow.

"You *will* propose, then, as planned?"

Neal let the leaf fall, tracking its topsy-turvy descent and cursing himself. He'd left London intending to propose to Muriel Pendrake on the Lizard peninsula.

But everything had gotten *mixed-up* along the way.

When he had finally arrived at the Lizard, with the correct Mrs. Pendrake, they'd spent days poring over rare algae. No intimate dinners. No picnics. They'd attended gatherings hosted by bird-watchers. They'd gone for rambles with the botanically inclined headmasters of local grammar schools.

Neal rubbed the back of his neck. He'd no deuced idea if he'd propose.

"Hark." Alan gripped Neal's shoulder, turning him.

Muriel had appeared, framed between the poplars at the other end of the rose garden.

When Neal reached her, he pressed her hand. It had only been two days since they'd parted company at Paddington Station, but he felt the warmth of their reunion.

"Hallo." She pumped his arm hugely, then waved at Alan, who approached at a snail's pace.

"Sorry I'm late," she said. "I decided to walk and got tremendously lost. I ended up flagging down a gentleman who'd been in the diplomatic service in China. We had a fascinating conversation about the laying of telegraphic cables. Gorgeous garden!" she called out to Alan as he came into range. "I think I came in the wrong way, but I loved that little bridge by the yew hedge."

In a matter of minutes, Alan and Muriel were strolling down the path like bosom companions.

Neal let the two of them pull ahead and sat on the edge of a fountain. He'd invited Muriel expressly to introduce her to Alan. Alan had the power to get her "Recollections" into the right hands. The question was—would he exercise that power? It depended on Muriel, on whether she, or her writing, impressed him.

As Neal watched them stroll, he could tell from Alan's gestures, his laughter, that he needn't worry.

Alan had taken a shine to Muriel.

Well, why the hell not? *He'd* taken a shine to her too. His mother would take a shine to her. His sisters, his brothers, his cousins—everyone would take a bloody shine to her. Wasn't that what he wanted?

When he finally stood and caught up with them by the tulip beds, Muriel was all smiles. She had an undeniably lovely smile. She was an undeniably lovely woman. It was undeniably lovely to be in her presence.

A butterfly fluttered past, winging for the trees, as though to underscore the point. She watched the butterfly with satisfaction.

Of course she knew it was a *Vanessa cardui*. They both did.

"We're off to Otis & Boyd's." Alan named the publishers and shot Neal a sideways look. "Otis is always in his office this time of day. He's mad for travel books, and he doesn't mind a bit of heft."

"Capital!" Neal tried to telegraph his thanks to Alan, and his enthusiasm to Muriel. He nodded at them both. "You two do that, then. I'll peel off to Varnham. Better if I check over the Borneo shipment sooner than later."

A silence descended, threaded with the buzzing of bees.

"You're not coming with us?" Muriel sounded not peevish, but disappointed.

"I'd just be in the way, wouldn't I?" Neal felt heat prickling his neck. Nothing to do with the sun. Everything to do with his awareness that he was, perhaps, acting a cad.

He glanced at Alan, but Alan had arranged his face into a careful blank. *No opinion here.*

In the libretto, Neal ended up with Lavinia.

But in real life, Neal and Muriel belonged together.

He'd already lived a libretto. He'd made too many dramatic mistakes. He'd turned his mother's hair white. He'd missed his father's final months, missed his very funeral. He'd led his best friend into a viper pit. He'd entered into disastrous affairs. He needed to make a sensible choice. And yet . . .

He'd fallen in love with a married woman he'd never see again.

No way around it, then. His latest mistake had already been made.

He couldn't pursue Muriel. He'd ruined himself for that life.

"You're better off without me." He said it with too much force, then tried to temper his tone. "I'll look forward to hearing all about it."

"At dinner?" Muriel tipped her head. "We could meet at the Criterion. Their curry cook is destined for a knighthood."

"Not tonight." *Christ.* He sounded a perfect ass. "I suspect I'll be occupied most of the evening with that shipment." He cleared his throat. "We'll see each other at your lecture on Saturday. We'll have dinner after that." He glanced at Alan. "You're invited, of course."

"Of course," Alan echoed, brows raised.

"And I'll ask Hitchens to come along."

"Why not Bidmead too?" Alan's mouth quirked. "We'll make a party of it."

Neal glared, but Alan was bending to pick a sprig of lavender.

After a moment, Muriel shrugged. "All right, then."

She didn't look terribly put out. But as they all three walked together toward the house, she sighed.

"It doesn't seem we're ever going to get a moment alone," she said. "But I don't mind speaking in front of the both of you. Neal."

No more smile. Her expression had become steely with determination.

Neal's collar grew tighter. Suddenly, he found it difficult to swallow. Alan slowed his pace, and he fought the urge to clutch his friend's sleeve, to prevent his dropping back.

"Neal. The answer is *yes.*" The air whooshed out of her. "I appreciate that you haven't pressured me, that you invited me to Cornwall, showed me Truro, that you were never impatient. That you let me arrive at my own conclusion."

A bird twittered. No, not a bird. Alan had started to whistle. Everything made sense, and nothing made sense.

What was she saying?

The sunlight, Alan's jaunty whistle, the green hedge, the exemplary woman beside him—the perfect pieces all fit together jaggedly. The gorgeous day was cracked with horror, visible only to him.

What had he done?

As Neal looked down at Muriel's face, a resplendent smile spread across it.

"It feels wonderful, doesn't it?" She sighed, this time with satisfaction. "When you've made up your mind?"

Not a word occurred to him.

At the house, it was she who pressed his hand. "I'm not worried about the details. But I needed to tell you. Once I knew myself, I was going mad holding it in."

They stood gazing at each other. He didn't know what to say, how to clear up the marvelous confusion he'd generated, and so he said nothing, letting the moment lengthen, until he realized that the script called for a kiss.

God above. Was he *engaged*?

Her chin tilted up.

"Muriel." How to let her down gently? "Muriel, I hold you in the—"

"Onward to Otis & Boyd?"

She was looking over his shoulder, at Alan. Neal turned, thrusting his hands into his pockets.

"Onward." Alan flourished his walking stick. "Or the doughty Otis, hardest-working editor in London, languishing for want of new talent, may retire early to his club."

"Fie on that! Not a moment to lose." Muriel fell into step with Alan, flashing a great grin at Neal over her shoulder. "Good luck with the Borneo shipment. More pitcher plants? Wonderful!"

The look Alan tossed over *his* shoulder was decidedly more quizzical.

After they disappeared, Neal stood stock-still in the shadow of Umfreville House.

*Caught between Pendrakes.*

Maybe Bidmead *would* do better with the scenario than he had. He couldn't do worse.

Christ, Neal had butchered things.

Finally, he shook himself and struck off, cutting across Hyde Park toward Varnham Nurseries, alone.

# Chapter Seventeen

The air sparkled. When Lavinia shut her eyes, colorful starbursts patterned the darkness behind her lids. The glasshouse smelled of turpentine and varnish, not flowers and fruit. Instead of plants, paintings abounded, stacked against the walls and mounted on easels.

But the light—the light was the same.

She walked a slow circle.

"What do you think of the portrait?" Lucy's voice made her start. She'd forgotten about Lucy. Also forgotten: the fuss she'd kicked up so Lucy would bring her out here in the first place.

She'd ambushed Lucy that morning in the breakfast room.

*Your aunt raved to me about your latest picture. I won't rest until I see it! I've been starving for art. Starving!*

"Oh." She tried to blink away the blue and red spots, focusing on a canvas at random. "Is that one it? Simply wonderful."

"Why did you want to come here?" Lucy watched her with a disconcerting intensity, her eyes glinting gold in the torrent of sun. "I had a feeling it wasn't to admire *Mouser at Rest*."

She gestured to a small picture on the easel in the center of the room. Lavinia squinted, then wrinkled her nose. Even unfinished, the painting unmistakably depicted Lucy's unappealing cat. She'd captured his all-too-human expression. He looked like an odd old man with fur.

Lucy caught her distaste and laughed. "It won't please the public either. Aunt Marian is partial, to me and to Mr. Malkin."

"The public is partial to Anthony in the buff," muttered Lavinia, glancing about at the other canvases on display. City scenes. But what of the dozen turned to the wall?

"May I?" She walked over and reached for one.

It *was* of Anthony. Far from nude. He sat, in trousers and morning coat, on a green sofa in a black-and-gold room crowded with cabinets and curios. He sat with a black-haired young woman who drooped over the sofa's arm.

Effie.

Suddenly, Lucy was beside her, lifting the picture away. Lavinia's cheeks burned. She'd been too forward, exposing the picture without waiting for permission. But Lucy didn't turn it back to the wall. She set it on an empty easel and stepped back, hands on her hips. She didn't look angry. Or rather, she did. She wore a terrible frown. But Lavinia had come to realize that this was just her face, most of the time. It meant she was thinking.

Would she speak?

Lavinia waited, boiling with questions, about the picture, about the broken look in Effie's eyes.

Effie had gone—abruptly, so far as Lavinia had surmised—to America. The subject had closed as soon as it opened.

Off-limits. Many subjects were off-limits at Weston Hall.

After that first night, Lavinia and Anthony had tiptoed around each other. They talked about Cranbrook—how best to approach him—but they didn't talk about George. Or Lavinia's father. A tacit agreement kept them quiet in those moments when conversation could only bring pain, exacerbate divided loyalties.

All week, quietness had predominated.

Finally, Lucy turned from the easel, a deep line between her brows.

"You remember her too," she said.

*Her.*

She didn't mean Effie.

"The Duchess of Weston?" Lavinia asked it a moment before she remembered that Lucy was now the Duchess of Weston. But Lucy showed no sign of confusion, or offense. She nodded and made a sweeping gesture.

"When she was alive, this was all filled with grapes and figs. Anthony describes it as a miniature Eden."

"Does he?" Lavinia felt again that lump in her throat. Lucy's lips curved up, not down, when she mentioned Anthony.

The tiny, frizzy, flinty woman was in love, in love with a man who loved *her.* Who'd married her.

It took effort to smile, but Lavinia managed.

"Fairyland," she said. "That's how I saw it. There used to be a lemon tree. I remember standing under the lemons." She stepped closer to Lucy, to the long-vanished tree. "One of my earliest memories. And happiest. Right here."

"That's why you wanted to come with me." Lucy tipped her head, adjusting a hairpin with no discernible result. "Not for the art."

Lavinia bit her lip. Denial would be futile. She'd longed for a last glimpse of the site that had launched her dreams. Strangely, vastly changed though it was, it didn't disappoint.

"It was a special place." She smiled a more genuine smile. "I'm glad to see it's still a special place."

"On days like today it's hot enough to cook a ham." Lucy fanned herself. "Anthony is threatening to build me a proper studio." She said it almost shyly, as though she couldn't believe her good fortune.

A rare moment in which her own assessment converged with popular sentiment.

Who in London *could* believe her good fortune? An orphan from Shoreditch. A devilishly handsome duke. It was something from a storybook.

Lavinia's lips flattened, but Lucy's gaze was wandering the glasshouse.

"I'll miss painting here, though," she said with a sigh. "Maybe we'll convert it back to a garden. Grow grapes and figs." She looked at Lavinia. "And lemons."

"You could go to Varnham Nurseries." Lavinia's voice scratched. She herself thought of going to Varnham Nurseries every day. Why? To torture herself? To remind herself that Neal was picnicking in a Cornish cove with Muriel Pendrake?

"Mmm." Lucy made a noncommittal sound as she drifted toward an easel. "There's time for all that. Now, I should finish this homage in oil to an unsung exemplar of feline kind. You can watch me mix paint if you're hard up for entertainment."

"I'm hard up for everything." The sour note in Lavinia's voice was unmistakable. Embarrassed, she dropped onto a marble bench. But the words kept coming. "I'm about to be divorced and déclassé, de-duchessed and utterly destitute."

Lucy stopped and turned slowly back around. "Not *divorced*." Her gaze was penetrating. "He might agree to nullity."

Cranbrook *might* agree, and save his pride in the bargain, if he could impute the nonconsummation to Lavinia's temperament. Or anatomy. So went Anthony's reasoning.

"In that case . . ." Lavinia wrapped her fingers around the edge of her marble seat. "*Defective*, déclassé, de-duchessed, and destitute. A wonderful option."

Annulment was scarcely better than divorce. But either was preferable to staying in her marriage.

"Not wonderful," she amended, bravado fracturing. "Least worst."

Oh dear. Tears. The light was webbing before her eyes. Lucy's scowl doubled, then trebled.

She should stop now. She heard herself rushing on.

"They'll never let me back in, my friends. First, the business with my father. I could barely show my face in London as it was. Now this. Agnes will pity me. Cora will disdain me. Elise will pretend I don't exist."

"Fine friends." Lucy put her hands on her hips. "You can do better." She looked—and sounded—the double of her very elderly, very waspish aunt.

"Better?" Lavinia felt her lips twist. "My friends are the best of the best. Rich, fashionable, eligible, titled—"

"*Terrible*," Lucy offered. "Tripe spouting. Intolerable."

Lavinia laughed aloud, then sighed. "I was intolerable too, I suppose."

"You suppose?" Lucy blinked at her.

Lavinia flushed. She'd been horrible to Lucy. And Lucy had repaid her with kindness.

"I *was* intolerable." Lavinia looked away. "I can see now that it's nonsense. *Society*. I've been telling myself I don't care if I'm shunned forever. Good riddance. But . . ." She hesitated, glanced back. Could Lucy understand the difficulty? "I was so popular for so long. That life is all I know." As soon as she said it, the enormity struck her afresh. What viable alternative existed? "I can't about-face and go to Girton!"

In the resounding silence, she had time to regret her outburst.

"Girton?" Lucy raised an eyebrow. "Golly."

"I'm not saying I'm empty-headed." Lavinia smoothed her skirt, too energetically. More of a stinging slap, really. "I *could* go to Girton."

"Admirable plan." Lucy gave a sharp nod. A moment later Lavinia heard her hairpin ping on the tile.

"Bother." Lucy prodded her pile of uncooperative curls, lifting her feet and peering beneath them.

"It's there, to your left. Oh, never mind, I'll get it." Lavinia bestirred herself from the bench. She had to crouch to feel for the bloody thing between the legs of the easel. When she gripped it with her fingertips, she wiggled backward and bumped into Lucy, who let her own crouch collapse into a sprawl. Surprised, Lavinia went down hard on her bottom.

The tile felt warm, even through her skirts.

Two duchesses, flopped on the floor.

But, such duchesses! Neither of them a proper lady. Lavinia supposed the floor was fitting enough.

"Your Grace." She handed the hairpin to Lucy with a sigh.

"Thank you." Lucy stabbed with the pin, then tucked her legs beneath her, making no effort to rise.

"Cat's-eye view," she remarked pleasantly. "We can all benefit from a change of perspective. So, you're going to Girton."

"I'm *not* going to Girton." Lavinia hugged her knees to her chest. She felt smaller, all the bright air and glass far above them. "I meant I *could* but . . ."

Why go on? It was all too obvious.

"Golly." She muttered it herself.

"What *are* you going to do?" Lucy looked at her sidelong. Her eyes were as sharp as ever, but the situation was utterly disarming. They sat on the ground, for heaven's sake, like girls at play with dolls.

"I don't know." Lavinia buried her chin between her knees. "I wish I *were* a cat."

Lucy giggled. No, Lavinia hadn't misheard. *Giggled.*

"You'd be a lovely cat," she said. "I'd paint a portrait of you to hang alongside *Mouser at Rest.*"

She *was* a peculiar woman. Easy to talk to, once you got the hang of it. Dropped to the ground. Forwent formalities. Said whatever crossed your mind.

Lavinia rather enjoyed her company.

"How nice it must be." She straightened her legs, propped herself on an arm. "To be able to paint."

"It is." Again a sharp nod from Lucy. This time, the hairpins stayed put. "But then, it's nice to do anything well."

Lavinia thought, suddenly, of saffron buns. Knowing how to bake them, and how to eat them. She thought of the way Neal slid plants into his vasculum. Of the way Neal . . .

She sat up straighter. "I suppose that's true."

"What can you do well?" It wasn't a challenge. Lucy was looking at her with curiosity. Convinced that Lavinia had an answer. That she had *something* to say for herself.

And she did. Didn't she?

"I can write," she said, surprising them both. She laughed. But it was true, and not so very ridiculous to claim when speaking to a woman *artist*.

"I can paint pictures with words," she said, chin lifted, a touch of defiance to preempt any disparagement.

Lucy wasn't in the least disparaging. She was *delighted*.

"You could become a columnist!" She leaned forward. "For *The Queen*. Make a name for yourself as an authority on fashion, on theatrical dress. You could interview Aunt Marian."

Lavinia blinked at this remarkable idea. She did know plenty about fashion. And Lucy's aunt had worked in the theater as a costume designer and dressmaker with some of her favorite actresses.

"I'd enjoy that, I think," she said slowly. But Lucy wasn't suggesting she write as a lark. "You mean, as a career."

"Author." Lucy raised her hands, as though framing the word. "You'd have an income, not much of one, in all honesty. But your lifestyle otherwise would be much improved. You'd do your writing in the Reading Room at the British Museum and meet the most interesting people. You'd go to fewer balls, but you'd join the Literary Ladies dining club."

Lavinia felt her heart accelerate. Lucy's bright, freckled face struck her suddenly as otherworldly in its beauty, a beacon of hope.

"I was thinking novels, more so than columns . . ."

"Even better! Do both. Columns *and* novels. Become a literary sensation. It's just the thing." Lucy scrambled to her feet. "All sorted, then." Grinning, she spun on her heel. "If you'll excuse me, I need to sort out this portrait."

Lavinia watched as she began to fiddle over a marble-topped table, opening boxes and lining up jars. Blood was humming in her ears. The caustic scent and the relentless hot light contributed to her giddiness.

She licked her lips. "How do I start?"

"Write!" Lucy glanced over, punctuating the sentence with a flourish of a funny flat little knife. "Write every day. Write a novel."

"Done." Lavinia rose like a shot. Swayed for a moment as the world darkened. She balled her hands into fists. The world returned, brick, steel, glass. Beyond the glasshouse walls, green grass, pink and yellow tulips.

"I have a novel." Or, part one, at any rate. On the last page, the pirate—his ship captured by agents of the tyrannical duke—lay in a dungeon foul, while the duchess schemed to save him from the gallows.

The tyrannical duke was patently recognizable.

As was the duchess.

"Excellent." Lucy smeared white into the purple on her palette, returning her attention to her easel. "Next, you publish it."

Lavinia swallowed. Scandal wouldn't begin to compass the effect. She was *already* a scandal.

She would become a sensation. Notoriety sold books. What did she have to lose?

She needed to make a clean copy of her novel. She needed to present that copy to a publisher.

She could see the way forward, see it as though this sparkling air endowed her with extra powers of perception.

She herself hadn't the faintest notion of the literary profession and its workings. She knew the name of a man who did, though.

And he happened to be an art critic.

"Lucy." Given that the question she was about to ask felt fated, her voice emerged with surprising steadiness. "Have you heard of Alan De'Ath?"

# CHAPTER EIGHTEEN

WALKING ABROAD WASN'T wise, not for a runaway wife. But opportunity didn't wait on wisdom. It had been five days since Lavinia's conversation with Lucy in the glasshouse, three since Alan De'Ath's visit to Weston Hall, two since Anthony's disastrous chat with Cranbrook.

In that time, a few things had become clear.

Annulment was not an option. Cranbrook had exploded at Anthony, accused him of conspiracy and adultery, threatened to storm Weston Hall and retrieve his property by force.

She'd been trying not to think of it. Trying and mostly succeeding, because . . . a literary career *was* an option. Or at least, Mr. De'Ath seemed to think so. He'd taken her manuscript and sent a note the very next evening inviting her to meet him and an *interested party* in Regent's Park on Saturday afternoon. She'd rather think about that, her sensational second life as a woman of letters.

When Saturday came around, she hesitated only briefly over her decision. Anthony might have tried to forbid the venture. His encounter with Cranbrook had left him tight-jawed and furious, and inclined to think her some kind of Helen, and Weston Hall some kind of Troy under siege. But, as luck would have it, he'd left the house early. Off to mastermind some act of Parliament with a bunch of rowdies from the House of Commons. The hotheaded, irreverent boy Lavinia remembered now seemed to relish statecraft. And, to her shock, by all accounts, he was proving an effective statesman.

Everyone trusted the lord without drawers.

Lucy, who'd spent the morning pacing the halls in an absolute snit about the latest disparaging review racked up by her friend Gwen Burgess, took no convincing at all. She stomped after Lavinia and hurled herself into the carriage.

Traffic crawled all the way to the park. As soon as they'd creeped to a stop at the southern end, Lavinia threw open the door, bolting past the startled footman. By the water-lily house, she forced herself to pause so Lucy could catch up. They were late. She prayed to God they weren't *too* late.

In a few strides, she outstripped Lucy again. She reached the conservatory and surveyed the circular garden, rings within rings. Couples strolled among the roses. A child wailed in his nurse's arms.

"Miss Laliberté."

*Hallelujah.* She turned.

Alan De'Ath sat on a bench in the shade of a mulberry tree. As she approached, he rose, snapping shut a small book.

"Have you been waiting long?" she asked. Stupid question. Her eyes fell to the book in his hand. He'd been waiting long enough to begin reading . . . She squinted. Something in Greek. She felt her spirits sink. Greek was worse than Latin. What must a man of his learning think of her novel?

"The minutes flew by." He dropped the book into a pocket and removed his spectacles, rubbing the lenses on his sleeve. Somehow, his gaze seemed sharper without them.

"By contrast, each minute in the carriage dragged for eternity." She gave a bright smile. "We went scarcely one mile, but it felt like a trip to China."

Her smile faltered. *China.* What an unfortunate figure of speech.

She was nervous enough without reminding herself how inadequate she was to the flora, fauna, and language of China.

"Well." She tried to recover, as Lucy finally reached them. "We're here now!"

"Tout à fait." There was only a hint of mockery in his voice.

At Weston Hall, he'd spoken with her exclusively in French until Lucy had broken in, scowling over her teacup. *She's not from France. It's a pen name.*

To which Mr. De'Ath had responded, with faux surprise: *Ah, un nom de plume. But, Miss Laliberté, my compliments on your accent.*

Her accent was decent.

His was downright Napoleonic.

Several times, as he and Lucy discussed art matters, she'd caught herself staring at him. He was so different from Neal, she could scarcely believe in their fabled friendship. He looked ten years older at least, bespectacled and bewhiskered, dressed in a plum-colored jacket and checked pantaloons. A wizened intellectual from some earlier decade.

Now that she saw him standing in the full light of day, she revised her opinion. *Wizened* did not apply. Formal, yes. Even priggish. Everything he wore was crisp and fine and stridently old-fashioned.

But he stood over six feet tall, equipped with shoulders broad enough to jam in doorways.

Scholarly pursuits didn't work such miracles on a man's physique. Was it all the swimming?

"I enjoyed your novel," he said. "A fine example of the genre. Transporting, actually. All those images of the West Country and the billowing Celtic Sea." His smile became brilliant. "It made me think I should take up an old friend of mine on his invitation to visit him in Cornwall."

More color must be flooding her cheeks. At the praise. At the mention of the old friend in Cornwall. She had a connection to Neal in Alan De'Ath. She could tell him—right now—that she knew the friend he spoke of. But to what purpose?

Someday—next year or the year after or the year after that—she might surrender to impulse and go to the Varnham Nurseries in London, or even the Varnham Nurseries in Truro, try to surprise Neal at work, beg a walk, an hour of conversation, for friendship's sake. He wouldn't refuse. He was so bloody decent. He'd have bright-haired children by then, and a house filled with dinosaur bones and lilies, and Muriel, like Lucy, would be kind to her if she came barging in, far kinder than Lavinia herself would be if the situation were reversed. Enough time would have passed that it wouldn't hurt, looking on from the outside, standing beyond that warm circle of regard, of love.

*Lie.* It would hurt like hot knives. She would have to fight the impulse with every fiber of her being. Now, with Mr. De'Ath, and later. She would have to stay vigilant.

"Thank you." Her voice was hoarse. The English grated in her throat far more than the French. "And thank you for trying to help me publish it."

"I do have a syndicator in mind." Mr. De'Ath brushed at one of his snow-white cuffs and the gold cuff link glittered.

"The *interested party* you mentioned?" She looked away, scanned the garden, the summer crowds drifting around the rings of roses and down the avenues of ornamental beds. "Will we be interrupting his family outing?"

Bankers did business in banks. Lawyers did business in law offices. But it seemed the literati did business everywhere. Why not, given that their business was interpreting the human condition?

Mr. De'Ath spoke smoothly. "He specializes in selling serial rights of novels to illustrated papers."

"Illustrations?" Lucy interjected. "The novel—isn't it a maritime romance?" She didn't wait for Lavinia's answer but addressed Mr. De'Ath. "You *have* seen Gwen's marine sketches. She displayed a few of them at the salon in March. You were taken with them."

"The studies of the river in pen and ink? I was indeed." Mr. De'Ath's eyes narrowed as he reflected. "Marine views, I believe she called them."

"She'd make the novel come alive! And illustrating it will raise her spirits." Lucy rose on tiptoe, most likely unaware, in her enthusiasm, that she was illustrating her own point. "I know she must be *dashed* by that review. You should go by her studio . . ."

Lavinia ceased to follow the flow of conversation. Gwen Burgess again. Finally, she cleared her throat. Wasn't *her* career the point of this excursion? She'd be better off if she didn't lollygag interminably in broad daylight. Sooner or later, someone who knew her was bound to wander by.

Or worse, someone Cranbrook had paid to hunt her down.

"This syndicator," she interrupted. "He's here? Do you plan to introduce me?"

"I do plan to introduce you. But first . . ." He swung his cane, pointing it at a building on the other side of the garden's inner ring, a humble affair in comparison with the massive conservatory, which towered in the foreground, all mortared brick, iron, and glass.

Lucy screwed up her face. "I can't countenance a lecture in my near future. Not today."

"I'd wager the lecture has concluded." Mr. De'Ath began to walk through the trees, setting a leisurely pace. "But there's work to be done on the libretto."

Lucy and Lavinia looked at each other, and Lucy shook her head.

"Don't ask me." She sighed, then set off after him. A moment later, Lavinia followed.

# CHAPTER NINETEEN

THE QUESTIONS AND comments started up the instant the applause died down. Muriel leaned on the lectern, beaming, as plump, dyspeptic Professor Murray—always popping up in lecture halls like a poison mushroom—delivered uncharacteristic praise from the front row.

Neal's knees began to vibrate as a pharmaceutical student stood and quizzed her about the medicinal properties of Chinese sage. Then Winston Reeves, a onetime colleague of Neal's father, took the floor. Reeves believed women incapable of rigorous scientific investigation; Neal's mother had once tossed him out of a faculty dinner by the ear.

"The ferns you described, the ones growing in the groves by the waterfall in Penang. They should be studied by experts. I hope you carried back specimens for the scientific community. I know a pteridologist who—"

"I did. I sent specimens to Kew." Muriel cut him off, nodding with enthusiasm. "In fact, I'm preparing a paper on their morphological features for the *Magazine of Botany*, with a focus on the reproductive structures. This species has helped me understand more fully the alternation of the spore-bearing and the sexual generations."

At the word *sexual* a few gasps and guffaws sounded. Reeves opened his mouth wider. Muriel continued smiling. "If you give me your direction, I'll see to it that a copy of the magazine makes its way to you."

Her air of indulgence chafed Reeve's vanity *visibly*. Neal could see him twitching.

How his mother would cackle.

"Ah," said Muriel. "I see a hand in the back."

The questions continued.

Neal felt an elbow in his side and glanced over at Simon Hitchens, who was giving him a significant look from the neighboring chair. He took his meaning and sighed.

Yes, Muriel was magnificent.

He didn't want to marry her, that was all.

Instead of communicating this directly, he'd been avoiding her. He'd like to have confided in Alan, but Alan had been avoiding *him*, or else had gotten caught up in his new writing project. He hadn't even come to the lecture.

As the questions tapered off and the audience disaggregated into chattering cliques, Neal rose and drifted forward, intending to offer Muriel his congratulations. Others had had the same idea. He joined the disorderly queue and stood rocking on his heels, hands in his pockets.

Muriel was gesturing broadly as she spoke to a round, whiskery man dressed in clashing plaids. Her former employer, and Varnham's biggest competitor, Robert Edevane. Neal looked away and saw Alan making his way down the side of the room. He went to meet him, frowning.

"I saved you a seat." He drilled his pointer finger into Alan's chest. "Which meant I ended up sandwiched between Hitchens and Bidmead, thank you very much."

"Bidmead turned up, did he?" Alan looked down his nose at Neal's finger. "I told Otis to haul him along, but you can never be completely sure of other people. They're so often unreliable."

Neal lowered his hand, teeth gritted. Of course, Alan had immediately pinpointed his irritation and decided to needle him.

"A life lesson for the ages," he grated. "But let me rely on you for a bloody minute, please. I've made a mess of, well, everything, and the situation with Muriel has—"

"Hold that thought." Alan turned from him to signal—without apparent success—to someone across the room. He shrugged and glanced back at Neal, a strange light in his eyes. "I shall return instanter." Before he angled himself into the crowd, he looked over his shoulder. "Don't run off."

"Don't boss," Neal retorted, hating his own petulance. He might have been ten years old and quarreling with his brother Jory. He struck out blindly toward the opposite corner of the room. Suddenly, he itched to escape. He couldn't stand another minute in the lecture hall, much less a dinner at the Criterion: Muriel, hoodwinked and happy; Alan and Bidmead, wherever he'd gotten to, crossing swords in a choreographed dance; Hitchens, the self-satisfied matchmaker, droning learnedly about iguanodons without one-tenth of Lavinia's intuitive genius.

No, he'd abscond at once. Write Muriel a letter explaining everything. Cowardly. But apropos. Their relationship had been, first and foremost, a correspondence.

He was heading toward the door when Muriel intercepted him. "Neal! You're not stealing away?"

He flinched, then recovered, clumsily. "What? No. No, wouldn't dream of it. Wonderful talk." He *had* found the talk wonderful. But as he continued to extol her eloquence and command as a lecturer, he could hear each phrase strike a false note. Damn his guilty conscience. He added insult to injury. But Muriel was glowing, ablaze with her triumph, insensible to his awkward demeanor. She wasn't one to be insulted or injured easily; she'd proven that several times over.

But he *would* hurt her in the end, when he dashed her hopes, revealed that he'd misled himself and misled her in the bargain.

The thought put a foul taste in his mouth.

"Never mind all that. I told him!" She almost sang the words. "I told Robert!"

"Robert?"

"Robert Edevane, of course." She beamed.

The room, overcrowded, overheated, felt smaller. The walls pressed in around him. Everyone seemed to be casting sidelong glances, smirking. The din of conversation dipped. Everyone was listening. His throat worked. *Dear God.*

"*Told* Mr. Edevane?" He spoke in a whisper. Damn his guilty conscience and double damn his consequent inaction. He'd let the situation lie fallow, and now new trouble had cropped up.

"I owed it to him." She didn't whisper. If anything, she spoke louder, to make up for his lowered volume. "He couldn't find out from someone else. After Esmé died . . ." She faltered briefly, the slightest hitch.

"There were many people who didn't consider that *I* was a competent general observer, plant collector, and botanist in my own right. Esmé and I had had offers of funding for future expeditions from Kew, from the Geographical Society, a half dozen institutions. When I went back to them, a widow, not one agreed to fund me. China is too perilous." She snorted. "No matter I'd spent six years there. Robert rehired me. He made me the *director* of an expedition. He gave me back my confidence in myself. Enough confidence that I can see I've outgrown his nursery. So yes, of course, I told him."

He stared at her. "But surely it's too soon. We need to talk more, or not *talk*. I'd thought . . ." He pressed his thumb hard into his eyebrow. "I'd thought to put something in writing."

His skin crawled, self-loathing rippling over him. Here he was, delaying. But what was the alternative? Reject her *now*? *Here*? Before an audience of colleagues and idle gentlefolk? If he waited, and wrote, she would receive his letter in private, where she could weep, or rail, or quietly absorb the blow, without interference.

But . . . who might she tell in the interim? He had to contain the damage, or the announcement would travel from one end of London to the other. Their wedding date might be printed before he'd revealed the engagement was inadvertent, a colossal misunderstanding. He continued staring.

"Writing? I expect something in writing, that goes without saying. I know how it works. I've done this before, as you well know." Her eyes narrowed with sudden shrewdness, and her lips made a firm line. Then she smiled. "There's Mr. Hewett. I have to tell him too."

She grabbed his hand and squeezed it in farewell, but he held on. He'd been left no choice.

"Muriel."

"Yes?" She looked at him, and all her virtues were written plainly across her countenance. Intelligence. Humor. Honesty.

She deserved honesty from him.

"I can't marry you."

She inclined her head, uncomprehending. She hadn't heard. He cleared his throat, raised his voice.

"I cannot marry you." He looked up toward the ceiling, wishing for a lightning strike. Then he straightened his head, met her gaze. She'd heard him. Her eyes grew wider by the moment.

"I'm proud to know you." He tightened his grip on her hand. "You possess a remarkable mind. And the greatest personal charm. You are . . ."

Her face was contorting. She would weep. Rail. What a wretch he was.

"I don't expect you to forgive me," he said. "I never meant to hurt you. I take full responsibility for . . ."

She drew in her breath, made a choked sound. He braced himself, brain teeming with curses. Hanging was too good for him. She kept choking, face flushed.

"Can't marry me?" She sputtered, blinking rapidly. Tears stood in her eyes.

He became aware again of the crowd. Heads had turned their way.

"No," he said desperately. "But please believe . . . if things had gone differently . . . But they didn't, and I . . . No. I'm sorry. I can't. I hope . . ."

"Ah! A mortal wound! I shall never recover," Muriel gasped. She was most undeniably convulsed . . . with laughter.

"I don't understand." He furrowed his brow, helplessly, maddeningly aware that the joke was on him, although he didn't yet see its contours.

"Neal, you possess great personal charm yourself." Muriel tried to still her trembling lips. "I hold you in the highest possible esteem. But I have absolutely no intention of marrying you, or anyone else. What sense would that make, when I'm bound for China?"

He released his breath. This whole time she'd meant . . .

"*Yes*," he said. "You answered *yes*."

He broke off. She'd answered *yes* to the question that had inaugurated their correspondence. Not to the question he'd never posed, the one that had seemed to him so obvious that it had become an inevitability, a trap.

Her smile was wry as she waited for him to grope his way forward.

"You're coming on with Varnham? You want the contract for the expedition to Sichuan? The one you turned down?"

She nodded. "I've had a change of heart. Going to Cornwall helped me remember how much I love being in the field. And how good it feels to get away from London."

How immensely, irrefutably compatible they were.

How utterly, absolutely *not* engaged to be married.

Humiliation, elation, chagrin—they came in waves.

Her smile gentled as she searched his face. "Getting to know you *has* been a part of it," she said. "I admire your vision for Varnham. I want to be a part of that enterprise."

Suddenly, she had to smother more laughter. "But you . . ." She squeezed his hand. "You imagined somehow you'd stumbled into a betrothment. Oh, my poor boy. You could have said something. But you worried I was too far gone in my swoon."

Her laughter rang out.

He felt as though he *had* been struck by lightning. A bolt of pure electricity couldn't make his face feel hotter. The tops of his ears were blistering.

"How did you even think it?" She was looking at him with curiosity, amusement, exasperation, and affection all mingled together. A sisterly look.

He tried to laugh, managed a puff of air.

She grasped his other hand, lifted both of them.

"Buck up," she said. "Your cheeriness is your chief appeal. Maudlin ill becomes you. Maybe you need a change of scene as well. Back to Brazil?"

He cleared his throat. "Cornwall will do."

A dark-haired, red-bearded man walked briskly past on the way to the door. Muriel twisted to watch his progress. "That's Mr. Hewett. I should . . ."

"By all means." He dropped her hands, and she was off like a shot. He stuffed his hands into his pockets, lifted his shoulders. Tried to look as though he hadn't just played the buffoon in front of God knew who. Idiotically, he pursed his lips, ready to whistle, like a schoolboy.

*Don't mind me.*

With a great show of casualness, he slouched in the other direction. That was when he saw her.

Lavinia.

She stood against the wall, pale hair swept back. Her face looked small and naked.

He straightened in surprise, his whole body flooding with awareness. He recognized the tilt of her head, the set of her shoulders. The haughty posture of the expert snob. He'd seen her hold herself just so to keep from shaking with fatigue. To keep from bowing under the weight of emotional burdens she'd never shared. She was so stubborn, so bloody prideful.

He was angry that she'd fled from him. Angry that she'd decided, in the end, that he was no different from the other men who'd hurt her. Same species, same variety. Deserving of nothing more from her than a hastily scrawled line.

He hadn't realized he was angry until now, when he felt it, hot within him.

Or was it hunger?

He wanted to put his mouth *there*, on her exposed neck, wanted to feel her pulse between his teeth as her fingertips dug into his skin.

Her eyes were locked on his. Only a few yards' distance between them. A smattering of lecturegoers.

She lifted her chin as he strode toward her. She used her beauty as a shield. He would have her defenseless, without armor, and show her how he could hold her precious and keep her safe. Together, they would strip down to the pith.

A man detached himself from the wall beside her, put his lips by her ear. Circled her tightly with his arm. Suddenly, they were pressed close, turning, walking away.

Neal turned too, turned before he could think. His blood roared.

She had attended the lecture with her husband.

Why? Why would she do such a thing? Hadn't she guessed he'd be in the audience? Or did she want to taunt him? Want to taunt her husband?

London thrived on these brutal little games.

He did not.

He bowled right between a pair of lanky students and continued, head down, heart thudding. A man moved directly into his path, a man whose brightly stripped cotton twill trousers made Neal snarl with recognition. His head shot up. Alan. Alan, with his arms crossed, walking stick threaded through them. He wore an expression of peculiar expectancy.

The Machiavellian fiend. Somehow, he was behind all of it. He was like a colorful spider, a peacock spider from New South Wales, delighting in casting his web, in observing his prey as they squirmed.

"How?" Neal stepped until they stood toe-to-toe.

Alan didn't bother to demur. Or to apologize.

"She came to me," he said, and shook his head, scolding. "You didn't mention she was a *littérateuse*."

Neal could only grunt. He should never have mentioned *anything*.

"Regardless." Alan smiled. "She called herself Miss Laliberté, but her Christian name and aura of mystery connected her at once in my mind with the false Mrs. Pendrake. Then I read her novel, which, I must say, made me blush, and that was that."

"Hogwash. When you go to the devil, he'll be the one blushing." Neal's throat felt tight. Memories were unfurling, embowering him once again in that fragrant green riverine world. He heard Lavinia's cry at the sight of the ship, saw her bedded in moss in the clearing, skin drinking the sunlight, felt his lips sliding on the silk of her, those lovely limbs twining around him.

Had she written of *that*?

"*You* are blushing," said Alan softly, and Neal bit the inside of his cheek.

"Careful, or I'll do more than blush." His voice emerged low and furious. "Who is she really?"

Alan shook his head. "I want to leave you something to work out on your own. I contented myself with engineering the encounter."

"Out of bloodless curiosity." Neal backed away from Alan in disgust. "And for the benefit of your dear friend Bidmead, so he can write a dirty verse about it."

"And for your benefit." Alan tutted. "I detected signs of pining. Frequent sighs. A misty gaze fixed on the middle distance. A slackening of the sidestroke and general waning of the sporting spirit. You were, quite frankly, in a lovesick state."

"Funny diagnosis from a man without a heart."

"Come, Neal, don't be an ingrate." He had the nerve to sound irritated. "I delivered to you the object of your desire."

Neal wanted to scream, took a deep breath.

"Indeed," he said. "Delivered her in front of Muriel, Bidmead, Hitchens, yourself—"

"Dramatis personae," murmured Alan, shrugging.

Neal's voice was a growl as he kept on. "—my foremost competitor, a handful of my father's fustiest colleagues, two dozen medical students, some Society grande dames, and last but not least, her bloody husband."

Alan started. "Husband?"

Neal's hands were fisted. "I suppose I was meant to punch him for the sake of performance."

Before Alan could respond, a small woman with hair like a Cornish hayrick burst through the crowd.

"Have you seen Lavinia?" She addressed Alan breathlessly. "I've circled the whole room."

Alan indicated Neal with his walking stick. "He has. Neal Traymayne. Lucy Coover. Or that's how she's known to the *haute bohème*. In polite company: the Duchess of Weston."

The diminutive duchess scowled at Alan before turning her fierce gaze on Neal. "Where did you see her?"

*Who is she to you?* Neal wanted to ask. Or better: *Who is she?*

Instead, he bowed. "Over there. Your Grace. With her husband."

Alan shook his head. "Would you believe me if I told you his presence was not my doing?"

"Would you believe me if I told you that I'm not interested in splitting hairs?" Neal looked from Alan to the duchess. She'd gone white, which made her face appear even more densely freckled. Cinnamon sprinkled on milk.

"Husband?" she echoed.

"Tall, blond." Neal resisted the urge to accumulate adjectives. Unworthy. Unappreciative. Unfaithful.

Lavinia had chosen to go back to him, and she seemed content to stay with him. It was none of his business.

"Try shriveled, gray, and liver spotted." The duchess picked up her skirts. She was still deadly pale. But her eyes shone with determination. "He must have sent a hireling. Well, I can deal with that." She bolted for the door.

Without a word, Neal gave chase. The duchess was propelled by some great emotion, and untroubled by propriety, but she was also short-legged and hindered by heavy skirts. Neal caught up to her easily and flanked her as she exited the building. She was swearing like a barmaid in an accent no one would ever describe as *aristocratic*.

At first, the sun hurt Neal's eyes and washed out the scene before him, so that the visitors to the Royal Botanic Society gardens moved like pastel shadows against a background of pale green. Then he focused, gaze sweeping from the observatory to the arboretum.

Lavinia and the tall blond man were nowhere to be seen.

The duchess confirmed this at the same moment he did.

"I would have bribed him." She groaned as she turned off the promenade, cutting across the corner of the rose garden. "I brought a *wad* of money in my skirt for just this eventuality. Dammit. Damn *him*, for a filthy, whoreson *villain*."

"That blond man . . ." Neal was just a step behind her, but his mind was still lagging, struggling to incorporate the new facts.

"He's a no-account minion," the duchess snapped. "I'm damning Lavinia's husband. She's been running from him since the very day they married. And now he's got her back. The *beast*. Dammit, dammit."

She started to trot, weaving around the statues. "We shouldn't have gone out in the first place. We knew he had his bloody police detectives crawling all about."

They reached the line of carriages, a black cavalcade stretching down the street.

"I need to get home." The duchess had begun muttering to herself. "I need to tell Anthony."

Neal had a strange, spinning sensation. It reminded him of when he and Jenni would twirl in the field until the horizon rushed toward them and the ground flew up beneath their feet.

The world made no sense. He understood less than he had before, about Lavinia, about her husband, about how her story of heartbreak squared with the reality.

But one thing was certain. She was in danger.

That knowledge leveled everything.

The duchess was giving orders to the coachman when he broke in.

"Forget this Anthony." He met the duchess's eyes. Long eyes. Their gaze was disquietingly sharp.

She wasn't a woman to take commands, from anyone.

"You said Lavinia's husband is a beast." His voice rasped. "If he hurts her . . . If we don't intercede in time . . ."

He'd never experienced such a violent fury. It burned inside him. His very teeth felt like coals in his mouth.

"We go there first," he said. "We stop him."

The duchess stared at him, hands on her hips. She nodded and turned back to the coachman. A moment later, she was springing into the carriage, calling over her shoulder.

"Hurry, then."

# CHAPTER TWENTY

THERE WAS NO reasoning with Granite-face and Tweed, the thugs. Granite-face had forced her from the lecture hall, and Tweed had helped pen her in the carriage. Tears had no effect. By the time they'd bundled her into Harcott House and locked her in the yellow sitting room, Lavinia's eyes were dry. She felt calm. Even as she screamed and pounded the door. It might have looked and sounded like hysteria, but she knew the difference. Part of her remained cold and untouched, calculating.

She wanted her mother to hear. She wanted to give her mother one last chance to disappoint her.

Or to surprise her.

To fly to her rescue.

After a time, she stepped back from the door and stood, neither disappointed nor surprised. If the past year had taught her anything at all, it was to surrender expectations. She'd learned her lesson at last.

Lucy's parents were dead, and hers were living. But she'd become an orphan too, albeit of a different stripe.

When the key turned in the lock, she didn't move, simply watched the door swing open, steeling herself.

Not Cranbrook.

The silhouette was feminine.

She broke in an instant, the word borne from her throat on a sob. *"Maman."*

"She's not here." Nan didn't enter the room. She held the door and beckoned. "Quick. He packed off the filth from his study, which means he'll be down any moment."

The pretty maid twisted to look over her shoulder, and Lavinia saw a flash of her flushed face, all rebellious agitation.

It was to be the chit to the rescue, then.

Lavinia was on her heels out the door, but the girl turned sharply, heading deeper into the house. Away from the front entrance.

Sensible move. If discovered aiding Lavinia's flight, she risked her position, her reference, perhaps more.

Lavinia caught her hand, which was fisted around the house-keeper's heavy key ring, stilling its jingle. She pressed it, too tightly, and felt Nan's thin fingers grind on the metal.

"Thank you," she said.

"He's a pig." Nan's round blue eyes bored into hers. They brimmed with indignation. Lavinia bit her lip. Cranbrook had dared to pinch and fondle *her*, a darling of the ton.

What abuses did he mete out to his maids?

She'd been focused on herself, her own woes. She hadn't considered that Nan was living a kind of hell in Cranbrook's service. That they might make a common cause.

"Old goat." Lavinia nodded her understanding. "That's what I call him."

For a moment, a smile flickered on Nan's lips. Then she tugged away her hand, tossed her head.

"Pig," she insisted. "I rather like goats. *Hurry.*"

"I won't forget this," Lavinia said hoarsely. It was the only promise she could make. She could remember, bear witness. Beyond that, she had no power.

Nan shot down the hall.

Lavinia spun and started in the opposite direction.

She was crossing the entrance hall when something made her stop short. A peculiar exhaustion. She was too tired to cry. And dear God, she was too tired to run. She'd done so much of both.

In her novel, her duchess had fled from her vile husband, but then she'd returned with a vengeance, plundering his estate, demanding recompense.

Lavinia whirled at the door and arrowed back into the house, charged up the marble staircase.

She had been waiting *years* to tell Cranbrook what she thought of him. That night he groped her under the table, she'd bitten her tongue because Papa wanted him for a client. That night he pressed against her in the library at the Sambourns' ball, she'd swallowed her cry because she wasn't meant to be in the library in the first place. She'd been waiting on George, who'd arranged the little tryst . . . and then neglected to appear.

All through the weeks of her engagement, she'd endured Cranbrook's foul kisses and roaming hands. On the train to Bodmin, she'd let him chafe her leg and take sick pleasure in her fear and pain. All because his money and his title were meant to save them, save her, her mother, her father.

To hell with them. To hell with all of it. She was saving herself now.

Her stomach kicked inside her as she turned down the hall. She passed doors shut tight in their frames, then reached a door that stood slightly open. The air in Cranbrook's study was close. It stank of him. Cologne. Whiskey. Animal excitement. Rotting flowers. Her nostrils flared.

He was an obscenity.

She hovered on the threshold. The study was dim, the curtains drawn. Her courage failed her. She couldn't take another step forward, couldn't keep her eyes trained across the room to where he sat behind his desk. But she could still speak. She had that power, at least.

"Goat." She hurled the word. "*Pig.*" Her heart pounded, and she swallowed bile. "You make me *ill.*" She found she could step into the room, after all. She was still staring at the carpet. Even in the gloom, she could tell it was red, red as roses. Strawberry red.

"You made me make *myself* ill, just so I could get away from you." She drew a deep breath. "Do you know what I was doing, instead of honeymooning with you in Fowey? I was gamboling by the sea with a handsome gardener." She shut her eyes—that feeling of being free, yet being held—it would sustain her now. "I didn't just abandon you," she said, louder now. "I gloried in my *adulterous* abandonment. You can divorce me, or not. I don't need the bloody High Court to tell me I'm not your property. I'm telling *you.* It's over. If you touch me ever again, if you touch Nan ever again, if you touch any woman, *ever,* I'll . . ." She made her shaking hands into fists. What? What would she do? Attack him with a cutlass?

She stepped forward, chest heaving.

"I *swear*," she said, and fumbled. "I swear that I'll . . ." She took another step as more words clogged her throat. She felt strangled by them. But maybe it didn't matter what she said. What mattered was her resolve, her fearlessness, her *power.* She forced herself to lift her chin, to stare straight at him.

She shuddered.

Cranbrook sat in his chair behind his desk, yes, but he sat slumped at an odd angle. His eyes gleamed unevenly, one slitted, the other bulging. His teeth showed in a yellow wedge.

His face was livid, his cheeks sunken.

Her shudder—it prolonged. Intensified. She was shaking, but she edged closer. Blood roared in her ears.

He didn't move. He didn't breathe. How long had he been like that? How soon after Granite-face and Tweed departed had it happened?

He'd suffered a fit, an attack.

She stood utterly still.

There was no way she could bring herself to reach out, press her fingers to his neck, or his wrist.

She stared at his hand, already waxen in appearance, fingers curled. It lay atop his desk. A bottle stood nearby. She could read the signature on the note propped against it. *Browning.*

That despicable tonic. For a cockstand, Browning had said.

Cranbrook had planned to drink his fill. To strut down to the sitting room. To make his *mark.*

Not today. Never again.

She backed up, slowly, feeling behind her. When she'd eased out of the room, she walked down the hall, not toward the front staircase, toward the back stairs.

The house was silent.

Maybe the staff had been taught to absent themselves once a woman started screaming.

Her chest heaved and heaved again as she descended to the ground floor, as she let herself out one of the doors in the south wing of the house. Without thinking, she let her feet propel her forward, into the garden. She needed to be surrounded by whatever was green and living.

The warmth of day washed over her. Unbelievable that the sun still shone. That birds still sang.

She was walking, and suddenly, she couldn't move. The enormity of what had happened overloaded her. It was as though her body had gone blank. She sank down onto a bench. She stared at Harcott House, the south facade. There was a trellis between the balconies, vines spilling over the diamonds of latticework.

Someone was climbing it. Not *someone.*

*Neal.*

She bolted upright. He was climbing easily, quickly, and then he was reaching out, catching the bottom edge of the balcony with his fingers, levering up his body in one smooth motion. One foot planted, and he was launched over the rail and out of sight.

# CHAPTER TWENTY-ONE

Now SHE COULD run. Running toward felt different from running away.

"Neal!" The shout tore from her. And he heard. Within the moment, he'd reappeared on the balcony and then he was clambering down, dropping the last few feet to the ground. She reached him, threw her arms around his neck, and pulled his head down close to hers. She needed to see him, to know that he was really there.

Tousled hair. Bumpy nose. Fringed brown eyes, the pair she saw every night when she shut hers to sleep.

He lay a finger on her cheek, the gesture releasing something deep inside her. She sagged with the sweetness of it.

"Are you all right?" He spoke steadily, to steady *her*. She realized it as she took in his expression. He was far from calm. There was murder in his eyes. "Did Cranbrook—"

"He's dead." Her own voice shook but didn't break. "An attack, I think. I found him in the study." She swallowed. "You came to find me."

He didn't speak. He simply gathered her to him, leaning into the shadow of the house, into the trellis itself, cool vines curling around them. For a long moment, she burrowed into his shoulder, savoring his solidity, breathing in his heathery scent, which reminded her of everything wild and free.

When she stepped out of his arms, it would break, the circle of protection. She'd have to face the world as it was.

She drew back, hands folded on her stomach, which clenched instantly. She looked up at Harcott House and felt dizzied, the edges of her vision going black.

"I can't go back in there." She aimed for a calm tone, but her voice shrilled. She drew a deep breath.

"Not yet," she amended. The coming days would be tense and hectic. Cranbrook's adult sons and daughters would gather, as would his friends and hangers-on. All of the people who'd attended the ill-fated wedding would congregate gleefully for the funeral.

Perhaps word would leak out, about her flight, her involuntary return. Speculations would circulate regarding the circumstances of Cranbrook's death. A new round of rumors, albeit different from the one she'd anticipated. Everything was different.

She couldn't imagine what it all would mean.

"Not yet," she repeated, and turned to Neal. He nodded and extended his hand. "Come along, then."

Their fingers intertwined. She sucked in her breath. She'd missed the feel of his warm, broad hand. His calluses had been roughened by his recent climb.

"You're lucky that trellis was well-anchored." She gave him a weak smile. "Or you might have broken your neck."

"I knew the trellis was stout. But I *am* glad we planted ivy." His smile strengthened hers. "It would have been a brutal climb if we'd planted rose."

She looked her question.

"Varnham designed the original gardens," he said. "And we've handled the major plantings and renovations since."

He was guiding her toward the privets.

"The south wall is all wisteria. Blooming. That was a treat."

She looked toward the back of the garden, enclosed by a high wall bunched with pale purple flowers. "You climbed the wall?"

"Didn't expect I'd receive much welcome at the front door."

She shook her head. "But how did you know to come here in the first place?"

"The duchess." Neal turned them down one green lane, then another. Lavinia didn't speak.

"Of Weston." He hesitated. "You are also a duchess."

"A dowager." Hysterical laughter bubbled up. She was *widowed*. Good God. Dizzy, she pressed closer to his side. "Where is she?"

"We split up. She did try the front door."

They must have missed each other, barely. Lavinia closed her eyes, then opened them wide. The bushes that enclosed them seemed tame after the blooming chaos of those rock-filled Cornish hedges. Nonetheless, it felt familiar. Walking with him amid so much green.

Familiar and strange.

He wore town clothes, dark jacket and trousers, well fitted to his muscular form. Any woman would notice the attractions of his figure, his bluntly handsome face.

He wasn't her discovery, her humble Cornish gardener. He was a man with wealth and social ease. A man who moved between town and country. A man with choices.

He'd chosen Muriel Pendrake.

She'd best not lose sight of that essential fact.

"Did she tell you I was once engaged to her husband?" She forced herself to pull away, to drop his arm. "That I was rich and spoiled and *intolerable* and that the money I took for granted was, by and large, robbed from his family? That the papa I loved wasn't who I thought he was?"

Lavinia hadn't realized she'd accelerated. She had to stop, wait for him to catch up. He came prowling toward her, slow and thoughtful.

"She said you were her friend." His steady gaze arrested her. Then his mouth tightened. "She said your husband was a beast. And a few other things."

Her breath whooshed out. "I'll tell you, then. I was born Lavinia Yardley. My father lives at Holloway Prison. My mother and I live . . ."

Where? What came next? She felt a flicker of panic and laughed again. And still he looked at her steadily.

"Tomas mentioned my father. Do you remember? The thieving architect? All true, by the way. The stories. Sometimes the rumormongers get it right." She curtseyed. "That's me. So wonderful to meet you."

His hands had slid into his pockets. He shook his head, a troubled line between his brows.

"I won't bow. Forgive my lack of courtesy. But we're already acquainted." His eyes hooded. "*Well* acquainted."

Her heart caught in her chest. She made herself smile.

"We are, and we aren't. In my native habitat, I'm a beribboned, *befeathered* little creature. The belle of the ball. Made in the same mold as your Elizabeth Davenport." Ridiculous, to hazard a guess, at this juncture, as to the identity of his former fiancée, but she couldn't help herself.

He acknowledged her attempt with a small movement, less than a shrug.

"I would never win over your mother." *Hush.* She knew better than this. Self-flagellation was but the flipside of self-indulgence. He'd said it, and she agreed. "But then again, I never impressed my own." She winced. So much for heeding him, or her inner voice. No stopping now.

"She wanted me to marry Cranbrook, and I did it. For her sake, and my father's." Shame bowed her head. "And because I didn't know what else to do. I was frightened by our poverty. I thought, in some ways, the marriage might be agreeable."

No one had forced her to make those vows. She could have been courageous. Legendary. Spit in Cranbrook's eye. Dared to pursue a journalistic career.

*I won't be your duchess. I'm off to work for* The Queen.

"You faced an impossible choice."

That one sentence unbalanced her. She looked up. Understanding, not judgment. That was what he offered.

"Your father's crimes aren't yours," he said, and she gave her head a disbelieving shake.

"I benefited from them."

"You paid for them, too." His eyes held hers. Funny, to feel *cradled* by someone's eyes. She'd always felt safer when she was with him. She realized she felt braver, too, worthier, even now that she'd stopped dissembling.

He knew everything. Or, nearly everything.

"The man I described to you, who I said betrayed me—it wasn't Cranbrook."

"No," he murmured. Of course he'd put certain things together. "I presume . . ." He didn't want to hurt her. That was why he spoke so delicately. "It was the Duke of Weston."

He made the obvious mistake. A cloud dimmed the light, darkened his eyes, blued the green hedges. She sighed.

"He would have been. He was the elder son."

She'd said enough to set up the tragedy. Neal's face turned grim.

"We did go to France together." She watched a shadow move over the grass. "But we hadn't eloped. We'd connived a rendezvous. And he didn't change. After I . . . After we became lovers, he continued . . ." She folded her arms over her chest. The *awkwardness*. "He continued philandering. And then he drowned."

An abrupt end, to his life. To her tale. She delivered it with odd brightness. She looked back at Neal.

"He drowned in the Thames, with a female companion. He'd stolen a yacht. I'm sure you read about it. You couldn't get away from it if you tried."

"Lavinia." He stepped toward her, his voice soft. She lifted her hand, palm out, to stop him, but he took her wrist in his fingers, brushed her palm with his lips. Sensation prickled through her.

"Cranbrook touched me as though he owned me," she whispered. "Even before I was his wife."

He leaned forward and pressed his lips to her forehead.

She breathed against his neck. "Today, when I went to his study, to *denounce* him, I thought, for the first time . . ." Another breath. "If George had lived, *this* is what he would have become."

Not a prince, in the end. An old goat.

George had taken pleasure wherever he found it. He'd never checked his appetites.

She'd hoped, ignored, made excuses.

A young, handsome marquess will be a young, handsome marquess.

But if he'd grown old and ugly? How would his behavior have struck her then?

It took Cranbrook to see George properly.

And it took Neal as well. Took a different kind of love for her to realize how thin and brittle that glamour had been.

His lips against her forehead felt so good, so right.

She found her resolve.

*She* could be generous, too. Like Lucy. Despite having lost everything.

She took both of Neal's hands.

"You're going to be happy," she said. "As happy as you deserve to be. I'm sorry for every snide remark I ever made about your mother, and fossils, and *Cornwall*." Holding his hands meant she couldn't dash away her tears, so she smiled through them. "You and Muriel are meant for each other."

Oh dear, her voice wobbled desperately. "I wish you joy." She turned, far too quickly, but really, what etiquette pertained after such a speech, in such a situation? "Well then. I have a husband to bury."

In her mind's eye, she processed past him. Measured. Solemn. Yet . . . she could hear her feet thudding on the path. She was most certainly running. Running away. Again. The hedges opened and closed around her in a mystifying pattern. She put her hand on the stitch in her side and slowed. Stepped out from the green corridor into a large enclosure awash with color.

Long, narrow flower beds framed a marble basin. Not a fountain, a planter. Its vivid, ruffled surface was all red and purple blossoms. In the center, a statue of a nymph lifted a vase from which yet more flowers bloomed.

She'd reached the heart of the maze.

At the sound of Neal's footfall behind her, she caught her breath to speak. "I took a wrong turn." She looked over her shoulder.

Another wrong turn.

*Devastating.* He stood in the gap of the hedges, eyes bright as sun, but darker. Scorched light. The sight of him made her heart cramp.

He strode forward. "Muriel and I—"

She interrupted, smiling so fiercely she thought her lips might bleed.

"Congratulations!" Of course. They were already engaged. No surprise there. She'd seen them holding hands in the lecture hall. Her cheeks ached. "I couldn't be more pleased for you. If you'll excuse me . . ."

He was going to ruin it, her largesse. She'd break if he uttered one detestable detail. She tried to slip around him, and he hooked her waist with his arm, moved her gently until they stood face-to-face.

She didn't let him speak.

"I *want* to be pleased for you," she gritted out. "Let me be my best self, I beg you. Another moment and I can't vouch for what I do or say. I'm not very good by nature at sharing, or losing, or being kind for no purpose, even about small things, and now I'm behaving commendably about the biggest loss I can possibly imagine, and so *don't* spoil it by detaining me or I will scream."

Her chest heaved. For a tense moment, they regarded each other. Then he grinned, eyes crinkling. The grin that made her whole body flush.

"Your best self?" He gave a one-shouldered shrug. "I enjoy all of your selves." Slowly, he bent his arm, drew her closer. "I am enchanted by them." His voice dropped. It was almost a growl. "I am maddened by them. Made sleepless by them. You are the most fascinating, unforgettable, impossible series of women I have ever met in my life."

She gaped, unsure if she'd heard him correctly. Her blood was crashing in her ears.

"In that case . . ." She swallowed hard. "I *hate* that you're marrying Muriel Pendrake. I don't care how much you have to say to each other about Darwin. I wish Darwin had never been born." She gripped his thick wrist and squeezed, the pressure almost vicious. "And I'd rather slice off my fingers than let you go. There. That's not even my worst self."

Laughter rumbled in his chest.

"I am *not* marrying Muriel Pendrake." His hands cupped her face. "Muriel and I are planning an expedition to China, for Varnham. I won't go myself, of course. She'll lead it."

"For three years!" The exultation in her voice embarrassed her. And amused him.

He cocked a brow. "Mmm," he said. "Yes, that's the standard contract."

She inhaled, and now as his spiced green scent billowed through her, nothing hurt. She felt bigger and bigger.

Oh, the wonder of it, Muriel would be back among her woody shrubs on the other side of the world, and Neal . . .

Where would he be? Truro? Penzance? Never far from Cornish flora, or from his family.

She'd reached it, the sharp edge of her happiness.

She was a series of women. But not one of them—of her—truly

met his specifications. What he felt couldn't survive long. Reality would wither his esteem, a little bit each day. When his mother loathed her. When his sisters found her ignorant. When his cousins learned she was a liar. When he wearied of her chatter. Of course, his goodness meant he wouldn't treat her ill. He wouldn't even put her aside. He'd marry her, and it wouldn't be the marriage he wanted, a marriage in which both parties agreed on bryophytes. She should protect him from himself. But not even her best self had the strength.

She was staring at him, memorizing the craggy planes of his face.

"You've been released from *your* contract." He stroked his hand down her throat. His calloused fingers lay on her pulse. She closed her eyes.

"Legally." She inhaled a shuddering breath. "Not socially."

The black behind her eyes was the black of mourning veils and hearses.

"What does Miss Laliberté care for social mores?"

Her eyes flew open. He'd arched a humorous brow.

"It remains to be seen," she said, a trifle stiffly. Bad enough that he'd discussed her with Lucy. What had Mr. De'Ath reported?

She sighed. "Many things remain to be seen."

"We know you can keep all your fingers." He teased her. That playful tone, its presumption of a bond of affection, of mutual understanding—it set off tiny bursts of delight inside her.

He stooped low, suddenly, and rose with a new expression.

"Would you keep this?" With quick, precise motions, he twisted the thin stem of a daisy around her ring finger, the bloom resting just below her first knuckle.

Her eyes felt too big for her face, too hot, too full.

He cleared his throat. This rough-hewn, forthright, confident man—for a split second, he looked almost shy. "Just until I replace it with a gold one."

"It is gold." Her voice was hoarse. She lifted her hand, put her nose to the brilliant disc, haloed by white florets.

And sneezed.

*Oh Lord.*

She blinked at him. "Was that a bad sign?"

"No worse than any other sign we've gotten. Better than most." He was grinning, such a gorgeous, giddy-making grin. "You and I will have to make our own luck."

Fine with her. Fate hadn't been her friend.

Until now. Come to think of it, she'd made a few new friends.

Words failed and so she hitched up her skirt and hopped, kicking her feet. Neal clapped his hands and laughed, but his gaze held more than gaiety. It had sharpened.

He devoured her with his eyes.

She felt a hot thrill. She commanded this look, this desire. She smiled and let her skirt swish back around her ankles.

"I practiced," she confessed. She had, on nights anxieties drove her from her bed in Weston Hall. She'd jigged, to exhaust herself, and to remember how it felt, to dance with him.

"No barrel." He tipped his head. "Pity. Formal gardens do have their drawbacks. Certain activities prove impossible."

She watched his chest move with his quickened breath. Her chest moved just as quickly.

"But others suggest themselves." The curve of his mouth beckoned.

She stepped into him before she was aware of what she did. She fit like magic into the lee of his chest. His heavy arms wrapped her. She was surrounded. Everywhere, his solidity, a strength that, even if it hurt, would never harm. When he kissed her—hard—bending her back, the force of it was just what she craved. With a jerk, he lifted her up, swept an arm beneath her knees, and began to walk. She strained upward to kiss the softness beneath his chin. So much of his flesh was dense, unyieldingly hard. She felt a weird frisson of power when she touched this vulnerable spot.

Here was a form of trust, his exposure of his most tender points. Her exposure of hers.

She kissed down his neck, twisting in his arms.

He knelt to settle her on the marble basin, parting her knees, wedging between them. She helped him shove her skirts around her waist, their hands fumbling together in the silk and lace.

"That cotton frock was easier," he murmured.

"It's like comparing apples to oysters." She sniffed. Neal was a marvel, but he offended against fashion. He laughed as he rolled down her stockings. When he touched her bare legs, his laughter quieted. He drew in his breath and glanced up at her, eyes shining between those long black lashes.

He banished the shadows, this man. The sunniness of his passion turned *her* to gold. Made everything radiant.

He pulled the stockings over her toes, catching her foot and nuzzling her instep. He raised her leg higher and she had to catch the edge of the basin or she'd have tumbled back into the flowers.

"Stop or I'll fall over." It came out half gasp, half giggle. "I'll crush the flowers."

He raised his brows, patently unconcerned. "I'll have to send someone out to replant them."

He rested her heel on his thigh and leaned forward, putting his palm on her sternum, just above the neckline of her gown. He pushed. Pushed her until she lay on her back, petals soft on her neck, her arms. He slid forward then, covering her. His broad, heavy torso mashed her breasts; the cradle of his hips dug into her belly. She exhaled, shuddering. Felt the jut of his erection, the rigid muscles of his legs. His weight drove her down, filled the air with the bruised honey of the flowers. He stroked her lips with his tongue, stroked inside her mouth. Then he was climbing down her body and over the side of the basin.

She heard herself make a strange humming sound as his rough fingers traveled up her inner thighs. She slitted her eyes, lifted herself on one elbow, and peered, but the froth of skirt and petticoat at her waist obscured her view. He had ducked between her legs. She could see only the bulk of his shoulders, the curve of his haunches, as he crouched.

This time, at the first intimate touch, she felt nothing akin to shame. She felt only eagerness—wild, wanton, shocking in its intensity. She dropped back into the flowers and rolled her hips up to meet his mouth.

The softness of her flesh and his suckling lips, the pulling, clutching pulse that throbbed there, where they merged. Dear God. The sensation. It gathered, more than physical. *Elemental.* She fanned her arms through sun-warmed blossoms, dug her elbows into the cool dirt, moaning as his teeth pressed into her, isolating the spot where his tongue now circled slowly, now flicked an agonizing rhythm. She spread her legs wider, opening to him. He could see, feel, taste every bit of her. She hid nothing. She gave all. And she took.

Pleasure shivered her legs. Harder darts shooting into her belly. The tension carried her beyond herself, made her call his name as knowing dissolved in a flash, a burst star sending heat streaming into her core. She arched with it, belly twitching, crying out again and again. His arm slid beneath her, and he twisted so he was under her and she straddled him, kneecaps grinding on the marble. He heard her cry of pain and levered them backward into the flower bed. The tickle of blossoms, leaves, stems, on her knees and shins made her laugh.

He wasn't laughing.

His face was hard with need, lips swollen. That look alone plucked the taut ribbon of her own need, a need she'd thought sated. Her hands shook as she unbuttoned his jacket. He shucked it hurriedly, and she scrabbled at his cravat, popped a button on his shirt, then gave up, sliding her hand into the gap. His skin was smooth, stretched tight over the densely knitted muscles of his chest. Her arm made a weird angle as she scratched down the rippled musculature of his abdomen.

He worked his own hand down the front of her dress.

They had no more subtlety, no more finesse. His fingers mauled her breast, rolled her nipple roughly so that a groan tore from her throat.

She felt the brush of his knuckle through the slit in her drawers as he freed himself from his trousers. Their eyes met. She held her breath, rose on her knees as his cock nudged her slick, beating center. She watched him as she sank down, watched the sweep of his silken lashes, the gape of his mouth.

It excited her, to stoke this need, to cause this wildness to build in him.

Their mouths fused, his hands closing on her hips. He filled her, stretched her, *grounded* her. He rooted inside her, and she bloomed all over him, twining her arms around his neck.

She surged upward until she was nearly emptied, then bore down, gasping with the thick, shuddering impact. His own gasps threatened to separate their mouths, so she gripped his jaw. She wanted her tongue inside him, to fill him as he filled her. His hands squeezed her hips tighter, moved her in a faster rhythm. He thrust up, twisting, striking something higher and deeper within her, and she clamped with her thighs, the sweetness of the friction nothing compared to this sudden clutching at the center of her being.

She tossed her head back and screamed. He folded her in his arms, kissed her so that she swallowed his words.

*I love you.*

It tasted like sunlight.

He began to buck beneath her, then he stiffened, jamming his hands in her armpits, lifting her up. With a groan, he rolled and spent himself. She held on to his shoulder as he jerked and settled.

Laughing, he flopped onto his back in the flowers, dragging her onto him, her skirts a hopeless tangle.

She pressed her ear to his chest, listened to his pounding heart. His fingers toyed through her hair. She was still warm and loose, with sunshine in her mouth, sunshine flickering through her limbs, and the sun above, weighting her down.

"You said you wouldn't let me go." He stroked down her spine.

She nodded, rubbing her cheek on the exposed wedge of his chest.

"I won't," she said, and felt a shudder of exquisitely delayed pleasure. She gripped a fistful of his shirt, brought the other hand to her lips, and kissed the daisy on her finger. The florets were mussed but intact.

She'd kept it. Would keep it.

In a moment, she'd rise and reenter the maze, slip back into Harcott House.

But not yet.

# CHAPTER TWENTY-TWO

NEAL FINISHED CHECKING over the labels on the new specimens, then walked through the palm house inspecting the pipes. Mrs. Buddington, a longtime Varnham client, was showing her grandchildren the giant bamboo. Neal greeted her and scooped up the youngest child so that he could pick bananas for his siblings.

"Especially hot, isn't it?" Mrs. Buddington sat on a bench, beaming mildly as the youngsters wrestled with their fruit, and Neal bowed his way out, with the excuse of seeing to the vents.

Before he turned into the hallway, an economic botanist attempted to draw him into conversation. What he wanted was after-hours access to the *Elaeis guineensis*.

"Certainly. Arrange it with the manager." Neal's eyes kept drifting over the man's shoulder. Pointless. The palm house was a construction of brick, steel, and green glass panels. He couldn't see out to the lawn.

When he did manage to exit the building, the view discouraged him. He waited, of course. Pretended to occupy himself with the herbaceous border of the main walkway.

But he already knew.

She wasn't coming.

Over the past two weeks, Lavinia had kept but three of their agreed-upon meetings. Her mourning occupied nearly all of her time. The funeral and related functions. No inquest, thank God. The Duke of Cranbrook was known to have suffered angina pectoris. His death in the early days of marriage to a young bride occasioned smirks, not suspicion.

Neal didn't like to think of those smirks. He'd too strong an urge to wipe them off the offending faces. Nonetheless, he was sensible of the good fortune. London didn't buzz with speculation about Lavinia's disappearance in Cornwall. Everyone who knew she'd been gone had kept quiet.

Last Sunday, she'd used the pretext of a walk in Hyde Park to visit him in the gardener's cottage at Umfreville House. She'd looked pale in black silk, demure and oddly distant, but once she'd shed her widow's weeds, once they were skin to skin, flooded with each other, everything rushed back. Her color. His certainty. The bed was narrow. They fit just barely on their sides, cramped and sweaty, but neither wanted to disentangle. They conversed mouth to mouth. Her news tumbled out.

The will had been read. No special provisions. Under the law, she was entitled to a dower's share of income from the ducal properties. Enough to finance a version of the life to which she was accustomed. The next Duke of Cranbrook was already preparing to move into Harcott House with his family. Lavinia's mother had found apartments near Grosvenor Square.

"I have my own money." She'd breathed it. At such proximity, he could only stare into her eyes, whirlpools of blue that could drown a man. "And I'm going to publish my novel, *soon*. Mr. Watt, he wants to run it in serial parts, in a weekly magazine, which means I need to write the rest as fast as I can." Her laughter blew lightly on his face. She *had* found time to meet with Alan's friend, the syndicator, but Neal couldn't begrudge her that.

She'd sobered and spoken with peculiar intensity. "I am becoming a *legendary* widow, wouldn't you say?"

"Legendary," he'd agreed, and hesitated. "Of course, you don't need to be a widow to be a legend. It's my hope that you're a widow for a legendarily short period of time."

She'd smiled in answer, a smile that looked so fragile he'd decided to support it with his own lips.

As his wife, she'd lose her title, and her deceased husband's income. She'd slide down the rungs of rank and, legend or not, she'd become common. Did that fact give her pause? Something had kept him from asking.

Sometime later, she'd pressed her face against his neck. "Do you know what else I am?"

"Besides a legend?" He'd put his chin on the top of her head.

"An orphan," she'd whispered. "Parents disown their children. I've disowned my parents. In my heart, they're dead."

He'd heard her rawness, the hurt inside the defiance. So, he'd bottled his first response. *Eventually your anger may ease. And if you're lucky, your mother and your father will still be alive, and you'll say the things to them you need to say, and maybe you'll be heeded. And maybe something will change. In you. In them.*

He'd said instead, "Whatever you are, you're not alone."

He'd meant it. He meant it still.

He was in love with the woman. If he had to make a case, argue points—why Lavinia and not Muriel, why Lavinia and not anyone else—he'd fail to convince. It exceeded the rational, the well reasoned. Upset his understanding of cause and effect. It was based on everything and nothing.

It proved that science needed faith.

Yes, these weeks had been trying. He'd stayed in London longer than he'd intended, meddling in matters his managing director was already adeptly handling; in essence, making more work for himself, *and* his employees, to justify his continued presence.

He'd stayed for her.

Every time she wrote that she thought she could slip away, meet him here or there, he went to that place and he waited. Most often in vain. He understood. She discharged a solicitor only to be besieged by a countess. Society was eager to condole with her in the hopes of extracting some delicious morsel of gossip. Perhaps, on some level, she enjoyed the attention. Much ink had been spilled in the gossip columns when the Duke and the Duchess of Weston paid not one but two visits. Lavinia had been cut from Society because of her father's malfeasance, the wrongs he'd perpetrated against the duke's family. Now that Weston himself showed Lavinia favor, her detractors couldn't use that old scandal against her. She'd been rid of the noxious Duke of Cranbrook and remained a duchess. He didn't fault her if she *was* enjoying the attention. A series of domestic upheavals had cast her down and then returned her to the peak. Such a dizzying trajectory was bound to produce a mix of emotions.

So, he didn't fault her. He was forced to repeat this to himself when, hours later, Alan's valet knocked on the cottage door to hand him a black-bordered envelope delivered to Umfreville House with the last post. Lavinia's mourning stationery. Neal ripped it open.

*My Dearest Neal*, the letter began.

*I spent the day barnacled with callers and couldn't get out the door.*

He took the letter inside, read the rest of it over a drink, then poured another and reread the concluding lines.

*On Saturday, the Sambourns host their annual garden party. My attendance is all but compelled, so I compel yours. Wouldn't my pirate like nothing more than to swarm up the back wall and drop down behind the holly trees? All eyes will be turned to the tennis court. No one will watch for the figure stealing down the path, except, your devoted, Lavinia.*

He stood, let the letter drop, and pressed his thumb hard into his eyebrow. He flung himself backward onto the bed. The linens diffused her scent, faintly. Rose and gardenia.

A sound rumbled in his chest, caught behind his ribs. He couldn't tell if it was a laugh or a groan.

LAVINIA SIPPED MÖET under an arbor. She felt like the black center of an anemone, a half dozen girls ringing her in a blaze of color. With her title, *plus* Anthony's seal of approval, she'd converted from pariah back to princess.

All afternoon, Cora, Agnes, and Elise had stood closest, chattering at her brightly. Cora's overlong engagement to a grouse-obsessed Scottish earl was nearing its conclusion. The wedding was scheduled, and Cora did *so* hope Lavinia could attend. Agnes, married years ago, kept her eyes on the tennis court so she could belittle her own husband's every move as he lost serially to opponents young and old, male and female. Elise's titters never ceased.

Tripe-spouting, intolerable friends. Lucy was right, of course. They'd been bred to it, just as Lavinia had. Perhaps they would read her novel—Miss Laliberté's novel. They would read of the pirate duchess—a spoiled girl who discovers a world beyond the drawing room, breaks every social taboo, and ends up richly rewarded for her transgressions with a life of love and freedom—and they'd long for broader horizons themselves. Bigger hearts. Muriel Pendrake wanted to *thrill readers and inspire new enterprises* with writing. Well, so did Lavinia. Only not for the sake of botanical discovery. For the sake of self-discovery, not just hers, but other girls' too.

What did Cora do well?

"Cora," Lavinia spoke over Agnes. "Do *you* still play tennis? I remember you were brilliant at it. You let the gentlemen beat you because they wouldn't ask you to dance otherwise. But you were better than all of them."

Cora looked surprised, and displeased. She'd always underplayed her athletic ability. And what did Lavinia imagine? That she'd leave the earl to his grouse, don a cricketing cap, and head for the greenest pitch, where she'd bowl her way into history?

The surrounding girls goggled briefly. Lavinia never used to say anything *odd*. Then Agnes sighed.

"I wish someone would let Stokes win." She referred to her husband exclusively by his surname. "It grows embarrassing."

"There's Miss Powell, by the refreshment table." Elise pointed with her champagne flute. "Maybe she can tell Sir Vincent to ease up on his serve. Though I don't know as that would help. Have you considered Stokes might require spectacles?"

"It's more than his vision. He holds the racket like he's wringing a goose's neck. He couldn't win *against* a goose." Cora rolled her eyes. Then she waved to Miss Powell, beckoning her over.

"You don't mind that Liz is joining us," she said to Agnes, who was absorbed in a brief volley. "Your husband's crushing defeat will bring her joy." She addressed everyone with a small, pink smirk. "It proves her fiancé isn't the worst tennis player in Christendom. Only the worst rider. Did you hear he was thrown into the Serpentine?"

A quick, mean-spirited anecdote followed, summarizing Sir Vincent's unfortunate morning ride in Hyde Park.

Lavinia hardly listened. She was staring as Miss Powell approached. A pretty blond flibbertigibbet. Lavinia had never wasted a thought on her, except to note that her prettiness was similar to her own, and to assure herself that she didn't suffer by comparison. She'd certainly never called her *Liz*. Or Elizabeth.

Elizabeth Powell, engaged to Sir Vincent, baronet.

Lavinia's hand flew to her chest. She'd taken to carrying Neal's silver cigarette case in her bodice, beneath the ruching of black lace. She imagined it as a shield, protecting her heart. It wasn't enough. She had to leave, now.

She opened her black parasol. "Sometimes my grief overcomes me," she murmured, and set off across the lawn.

The Sambourns' property was large, with a slight slope atop which the house towered. Croquet at these parties was something diabolical, and she gave the match a wide berth. Debutantes in pale summer silks were drifting back and forth from the tennis courts, as older ladies and gentlemen seated in basket chairs or reclining on turkey rugs inspected them languidly and commented among themselves. An embowered band played familiar tunes of dutiful merriment.

Same old ton. Perhaps this summer's hats were bigger.

The gardens stretched behind the house. Roses had been trained up the back wall. The vines bloomed profusely, spiky with lurid red thorns. She'd forgotten the roses. They foretold a brutal climb, brutal indeed. She couldn't warn Neal, so she returned to the edge of the patio to wait. Surely, he'd come soon. She turned her head, and she saw him. He stood *inside* the house, stood by the piano, laughing with the Sambourns' eldest son, Graham. They both wore short cream-colored jackets and knickerbockers.

He didn't need to swarm up the back wall, like a pirate. He'd walked through the front door, like a gentleman. A gentleman who'd once been engaged to Miss Elizabeth Powell, a facsimile of Miss Lavinia Yardley.

She stepped quickly off the patio. *She* was the one stealing down the path. She grabbed bunches of her gown in her left hand and flew through the garden toward the back wall, so quickly she could feel the drag from her parasol. She let it go, let the handle sail over her shoulder. She reached the wall and stood for a moment, blinking at the stone and the roses. Now would she swarm up? Her little fantasy had turned inside out and reversed—unhappily.

She already felt too hot and her skin prickled at the very sight of the thorns.

"Roses are worse than cats." Neal spoke right behind her, and she turned. He was twirling her parasol, grinning. "If that's a Worth gown, you'd best think twice."

"It's not a Worth." She gave the skirt a shake. The gown was simple, crepe de chine and black lace. "It's a Stirling. Lucy's aunt designed it for *the* Celestia Jordan. To play Ophelia. But she wanted white."

Neal lowered the parasol, eyes sliding over her. "Lovely."

"It's not lovely." She stood stiffly. "Lovely is trite. Lovely is . . ." Elizabeth Powell. Lavinia Yardley. So much for dreaming she could change. She was a ninny through and through.

"Lovely," she muttered, and suddenly she was gasping for air. Neal tossed the parasol into the pansies and stepped forward. She stumbled back, would have gotten herself pricked and tangled in the roses, but for his quickness. He folded her into his chest.

"Easy now," he said, soothing.

"She's here. Your Elizabeth." She clung to him. He was silent.

"It's a small world," he said at last, and held her tighter. She could feel his chin pressing through her widow's cap.

"It is, isn't it?" She'd been writing of the wider world, but in the end, the small world of the ton was what she knew best. She would let Neal down in Cornwall. Another Elizabeth Powell. Seeing the girl had made it patently obvious. She struggled to calm herself.

"Still," she said, stepping back from him, "I didn't think you'd have an invitation to the party."

"Graham Sambourn and I were at Oxford together."

She bent her lips into a smile. An Oxonian gentleman. Where was her brawny-armed, unkempt Cornish pirate? Neal's muscles swelled his jacket, but he looked combed, clean, and wholesome. He was even wearing special sporting shoes with laces. He'd planned to play tennis, to participate in the party. Whereas she'd imagined they'd linger in the bushes, where fantasy ruled and daily pressures dissipated to nothing.

"You shouldn't stay," she said. "Poor Elizabeth."

"If I thought my presence would make her awkward, I'd go." His gaze was as straightforward as ever. "I assure you it won't. I saw her last week, in fact. Varnham is making her wedding bower."

"You didn't tell me."

"I've hardly seen you. It didn't seem important." He studied her face. "Please believe me—there's no cause for concern."

She couldn't speak. She couldn't nod. She *was* concerned, not that he'd choose Elizabeth over her. She was concerned that in choosing her, he chose just as foolishly, as regrettably. She'd been trying to tamp down that fear since that awful, wonderful afternoon in the garden at Harcott House. She'd never known anything as good as his love. She'd lucked into it. She'd accepted it, a selfish act.

Her love wouldn't be enough for him in the end.

As the silence lengthened, he tugged ruefully at his short, sporting tie. "If my presence makes things awkward for *you*, I'll go as well. I only came here because you compelled me." The corner of his mouth kicked up. "My pirate queen."

She almost catapulted into his arms. He wanted her, and she wanted him. Forget the rest.

*I compel you to follow me*, she'd say. *Behind these holly trees.*

He cleared his throat. "Elizabeth is here. I should tell you, so is your mother. I saw her in the house. I think I'd have recognized her, but I also heard her addressed."

She jerked, a catapult arrested. "Oh." She should have predicted it.

"I walked on," he said. "But I would like to meet her."

"I wouldn't like it!" She snatched up her parasol. Anger, anger fortified. Hadn't he listened? Did he still fail to understand what her parents had done, to *her*? "You *should* go."

Whatever Neal saw in her expression made him catch his breath. He laid a gloved finger under her chin, tilted her head up.

"I love you," he said, looking into her eyes, and then he kissed her, long and deep. His lips teased her. She fizzed all over, golden bubbles rising from her toes.

She wasn't intoxicated. She was a flute of Möet. Delicious, ticklish, effervescent with his kiss. He pulled away.

"I would like to meet your father too," he murmured.

One by one, the little bubbles popped. She flattened inside.

"You're a fat-wit." She swung around, resting the parasol handle on her collarbone, presenting him with a big black dome. She spoke to the roses on the wall. "My parents are awful people."

*Look what they produced.*

"Don't think you'd be welcomed with open arms." She gave a broken laugh. "They won't see it as gaining a son. They'll see it as losing a duchess. My title is the only thing they have to show for decades of striving, and conniving, and stealing, and . . ." Her throat constricted.

*Selling their souls.*

"I don't expect or need them to embrace me." Neal lifted the parasol gently, higher and higher. She released the handle and felt the rush of air as he cast the black silk contraption aside. His fingers wrapped her shoulder. She turned from the roses. She would always prefer his face to flora.

"I want to know them," he said. "So I can know you more fully."

"And love me less." She bit her lip. She'd imagined it would start with his family, the diminution of his love, but it could just as well start with hers.

"Never," he said. "I can help with—"

"You can help by leaving it alone," she snapped, and he took a deep breath.

"I will," he said. "For as long as you want."

She almost looked away from the brightness in his eyes.

"There isn't long, though," he said. "For other things." He tipped back his head, gazing up at the blue sky. "Today is St. John's Day. Midsummer."

Her lungs folded up inside her chest.

"You're missing the celebration," she rasped. "Golowan."

His mother's last. That was what he'd said to Tomas and Kelyn. He was missing it because of *her*.

"It goes until St. Peter's Day." He sensed her agitation and his mouth softened into a smile. "I haven't missed it. I'll leave for Penzance on Monday. I wanted to see you before I left." His smile widened. "To ask you to come with me. There will be barrels aplenty, but they'll be tar barrels, all ablaze in the streets. We do our dancing with linked arms around the bonfires, the whole parish. Jenni and Johannes, her husband, always bring rockets and fire wheels."

"I can't." She stared at him. Her scalp itched beneath the cap. She felt sweaty, clammy, distinctly unwell. "How would I explain it?"

"You're imaginative." He lifted his brows. "And who's to stop you going?"

No one. No one but her. She had to stop herself.

His mother's last Golowan. And he wanted to turn up with a flibbertigibbet of the first water. Maybe *he* saw her differently. His mother wouldn't. She'd be devastated.

She shook her head. "Cranbrook's son. He'll be moving into Harcott House. And we have another meeting with the solicitor, on Wednesday."

"Ah." Neal rocked back on his heels. "I didn't realize you were so averse to canceling appointments."

She flushed. His speech was rarely barbed.

"My husband, a *duke*, died not two weeks ago," she said. "I have myriad obligations. You know that."

His jaw muscles had flexed. His cheekbones stood out like boulders.

She bent to pick up her parasol, then stood in its little circle of shade, looking at his silly shoes, and the white hose clinging to his muscular calves and the bottoms of the knickerbockers.

"I know that you would sacrifice to become my wife," he said quietly.

She raised her eyes. He thought she shied away from sacrifice when she was *trying* to do just that.

"Not financially," he went on. "I haven't explained, formally, my situation, but I'm, Christ. I'm a wealthy man. I don't have the way of wealth. Much of the time, it makes my skin crawl. But insofar as I can put the money to good uses, I'm grateful. I would give every penny to anyone in my family, or yours. Your mother, your father. I will provide for them. You'll have a study in Truro where you can work on your bloodthirsty novelizing, until the cows come home." His lips tugged in a smile that faded, leaving his face again with that stark look.

"You told me you were Lavinia, *just* Lavinia. You told me that you didn't want your father's name, or your husband's." He drew a breath and held it several beats longer than she expected.

"A title is different," he said. "Titles open doors. I know that. Doors *should* open to you. My astonishing, marauding duchess with your bluebell eyes."

She tipped back the parasol. Her lips felt bloodless.

"A daisy doesn't tie you to me. If you've realized you want to let go, let go." His eyes held such unlikely light. "You're a dreamer. Don't let any of us tell you what to dream."

She tried to speak, croaked something unintelligible. Her heart beat that familiar doomed rhythm.

He was better than any dream.

*Tell him so.*

He thought her fickle. He thought she'd rather remain Duchess of Cranbrook than transform into Mrs. Traymayne.

*Mrs. Traymayne.* The syllables sang in her ears. *Mrs. Traymayne.* Novelist, wife, mother, barrel dancer, baker and eater of saffron buns, traveler of the world, barring China. More and more unfolded as the name repeated. *Mrs. Traymayne.* It heralded a lifetime of small and large pleasures and challenges, adventures.

She had to moisten her lips with her tongue to peel them apart. She wasn't fickle. She wasn't selfish, either. Not anymore. She would destroy Golowan, dash his mother's hopes for him, ruin their time together.

"I love you," she said. "I'd go with you, of course I would, but . . ."

Something shifted in his expression. Everything stilled. He was entirely focused on her. Even her heart seemed to stop.

His smile took its time reaching his eyes. When it did, they crinkled. She ached to put her fingers on those creases, to kiss his cheekbones, the bump on his nose, his full, firm lips that smiled at her despite everything.

"Well," he said on a breath. "I didn't oblige you coming in, so I'll oblige you going out."

He glanced up at the wall.

"The roses." She made weak protest.

"Gloves." He raised his hands. "Fashion with a purpose." He raked his fingers through his hair, disordering it. He looked more like the man she'd first met.

"Neal," she said. "I'm sorry." He froze. They stared at each other. He wasn't smiling. He lunged forward and plundered her mouth, a piratical kiss that made the parasol drop from her nerveless fingers.

"When . . . when you're back in London . . ." she stammered as he released her. His lips were glistening, eyes hooded. But his wildness had subsided. He touched her cheek.

When *would* he be back?

She opened her mouth, but he'd already retreated several feet. He bounced on his toes and ran forward, launching himself at the wall. He seemed to bound straight up it, barely using his hands, feet finding invisible crannies. When he reached the top, he hoisted himself, swung a leg over, and paused, looking down from his perch. He tugged fabric from his pocket. Not a decorous linen square. One of his ridiculous kerchiefs. Blue. He waved it at her, in goodbye, or perhaps, she thought, watching it ripple, as though it were a flag.

Then he was gone.

## CHAPTER TWENTY-THREE

THE FIFTH DUKE of Cranbrook arrived Sunday afternoon to take possession of Harcott House. Lavinia liked him scarcely better than his sire. He was a handful of years older than she and insisted on calling her *Mother* with a lasciviousness that made her insides roil.

"You always have a home here," he said at dinner, foot pressing hers under the table. Lavinia hadn't planned to observe a proper mourning period before marrying Neal. Four months at Harcott House, she'd thought. Perhaps five.

Now the prospect of remaining through the cheese course made her skin crawl.

The next morning, she woke early and walked in the gardens, turned and turned through the green hedges. With every turn, she expected to see him. Neal. Framed by twigs and leaves, grinning. Leveling her with those bright brown eyes.

But no, he'd have boarded his train by now. By now, he might have decided he didn't want to marry her. She hadn't let him go, but then, she hadn't gone with him. A selfless act. One that made her more worthy of him, and that might mean she'd lost him.

Was it selfless? Or was it cowardly? She feared seeing his cousins and owning up to her lies, feared getting quizzed by his mother on the morphology of the *Plesiosaurus*. She feared that his sisters would sniff out the feathers on her, years of winged hats, and gape with wounded horror. She'd endure their ridicule, but why? So Neal could make known his ridiculous decision.

He'd chosen the kind of wife who faded.

She kept walking, eyes welling, spilling over.

Tragic Lavinia, watering the garden with tears.

*He* didn't think she'd fade for him. He had once called her a *wordsmith*. When she'd spun out ideas about what to name that ointment of his, he'd eagerly jotted down her phrases. He took advice from her. He appreciated her imagination. He made her feel essential, like earth and atmosphere. With him, she was water and salt, electricity and light, moss and silt. She was the tender new shoot unfurling from something deep and ancient and nourishing. *Lovely* didn't begin to describe it.

Maybe she should trust him, trust that.

She entered the heart of the maze and roamed between the hedges and the narrow flower beds. She sat on a bench facing the enormous planter. It was bursting with new plants, concentric rings of pale green and pale pink leaves.

Where was Neal's train now? Reading? Didcot? Swinton?

LATER IN THE day, she went to Weston Hall to beg a position for Nan and discovered Anthony slumped over his desk behind a mountain of wadded paper. He was not a bookish man, and his statesmanship clearly cost him. She drew a chair close to his and tugged his latest effort from beneath his elbow. The beginnings of a speech on local self-government in India.

Indian self-government, not her area of expertise. Sentences, however . . .

"Once I figure out what you mean here," she said briskly, pointing. "I'm sure I can make it sound much smoother."

"I don't want it to sound smooth." Anthony batted away the paper.

Lavinia frowned. "Then I shall make it thunder." She picked up his pen.

Anthony looked at her, startled, then kicked back in his chair with a laugh. "All right, then. Make it rain fire."

"Gladstone will tremble in his boots!" She positioned herself at the end of his desk, the paper spread before her.

"Actually." Anthony cleared his throat. "I've joined the Liberals."

"Have you?" asked Lavinia absently, brows coming together as she tried to decipher his opening. His script was bad, his syntax worse. "Well, I guarantee someone will tremble. I am a writer of bloodthirsty prose."

Hours passed. Hours of struggle, and some hilarity, during which she experienced her selves layering over one another. Her childhood self, bickering with Anthony, demanding her way. Her writerly self, newly confident, exploratory. At the end of it, they'd produced a legible document Anthony could read on the floor.

Lavinia sailed downstairs to take tea with Lucy and the members of her painting club, immensely pleased, Nan's future secured, and a blow struck against authoritarian rule in the colonies. Tea turned into dinner, and by the time she left Weston Hall, she had in her possession several sketches by Gwen Burgess that answered to her descriptions of her novel's most gripping scenes.

She'd feared the return to London, but here she was, reconstructing her life, different from the one she'd lived before.

Now she feared a return to Cornwall. But if she went, if she joined Neal, couldn't she construct a life there too? One that was good for both of them?

Maybe she couldn't. But couldn't *they*? The two of them, together?

Back at Harcott House, she stood at the window in the guest

chamber, waiting for the sky to grow dark. But it didn't. The sun had stalled. The day stretched on and on. So much light.

Midsummer.

His mother's last.

She scarcely slept.

In the morning, she called for the carriage and rattled into the north of London. When she stepped out, her heart was pounding. She paused on the street looking up at Holloway Prison, its turrets, then passed into the courtyard, stopping before the entrance, an enormous arched door flanked by twin griffins, stone keys clutched in their stone claws. A guard approached, and she ducked her head, retreated.

It wasn't time.

She wasn't ready to talk with her father, to hear his answers to the questions she now knew to ask. She could take longer, however long she needed. When she *was* ready, she'd welcome Neal's support.

Neal was in Penzance *now*. Maybe her support didn't measure up to his. Maybe she did the right thing, for him, keeping away. The selfless thing.

Being selfless wasn't her strong suit.

Neal loved her for her selves. Shouldn't she bring all of them to bear, rush to him with everything she had?

She paused by the gates, eyes drawn to the yolky yellow heads of dandelions in bloom. The leaves, they *did* have purple spots. It wasn't just that they were filthy.

She stained her gloves scrabbling in the dirt, levering the whole plant out. The footman's eyes widened to saucers as he opened the door for her to climb back into the carriage.

She smiled at him.

If she took the train tomorrow to Plymouth, overnighted in a hotel, caught the first train the next morning to Truro, and changed at the station to the West Cornwall Railway, she would get to Penzance before St. Peter's Day.

She had so much light on her side.

———

THIS GOLOWAN, THE house was overfull with Traymaynes. The dining room couldn't hold the whole boiling of them. The children didn't stand still long enough for a head count, but Neal knew they numbered nine, if he didn't include the one Nessa and Cyril were expecting.

Nessa had made their happy announcement the previous afternoon on the quay. Neal's mother had been walking slowly, one hand on her Newfoundland's shaggy back, the other arm linked through Neal's, head turned to watch the children load into a boat. Before she let him go to embrace her daughter, Neal felt her tremor.

She was smiling, but her eyes brimmed.

Bittersweet, these few golden summer days together. By the time the season came around again, they'd celebrate a new life among them.

But Heddie Traymayne. Where would she be?

It was a metaphysical question, or a religious one. Or a scientific one, as Neal sometimes thought. The body went back to loam, and flowers grew. Reverend Curnow might say she'd be with them still in spirit, looking down with her beloved husband at her side.

Neal didn't believe it, not quite in those terms. But ever since he'd arrived in Penzance, he'd been hearing his father's voice. He'd heard it loud and clear right then.

*Well, my lad, when will you make* your *happy announcement?*

He didn't know how to answer. *Did* he have a happy announcement? During his last imaginary conversation with his father, he'd boasted about his future wife. A lot had changed since that afternoon in Kyncastle.

He hadn't known what to say, when Emmeline had asked after Muriel at dinner on the day he'd arrived. He'd stuttered under his mother's gaze, which made things worse. Tomas and Loveday leapt in to sing the praises of Muriel Pendrake.

"She's in London," he said at last.

His mother had leaned forward eagerly, but before she could speak, Molly, Alice's middle child, burst into the room, soaking wet. The turkey had chased her into the pond.

"Because she's got dirty feet!" yelled her brother, John, running in behind her. No longer the center of attention, Neal had risen to help Kelyn and Loveday carry empty plates into the kitchen.

Today, the family roved outdoors, crossing the brook and wandering up through the orchards and across the fields to the sea. The adults picnicked while the children—and Neal—splashed in the water. After Neal changed out of his wet clothes, he found Perran, Jory, Nessa, Cyril, Jenni, Kelyn, and Emmeline gathered on the lawn in chairs set up in the shade of the elm trees. The twins had been caught eating grasshoppers, and Perran and Jory were assuring Kelyn that no harm ever came of consuming insects.

Neal caught Jenni's eye, and she stuck her tongue out at him.

"You used to eat flies," she said. "Do you remember?"

Ah, the family's favorite game was about to commence. Tease baby Neal. He knew how to play, though.

"I still eat flies," he said, and smiled blandly. The sound of wheels on gravel made him turn his head.

A cab was rolling up the lane. Neal glanced at Perran, who shrugged his shoulders.

Their mother's sisters, nieces, nephews, and cousins had visited for St. John's Day and gone on to Uncle Arthur in Penryn. Everyone else was here, except William, who'd stayed behind in Kyncastle with the cows.

Was it William come to join them?

The cabman reined the horse and jumped down. The trunk he lowered onto the grass looked familiar. The cab door opened, and Lavinia stepped out, cradling a hatbox.

Neal stood, heart pounding. She was standing down the slope

from them. Had to look up at the boiling clan. Thank God they weren't *all* on the lawn. She would think a mob confronted her.

Emmeline ran forward before he did. "Muriel!"

Neal felt a jab in his side.

"I knew it," Jenni said, and jabbed him again for emphasis. "I knew it from the way you *didn't* speak of her. Quiet as a clam." She winked at Nessa. "Neal has a sweetheart. I thought he'd given up after that Elizabeth."

Nessa swatted at her. "Why don't you stay quiet as a clam for once?"

"Because I don't want to deny you all the benefit of my insights and observations." Jenni swatted back. "She does *look* rather like Elizabeth, though, doesn't she?" From her muffled squeal, Neal could tell that Nessa had stamped her toe.

Emmeline and Lavinia were walking toward them. Kelyn came around the table as Tomas struggled to his feet, a twin under each arm.

"Do you remember this pretty lady?" He gave a few bounces and the boys shrieked and kicked.

"Dear Muriel," said Kelyn, a crease between her brows. "But you're in mourning. I'm so terribly sorry. Neal didn't tell us."

"Oh, that. It's nothing." Lavinia placed the hatbox on a chair and smoothed her skirts. The black silk set off her pallor. Her eyes flitted and she licked her lips, ill at ease.

"My husband," she added, unnecessarily.

Everyone had to have noticed the widow's cap. It perched on her shining hair. Neal saw Kelyn glance sharply at Tomas, who tilted from side to side in a modified shrug.

They'd met Muriel Pendrake as a widow. One didn't expect that a widow could be widowed. Did one?

He opened his mouth and shut it again. If Lavinia had given him a lick of warning, he would have prepared the way. Confided in

Jenni, perhaps. Come up with a plan for approaching his mother. For explaining to his cousins.

She never made anything easy.

He wanted to shake her. Since he'd left her in the Sambourns' garden, he hadn't known *what* to think, about her, about *them*, their future.

He wanted to fold her in his arms. Carry her to that sheltered stretch of beach where he could look back and forth between her eyes and the waves, gauging their relative blues, until his air gave out and he had to sip the breath from her lungs.

"Mrs. Pendrake." Jenni spoke warmly. "You are an inspiration. I hope to go to China one day, to the Peking Observatory."

Neal started. Bad beginning. Quite bad, in fact. Lavinia's skin was taking on a sickly cast. He should intervene. Say something before Jenni started asking about the egret density on the Yangtze River.

"We've heard all about you." Jory chimed in. "And owe you a debt of gratitude. You saved our little brother's life in the harbor."

Now Neal felt his jaw drop. He hadn't realized his cousins and siblings had conferred in such detail about his and Lavinia's visit to Kyncastle.

"Which makes you an honorary Traymayne," continued Jory. "We've each of us saved Neal's life. If you haven't noticed, he likes to get into scrapes. There was the time—he was five, I think, or six—he tried to ride Mr. Knight's sheep, right there, in the field just up the hill." He waved an arm, warming to his story. "He climbed a fir tree and jumped onto a ram's back, an evil-tempered old ram. Boreas, his name was. Well, Boreas bucked like the devil, tossed Neal ten feet in the air. He landed plumb on his head. Knocked him totally senseless. He was about to get trampled by the flock, but I jumped the fence and—"

"I'm all for embarrassing, Neal," interrupted Nessa. "But we should let Mrs. Pendrake get settled first, and we should introduce ourselves. I'm Nessa, Neal's sister, and this is my husband, Cyril."

"Perran," said Perran. "There's about two dozen of us, all told. Good luck with the names."

"Mrs. Pendrake is here?" Neal's mother had emerged from the house, where she must have been reading in the sitting room window seat. Her spectacles still perched on her nose.

This had to end, this confusion.

"Not precisely." Neal blurted it out. Lavinia shot him a strange look. A mixture of apprehension and something sweet and hopeful. He saw that she was twisting her gloved hands. What was wrong with him, leaving her to stand there while his family studied her like an interesting exhibit with an indecipherable label?

He shook himself and jogged to her, reaching out. Her fingers twined around his, the grip fierce, slightly desperate.

"Mother," he said, facing her, then sweeping the entire group with his gaze. "*Everyone.* I am delighted to introduce you to . . ."

He swallowed. "My fiancée." *Almost there.* "The Duchess of Cranbrook."

Shock. Even the insects stopped buzzing. Not an entomologically accurate statement, surely. But Neal heard *nothing* in that moment. Silence reigned.

Lavinia curtseyed. "Please call me Lavinia."

"A *duchess!*" Emmeline clapped her hands. "So you *do* know Sarah Bernhardt and the Prince of Wales! I thought you must be lying."

"She *was* lying," said Kelyn softly. "Lying about quite a bit more than who she knows. She lied about who she *was*. Neal, were you a part of this deception?"

"No," Lavinia spoke up before he could answer. "I lied to everyone, including him. To run away from my marriage. I borrowed Mrs. Pendrake's identity. She's got it back, though. Don't worry. She is every bit as extraordinary as ever and doing all sorts of inspiring things to advance science and women's education, and I'm sure you'd all adore her. She's exactly the sort of woman Neal should marry, and if I thought she'd truly make him happier than I could, I wouldn't stand in their way. Because I love Neal."

She paused to gulp air. "I would have come sooner, but I wanted to spare him embarrassment. I knew he'd disappoint you all, turning up with a *debutante*. But I was disappointing him, staying away. So I'm here to tell you that I may be a flibbertigibbet, but I love him with every particle of my being. I make him laugh, and I *am* prepared to race to his rescue whenever he tries to get himself killed, and we don't know about any of the same things so we'll never get bored with each other, which we might do if we were just agreeing all the time on the right way to pack bulbs or rehashing the life of Darwin!"

She had to gulp again and this time the pause was punctuated by Jenni's snort. Lavinia looked at her, brow furrowed.

"I think it might be best to marry someone with whom you have very little in common, to keep things from getting dull," she continued. "And he loves me."

Neal's mother sat heavily in a chair, hand clutching the snow-white braid that hung over her shoulder.

"Forgive me," she said. "My brain has been sluggish of late. You are not a botanist. You are a duchess who abandoned her husband. That husband, I assume, given your attire, has since passed on."

"Correct," said Lavinia with touching concentration. She looked like a schoolboy summoned to a difficult recitation. "I am a dowager."

"And after meeting my son under false pretenses, you now intend to marry him, in part because you have so little in common." His mother's voice was as dry as fossils in sandstone. "Your interests are . . . ? Not botany, I take it."

"Fashion." Lavinia had gone rigid. "Particularly theatrical fashions. Dancing. France. I speak fluent French. Novels—reading *and* writing them. I've completed a romance, in fact. A romance of the high seas. I like to shop."

Neal's mother looked like she'd been presented with a reconstruction of a dinosaur with the head at the wrong end.

"Will you introduce *me* to the Prince of Wales?" asked Emmeline.

Jenni and Nessa were exchanging glances. Perran was mouthing *romance of the high seas* at Jory, who was trying to hide a smile. Christ. The Traymaynes *were* a judgmental lot. Terrible snobs. Assertive. Righteous. Eager to boss the family baby, who, left to his own devices, tended to land in trouble. Neal bit the inside of his cheek. This old dynamic. He rebelled or he tried to please. It was hard to know his own mind, to separate his convictions from all their strong opinions.

*Bollocks*, said Neal's father. *What's hard is your head. Don't just stand there like a post. Do you love the woman?*

"Lavinia's right," said Neal. Eyes swiveled. Suddenly, he was at the intersection of all their gazes. Lavinia's was the one that drew him.

"I love her," he declared, watching her eyes widen. "It's an incontrovertible point. Not open for debate."

*Yes. That's it.*

He grinned. "If that hatbox she brought contains a hat with the last dodo bird stuck on top, I'll still love her."

Jenni sucked in her breath. "Crikey."

"I'd mind it, of course." Neal couldn't help but laugh at the image. "We'd have a rip-roaring fight, perhaps." He sobered. "But I'd trust, when it was over, that we'd both see the world through slightly different eyes. And we'd love each other all the more."

Color flooded Lavinia's cheeks. She took several steps backward, as though she needed room to take him in. To take *it* in.

He realized in that moment that he'd surprised her. Her eyes were brilliant. Glorious.

"The last dodo," repeated Jenni, frowning and laughing at the same time. "If any part of a dodo is in that hatbox, we're taking it to the Natural History Museum."

Suddenly, Lavinia laughed too, her shoulders loosening.

Neal's next realization was more astounding, more humbling.

She hadn't been sure that he was sure of *her*. She hadn't fully expected him to speak up, to speak back. To present their love as an article of faith.

Her doubt made him ache. But the joy spreading now over her face—it acted as a balm. He'd never seen anything as beautiful.

"No dodo." Still laughing, she lifted the lid off the hatbox on the chair. "I dug up dandelions." She said it breathlessly.

Perran, Jory, Nessa, and Jenni crowded around the chair to peer inside the box. Lavinia had lined it with newspaper covered liberally with damp dirt. Neal touched the soft flower head of the wilted dandelion plant.

He had the inane idea that the wind might blow and take his heart along with it, like dandelion seeds. He felt as though the world were making a wish on him.

A wish for love.

He lifted his head and met Lavinia's eyes. Bluer than the sea, and deeper.

He cleared his throat and glanced at his mother, who had cupped her chin in her hand. Her eyebrows were lifted well above the frames of her spectacles.

"I discovered a new dandelion species in Kyncastle." He felt oddly shy, with Lavinia and his family gathered so close. "Somehow—Father didn't collect it. I'd hoped I could bring you the journal with my published description, but it won't be out until July."

His lungs felt hot and tight. He went up to his mother's chair and took her hand, so thin and cold.

"I named it for you," he said. "*Taraxacum hedrae.*"

Slowly, his mother's eyebrows lowered. Her eyelids curved down as her smile lifted her lips. It was that expression he'd been observing these days—bittersweet. Her hand tightened on his.

"I wanted to press a good specimen for you," he said. "I didn't find any, though, when I was just in Kyncastle."

"So Muriel brought a plant." Kelyn walked to the hatbox and lifted it. "She brought you a plant to press and give to your mother." She passed Neal the hatbox, then turned to Lavinia. "That was kind of you."

"But didn't she come from London?" Jenni folded her arms. "What's the distribution of *Taraxacum hedrae*?"

Jenni thought too quickly. She never left him enough time to develop a strategy. He sighed.

"I doubt it grows in London," he admitted. He didn't want to say it and hesitated, too long. Lavinia's face was already falling.

He looked into the hatbox. "This isn't *Taraxacum hedrae*."

"The purple spots, though." Lavinia started forward, shoulder pressing his side as she studied the plant. "There." She pointed.

Where to begin? It wasn't even close.

"Give it here," said his mother. "I believe I am the intended recipient." She took the hatbox from Neal's outstretched hands and settled it on her lap. She addressed Lavinia. "You brought this all the way from London?"

A rhetorical question, but Lavinia nodded.

"Why a hatbox?"

"I don't have a vasculum," said Lavinia. "I *am* interested in botany, but I only learned of my interest recently. I have learned several things about myself only recently."

She took a breath. "For example, that I would rather have a daisy wrapped around my finger than wear a duke's diamond."

She fisted her hands and crossed her arms, fists shoved beneath her biceps. She'd begun to tremble.

"When Neal told me about the dandelions he'd named for you, I knew. I knew how much it meant, how much he loved you. And I knew that I wanted to live that kind of life."

Tears spilled over her lashes.

"A life where love is common as weeds," she whispered. She looked around at them, the members of his family, all staring back at her. "You're so very lucky."

Her eyes locked on his. She smiled, a smile that lit her like summer sun.

He had promised her they would make their own luck. Dammit, they were starting now. If he kissed her, Perran, Jory, and Jenni would never let him live it down. The teasing would be pitiless.

If he didn't kiss her . . .

But there was no world in which *didn't kiss* was an option.

He pulled her against him, slid his fingers into her hair, sought her lips. They parted beneath his, full and soft and salty-sweet. Her face was wet with tears but she laughed into his mouth. Surprised again. He liked to surprise her. Right then and there, he made it a goal to surprise her every day.

She wound her arms around his shoulders, and he dipped her back, kissing her through his grin. When he straightened and released her, he kept ahold of her hand, aware of their audience. Jory was pounding Perran's shoulder, smile stretching from ear to ear. Tomas and Cyril were inspecting their shoes. Kelyn was blushing, and Emmeline sighing. Nessa and Jenni looked amused. His mother—his mother had tears slipping down behind her spectacles. She had her arm wrapped around the hatbox as though it held something precious.

Which it did. A common, precious weed.

"I think it might be *Taraxacum hedrae*," she said, her voice rasping. "And I should know." She addressed them all, then looked at Neal.

"Neal." She smiled as she wiped her eyes and lifted her chin. "Go buy that girl a proper ring."

———

DURING DINNER, LAVINIA became even more hopelessly confused. She tried to talk to Jenni about bugs and Nessa about stars, mixed up Mary and Maude, abandoned hope on the children. The merry racket of the meal overwhelmed. Elbows bumping, serving spoons clattering. Incomprehensible jests. She felt the curiosity of Neal's family members like a persistent tug. She also felt their welcome flowing toward her.

They wanted to get to know her better, to put the missing pieces together. She wanted to get to know them better too.

Not tonight, though. They had tomorrow for that.

After dinner, she and Neal walked up through an orchard of twisty old trees and down a lane lined with flowering hedgerows. The hedgerows smelled like honey, and the glowworms spangled the greenery with tiny lights. Where the lane ended the fields stretched down to the sea. The sun had sunk below the horizon, but the sky still blushed with color, lavender above the dark waves.

Neal led her along the beach, past the piles of sticks laid for the St. Peter's Day bonfires. Tomorrow, the beach would be thronged with revelers and the night would glow with flames. Fireworks would shower the sea with sparks. She'd celebrate with the Traymaynes, celebrate togetherness, and the zenith of the year.

Tonight, the beach was empty. The sand was soft beneath the blanket Neal spread in the lee of a boulder. Soon, experience reconfigured. His rhythm was her rhythm, her rhythm was his, and *their* rhythm was the rhythm of their surroundings.

There was a high tide of kissing, and a low tide of kissing, but there wasn't ever a cessation of kissing. Sometimes, it was only this: the drowsy, sweet tangle of tongues. The drift of fingertips over skin.

"I found us a house in town." Neal's thumb stroked up and down her throat. "Before I left. I do enough business in London to warrant it. And we can't have you languishing for want of theater, and shopping."

She sighed. In his arms, she wanted for nothing. But he was right, she wasn't done with London. She was ready for her new life to begin, there, and in Cornwall too.

Her lips worried the lobe of his ear. "Where in town?"

"Kensington," he sighed, then yelped as her teeth closed on his neck.

"Not Kensington." She licked the little indentations she'd left in his skin. His neck was beyond irresistible. It was edible.

"Mayfair," she said.

He rolled on top of her, his weight exerting a delicious, indelicate pressure. He claimed her lips, tongue filling her. When he could speak again, he said, agreeably, "Very well. I decide in Cornwall. You decide in London."

She pushed at his chest and he let her topple him. She straddled his hips, kissed his fingers when he reached up and laid his hand on her cheek.

"So, in Cornwall, we'll tramp about getting horribly freckled and host dinners for botanical reverends, and in London, we'll go to balls and the theater and salons for artists and writers."

He gasped. "Exactly."

"You'll have to grow extra lemon trees. Lemon juice cures freckles."

He pulled her forward so she was stretched on top of him. She turned her face, cheek on his chest, and watched the shimmer of the breaking waves.

"If we could sail right now, anywhere in the world, under the Jolly Roger, I wouldn't." She tipped her face just enough to kiss his chest. "I'd want to stay right here."

His arms closed around her. It felt good. It felt better than good. She rose and fell with his breath.

"When we marry, I won't be a duchess anymore."

"Mmm," he murmured, hand heavy on the back of her head. "I'll kiss you and you'll turn into common Mrs. Traymayne. It's like a fairy tale in reverse."

She laughed, startled. It *was* a fairy tale in reverse.

It was the happiest ending—the happiest beginning—she could imagine.

"Kiss me now," she said, and he did.

# Author's Note

AFTER I FINISHED *The Duke Undone*, I had no intention of revisiting Lavinia Yardley, the novel's most unwitting antagonist. As a reader and a writer, I'm drawn to heroines who are outsiders and iconoclasts. I heartily endorse their ambition, their ideals, their big, brave plans. Lavinia seemed too small-minded to hold my interest. She didn't question and defy social conventions. She was a Society insider, pretty and popular, a nineteenth-century mean girl. I dismissed her, and then that dismissal began to irk me. Everyone has hidden depths. I decided to follow Lavinia beyond *The Duke Undone* to see how she'd respond to her changed circumstances. I'm so glad I did! She ended up challenging my assumptions and winning my heart.

*The Runaway Duchess* is set in a version of Cornwall that deliberately blends fact and fancy. I first went to Cornwall in my imagination, through the novels of Daphne du Maurier, from which I borrowed a bit of atmosphere, and also an inn, and a ship. Much later, I explored the Cornish coast in real life. In 2019, I co-taught a summer course in London called Literature of the Witch. We took our coven of students west to see Arthurian ruins and to wander the Museum of Witchcraft and Magic. It was a weekend of adventure, and misadventure. We got lost in the woods trying to find St. Juliot

Church, restored in the nineteenth century under the direction of architect (and writer!) Thomas Hardy. We trembled with mortal terror while hurtling in cabs along winding roads hemmed by hedgerows. We sheltered together in the lee of a rock as a sudden, shockingly violent storm churned the harbor and lashed us with wind and rain. Many of my real, and unreal, experiences in Cornwall filtered into *The Runaway Duchess*. I invented Kyncastle and Mawbyn, but both villages are composites of actual places, including two that we visited on our trip: Boscastle and Tintagel.

Varnham Nurseries is modeled on Veitch Nurseries. In the nineteenth century, Veitch Nurseries employed nearly two dozen plant hunters and introduced over a thousand plants to England. Muriel Pendrake owes something to the famous botanical artist and plant hunter Marianne North (1830–1890). A permanent exhibit of North's paintings hangs in the Marianne North Gallery at Kew Gardens.

If I had to recommend just one book I discovered while researching for *The Runaway Duchess*, it would be *A London Child of the 1870s* by Molly Hughes. This vivid memoir of Victorian life invites readers into the Hughes family and shows us London—and Cornwall— through Molly's eyes. I found it warm and moving, and invaluable as a resource, illustrating the everyday goings-on of a middle-class family not entirely dissimilar to the Traymaynes.

# ACKNOWLEDGMENTS

THANKS TO MY clear-eyed agent, Tara Gelsomino, who always sees more than I do. Thanks to my brilliant editor, Kate Seaver, and the extraordinary Berkley team, including Bridget O'Toole, Jessica Brock, and Mary Geren. And thanks to the Berkletes—you bowl me over with your talent and derring-do!

I'm wildly lucky to work with fabulous colleagues and students at Wake Forest University. All of you have my deepest appreciation! Sarah Hogan, our midsummer dreams magicked this book into being. I'm so glad we shared a London June. I'm so glad we shared it, too, with such intrepid students. I loved every minute, except for the minutes in the dead of the night when the fire alarms kept ringing.

I first spoke the plot of this book aloud to Julia Scarborough in Bushy Park as the royal deer bounded in the distance. Thank you, Julia, for listening and for always asking the right questions and offering the most specific, spellbinding details. I found inspiration for this book, and other books, with Joanna Howard at the Poet's Stone. Thank you, Joanna, and our holiday together! Marcia Underwood is my modern model for Muriel Pendrake. Marcia, thank you for wandering the neighborhood and for patiently repeating the names of all the flowering shrubs. Radhika Singh, your Gchat was my favorite romance. Thank you for accompanying me through evolving genres and forms. Mir Yarfitz, you now know all the tropes! Thank you for being a cinnamon grump.

And finally, boundless love and most profound gratitude to my friends, to the Wolves, and to Ruoccos, including Blackberry. *Spem in alium!*

# The Runaway Duchess

## Joanna Lowell

## Questions for Discussion

1. Neal tells himself that "intellectual affinity and common interests" matter more than physical attraction when it comes to choosing his wife. How does this idea strike you? What would you prioritize if you wanted to form a long-term relationship?

2. As a wealthy young woman in Victorian London, Lavinia struggles to meet a particular set of social expectations and embody the feminine ideal. Why does she try so hard to conform? In your own life, how have you found yourself embracing (or rejecting) certain norms? How have others reacted?

3. After reading Muriel Pendrake's manuscript, Lavinia objects to the very idea of traveling the world to slap Latin onto birds and flowers. How do you understand her objection? What's your own perspective on the historical development of scientific knowledge?

4. Paris is often described as the city of love. Lavinia adores Paris, but by the end of the book, she sees beauty and romance in the Cornish countryside. What makes a place romantic? What's the most romantic place you've ever been?

5. Lavinia feels betrayed by both her mother and her father. Should she forgive them, and if so, what might forgiveness look like?

6. Neal attributes his parents' happy marriage to their ability to agree on what's important, in their case "dinosaur bones, bryophytes, and children." He and Lavinia disagree on many things. What three things do you think they can agree on? Why would those things be important to their marriage?

7. Lavinia decides to write a romance about pirates. Why do pirates appeal to her? What do you think she'll write next?

8. Neal describes his courtship with Lavinia as a "fairy tale in reverse." What are the fairy-tale elements in the book? What do fairy tale and romance have in common?

9. What's your favorite plant and why?

**Joanna Lowell** lives among the fig trees in North Carolina, where she teaches in the English department at Wake Forest University. When she's not writing historical romance, she writes collections and novels as Joanna Ruocco. Those books include *Dan, Another Governess / The Least Blacksmith, The Week,* and *Field Glass,* coauthored with Joanna Howard.